MW01610596

Acknowledgements

Writing a novel is not a work that's done in isolation. Many people contribute to an author's work and it is to those people that I wish to express my thanks.

God has provided my husband a plethora of opportunities to grow his patience as I slipped into the world of Andrea Wilton and Brian Strait again and again. His unswerving support is greatly appreciated as he encouraged me to be all that I could be.

Colorado Christian Writer's Conferences are my training ground and I have learned a ton of things that I really didn't know I needed to know when I began writing. I look forward to honing my skills at future conferences.

My editor for this book has been the greatest encouragement. Karissa Derksen worked tirelessly to make sure my scenes were consistent and that words like Brian and from did not come out as brain and form. Her questions about characters tickled my writer's ego and when she told me she'd begun to dream about them...well...what can I say.

I thank my readers for continuing to ask about the book and wonder when I would complete another mystery. Their excitement over the first one, Mind Trap, kept me at the task of finishing this work and beginning on the sequel.

I hope that each of you will not only enjoy this book but also remember that your spirit can still be fed even when reading for entertainment.

Copyright © 2009 by Barbara Ann Derksen
First Edition

All rights reserved. No part of this book shall be reproduced,
stored in a retrieval system, or transmitted by any means without
written permission from the author

-A Wilton-Strait Murder Mystery-

God bless Cathy
Barbara
(from Steinbach)

Prologue

The intruder shoved her up the stairs. Diane Michner stumbled. She grabbed the stair treads for support. Tears of fright blurred her vision.

"Hurry or I hurt the kid." His rumbling threat released hot breath across her neck. She scurried faster. An arm, covered in monstrous tattoos that bulged beneath the sleeve of his dirty t-shirt, circled the tiny wiggling torso of her three year old son. Jeffrey whimpered. The thug pushed her again.

"Mommy!" Jeffrey screamed, large droplets of tears coursing down his pudgy cheeks.

"Quiet." The man gripped the boy's arm and squeezed. He shot a glance at the woman. She bowed her head in submission and headed toward her little boy's bedroom.

"H-h-how long will we be g-gone?" Her eyes traveled over the little blue train stenciled on three walls of her son's dream room.

"Never mind. Get the clothes." He motioned with the boy's body, whipping him toward the folded doors of the closet. Jeffrey whimpered.

She yanked the door open and snatched a large suitcase from the top shelf. Her tears dampened pieces of clothing from her son's chest of drawers as she threw them into the case. With downcast eyes, Diane glanced toward her son and then back to the task at hand. In a haphazard fashion, she added some of the outfits hanging inside the closet door and seized his fluffy brown teddy bear from the bed. Jeffrey whimpered again.

Obediently she turned toward the doorway where the intruder fought to retain hold of her struggling child.

"P-please. Don't hold him so tight," she pleaded. "You'll hurt him." Her arms ached to hold her frightened son, to protect him from this man who didn't care if he injured a small child. "It's okay, Jeffrey. Please don't cry."

The man used his elbow to point her toward the next room. "Get a move on." His grip on the child's body enticed her to hurry.

The trio moved quickly down the hall towards the bedroom she shared with her husband of five years. She sucked in an anguished breath as she stumbled against the doorframe of the closet. She seized another suitcase and shoved in pants, shirts, and undergarments for both of them, then closed that case and looked at the man. Her eyes begged as her arms reached to hold the tiny boy.

The man thrust Jeffrey at her and grabbed the suitcase, as she wrapped grateful arms around her son's trembling body. She could feel his terror. The thug pushed Diane toward the hallway. She shifted the boy's weight to one arm but stumbled, almost losing her footing. She reached out with her free hand to steady herself against the wall.

Moving toward the staircase, the villain picked up the other suitcase standing just inside the boy's bedroom. "Get going." He motioned for her to descend the staircase toward the living room.

When she reached the first floor, Diane gasped. Two large men twisted a rope looped tightly around her husband's neck. Another coarse length of rope tied Trent's hands and wrists together, behind his back. The muscles of his upper arms stretched painfully beneath the sleeve of his cotton shirt. He grimaced, pain written on his face. Bright red oozed from a cut above his eye, the evidence of a battle lost. Blood congealed in his eyebrow and then trickled down his face to drip onto his collarbone. A jagged piece of cartilage stuck out from the bridge of his nose, blood coagulating near his upper lip.

A tormented groan escaped Diane's lips, as if from the depths of her heart. She shuddered and cuddled Jeffrey, trying to shield him from the sight of his father. Her body churned with unfamiliar hatred as she looked on the three men who had invaded their peaceful home. She watched as they laughed. The one nearest caressed her cheek. Her skin crawled in revulsion. She yanked her face out of reach. The intruders laughed harder.

*****

Trent struggled toward his wife. He watched anguish seep from her eyes, a torment that matched his own. Had he brought this to their home? What did they want? The thugs yanked him back as viciously as they would a dog on a leash. He twisted, desperate to reach her side. Jeffrey's eyes seemed so large that Trent could almost feel his fright from across the room. His own eyes cautioned his wife not to arouse their anger.

By the look on Diane's face, he knew she wanted to scratch their eyes out, to inflict as much damage on them as they had on her family. He watched tears fall unchecked as

Diane turned accusing eyes on him and then turned her head towards their son.

****

Diane glanced up again at her husband and saw a tear slide past the corner of one eye. His helplessness was evident in the slump of his shoulders. The men were too strong. "Diane..." His voice croaked. The rope strangling him ended further communication. He saw the slight nod of her head. She offered him understanding. He had tried to protect his family but failed.

Diane glanced around at the destruction of her tidy home, a sanctuary they had built together. Two plants dripped black dirt onto the carpet, evidence of her husband's struggle. The coffee table lay at an awkward angle in splinters, and two sofa cushions exploded with feathers everywhere. She ached to have control over her life again as evening shadows crept from the corners of the room and the smell of overcooked food lingered in the air.

"Did anyone think to turn off the stove?" She made a move toward the kitchen but a large beefy hand stopped her.

Her subjugator grunted beside her. His nod told one of the others to check it out.

Diane's focus switched. She watched the thug drop the bulky suitcases and then flex his muscles. His grin, when he caught her watching, caused her stomach juices to curdle.

"Now, we go outside to your car. I will hurt you and your son if you make a fuss or attract any attention. Understand?"

Diane nodded once. "Why are you doing this?"

"Not your business." He pushed.

"Not my…" She stopped in her tracks but her captor raised his arm as if to strike her. Diane used her free arm to swipe at tears betraying her fright. Her eyes traveled down the sidewalk toward the SUV. Her husband groaned, loud enough for the neighbors to hear if they'd been home, as the butt of a gun connected with his right shoulder. She saw his knees buckle. They were defenseless against these men. Her husband stumbled against the side of the van but no longer labored to free himself.

Diane cried in anguish, not caring this time who heard. She stared as they grabbed her husband's shoulder and squeezed. They lifted him bodily into the backseat.

"We take your car." Diane jumped. Her escort's hot breath drifted across her neck as he thrust her through the door. The thug let the front door slam behind them. He threw the suitcases into the backseat of the station wagon parked near the front entry of the house. He motioned for her to secure the little boy into his car seat.

"You drive. Follow them, and nothing will happen to you or your man. Make a wrong turn, and you won't live to see him shot." The brute spoke the last word as if a gunshot erupted from his mouth and then he sneered. He plunked himself in the passenger seat.

Diane's eyes looked, maybe for the last time, towards the home she had come to love. She searched for any means of escape and then slumped in the driver's seat. Her instincts told her they would carry out their threats. Her hands trembled as she inserted the key into the ignition. The motor roared.

She placed the car in reverse and swiveled her head to linger on the tear-stained face of her little boy. Her heart felt as if someone had punched a hole in it and all the blood drained away. Her mind filled with black hatred, hatred so strong that she knew if she'd had a gun in her hand, she'd use it. Instead, she backed out of the driveway and followed the SUV containing her husband. She made a quick study of the home her family had occupied for the last five years, longing to wake from her nightmare. Will we ever come home again?

Chapter 1

Andrea Wilton skipped up the steps of her best friend's house just as the street lights came on. She rang the doorbell and then smiled to herself. *What a day. Did I really do that?* She pushed the buzzer a second time, impatient. *Jason Dwyer asked me for a date and I turned him down. Where's Diane?* She grabbed the doorknob. With little more than a slight turn the door opened. Andrea stuck her head inside.

"Diane, I'm here. Diane?" Silence. "Diane, Trent, where are you guys?" Andrea stepped inside. *They wouldn't go out and leave their door unlocked.* "Diane, Trent, Jeffrey." Andrea looked around as she stepped farther into the living room. She gasped. Her hand went to her mouth automatically as she spied the broken coffee table, a couple of plants on their sides spilling dirt all over the floor, and a torn curtain. *What's happened?*

She walked, her steps hurried, toward the kitchen. The table was set for dinner. Food, cold and unappealing, remained in pots on the stove. Andrea returned the way she'd come and began to ascend the staircase toward the bedrooms. Just then the doorbell rang. She sighed in relief. *There they are.* She almost ran toward the front door. *Why are they ringing their doorbell?* "Hey you guys…Brian, what're you doing here?" Her voice filled with disappointment.

"Well, that's some welcome. Maybe I should be the one asking questions. What are you doing answering the Michner's doorbell?" Brian eyes twinkled as he rested his weight on one leg and placed his hands on his hips, clearly waiting for her answer.

"I…well…the Michner's aren't home. But some…"

Brian straightened. "What do you mean…they're not home. I was supposed to meet…"

"They're not home but something's wrong. I mean, look at this place." Andrea grabbed Brian's arm and tugged him into the living room. She watched his look change from friendly to startled in a second as he surveyed the destruction in front of him.

"Diane would never leave her house like this, especially if they were going out of town, which I doubt, since I had arranged to meet Trent here, tonight. How did you get in?" Brian's consternation was evident.

"The door was unlocked. I came over to talk to Diane. Is there something wrong with that?" Andrea glared at the man in front of her. Brian's need-to-know attitude had always irked her.

"They don't…"

"I know. They don't leave the door unlocked when they're not home. Check out the kitchen." Andrea led the way. She pushed the swinging door open, then stepped aside to allow Brian to see what she was concerned about.

"Wow. It sure looks like they left in a hurry." Brian walked over to the stove and lifted one of the lids on a pot. "Potatoes. Still in the water." He felt the side of the pot. "Still warm, too. Strange."

"Everything about this is strange. I think we should call the police." Andrea reached for a phone sitting on the counter.

"Wait. Andrea what if they just had a family emergency. Why don't we call the hospital first. See if they're there."

"Good idea. You call." Andrea handed Brian the phone. He punched in the numbers and then waited.

"Hi. I'm checking to see if a Diane and Trent Michner came in this evening." He listened for a minute and then hung his head as he punched the off button. "I was hoping…" He looked at Andrea. "I don't really know where else to call. Do you?"

Andrea's face crinkled a little as she thought for a minute. "We could call her parents but I'd hate to alarm them. But then…"

"Right. How else are we going to know? I'll use my cell phone to call Trent's folks."

Andrea and Brian each made their calls. Both sets of parents knew nothing about any family emergency that would call Trent and Diane away so urgently.

"Brian we have to call the police. Maybe they have

some way to find them that we've not thought about."

Brian hesitated. "I think someone has to be missing for 24 hours before the police will get involved."

"You're probably right. Should we wait until tomorrow, after work, to contact them? Maybe Trent and Diane will be home tonight yet and we'll look really foolish for thinking the worse. I sure hope that's the case, anyway."

"Why don't I meet you at the police station if we haven't heard from them before the end of the work day? Say about 5:30. Then we'll see what the police have to say."

"It's sure going to be hard getting to sleep tonight. Brian, can we pray about this now?"

"Sure. Lord, I know you know where the Michner's are. It doesn't look as if they've been gone very long but Lord please keep them safe and bring them home soon. In Jesus name. Amen."

"Thanks Brian. See you tomorrow." Andrea walked out the door and down the steps, the same route she'd taken just a half hour before. What could have happened to the Michners?

****

After a long night and an even longer day at work trying to concentrate on her boss's letters and appointments, Andrea phoned the Michner residence for the fifth time that day. No answer. She let it ring five or six times before hanging up. Even the answering machine was not working. She grabbed her handbag, threw on her coat and left the building just as Jason Dwyer drove past. He looked toward her but kept on going. *I guess he's still miffed that I said no.* Andrea continued toward her car, unlocked the door and sat down. She turned the key, put the car in gear and headed downtown. The police station was on Main Street.

All the way she prayed. Her heart was so heavy. *Lord, protect them, wherever they are.* The short drive took her past Freiman's, a large department store. Andrea remembered the last time she and Diane had shopped there. It was just before Jeffrey's third birthday. They'd had a lot of fun looking for the perfect gift and then all the decorations for the party. Now... Andrea didn't want to finish the sentence.

She parked across the street from the main entrance to the police station just as Brian stepped out of his car. He nodded in her direction. She joined him on the sidewalk. Together they entered the building, neither saying what was on their hearts at that moment.

Andrea laced her fingers together to keep them from shaking. Her large eyes surveyed the room. Dark blue uniforms surrounded the tops of antiquated, scared desks, hidden by a conglomeration of paperwork. People were everywhere; some wearing handcuffs, others filling out reports. Large overhead fans moved the stale, sweat-filled air. The noise level forced everyone to shout.

She followed Brian towards a scowling uniformed officer. His desk was situated closest to the entrance. Andrea moved to stand beside him so she could hear.

"Sergeant, we'd like to report some missing people." Brian looked directly at the cop who didn't say one word, just picked up the phone at his elbow. The commotion all around them drowned out the officer's voice but Andrea watched as the policeman's lips moved in conversation. The sergeant hung up. He motioned for them to follow as he opened the gate located in the railing that separated the squad room from the entry. Brian and Andrea walked through.

The sergeant led them in a zigzag fashion, dodging

desks and bodies, to an office on the far right of the main room. On the worn brown wooden door, highlighted by a smoked glass window in the center, were the words *Lieutenant Kurshner* emblazoned in bold black letters across the glass. The sergeant gave a light tap on the door.

"Come in." A man's voice with a deep base sound to it answered from the other side of the door.

The sergeant opened the door. "Lieutenant, these two people have a missing person to report." He backed out, making room for Andrea and Brian to enter. The two made their way past the sergeant as he ambled back the way he had come. They sat in empty chairs at the lieutenant's invitation.

"My name is Lieutenant Kurshner." He smiled, crinkled lines showing on his kind face. "What can I do for you?" Middle aged in appearance, his short graying hair gave the impression of a former life in the marine corp. He soon made them feel at ease. Brian and Andrea began to talk at once.

"They never take Jeffrey with them when they go out in the evening." Andrea moved to the edge of her chair, trying to inject her knowledge into the head of the lieutenant

"They always tell me their plans if they're going somewhere." Brian's brow furrowed as he concentrated on the details of his statement.

"One at a time. Please!" Lieutenant Kurshner raised his voice, making himself heard above their outburst. "Now, who are you talking about? You go first." He pointed to Brian.

"The Michner's. Trent and Diane and Jeffrey, their three year old son. They're missing. Trent has been my best friend since second grade. I am as much a part of their family as a blood relative. Andrea is Diane's closest friend. They would have told both of us if they'd planned to take a trip somewhere."

"And--" The lieutenant focused on Brian.

"I went over to their house early last night to finalize plans for a fishing trip that Trent and I were planning. Andrea answered the door and neither Trent nor Diane are anywhere to be found. That's not like Trent. When he makes plans with someone, unless he phones to cancel, he's always there."

Andrea grimaced. Her body felt as if she'd been up all night and her emotions tied her in knots. "I went over there to tell Diane some important news but…I tried the door and it was unlocked so I went inside."

"The door was unlocked?"

Brian spoke before Andrea had a chance. "Yes and that's another thing. They never leave it unlocked when they go out."

Andrea jumped in. "And they never take Jeffrey with them when they go out in the evening. Diane would have told me their plans when I talked with her the night before. Diane and I tell each other almost everything.

"They do." Brian interrupted and interjected a smirk. "Trent and I have to make an appointment to get any phone calls in."

"Yah, right." Andrea shot him a look that told him to shut up. "Anyway, Brian and I decided to come here right after work. As far as we know they've been missing for over 24 hours. The house was a mess. Diane always left her home in immaculate condition, even when they go on a trip." She shivered.

"I already told him that." Brian wrinkled his brow and

then continued, "While I waited for Andrea to show up, I remembered a phone call I received about two weeks ago asking me if I knew Trent Michner."

"Brian, you never told me that. Who called and what did they want?" Andrea jumped at him, interrupting his version of the story to the lieutenant.

"Hold on Andrea. I'd just thought about it before you got here." Brian appeared agitated.

"Go on. Go on," pressed the police officer, impatient at their interchange.

"I told the caller that I knew Trent, but then they wanted to know if I talked about his work with him. I asked for their name but they immediately hung up. That made me suspicious, so I called Trent. He explained that the work he did was secret. I can't imagine what's hush-hush about laundry soap but I really don't know what it is Trent is working on. He's trained in biochemistry, so I imagine it's something along those lines."

Lieutenant Kurshner continued prodding for answers. "Is there someone who would have any reason to harm them?"

"No way." They both answered at once again.

"One at a time, one at a time…if you don't mind." The lieutenant drummed his pencil on the desk. He looked at them, waiting for one of them to continue.

"There is no way anyone would want to harm these two. And who could possibly have anything against a three year old?" Brian raised his voice in agitation. "It's obvious, to us at least, that something is seriously wrong here."

"I think you're right." The Lieutenant scribbled notes on a clean sheet of paper, beginning to take their concerns to heart.

"You do?" Andrea's voice squeaked. Tears quickly filled her eyes.

"Yes, I do. Now can either of you think of anything else?"

Andrea blinked, hoping no one would notice her emotional state. She jumped to answer the lieutenant's question. "Diane did seem preoccupied, now that I think of it, the last time I talked to her but when I asked her what their plans were for the weekend, she said they were planning a quiet few days at home."

"Let's see. That makes them missing since…when did the two of you last talk to either of them?"

"I talked to her the night before last."

Brian thought a while and then said, "That's about the time I talked to Trent too. By the way, Trent works for Hartford Industries. Maybe they know something."

"What's Hartford?" The lieutenant raised his head to peer at Brian for a short moment and then continued writing everything they said.

"It's a plant just west of here, on Highway 10. I work there too, as an office manager. We manufacture chemicals for different uses, from cleansers to laundry soaps. I never go into the labs. Trent regularly changes the subject whenever I try to ask him about his work. I just thought that maybe he didn't want to bring his work home."

Continuing to write as fast as he could, the Lieutenant asked, "Would he normally be working today?"

"Yes," replied Brian, "and so would Diane. She worked part time for the Times. She wrote human interest stuff."

"She's a really good writer," Andrea added.

"Well, I'll get in touch with the Daily Times as well then. What's the address of their house? I want to check things out there. If things are as you say, we'll need to have the forensics team go over the place with a fine tooth comb including dust for fingerprints."

"We'll take you there." Brian began to rise from his chair.

"No, that won't be necessary. I'll call you as soon as we know anything."

"You think something bad happened to them, don't you?" Andrea's worse fears surfaced right in front of her.

"We can't tell anything yet, but we'll call you." The Lieutenant repeated as he grabbed his coat.

"We're coming too." Andrea got up and moved toward the door as she watched the concern on Brian's face, a concern that matched what she felt. While they had come to report their friends missing, she had secretly hoped that the police would allay her fears, not confirm them. If this situation concerned an experienced cop, well…maybe…

"As I said, that won't be necessary." The lieutenant looked at them more sternly this time as he moved with them toward the door of his office.

"We're coming." Brian's obstinate streak rose to the surface. "If they've returned, we want to see them. If they haven't then--. In the meantime, we know what's out of place and what isn't. We're coming."

"Fine, fine. Come along then. We can eliminate your fingerprints from the rest, I guess. We can all go over in my squad car or--"

Andrea blurted. "No, we came in separate cars. We'll drive our own to the Michners so we'll have our own cars for the drive home. Uh, right, Brian?"

"Sure. Sure. That's fine with me." Brian seemed preoccupied. "Lieutenant, do you handle missing persons or do you handle crime scenes?"

"If I find this is a crime scene, I'll turn it over to the boys that do this all the time but…"

"What else could it be?"

"One never knows. People run away for all types of reasons…like taxes."

"Well…these people didn't run away. I know them too well."

"We'll see." The trio left the lieutenant's office and the police building.

Chapter Two

Four cars formed a convoy back to the Michner residence; Brian's, Andrea's and the lieutenant's with another police vehicle taking up the rear.

The short drive seemed to take forever. Andrea's anticipation grew with each corner or street they passed. The solution to the puzzle of her friend's whereabouts seemed far off. She wanted the Michners to greet them on their return to their home with a simple explanation for their absence. She wanted it so bad, she could almost taste it. No one noticed the mustang following a few car lengths behind.

Lieutenant Kurshner pulled his car into the Michner driveway, followed closely behind by a black and white police cruiser. Brian parked his car on the street just as Andrea pulled in on the opposite side. As the worried couple walked toward the house, the police officer driving the lieutenant's squad car shut it off. The lieutenant walked beside Brian and Andrea up to the door of the still silent house. No one greeted them.

The lieutenant snapped on plastic gloves. He rang the doorbell. No answer. He gingerly placed his hand on the doorknob of the house, careful not to smudge a print if it existed on the knob. He told Andrea and Brian not to touch anything.

"We'll need to take your fingerprints so we can eliminate them from any we might find inside." He spoke as if the conversation had never been interrupted with the drive from the police station. He entered the unusually quiet home. He scanned the room and then turned to the uniformed cop just emerging from the second police car.

"Sergeant, radio for a forensics team. We'll want them here asap."

"You do think something bad happened." Tears pooled again in Andrea's eyes. Brian placed a comforting hand on her arm but she shrugged it off. She didn't want to be comforted. *I want Diane to come walking out of that kitchen.* A silent tear slid down her cheek.

Brian, Andrea and Lieutenant Kurshner didn't have long to wait. Within minutes, two more black and whites pulled up to the curb outside with a third car in between. Several officers and two suits walked into the house. One of the detectives carried a large bag which he deposited in the center of the living room carpet.

"Make sure you dust for prints each step of the way into the house." The man shook hands with Lieutenant Kurshner while he barked orders to his team. "and take scrapings of all samples of blood droplets. Well Bryce, tell me what we have here." He snapped on plastic gloves.

Blood, they found blood? Andrea felt sick. *We should have called the police last night.* She looked toward Brian. "I didn't notice any blood, did you?" she whispered.

25

Brian spoke in equally hushed tones. "No but then I wouldn't know what blood looks like."

The Lieutenant walked with the detective through the house toward the kitchen. Andrea's tears continued unchecked down her cheeks while Brian looked on with dazed confusion. This nightmare was real. She had a hard time realizing she wasn't dreaming. She watched policemen spread a fine dust over furniture and then whisk it off to reveal prints that Diane would have scrubbed to erase had she been there. The lieutenant returned.

"Folks, this is Lieutenant Smithen. Rory, these are the people who reported the Michners missing. Brian Strait and Andrea Wilton. Close friends."

Lieutenant Smithen reached toward them to shake hands. "Tell us what's out of place."

"There's a lot of stuff that isn't where it usually is. But we.. I mean…I didn't move anything and I didn't see Brian move anything."

"I picked up one shoe…" Brian turned to the lieutenant. "…one shoe in the corner of the living room and that was just before we left. I didn't think anything of it. Just a shoe." He squared his shoulders and turned his back to Andrea.

"Show me but don't touch anything." The lieutenant waved his hand for Brian to precede him toward the front window. Andrea followed.

One of the policemen picked up the shoe gingerly, careful not to smudge any prints. As he turned it over, a small round pebble fell out and rolled across the floor. "Was this in the shoe when you picked it up earlier?"

"I didn't turn the shoe over so it could have been…I

don't know. Could this mean something?"

"Well, it could mean something or it might mean nothing. We'll know more when the lab is finished here."

Lieutenant Smithen picked the stone up at the same time as he pulled a plastic bag from the pocket of his sports jacket. He placed the pebble into the bag and sealed it. Then he tucked it back into his pocket. "Let's go upstairs."

Andrea and Brian led the way. As they approached the first bedroom, they gasped. Clothes were scattered everywhere. Nothing hung in the closet and the dresser drawer was open and empty.

Both police lieutenants, along with members of the forensics team, scrutinized each of the bedrooms. They dusted for prints, and picked up anything that looked as if it did not belong. They took pictures of each room.

Andrea took a quick look around the upstairs before returning to the first floor. Her heart felt as if it had been ripped from her body and replaced upside down. She moved quietly, with sad, doe-like eyes into the kitchen. Plates, pots, and a table set for a family dinner greeted her just as before. An officer motioned for her to join him and he quickly explained the procedure for fingerprinting. Andrea reluctantly extended her right hand and the process began. An involuntary shiver walked quickly up her spine, tickling her back bone. This new experience she'd rather not have.

Ten minutes later she re-entered the small blue and white checked bedroom on the second floor, wiping the ink off her hands. "Your turn Brian."

Brian nodded in acknowledgement. "Lieutenant, how long will this take?"

"Since you are both here anyway, why don't you walk me through the rest of the house and point out any discrepancies. Then the two of you can leave for home after you get the prints done? We won't know anything until after the lab comes back with their report, and that could take a couple of days."

"That long?" Andrea placed her right hand on her hip punctuating her impatience. "The Michner's could be anywhere by then. Can't you hurry the process?"

"Procedure." The lieutenant moved down the hall toward the stairs. Andrea followed, waiting for a clearer explanation. "We need to be thorough and that always takes time."

The trio descended the staircase followed by Lieutenant Kurshner. "We'll place phone calls to the hospital…

"We've already done that." Brian was firm in his response clearly siding with Andrea about speed.

The lieutenant continued impatiently. "… the airport, and all other means of leaving this town. After we get their plate numbers from the data base, we'll put out an APB on their car. That can be done while we're waiting. Now walk me through and then get out of here. Leave the police work to us."

After they had pointed out anything they thought important for the lieutenant to know, Andrea followed Brian into the kitchen. She watched as his fingers were inked one at a time just as hers had been. *Just a few hours ago, we were planning on having a conversation with them, and now here we are getting fingerprinted.* Andrea sighed She watched Brian walk from one appliance to another wiping the ink from his fingers. His hand moved to touch first this one and then that, but he pulled back each time. He did not appear any happier than she. The duo moved down the front hall to the door leading outside.

"Andrea, I know we don't know each other really well

but we need to work together, try to trust each other."

"You're right, I don't know you. B-b-but I guess you're also correct in that we've got to stick together. All right, truce." She held out her hand for a handshake and Brian grabbed hers in a tight grip. "Besides, I never heard Diane say anything but nice things about you."

"Same here. Trent valued your friendship. Call me, if you need anything, ok?"

"Uh – sure. Sure, I'll call. Lieutenant, will you call us if you find out anything? By the way, which one of you will call?" Andrea and Brian were just about to reach for the door-knob when a plastic gloved officer opened it for them.

"I will." Lieutenant Smithen looked in their direction. "This is my case now."

"We'll be in touch." Brian and Andrea gave a half-hearted wave as they walked through the open door. They paused, with shoulders slumped, on the front porch and then walked down the drive towards their cars.

****

Smithen watched the two worried people through the front window. He wondered how they were involved, if they were. He also wondered what they hadn't told him. They gave all the appearance of genuine concern, almost fear. And yet they were adamant when they said the Michner's had no enemies. Someone didn't like them. The blood told that version very clearly.

As his detective sense worked in overdrive, he also noticed a black car parked across the street about half a block away. He could see two men sitting in the front seat. They watched the house as if they had a personal interest in the goings-on.

"Sergeant, go out the back door. See that car just down the street? See if you can get a plate number." The sergeant walked to the back door.

****

Knuckles whitened as his hands gripped the steering wheel. Jason smoldered with rage. *So she wouldn't go out with me but she has time for this shmoe! Well I'll show them.* He ignored the restraining hand and the tone of displeasure from his partner. With the car still in park, he revved the motor. His thoughts of failure consumed him. A rage in his head drowned out all sound. Women threw themselves at him. But not this one. *SHE refused to go out with ME.* His false sense of self left a bruised ego in its place. *I'm usually the one who ignores them.*

Weeks of work had gone into developing a relationship with this woman. His partner grabbed his arm again but Jason shook it loose, intent on the task at hand. His rage burned. *It's not supposed to be like this. I seem to have no control over this broad. I thought I had succeeded is getting her to like me.* He floored the gas pedal as he shifted into drive. *I'll show them.*

****

Andrea shrieked, "Brian, watch out!" The car picked up speed. Brian watched, mesmerized, as the vehicle headed straight for him. Halfway across the street, headed toward his own car, he darted for cover. The offending car's right fender breezed past his leg missing him by a fraction of an inch.

"Hey." He shook his fist at the careless driver. The thought of 'what next' crossed his mind as he watched the car disappear around the next corner. He dusted off his pants. Andrea ran to his side.

"I'm fine, no thanks to that idiot." He saw her look of panic disappear.

"I thought that guy would hit you for sure. Some people just don't know how to drive. Boy, what next? Are you sure you're ok?"

"Sure. I'm fine. But I won't be if I don't get some rest tonight. I don't know about you but I'm exhausted. See ya later." He waved his hand, smiled, and proceeded to get into his car. She did the same. As she placed her car in gear for the trek home, she thought about the quiet life she used to lead before yesterday. *Wondering what to make for dinner was all I used to worry about. Now, the Michners are gone without a trace and Brian could have been hit by that car.*

****

The lieutenant, unable to get a license number, wrote down a description of the car. Something about the way that car drove seemed deliberate. His long years on the force had his instincts in overdrive as he returned to the task of searching for clues. That car may be connected to this case. *But how?*

Chapter Three

Andrea trudged up the stairs to her front door. *I can't believe this is happening.* She fumbled with her key, inserted it into the lock, her right hand shaking as the emotion of the day surfaced again. "They've got to be alright, they've just got too." She spoke out loud to her dogs, dependable doorway companions, as she pushed the door open. She slammed it behind her and then cringed as the solitary pane of glass rattled.

Ignoring their enthusiastic welcome, she walked past Patches and Pokey, down a short hallway to the kitchen, dropping her keys on the hall table as she went. She kicked off her shoes, and entered the sunny yellow room, her favorite. This time, the room did not sooth her tired spirits as it had done every day since she'd painted it. It only reminded her of Diane, the person who'd help her decorate the space.

She sat heavily on a chair in the alcove overlooking the backyard. Tears flowed freely now that she was out of site. Patches laid her head on Andrea's lap. What can I do to help, her eyes seem to say. Andrea patted her head.

Where are they? What had happened to them? The questions flowed through her mind like an old fashioned ticker tape. She glanced down the hall toward the front door, willing her friends to walk through.

Andrea hiccupped. "I'll bet you girls want to go outside. You've been cooped up all day, haven't you?" She opened her back door and Patches and Pokey escaped into the early evening air. *Diane loved to watch the dogs run around out here.* While the dogs were still outside, she filled their water bowls with fresh water and added some more dog food to the stuff left over from that morning. Once they were inside again, she prepared a sparse dinner for herself. She took a bite but realized her appetite was non-existent. *It tastes like cardboard.* She threw it into the trash.

The police seem to be in no hurry to find Trent and Diane. Where'd that thought come from? Andrea swiped a stray hair from her forehead. She adjusted her living room blinds so no one could see inside her house and then sat on the sofa next to the phone. *I wonder if we could...would the police be upset if...* She picked up the phone.

Marcia Dixon had gone to college for her undergraduate degree with Andrea and Diane. She had moved to Boston to pursue a degree in law but had then entered a law practice in town about a year ago where she became a well-known criminal attorney. The women had lunch together often. Andrea wanted some advice.

"Hi Marcia. How are the wedding plans coming?" Andrea replied to the friendly greeting on the other end of the line.

She listened as her friend talked about the details of her wedding with Jonathan Fry. A psychiatrist, Jonathan and she became re-acquainted during another case when Marcia had enlisted his help for her client. Now they were getting married in three months. Andrea and Diane had tried to share their faith with the two but so far, neither seemed interested. The women hadn't given up yet.

"Marcia, I called for a specific reason. Sorry to cut you off but…"

"Andrea, what's wrong?"

"Diane and Trent, along with their son, are missing…"

"What? Are you sure? Where have you looked?" Andrea moved the phone away from Marcia's high pitched demand for answers.

"Not a trace so far. We reported it to the police but… they seem to not be in any hurry and I have this feeling…time is important."

"It usually is to those involved in a missing person case, Andrea. The police will get there but they have a procedure…"

"Yes I know. Procedure. Marcia, what if I tried to find them myself. Could the police stop me?"

"As long as you don't interfere with an on-going investigation…no. But…"

"I can't just sit here. I have to do something."

"Yeah, I guess I'd do the same thing. Call me if you need anything and keep me posted, Ok. I have to go. Jonathan is picking me up so we can meet with the photographer. Andrea, I know you are a praying person. Pray that they'll turn up soon. The longer they're missing the less their chances for survival." Andrea caught the worry in Marcia's voice.

"I didn't need to hear that but thanks Marcia. I'll be in

touch." Andrea hung up. She stood and touched each piece of furniture in the room, remembering the shopping spree. Diane had helped her purchase the furniture when she'd moved to town eighteen months ago. They'd had a blast. Now…

Andrea shook herself. *They're in God's hands. I need to look upward, not inward. There's got to be something I can do. I am so afraid for them.* Inside a still small voice reminded her that fear was not from God. "Yes Lord, I know." Andrea sat, folded her hands, and began to pray. The dogs walked quietly to her side, finished eating for the time being, and lay at her feet. "Lord protect them, please."

****

The motor boat skipped over smooth stones as it slid onto the beach. Three men hauled two people, blindfolded, out of the boat. The woman held a small, sleeping boy. A second boat arrived minutes later with four more men, all rough looking and intent on their destination. The captives were forcefully steered up the shoreline on a path leading to a rough hewn cabin surrounded by several sheds of varying sizes. The woman tripped and almost dropped the boy but one of the thugs steadied her, not very gently.

Once they had arrived at the door to the cabin, the blindfolds were removed. Rough hands pushed the couple inside. Diane Michner peered into the darkened interior. Furnished with a double bed and a cot, two chairs and a table, the cabin looked like anything but a vacation spot. Placing Jeffrey on the cot, she rubbed her tired eyes in an attempt to adjust to the dust laden air. She looked at her husband with questions in her eyes. How had this happened to us?

The men left. She heard the lock click as the door closed. Stealthily, she moved to the portal, grabbed hold of the handle and pressed the latch. Nothing happened. It held. They were locked in.

She walked to her husband's side. "Let me look at those cuts and bruises." Feelings of blame and resentment surfaced while she worked. "Nothing looks as if medical attention is needed except for the cut over your eye. Antiseptic and a bandage would help." She moved her head clockwise around the room. Trent remained silent.

Diane spied some supplies on a shelf near a small counter. Taking a couple of short steps, she found a first aid kit. She plied the lid open and returned to her husband's side. "We've been traveling all night. I don't know what direction we've gone except the weather is considerably warmer here. How could this happen to us?" How could you let this happen. Tears blurred her vision not for the first time since their nightmare began,

Trent folded his arms around his wife's petite body. Jeffrey, now awake after hearing the men leave, scurried to their side and held his arms up. His face was streaked with dirt and tear tracks. Trent picked him up, looked around and sighed. "I don't know what's going on for sure…but…"

"But you knew Max represented a dangerous element. Why didn't you just tell him to forget it?"

"I did and now look where we are." Trent's comforting arms softened his sharp retort. Diane swiped at fresh tears. She looked toward him with fear written all over her face.

"What are we going to do?"

"I don't know. We'll think of something. If Brian showed last night…he'll be looking for us…I hope."

Chapter Four

Another twenty four hours passed and still no sign of Trent and Diane. Neither Andrea nor Brian knew what to do about it.

"Andrea, the police haven't got any leads." Brian's exasperation traveled through the phone lines like mustard from a squeeze bottle. "I'm going nuts just sitting here and I'm not getting anything accomplished at work."

"I know. I feel the same and my work today left a lot to be desired. Mr. Forester, my boss, tried to tell me they went on a vacation. Can you imagine? Brian, we have to do something." Andrea fiddled with the microwave as she heated some macaroni & cheese for dinner.

"What? What can we do?" Brian snapped, impatience lacing his words with anger.

"Don't bark at me. I just know I can't sit here day after day waiting for the police to get off their duffs and find them. We've got to think of something...anything."

Brian quickly apologized. "I feel so helpless."

"Brian, I have to go. Someone's at the door. Call me if you think of anything." Andrea replaced the receiver and walked toward her front door. The doorbell peeled again, more insistently this time. "I'm coming, I'm coming."

The dogs raced toward the front door just ahead of her. Reaching for the doorknob with one hand, Andrea held onto Patches collar with the other. The dog acted as protector whether Andrea needed one or not. She opened the door to see her next-door neighbor standing in front of her. He looked troubled. He pushed the glasses sitting on his nose further up his face with his index finger.

"Hi Max, what can I do for you? Need some sugar? Where's your bowl?"

"Hi, Andrea. No, I just wanted to say, I'm so sorry. If I'd known this would happen--"

"Sorry about what, Max? Come in, why don't you?"

Max backed away from the door. "No, I just came to give you this." He handed her a small piece of paper. Puzzled, she began to read the note. THWACK. Max slumped forward, and fell face down on the carpet in her entryway. The note fluttered to the floor as her fingers and then her whole body went numb with shock. A pool of dark red seeped from the side of his neck to form a river the congealed as it ran toward the hallway table. Andrea shrank from the sight but then moved to try to roll Max onto his side. Her efforts were in vain.

The bullet had made hardly any sound but the ragged

hole it left convinced Andrea Max was hurt…bad. She felt the rise of panic like a thick mass growing in her esophagus cutting off her ability to breathe. Impossible to think. The pit of her stomach filled with bile. She sat down hard. She shook her head to clear the fog. " Max. Max, answer me." She heard her voice shouting from a long distance away as if she were in a room padded to stifle echoes. She strained to wrap her arms around his shoulders, only managing to lift his head. He's too heavy. Sticky blood soaked her pants and ran warm over her legs. She couldn't make him hear her. Large sobs rumbled up from her chest. Tears streaked in rivulets down her face. She spotted Max's note laying beside him. She picked it up with bloody fingers and then, without a thought, put it in her pocket.

Andrea scooted back, away from the front door and Max's still, lifeless body.. She had to get away from the blood. Her back rocked the table near her. The phone dropped. The receiver hit her shoulder and she stared at it, wondering where it came from. She picked it up, inspected it as if it could tell her what to do next. She tried to replace it. Her sticky, blood-soaked hands would not release it. Red oozed over the once white instrument just as it did everything in the hallway. *Help. Need to get help.* Her senses began to clear. She shook her head again and then again, blinking her eyes, trying to focus. She dialed "9-1-1".

"Operator...help me--er us or--

"Slow down, Ma'am. What's seems to be the problem." Andrea heard the operator as she used her best calming voice. "Tell me where you are, please."

"I'm at 1020 Topeka Bay, right off Euphoria in Simpson Heights. My neighbor has been shot. Right on my doorstep."

"Is the shooter still there? Can you see anyone?" The operator's voice rose a little and squeaked with apprehension.

"It came from somewhere outside, I think. No, I can't see anyone. I'm sitting on the floor."

"Stay out of sight of your door, ma'am. The police and ambulance are on their way. In fact you should hear the sirens at any moment."

Andrea heard the distant sound of a siren coming closer and closer. "I hear them. I'll hang up now. Thank you."

****

Cars roared to a stop outside the address given them by dispatch. Officers looked around before exiting their cars. With one man in the lead, several policemen, their guns drawn, inched toward the house, keeping a low profile. The front door lay wide open. They moved with caution, pointing directions at one another. Inside they saw a woman on her knees beside a man in a pool of blood. She had a steady stream of tears running down her cheeks.

"Help him, please?" she said, looking at them with large eyes full of sorrow. They glanced at the fallen man but moved furtively past to inspect the rest of the house. "There's no one in here. The shot came from outside." Her voice fell on deaf ears as they continued their survey of the house.

"Clear." One officer shouldered his way into the kitchen while another took cautious steps up the stairs to inspect the second floor. "Secure." They holstered their guns and returned to the woman's side. One police officer reached out the door and motioned the ambulance attendants, who had just arrived, to hurry.

****

The EMTs approached the victim and extricated the hands of the distraught woman from around the fallen man's neck. One technician moved her to an adjacent room while, the first technician, the one who seemed to be in charge, took a good look at the injured party. He felt for a pulse and then used his stethoscope to check for a heartbeat. Nothing. He shook his head. He snapped his medical bag shut while another man reversed his steps, and took the equipment back to the ambulance. It wouldn't be needed this time.

****

A grizzled looking EMT, hauling a plastic tarp, led Andrea toward the sofa in her living room. He placed the blue sheet of plastic on the sofa and then ushered her down to the soft cushions. Treating her as if she were fragile, he put a cushion behind her back and told her to take a few deep breaths while he felt for her pulse. His gentleness seemed so uncharacteristic and yet the term Teddy Bear came to Andrea's mind as she watched his hands on her arm.

"Are you hurt, miss?"

"No." She hiccupped. "This blood is from Max." She seemed dazed. "He's been shot." Andrea looked down at her blood covered hands. She turned them this way and that as if to figure out why they felt sticky. Red stains soaked through her pants and caused them to stick to her legs. Her shirt had pulled loose from her pants and was torn with more red stains soaking through the fabric. She couldn't control the tremor in her hands and legs.

"Here's some water." The kind face of her Teddy Bear looked on with compassion.

"I-I'm okay." Tears slid down her face. "I'm s-sorry. I've never s-s-seen someone shot be-before. Poor M-Max. You know, he-he's my c-closest neighbor. Who c-could've wanted to t-take his life?" She reached for a tissue from the table beside the sofa. Her hands shook so badly she could hardly blow her nose. Her body trembled with the jerky movements of a Parkinson's patient.

"Is there someone we can call to come stay with you?" asked the worried paramedic. "You shouldn't be alone at a time like this. Besides until the police find out who killed your friend, you could be in danger."

"Oh, you're a big help!" A burly detective, who towered over the scene, blustered from behind the paramedic. "Why don't you wait outside until the medical examiner has finished with the body. We'll look after this lady since she appears to be okay." Andrea reached out to the man as if to a lifeline but she watched as he cleared away his equipment and moved toward the front door. The police officer watched as well, shaking his head, and then opened his pad.

"My name is Lieutenant Maxwell. While we wait for the county attorney to arrive and the criminal investigation team, let's get some of the preliminary questions out of the way, if that's okay with you. Would you like someone to get you some coffee before we start?"

"N-no, I don't n-need anything right n-now. Um... maybe a glass of water." The lieutenant motioned the request to an officer. The quiver in Andrea's voice quieted a little but he kept his eye on her as he asked his first question. Once Lieutenant Maxwell determined Andrea's relationship with the victim, he gathered background information on her. A uniformed man brought her some water. Andrea wrapped her hands around the cool clear glass. His next question reminded Andrea why he was there in the first place.

"Do you know any reason why someone, anyone, would want to kill this man?"

"No I don't. I really don't...err...didn't know Max all that well. He came over a few t-t-t-times." She pronounced one word at a time to keep a tight control on her emotions. "You know, for coffee. Sometimes he would stop by for s-s-some baking ingredient that he needed for a recipe. He's always running out of sugar or something. Anyway, he seemed to bake a lot for a man living alone. Other than that, I never saw him. We didn't socialize in the same circles."

"Why did he walk over here today?"

"He came…um…I'm not sure exactly why he came over today. He'd just arrived when s-someone s-shot him." Tears started again as Andrea thought about what she had just said. "Could someone w-w-w-ant to kill me as well? Maybe t-they m-missed."

"What would make you think that?"

"Well, my closest friend disappeared two days ago and now this. I guess I ..I.. Things are not as quiet as they usually are around here. I'm just a little on edge."

"Do you know of anyone who would want to harm you?"

"N-n-no? I mean NO. I get along with everyone. I've only lived here for a little over a year. I live a pretty quiet life… work…church…that kind of thing."

"Boyfriend?"

"No…no one special. Jason Dwyer from work asked me out a couple of times but I've never gone out with him… yet."

"Could he be the jealous type? I mean, could he think you preferred Max…"

"Never. I don't have a relationship that is that close to

anyone…except Diane Michner."

"And that's the lady who's gone missing?"

"That's right. Brian and I reported them missing just yesterday."

"Who's Brian?"

"Brian Strait. He's Trent's best friend. Trent is Diane's husband and he's missing too along with their three year old son. So Brian and I went together to the police station."

"Who did you talk to there?"

"Lieutenant Kurshner at first but Lieutenant Smithen took over from him, I think."

"I'll talk to him when I get back to the precinct then. To answer your question about whether or not you are in danger, at this point it's hard to say what's going on. I really don't know what to tell you about anything and won't know until we are further along in the investigation. A murder is always so full of holes in the beginning. Later those questions get answered, but until then, there are too many to even speculate. What more can you tell me about Max?"

"Max. Shuster is his last name. All I really know about him is he's thirty-five, single, and a good neighbor. Whenever I needed a man's help, Max was willing to try to fix it. He's not always good with mechanical things but he tries. He travels a lot, too."

"Did you know any of his friends or business associates?"

"No, I've never met any of Max's friends."

****

The detective looked toward the body laying in the entryway. The man appeared to be about 5'10", had a bushy mustache that gave him a mysterious appearance, but dressed with a conservative flair. His thick hair was beginning to gray at the temples. He could not see any other distinguishing marks from that distance. The coroner would have to fill in the details. He glanced back at Andrea.

****

"Max always seemed to me to be a man with things to do and places to see. He traveled a lot and he knew about stuff." Andrea screwed up her nose in an attempt to concentrate on the detective's questions. "You know. He's someone who always has a ready answer for any question."

"What kind of questions?" The detective peered at her over the rims of thick eyeglasses. He sucked on the end of his pencil as he waited for her to sip from the glass of water she held in her hand.

"Oh, you know, about stuff like you would read in the newspaper. Current events, EPA, things like that. Just conversation between friends."

The police officer stood and held out his hand to Andrea. "Maybe you should stay with someone else for a few days until we can get some answers to our questions."

"There is no one to stay with. Diane's my only close friend." Andrea hung her head and felt the tears flow freely again.

"It'll take us most of the night to clear this crime scene before you can begin cleaning up all that blood. I'd get a professional service in, if I were you. Why not check into a motel tonight."

"Fine, I guess I could do that."

"Do you want us to take you to one?"

"No, that's okay. I need my car with me, but do you think one of your officers could follow me--just in case. Could someone check on me occasionally through the night as well?"

"We can have someone follow you, but we're too short handed to post a guard or anything else. I wish we could. The regular patrol car in that area could check though, but they only pass by about once or twice in the evening."

"That's okay. At least that will make me feel a little safer," said Andrea. She walked toward her bedroom to gather some things for an overnight stay. Throwing nightclothes, a fresh outfit for the next day, and her toiletries into a suitcase, she trembled, and tears that had not really subsided, flowed once again. Her heart ached for Max. She missed him already.

A glance in the mirror almost frightened her. She looked like someone from a horror movie. She reefed off her blouse, and walked into her bathroom. She knew she would never wear these clothes again so she opened the vanity door and threw it into the waste basket under the sink. She emptied the pockets of her pants on the counter. Her shoes and under-clothing followed her blouse into the garbage before she stepped under the hot spray of her shower.

Heart wrenching sobs filled the shower stall as quickly as the hot spray washed away the last signs of Max Schuster's blood. Her body trembled and bile from too much stomach acid burned it's way up her esophagus. She retched and then gagged again. Nothing. Swallowing repeatedly, she soaped every inch of her body, breathing in the clean scent of her favorite bath soap and then soaped herself again. Finally, she felt in control and stepped out to complete the task of packing for the night. She replaced everything into the pockets of her clean pants for the journey to a safe motel nearby.

Chapter Five

Andrea stepped into her living room. Police were everywhere, dusting for prints, examining the body…*Max, not a body*. A couple of other men in plain clothes searched every inch of the foyer. *My house is under a magnifying glass.* She sniffed and then watched as one of them pulled a piece of dust from under her sofa. *So much for being a clean freak.*

Two men approached Max's body with a large black heavy plastic bag. She struggled with them as they lifted Max into it, zipped it up, and then placed the package on a gurney ready for transport.

"Miss. Miss." An officer stood right in front of her. Her eyes shifted to his face. "You can go now. You should be able to come back tomorrow. The crime scene will be cleared by then."

Crime scene. A shudder escaped. How could she ever feel safe in this house again? She felt a shiver walk its way down her spine. Was someone watching her. She collapsed into the nearest chair. *I've gotta get outta here.* She grabbed her suitcase and began to walk the short distance to her front door. Blood, everywhere. *Poor Max. Now he's on his way to the morgue.* She saw him fall again…and again, like a bad movie playing the out-takes over and over.

She shuddered…then dropped to the floor in a heap. "What was that?" she heard herself begin to scream and within seconds an officer was at her elbow.

"A backfire, miss." The officer placed a comforting hand on her shoulder.

"How do you know that? Maybe…" Her hand shook as if the bones in her body were reacting to an earthquake. She looked into the kind face of the officer who would escort her to the motel. "I'll…I'll be alright." She refused his offer to help her stand and grabbed her bag once again.

The fresh air smelled so good. *The dogs are outside.* They didn't like Max so she always gave them some freedom when he came over. "I need to get Patches and Pokey from the backyard before their barking disturbs my neighbors. I'll take them with me to the motel."

****

The officer, rather short and stocky, watched as the dogs greeted her with tails wagging, tongues drooping from the side of their mouth. The leashes clicked into place and then she led them toward her car. *What luck. I'll know where she's staying.* He smiled, a cover for the thoughts traveling around his head. *We'll have to keep a close eye on this one. The boss will want to know what we've done with her.* He polished the badge hanging over his heart. *Some cover.*

****

Andrea stowed the dogs into the back seat. Tears blurred her vision. She plunked down into the driver's seat. Swiping her hand across her eyes, she swiveled her head and nodded to the police officer waiting in his car to follow. Her spine tingled with an uncanny sense that someone watched her every move. *I'm getting paranoid*, she thought. *Who'd want to hurt me?*

Short minutes later, the neon sign for the Days Inn Motel flashed a greeting. She registered, returned to her car for the dogs and suitcase and then with a wave to her protector, she entered the motel for the night. She wrinkled her nose. Stale cigarettes. The door to her room opened first try. She quickly slid her suitcase inside and guided Patches and Pokey to their home for the night. She snapped the lock in place but then noticed her room had an outside entrance as well. She checked that lock to make sure it was secure. She closed the curtains.

Andrea collapsed into the only chair in the room. Tears streaked slowly down her cheeks. She was too tired to sit straight. She wrapped her arms around herself. *What happened to my neat little world...my safe world?* The nausea erupted again and she contemplated a trip to the restroom. She scratched Patches head resting on her knee. *It's funny how dogs know when something's wrong.* "You guys are all the medicine I need." The dogs wagged their tails.

She remembered the note. She reached into the pocket of her pants, opened the crumpled page and read. *They've taken Trent and Diane Michner against their wills. If anything happens to me, go to the bank on Main St. & 16th. Blvd. The safe deposit box vault - use a key. Hidden under the flowerpot on my back deck. Your name on the deposit box signature card. Use the information and money inside box to find Michners. Don't contact police. May be involved.*

"He knew his life was in danger!" she squeaked. "They've taken Trent and Diane? Who are *they* anyway?" Her agitation sent the dogs skittering to the other side of the bed with tails drooping. "They're connected. Trent and Diane are with people who are capable of murder." *Max is right, I have to find them…now.* She paced around the small room, bumped into the bed every time she came close to it and nearly stepped on the dogs twice.

"Brian… I need to call Brian. He'll want to know about Max, the note, everything." She reached for the phone on the bedside table, all the while arguing with herself. *Could she do this? Should she do this? Let the police…but they may be involved Max said.* She wondered how Max knew her friend. "Right, he works…worked at Hartford too." Brian works there too. Maybe Brian knew more than he had this morning about the Michners. She finally dialed the number he had given her.

Before he could say more than hello, Andrea stumbled over words that rushed on top of each other to be heard.

"Andrea. Slow down. Take a deep breath. What time is it anyway?"

Andrea ignored his question and rattled on. "Someone shot Max Shuster on my doorstep tonight, and…he works at Hartford, too. Did you know him? There's a connection." Andrea shouted, almost hysterically.

"Andrea…Andrea…slow down. Breathe."

Taking a deep breath, she calmed a little and then continued. "As I said, Max is my next door neighbor...was my next door neighbor. All I really know about him is his address and his name. And he isn't married. He travels all the time for Hartford and to the Caribbean occasionally to scuba dive. Sometimes, he borrows something for a recipe he's preparing. He seems very nice. I guess I should say seemed. It's so hard to believe he's dead. One minute he and I are talking and the next…lying in a pool of blood…dead. I don't even know if he had any family. He wants me to solve his murder! Me, a secretary! He left me a note." With that said, Andrea sucked in another deep breath.

"What note?"

"He slipped a note into my hand just before he was shot."

"What's in the note?" She read it to him. She heard a gasp on the other end of the phone line.

"He said Diane and Trent were taken? By whom?"

"He didn't say by whom or where they were taken. Just that they were taken. He left me some money."

She read that part of the note again. "I need to go to that bank after I find a key to a safety deposit box by his back door. What am I going to do?"

"How did he get your name on the safety deposit box?"

"Oh I don't know. That's what's in the note."

"You are going to take this new information to the police, aren't you?"

"Max said I couldn't trust the police. They may be involved. So no, I've not said anything to them and I'm not sure I will."

"Andrea."

"I know. But what can I do? If the police are involved in this…"

"I don't like this. What if Max is one of the bad guys?"

"Max is not a criminal. He's the kindest, gentlest…"

"Yes, but he did say he was sorry. He is involved and you already admitted you don't know him that well."

"Look Brian, I plan to go to the bank first thing tomorrow. Since it's Saturday, they close at noon. Do you want to meet me there?"

"Fine. But if you still feel uneasy about doing the detective work as Max wanted, then will you tell the police?"

"Maybe."

"But.."

"Maybe. That's all I can promise now. Are you coming or not?"

"Okay, okay. Where is it and what time?"

"How about 8:30 tomorrow morning. That'll give me time to get home, change, and find that key. The bank is the Terrace Bay National Bank, located at Main St. and 16th Blvd."

" I'll be there. Are you okay for tonight? Do you need me to come over?"

"No, I'm okay. I have my dogs, Patches and Pokey, with me. Anyway, I feel better than I did 30 minutes ago. Brian, you will help me, won't you?"

"I guess so. If it means finding the Michners. But I still think we should notify the police."

"And what if they are the reason the Michners are missing?"

"It seems so preposterous. I guess. Anyway, I'll be

there tomorrow, and we can decide the next step then, okay?"

After she hung up, she slowly dragged the rest of her toiletries from her overnight bag and placed them on the bathroom vanity. She placed the outfit she'd worn on a hanger and slipped into pj's. Her head had taken on the thudding dull achiness of too much crying, while her eyes continued to burn with unshed tears.

She crawled between the cool sheets, pulled the covers almost over he head. Weariness seeped from every pore on her body, but would sleep elude her for the second night in a row. Thoughts of the chaos her life had become roiled in her head like a bubbling caldron. Her mind stewed on first this thought and then that. She needed to make some decisions. *I've always trusted the police. Never had much to do with them but...could I trust Max? Wasn't he involved?* An hour later the sheets looked like a couple of kids had had a blast jumping all over the bed. She untangled herself, padded barefoot to the bathroom and picked up the packet of sleeping medication that the EMT's had left. That might help.

Andrea lay down again, turned on the television, and curled herself spoon fashion around the dogs. Before long with heavy eyelids, she snapped the remote off and slept. Her eyes popped open. When she looked at the clock, she'd slept for only an hour. *Five o'clock.* She groaned and reached for the note. What did that safety deposit box contain?.

****

Rubbing sleep deprived eyes, two men watched Andrea's motel from a distance. Each time a police cruiser passed during the night, they scrunched down to avoid detection.

"That broad needs to be gone." The larger of the two twisted his back this way and that to relieve the kinks. "She's gonna get in our face, I just know it."

"Sure and if we do that, you think the police won't get in our face."

"Yeah, well…"

"Yeah well nothing. We was told to watch. So we watch. That's all."

"What if we scare her?"

"Like how?"

"Well, she loves those dogs. Why not hurt one of them." The bulk of him shook with the gleeful thought of hurting anything.

"Maybe…"

"It'll work. You'll see."

"Naw. I don't like hurting dogs. I like dogs. Think of something else."

"Maybe a note pinned to her door, letting her know we was here."

"And exactly what door is hers?"

Well…well, then her car. The windshield wiper."

"Yeah, I like that. She won't feel safe anywhere and maybe, just maybe, she'll keep her nose out of our business."

"What should I write? How do you spell Miss?"

"Give me that. What are you…being polite yet?" The take charge guy wrote quickly, opened the car door as silently as possible and then stealthily crossed the parking lot of the motel. He slipped the note under Andrea's windshield wiper. Just as quickly, he sat back in the driver's seat of the black mustang. The engine roared to life. "It'll be daylight soon. We'll move the car over there." The large man pointed to a clump of trees with a road intersecting the vegetation. "We can watch from there."

"Good. We can follow when she leaves." He polished his badge again.

****

Andrea slipped into the bathroom and then returned to the warm comfort of the bed. She lay watching the first light of dawn peak through the crack in the drapes. Her leg muscles cramped so she stood quickly, flexing her foot until the pain decreased. She leaned into a stretch to get the kinks out of her back. A shower would feel good.

An hour later, she walked briskly across the parking lot with her suitcase, deposited it into the trunk and then started the engine before she brought the dogs. She looked up as the car hummed to life and saw it. A note stuck under the blades of her wipers.

Sliding out of the car, her fingers grabbed the paper. She turned it over. *You're next*. Andrea slammed the car door, left the motor running, and raced back toward the hotel. She'd left the door wide open with the dogs tethered to a chair.

She stumbled to the bed. The murderer was out there. He was stalking her. He must have followed her last night. The police hadn't seen him or them or…maybe they didn't want to. Andrea picked up the phone,

"Brian, they were here. The murderer was here last night. They left a note."

"Huh, oh Andrea. What time is it? Never mind. What's this about a note?"

"Someone left a note on my windshield. It says I'm next."

"I'm coming over there. What motel did you say you were at?"

"The Days Inn on 63rd."

"Andrea, call the police. NOW."

Andrea hung up, dialed again and asked for homicide. The police sergeant answered in a tired voice. "Hello, homicide division. What can I do for ya?"

"Hello, I'm Andrea Wilton. A friend was shot at my house last night. I stayed at a motel but when I tried to leave this morning I found a note on my windshield. It says I'm next." Tears began to flow anew as reality hit. "I'm so scared. They're out there."

"Miss, stay calm. I'll have a squad car there in a minute or so." The phone line hummed as he disconnected and Andrea sat dazed and confused. *Why would someone want to kill me? I know nothing about anything.* She peeked through the curtains toward her car. All was quiet or so it seemed.

A few birds flew by and streaks of sunlight promised a nice day. Andrea sighed. Just then Brian's now familiar car pulled up beside hers. He reached into the vehicle, turned of the ignition and looked toward the motel. Andrea rushed to open the door a crack and signaled for him to come in with shaking fingers.

As he approached the door, a marked black and white pulled in. The officer got out and walked over to her door as well. "Are you Andrea Wilton?"

"Yes. That's my car and this is the note."

"Oh, I wish you hadn't touched it. We might have gotten some fingerprints off it. Oh well, let's see." He stuffed his hands into plastic gloves and turned the paper to the light so he could read. Then he dropped it into a plastic bag.

Where would we be without plastic? Andrea giggled nervously.

"Who are you?" He looked at Brian.

"A friend. Andrea called. I came."

"Well, I'll drive around and check things out. In all likelihood they're long gone by now. It's too light and these guys like to keep to the dark places." He retraced his steps and drove off the lot.

"Brian, thanks for coming. I was so scared."

"That's ok, Andrea. I should have come to stay with you last night.' Brian looked sheepishly at the floor. "All of this is just so strange. What happened to normal?"

"I agree. Since we discovered the Michners gone, life has been anything but normal. Brian, this whole business has me so scared for them. These people aren't just playing. They mean business."

"There's the cop. That didn't take him long."

Andrea stood close to Brian, slurping up the warmth of knowing she could trust someone. Because the Michners had, she did. It was that simple. The police officer approached.

"I see nothing out of the ordinary. All's quiet. Why not go home, keep you eyes peeled and all doors locked. Maybe it would be a good idea to stay somewhere else tonight since they probably know where you live. I'll pass this information on to the detective in charge after last night."

"Thanks officer." Andrea grabbed the dogs and began to move toward the door.

"Where do you think you're going?" Brian spoke loudly enough that the officer turned back toward them. He waved and the officer left again. "I'm not letting you out of my sight until after we've gone to the bank and I have you settled somewhere safe. I don't have that many friends that I can lose any more." Brian's face looked as serious as Andrea had ever seen him.

"Are we friends?" She felt warmth rise along her collarbone and infuse itself on her face, she was sure, like a beacon.

"Well, I feel responsible for you in Diane's and Trent's place. Besides, I do think of you as a friend. We go to the same church so we're even siblings. You know. Sons....and daughters of God."

"Oh Brian, you say the nicest things." Andrea batted her eyelashes in an attempt at humor. "I do consider you a friend. Maybe not as close as the Michner's, but a friend nonetheless. I trust you anyway. Now let's get out of here."

Chapter Six

Andrea looked at her watch. Eight o'clock. She groaned audibly. "It feels like half the day is over." She looked toward the man who'd not left her side all morning.

"Max's instructions were certainly easy to follow. Now I hope that it won't be difficult to get into the box at the bank. It's hard to figure how he got your signature without you knowing about it."

"Do you doubt my word?" she snapped. "Oh, I'm sorry. I'm just so tired. I know. I have no idea how he did that but let's hope it works." Andrea closed her eyes for a moment as they pulled into the bank parking lot.

"You don't look as if you hardly slept last night." Brian gave Andrea a steady glance. "Have you thought any more about the police?" He spoke in a whisper as he gently guided her through the door into the brightly lit building.

Andrea looked around to make sure no one could overhear their conversation. "Let's talk about that after we see what's in that safety deposit box, okay?" She approached a woman at the counter. "Can you help me get into my safety deposit box?"

"Certainly. Just sign here." The woman handed her a blank piece of card stock which she signed *A. Wilton* in her usual scrawl. "I'll just verify your signature and then we can proceed to the vault." The woman walked over to a wheel containing hundreds of cards and found the one she searched for. She placed the card with Andrea's signature next to the one on the wheel and smiled.

"Everything seems to be in order." She motioned for the two of them to follow.

"I feel relieved and curious all at the same time." Andrea whispered to Brian as they walked past some bank clerks, a few small offices, and a copy machine. The large steel vault was in front of them. Andrea inserted the key she had into a box that the clerk indicated was hers and then the clerk inserted her key. The woman withdrew a fairly large metal box, handed it to Andrea and then directed the couple to a small cubicle.

"Well, come on, open it." Brian rubbed his hands together in anticipation. His eyes sparkled.

Andrea couldn't help the chuckle that escaped. "You're excited and I'm feeling like an intruder." She lifted the cover. "Wow." She carefully lifted out the top document. "Ten thousand. Are each of these worth that much? She scanned the contents further. "There must be…"

"Thousands…hundreds of thousands. Where could Max have gotten this kind of cash? I handle the payroll at Hartford. He doesn't…er…didn't make this kind of money." Brian sat back on the chair he'd been leaning from.

"Max didn't live an extravagant lifestyle. At least he never seemed to act as if he had this kind of money." Andrea looked directly at Brian for the first time since they entered the bank. "Could these be phony?" She noticed a crumpled piece of paper near the back corner of the box. "What's this?"

She pulled it out and opened it, holding it so the light would allow Brian to read it also. *Andrea Wilton:*

I am so sorry but I have no one else to turn to. About a year ago I began saving these because I knew the people I'm involved with would eventually kill me. No one can guess what they have coerced me into doing. It's vicious. You will need to fly to Haiti. I think that's where they've taken the Michners. DO NOT go to the police, ever. Be careful. You could become a victim too.

"He wrote this note since the Michners disappeared. Haiti? I can't go to Haiti. I don't even know where that is."

"And he's certainly blunt about the police. What's that about coercion and *it's vicious*? Who are these people? And more importantly…"

"We're not going to the police with this. Marcia Dixon…you know her…she said that as long as we don't get in the way of the police, we can look for the Michners all we want. We certainly won't be in the way if we go to Haiti."

Andrea grabbed one of the bonds. She held it up to the light. "I'm not sure what I'm looking for." She turned to Brian.

"Doesn't Max's warning scare you a little?" Brian turned in her direction and placed his hand on her back. His touch felt comforting. Curious.

"I've never been so scared in my life. But what are we supposed to do? He says his murder is tied to the Michners. I want to know where Diane and Trent are. Don't you?" She whispered, afraid someone might be listening. "Y-you don't think we're capable of finding them, do you?"

"It's not that…" Brian spoke loudly but then softened his voice a little. "I just think we…you… need to really think this through carefully. And I certainly don't think you should go to Haiti all by yourself." Brian folded his arms across his chest."What do you know about defending yourself against people like this?"

"Well…not a lot but if Max…"

Brian stood as if ready to leave. "Well, at least I have a license to carry a gun." He walked through the doorway of the cubicle.

"Are you saying you'd be willing to come with me?" Andrea quickly grabbed one of the bonds and closed the lid to the box. She stuffed the bond into her purse and returned the safety deposit box to the vault making sure it was locked up and safe..

"Maybe…what are you doing?" He followed as she returned to the main part of the bank.

"I'm going to verify that these are real before I make any decision." She stalked purposefully toward the nearest bank clerk.

Brian grabbed her arm mid stride. "Are you crazy? If the bank suspects that you know nothing about these bonds, how are you going to explain that they have your signature on them? Just deposit one and see what they say."

"Fine…" Andrea shrugged out of his grasp.

A few minutes later Andrea watched the clerk complete

the paperwork for her new account. She looked toward Brian as he stepped up to the counter beside her. "This is so unreal!" she whispered. "Things like this just don't happen. I've always lived a very quiet life ….Oh, my gosh…my job. I can't just up and leave. What will Mr. Forrester say when I tell him I'm going to Haiti to find my friends?"

"Let's take this a step at a time. We need to think carefully, look at all the ramifications. We'll talk when there's no chance anyone can hear." Brian placed his index finger over his lips shushing her.

Andrea inhaled a deep breath. "Brian," she whispered this time, "will you come with me? There's more than enough money to cover your expenses as well. I don't know who else I can trust, do you?"

The clerk handed her the receipt for the deposit. "Thank you Miss Wilton. If there is anything further we can help you with, just ask." She smiled and then turned toward another task as Andrea and Brian left the way they'd come.

"I see your point." Brian opened the front door of the bank. "I think we should pray about this before we make any definite plans."

"Do you mean now?" Andrea stole a furtive glance around the parking lot.

"Yes, why not now? We need the Lord to be the decision maker on this, I think. Then we know it'll be the right one." Brian bowed his head. "Lord, you know where Trent and Diane are. You also know all about Max and what's going on here. Please give us clear direction. Help us make the right decisions."

Andrea felt a sense of peace for the first time since all this began. If Brian could rest in God then so could she.

"Let's take your car...oh that's right. Mine is still at the motel." They walked toward Brian's car.

"Let's stop at the police station on the way. I'd like to know if they've found out anything yet." Brian opened the passenger door for Andrea to get in.

Brian got in and started the car. "I'm still not convinced the police are the bad guys here."

"I won't get them involved. I have a gut feeling that Max is right. How could those thugs have known where I was staying last night?"

"They could have followed you and besides…"

No, Brian. No Police….please?"

"All right for now." He pulled into traffic and headed toward the police station.

"Brian, I'll need to make arrangements to convert some of that currency to Haitian currency. Maybe US dollars are good enough. There's so much to find out before we actually leave." Andrea's head hurt from lack of sleep.

"I'll need to arrange for time off work and…"

"On Monday, I'll add two more bonds to the amount I just deposited. We may need more than $10,000. I'll also get some cash and some travelers checks." Andrea leaned her head against the head rest. In no time at all the rhythm from the engine lulled her to sleep.

Brian looked over and shook his head. Their lives had changed drastically in the last two days and it seemed it would change some more before this nightmare was over. *Haiti, huh? Well I do want to try out some scuba diving in those beautiful Caribbean waters.* As Andrea pointed out, someone had to find the Michners. He hoped going to Haiti wouldn't be a wild goose chase. Why would the Michners be in Haiti?

Chapter Seven

"Now where are those two headed?" The driver of the black mustang growled his displeasure.

His passenger blinked sleep deprived eyes. "Can't someone else do this today? We haven't slept in hours."

"Quit your whining." His grip on the steering wheel tightened. "There is no one else. You'd better not nod off. The boss'll have your head. Now keep your eyes on that gadget." The location detector they'd placed on Brian's car, while he and Andrea were in the bank, beeped steadily.

"These two are trouble. I just know it." A large man, he slumped deeper into the front seat. The blip from the device was making his tired eyes water.

"Yes well…we have ta make sure they don't cause any."

****

Andrea eyes popped open and she began talking as if she'd never fallen asleep. "Do you think we'll need Haitian money?"

"Good morning to you too. Feel refreshed? I don't know about the money but I'm sure they'll be able to tell you at the bank." Brian rubbed the back of his neck. It felt as if they'd been up for hours.

"Do you have what you need for a trip to a tropical country?"

Brian frowned in her direction. "I can't help thinking we're in over our heads here. What if…"

"Brian, if the police are involved, like Max said, they aren't going to spend a lot of time looking for Diane and Trent, now are they? Are they even coordinating their efforts, what with Max's death and all?"

"I guess that's something we need to find out. Do you have any idea when you want to leave? I need to get a leave of absence from work. You probably will too."

"They probably won't give me any leave. I'll…just have to quit." Andrea's inhaled as the words sank in. "I love that job but…Diane means more to me than a paycheck. I can always get another job but I can't replace her. I want to leave as soon as we can work it out."

Brian scowled toward the windshield and then glanced at Andrea. "I hadn't thought of you as tenacious before. You're like a dog delighting in a ham bone. This won't be a pleasure trip you know."

Andrea's voice squeaked. "You think I'm enjoying this?" She sputtered her indignation. "Why I'll…"

"No, I don't think you're enjoying this. Calm down. I just want you to be clear. Is this the direction you want to go? I agree. We shouldn't involve the police any more than they are already. Besides, they may consider it strange that you withheld evidence anyway."

"I did not withhold evidence. I forgot about it."

"Well anyway, do you really think you can trust Max and what he says?" Brian maneuvered his car into a parking spot across the street from the police station. He glanced over at Andrea, a look of concern creasing his forehead. "Do you even know him well enough to judge?"

"I have no reason to doubt him, but … well… I just don't know!" Andrea opened the door on her side of the car. Brian turned off the motor as the two walked into the familiar building. Conflicting thoughts skittered across her brain as she watched the officers in the room. *Because of Max's doubts, I'm not sure we can trust the very people I've spent my life believing are here to help us.*

A few minutes later they were seated in chairs across the desk from Lieutenant Smithen. "No new developments. We found out that Hartford Industries is a government facility, one classified as top secret. We'll need special permission to get inside the lab to find out what Trent worked on." He settled back into his own chair and scratched the side of his head. "And then we still won't know if something terrible happened to them or if they simply went on a last minute vacation."

Andrea opened her mouths to protest but then clamped it shut. Max's note.

"As for Diane Michner's work, she's researched an investigative piece. The newspaper editor doesn't know what it's about, though."

Brian sat forward in his chair. "What about Max Schuster's death? Anything?"

"Do you think there's a connection?" Andrea sat forward in her chair.

"No…well, I'm not sure." The lieutenant rose from his chair. "We'll get in touch with you if we hear anything and we'd like you to tell us if the Michners contact you."

The duo walked slowly out to the car. "Does it sound to you as if they know what they're doing?" Andrea sat in the front seat. She watched Brian walk around to his side of the car and open his door. "Brian, did you believe the lieutenant?"

"I don't know. The lieutenant didn't make me feel too confident, that's for sure. After all, both cases do involve you. I wonder if they're taking Trent and Diane's disappearance seriously enough."

"I know." Andrea watched the houses they passed and the kids playing in the yards, not a care in the world. *Trent and Diane didn't think their life was in danger either.*

"It's frustrating. We're no closer to the truth than when we first asked the police for help. I guess the only way to find out the truth is…to do things Max's way. That is, if we can believe all that Max said."

Brian turned down the street where the motel was located. "It's been almost two days since…"

"…since Trent and Diane were kidnapped." Brian looked at her with a frown. "Well we might as well use that term. Max said so."

"I just hate to think…"

"Well Max's truth is a place to start anyway. I find it hard to believe that someone wants to harm the Michners, too but… Do those people think that no one'll notice the disappearance of a young family? And then there's Max. I guess we'll find out something soon enough." Tears of frustration and lack of sleep started to run down Andrea's cheeks. She swiped at them with the back of her hand. She sniffed and then looked out the window on her side of the car.

****

Brian reached a reassuring hand toward Andrea, but pulled back. "You're not the only one perturbed by this thing." He looked out his rearview mirror. Then looked again.

There… two cars lengths back. He saw the fender of a black mustang as it peeked around the car in front of it. *Is it the same car? The one that almost hit me? Nah, there's lots of cars like that one.* He glanced at the street in front of him and then back toward his rear view mirror. 2004, all black…just like that car two days ago. *It's got to be the same one.*

Without a word to Andrea, Brian pulled into the motel's parking lot. The black mustang parked down the street. It was almost as if they didn't care that Andrea and he might see them. Andrea seemed not to as she exited his car and slid into the driver's seat of her car. She lowered the window. "Goodbye, Brian. Thanks for coming to get me this morning. Those guys had me spooked."

"I'm just glad you felt comfortable enough to call me. Will I see you tomorrow?" Brian leaned his arm over the open window of his car.

"Church, right. It'll be good to do something normal."

"Great. See ya there?" Brian shifted the car into drive.

****

Brian dropped his head, pretending to look at something in his lap. He glanced up in time to see the black car speed past. Two men were inside and they watched Andrea's car intently. He pulled onto the street. *Now we'll see who's following whom.* A short distance later Andrea pulled into her driveway and the Mustang continued on as if it never followed her in the first place. *Two can play this game.* Brian pursued at a safe distance into dense traffic. *It's gone.* He drove up and down a couple of nearby streets but no luck. He decided to head home. He'd bet his life those guys were tied to Max's murder. *It may be my life.* He settled into his seat for the short trip home, uneasiness seeping from every pore.

****

Andrea shuddered as she tiptoed around the dark stain where Max's body had fallen yesterday. The dogs stood in the living room, the smell of blood keeping them at a distance. She patted their heads and looked around her hallway. *Boy, what a mess!* Andrea picked up the phone book to look for the number of a professional cleaning service. Not open until Monday morning. Her to-do list for Monday was getting longer.

****

Jason Dwyer pulled his cell phone out of the pouch attached to his belt. "Lo, what da ya want? Er...Demos?" He stood, straightening his body almost at attention. He held the phone a few inches from his face. Anger, thick enough to melt the phone lines, poured over him. He hiccupped. "Yah, yah. I know. Now we got the chemist, we don't need her anyway." He shook his head in agreement. "I'll take care of it." He shifted his weight from one leg to another. "Tomorrow. I'll take care of it tomorrow." The line went dead. *The bimbo was gonna get hers… tomorrow.*

Chapter Eight

Fluffy cumulus clouds floated overhead as Andrea entered the church building for the early service the next morning. She spotted Brian speaking to a couple near the hallway to the Sunday school rooms. As soon as he saw her he moved down the aisle toward her.

"May I sit with you this morning?"

"Sure but…let's not give anyone a thing to talk about…ok?" Andrea winked and then turned to the bulletin insert to read about upcoming events.

"How did you come to know the Lord?" Brian spoke in a reverent whisper as people filled the pews to their right and left.

Andrea leaned toward him and spoke in a soft whisper.

"In our sophomore year at college, Diane invited me to her parent's home for Easter. I discovered just how 'religious' they were. Her folks went to church the Friday before Easter Sunday as well as Easter Sunday. And then they told me that Jesus had died for my sins."

"I'll bet you didn't like to think of yourself in that light."

"How did you guess?"

"Andrea, I'm beginning to see how strong and self-sufficient you are. I'm sure you thought of yourself as OK."

"I did. In fact, Diane quickly changed the subject because she knew I was not comfortable with that conversation."

"So how did you finally learn you needed a Savior?"

"On the ride back to campus, Diane asked me how I felt. I had lots of questions. To make a long story short, I discovered my arrogance…to think I could do without God in my life."

"Isn't it amazing that we think we can leave our Creator out of the equation?"

"Is that what happened to you?"

"Something like that. Go on, what happened next?"

"Diane led me in the prayer of salvation. I agreed that I had turned my back on God. That continues to be my biggest failure but there were others…like pride in my accomplishments or thinking myself better than others. I asked Jesus to take control of my life then and there and I've been an avid follower ever since."

"Praise God. For both of us. I came to know him just before I moved here. I believe God wanted me here so…I moved." Brian smiled a look of peace and contentment.

"Diane introduced us, remember but…back then…you seemed to be so focused on your job, you had little time for anything else including the Michners. I'd see you sometime at the Michners but you and Trent were always doing your thing and Diane and I often took that opportunity to go for coffee."

"Trent knew me from our high school and college days. He respected you so much that he warned me not to get too close. I guess my reputation has not always been spotless but… after I met Christ…I didn't want to be that kind of person anymore. Trent wasn't so sure that I had changed…yet."

"Do you remember when you first visited this church?" Andrea noticed curious glances from nearby worshipers.

"I do. I moved here after being best man at Trent and Diane's wedding. I met you there, didn't I?"

"I'm glad I made such an impression. I was Diane's Maid of Honor." Andrea turned her attention to the worship team who'd just begun to lead everyone in praise songs to the Lord. The music had her spirits soaring. She noticed Brian's beautiful singing voice. She also detected his serious, heart-felt praise of the Lord.

Andrea, aware of a strange twinge in her stomach, considered this new piece of information. Sitting right next to Brian in church was a new experience. *One we'd better not repeat if we don't want to be the latest topic of conversation for the romantics in the congregation.*

The sermon, uplifting and inspiring from start to finish, focused on what Jesus would do if He lived in the world today.

The idea intrigued Andrea. What would Jesus do if faced with the dilemma that she and Brian were faced with?

After church, Andrea waved good-bye to Brian. "I'll see you Monday after work."

"Good. If you hear anything, call me. I'll do the same. Okay?" Andrea nodded her head in affirmation.

It took Andrea only a few minutes to drive home. When she turned down her street, the whole block looked like the parking lot of a police station…except for the fire trucks. *Someone's house is on fire.* She drove on down the block hoping to be able to pull into her own driveway. The closer she got, the more fearful she became. *It's my house.*

Andrea slammed on the brakes The angry orange flames were shooting out of every window in her home. She watched, as if in a dream, as men in yellow fireman's coats ran here and there. Various pieces of equipment lay all over the sidewalk. Her hand covered the involuntary cry of dismay when she saw fire bursting through broken window panes and smoke erupting through the shingles on her roof.

"Patches, Pokey." She screamed as she raced towards the inferno. Terror filled her eyes. She searched the crowd… people mesmerized by the blaze from her home.

"Wait, miss. You can't…"A policeman moved to block her path.

A fireman raced after two dogs when they broke away from their tethers. "Hey, come back…" Patches and Pokey lunged for their mistress.

"Oh my pretty girls." Andrea breathed a deep sigh of relief but then coughed as the acrid smoke coming from her residence filled the air. She dropped to her knees and hugged her animals tightly. "Are you hurt girls? How did you get out?" Her hands did a careful inspection for damage. "Thank God you're safe."

She glanced over their heads. Tears blurred her vision. She watched the roof collapse and ashes spew into the air. She turned to the policeman who'd tried to stop her. "What happened? My house." Her hands waved toward the scene.

"All I know, miss, is what the neighbors told us. An explosion caused the whole house to burst into flames. We won't know the cause until the Fire Marshall completes his investigation. Uh-h-h, do you normally let your dogs roam free when you go out?" He steered her toward the running board of a nearby fire engine. Andrea sat.

"No...I-I don't." She began to shiver from emotional overload. A nearby paramedic wrapped a blanket around her shoulders. "They're inside until I come home. I've no idea how they got outside. Maybe one of the neighbors?" Andrea didn't care how they got out as long as they did.

She watched her peaceful afternoon go up in smoke along with her house. Nothing left...except the clothes she had on...and her dogs. Two firemen leaned against the side of a fire truck, oxygen masks over their faces. Others chopped holes into the siding. Flower beds, trampled. *What next?* But her dogs were safe?

A neighbor placed a comforting arm around her shoulders, squeezed her regret and left. Another asked if she could call anyone.

"No, I have my cell phone." Andrea's attempt at a smile failed miserably.

Tears again. *Does a body ever run out of tears?* Andrea watched a tall, robust man walk toward her, his uniform a combination of soot and polish. "It looks like whatever exploded engulfed the building in flames long before the department could arrive. It could be a severed gas line or...do you have any enemies, Miss Wilton? Could someone want to harm you? I mean...someone had to let the dogs out and since you weren't home..."

Maybe someone was aiming for you. The memory of Friday night filled her with terror. The police had suggested the same thing, hadn't they? First Max and now her home. "I-I don't know. I d-don't think so but...F-Friday, a man..." She hiccupped. "M-my next door neighbor was killed on my door-step. One policeman suggested that maybe the bullet was meant for me, but I ..."

"It's just a thought...part of my investigation. Try not to worry too much tonight."

"I don't have any enemies. I ..."

"Except for a neighbor getting shot on your doorstep, right?"

"...a-a-and my best friend disappeared four days ago along with her husband and small child." Andrea's voice shook as she grimaced. Her life didn't sound so peaceful even to her ears.

"I'm sure this isn't going to help any. Anyhow, it's too early to tell anything for sure, but, what you've told us may point to the reason for the fire. Please let us know where we can reach you, Miss Wilton, in case we have any more questions."

"I will." Andrea gawked at her home one last time re-membering why she'd bought it in the first place. A sanctuary. A place to come after work. To put her feet up and relax. Now look at it. Sobs garnered strength as she watched firemen tram-ple through her things, picking up this charred piece of something and then another. *What is happening to my life?* She looked toward the faces of her neighbors and wondered if the culprit, if there was an arsonist, stood in the crowd watching her misery.

She stood. Pain erupted behind her eyes. She dried her tears on her sleeve. Crying served no purpose. Soot filled the air. It covered her hands, her clothes and her dogs. She grabbed their collars to steer them toward her car. *At least I still have a car.* She brushed the soot off the dogs' once glossy coats and then corralled them into her back seat. Her limbs seem to buckle as she fell rather than sat on her front seat. She rested her head on her steering wheel. The cool plastic felt good.

****

Brent Morrison, the fire marshal checked all the gas lines and electrical circuits, but found nothing to indicate something of that nature caused the fire. He decided to sift further through the ashes. Kicking hot coals aside with the toe of his boot, he moved a piece of charred wood. Studying a partially burned out wall, he began to see a burn pattern.

"Charlie, check this out." He called his assistant who immediately crossed from the right side of the house to stand beside him. "See the pattern?"

"It looks like the fire started over there." Charlie pointed toward the kitchen counter, where the back door used to be. A charred tin bucket lay on its side. Charlie picked it up gingerly holding it between his thumb and index finger, hoping not to smear any prints.

"That smells like gasoline." He held it for his boss.

Brent bent his head toward the bucket and took a long sniff. "Sure smells like it." He kicked at some debris. "This looks like the ash from a rag or maybe two. I'll bet that's how this fire was set. He inserted a rag into the gasoline but left it hanging over the edge of the bucket. Then he lit it. That would give him time to get out of here before the fuel ignited. The explosion was probably caused by the gas lines to the furnace erupting, however."

Charlie wrapped the bucket in plastic. "When the lab checks this over, I sure hope they find some latent prints. I'd like to catch whoever did this."

****

Andrea took her dogs to their favorite kennel. "Make sure they're fed and watered right away. I don't know how long they've been outside without any water."

"I'll take good care of them." Jane Moyers had looked after her pets ever since she moved to town.

"I don't know when I'll be able to take them home…or even where home will be, for that matter. I do know I'm going out of town for a while so you will have them for at least a couple of weeks. Is that okay?"

Jane agreed to make them feel right at home for as long as Andrea needed. "You can visit whenever you like."

Andrea hugged her pets. They were settled. Now it was her turn to find sanctuary for the night. Choosing someplace close to work but in the busiest part of town, a larger hotel than the night before with more amenities, Andrea locked the car and walked toward the clerk at the front desk.

"A room for one night? Certainly Ma'am," he said. *At least my bank account is liquid enough that I can afford to stay here.* The room clerk handed her the key that opened her door on the sixth floor. She peered out the window overlooking the brightly lit downtown streets. *If the situation were different…*

but…it wasn't so… Tomorrow she would look after the clothes situation but for now, a good long soak in a hot soapy tub of water would suffice.

The muscles between her shoulders ached. Andrea felt and tasted grit. She took off her soiled clothes, placed the bathrobe located on the back of the bathroom door closer to the tub, and then turned on the tap to fill the large whirlpool with warm water. She splashed in some bath wash to make bubbles. *Oh boy. This is going to feel so good.*

Andrea slowly slipped her big toe into the warm soapy suds and then sank bodily into the depths of the tub. Slowly tight muscles relaxed in the pulsing jets of steamy water but visions of her loss encompassed her like the soap bubbles in the tub. She groaned. *Stop crying.* Her eyes pooled. Deep, from the bottom of her soul, sobs volcanoed to the surface. Everything familiar was gone. Even Diane. She had never felt so alone.

She cried a long time, for possessions but more for the intrusion into her life. *Lord, why?* And then she became aware of a whisper, *"Why not."* She sat up. Tears subsided. She looked around. She lay back into the warmth again, feeling the comfort. *The Lord has provided, hasn't He?*

She hadn't realized just how tense she felt. It as if she'd been beaten. Her muscles began to loosen up. Andrea closed her eyes. She concentrated on the shopping trip tomorrow. It had been a long time since she'd been able to afford new clothes. *Brian.* I wonder what he'll say about this latest development?

Chapter Nine

"It seems that I am phoning you all the time." Andrea heard a big sigh on the other end of the line.

Brian was quick to ask what the problem was this time. "I thought you would want to know..."

"What, what?"

"My house burned down this afternoon." She heard a very audible gasp on the other end of the line before she continued. "I've lost everything except my dogs." Silence, long and telling. "Brian, are you there?"

"Yes! Yes, of course. Man, what next? Do they know what started it? How did the dogs get out?" Brian rattled the questions off like an interrogator.

"They don't know what started the fire yet but it seems to be an explosion of some sort. They're guessing a gas line erupted. Anyhow, they'll know by tomorrow. The dogs on the loose is a puzzle, but I'm sure glad they were. I guess I'll spend tomorrow buying new clothes as well as luggage." Andrea yawned.

"Do you want to postpone the trip until they discover what happened to your house?" Brian asked. "Maybe that way, there would at least be something we have an answer for."

"I agree. I…" she sighed into the receiver.

The catch in her voice gave away the extent of her emotional stress.

"Andrea, do you want me to come over? I'd be more than happy to, and we could go get something to eat."

"N-no, I'll be fine, and I'm really not very hungry. I just feel absolutely exhausted, and yet I really haven't done any hard work today." She sighed again. Andrea opened her mouth to say goodbye but nothing came out.

" Well…if you think you'll be okay… Do you have any more of those tranquilizers that the EMTs gave you the other night? Why not take one and try to get a good night's sleep? Tomorrow, things will be clearer." Brian worked hard to inject a positive note in his voice.

"If I get hungry I'll call room service. Brian, we have to find the Michners. Every time something else happens, I get more fearful for them. These people are vicious."

"You think this is arson and tied to the Michners?" Brian's voice rose with his own emotional state of stress.

"What else?" Andrea let out a large sigh of resignation.

"I'll call you tomorrow." With that she said goodnight. Moving toward her handbag on the table in front of the window, she extracted two tiny pills. Swallowing, she thanked God for good friends and medicine that would help her sleep. She rinsed the charcoal from her dress and hung it over the shower rod. It didn't take too long for sleep to overtake her emotionally drained body.

****

Sun peeked through the draperies. Andrea opened one eye and searched the room for anything familiar. *Oh yeah. The fire.* Her eyes didn't want to open more than a slit. The light hurt. She crawled out of bed and staggered. *Sedatives. I hate taking those things.* She was on her feet. *The dogs? Oh yeah. The kennel.* The loss of all her possessions made her feel as she had when her parents died; set adrift, no anchor. She'd hoped she'd never feel this alone ever again but…what if she had been at home when that gas line, or whatever, exploded? She'd be dead.

She checked the bedside clock. She slowly stretched from side to side to relieve achy limbs, expelling the numbness from the crumpled position she'd slept in. Speaking of crumpled. Andrea spotted her dress hanging in the bathroom. *I need an iron. I'll call the front desk to see if they have one after I've had a chance to shower. At least they'd provided a bathrobe.*

She wriggled her toes. All she had for footwear were the high heeled shoes. She looked at her reflection in the mirror. Her hair could use a good shampoo. She quickly stepped out of the underclothes she'd slept in and stepped under the hot stinging spray of the shower. *This feels so good.*

Allowing the hot water to wash away her body stress, Andrea mentally made plans for the day ahead. *Before I go to the office, I'm going to have to find some suitable clothing. I'll call in and let them know I'll be a little late. Some of Max's money is going to come in handy when I shop for those new clothes.*

****

As soon as Andrea sat down at her desk, Tom Forrester's door opened. He motioned for her to enter his office. "Bring a cup of coffee with you. I heard the news on the TV this morning."

Andrea poured herself a fresh cup and walked briskly into her boss' office.

"How are you, Andrea? Is there anything I can do to help?"

"No, not really except…"

"Yes."

"Well, I need some time off…about two or three weeks should be enough."

"Oh, Andrea…I don't know. You've been here such a short time. What do you need the time for?"

"The fire just complicated our plans. Brian Strait and I have decided to go to Haiti to search for Trent and Diane. We believe that's where they've been taken."

"Taken…but I thought…"

"I know. Everyone, including the police think they left for a last minute vacation. We have reason to believe otherwise."

"Andrea, I'm not sure this is something you should handle yourself. Let the police find them."

"I can't." Andrea clamped her mouth shut. She'd already told him more than she'd planned.

"Where are you staying?" Tom Forrester crossed his legs. He seemed in no hurry to begin his workday.

"I found a comfortable room at the Viscount Gort but I intend to relocate to something a little nicer tonight."

"That hotel is pretty expensive."

Andrea crossed her fingers behind her back. "I have some money saved." Her lie felt wrong but Andrea knew that telling Mr. Forrester about the money would have only caused a string of questions. She filled him in on the suspicions of the fire department.

"The Fire Marshall hasn't confirmed arson yet. I'll call him later. Until he knows what happened for sure, I plan to stick around. I want to inform my insurance company before I leave town. As soon as I know what course of action I need to follow to have a home to return to, I will leave town. Could take a day or two, at the most."

"Andrea, I will miss working with you. We were a team. I know the company will not grant a leave with your short work history here. I'm sorry."

"I am too. But I need to do this."

"Why don't you pack up now then. That'll give you the rest of the day to make those decisions. I hope you decide to let the police handle this. I think you're out of your league here." His utter lack of support for her trip surprised her but it did sound like a wild goose chase, even to her ears.

"I'm sorry about not giving you more notice …"

"Oh forget that. One of the other girls will fill in. When

you get back, check with me. If I haven't hired anyone, the job is yours. You're one of the best secretaries I've had." Tom Forrester stood and reached across his desk to shake hands. "Now be careful." He ushered her out of his office and even waved. She stopped at her desk. Andrea quickly emptied her personal items from the desk and stuffed everything into her new handbag, one that matched the shoes she'd bought that morning. She picked up her keys and left the building.

First stop…the bank. Determining, with the bank clerk's help, that American currency was used in Haiti, Andrea asked for two books of traveler's checks in the amount of $3000 each.

"But miss, two books? We could put all $6000 in one book. And what denominations did you want the checks?"

"I need two books. A friend is traveling with me. Make the checks in denominations of $100 each."

"If you want your friend to be able to cash the checks without your signature, she'll need to sign her checks."

"It's a he."

"Pardon?"

"My friend. It's a he."

"Oh, I just thought…"

"We'll come back later today to pick his up then," She took the list of things to do from her purse and crossed bank off. One task completed; several more yet to do. "Er-r could he come in alone to sign those checks?"

"As long as he has proper identification. We close at five."

Andrea walked out, stuffing her book of checks and some more cash into her handbag. She sat in her car thinking about her next stop, reading her list to make sure she hadn't forgotten anything. She decided to phone Brian to let him know that he had to go to the bank to sign his checks. Using her cell phone, she punched in the numbers for Hartford Industries. An operator answered. "May I speak with Brian Strait?"

"One moment, please."

Comfortable, safe, trustworthy. His voice spoke interrupting her thoughts. "Uh, Hi Brian. I'm in the bank parking lot. I took some money out of the account and had them make up some traveler's checks for us. I've left a checkbook for you at the bank but the checks have to be signed by you before they will let us leave with them. Can you meet me here or…?"

Brian chuckled on the other end of the line. "You know, for a quiet woman, you can sure talk a mile a minute sometimes. I'm glad to see that you are feeling a little better today."

"I am. In fact I'm having fun…shopping."

"You women are all alike. Give you a shopping mall and you're in seventh heaven."

"As if you guys don't like to spend time shopping. I seem to remember you and Trent taking an inordinate amount of time looking for some fishing equipment about two weeks ago."

"Yes…well…that's different"

"Oh, sure. Are you going to answer my question or not?"

"As it turns out, I am free today. I just told my boss that

I would not be working for Hartford anymore. He told me to clean out my desk today to make room for someone who will do the job. I think he's kind of miffed. Anyway, I'll be finished here in a couple of minutes, and then I'll see you at the bank. Okay?"

"Sure. Hey…maybe I'll go back inside and check out some of the money transfer information. When we're in Haiti we may need to transfer a little to a bank account there…since we have no idea how long we'll be gone."

"That sounds like a plan. I'll see you there."

****

Twenty minutes later, Brian walked through the door to the bank. He winked. Her heart felt as if it had a bubble in place of a beat. *What's that about?* She placed her hand over her heart and smiled in his direction.

"What's with you?" He stopped signing the checks the clerk had placed in front of him to glance in her direction.

"I feel kind of free, don't you? No job, no responsibility, no…"

"No means of support except…"

"Yah, I know." She lowered her voice considerably. "Max's money. Anyway, we can enjoy it for a little while, can't we?" They walked towards the exit and out to the parking lot.

"I hope this will cover our initial expenses." Andrea moved towards her car. "If we need more, I deposited enough in the account I think. The clerk said that if we need to transfer money, all we have to do is wire the amount and the bank will handle everything."

"I'll bet you feel better just knowing you have enough to buy a house when this is all over. I know it won't replace the memories, but .. well .. we'll be making some new ones anyway, won't we?"

"I sure hope they're not all bad ones."

"I hear that Haiti is quite pretty in some spots. A lot of poverty, though."

"Yes, well. We'll need to keep focused, I'm sure. I expect that there'll be plenty of distractions."

"At least, the trip will help get your mind off what you've lost this past week. Have you given any thought about when you would like to leave?"

"Not really," she replied. "I want to wait until I hear from the Fire Marshall."

"Someone could very well be trying to warn you to mind your own business. Of course, we could both be paranoid too." Brian placed a reassuring hand on Andrea's arm. "Um, I didn't want to scare you yesterday but…remember that car that almost ran over me in front of the Michners? Well, Saturday, it followed us to the police station. After I dropped you here, it followed you and I followed it past your house. They saw where you live."

"Brian, did you not think I needed to know that?" Andrea's voice trembled.

"I wasn't sure they were part of all this but now… I followed them until I lost them in traffic. They don't seem to be anywhere around today. I wonder if they've changed cars."

Andrea closed her eyes and chanted, "We're doing the right thing. We're doing the right thing" And then, "Yes. We are. Max said this is tied to Trent and Diane. We need to find out where they are so we can get them out of whatever mess they're in."

Brian fingered her chestnut colored hair. He pushed it behind her collar. "You know, you're one brave woman. After all you've been through, you're still thinking only of Diane."

"And Trent. They're a couple, remember. Anyhow, I don't know how brave I am. I have no idea if I have what it takes for something like this. If you weren't going with me… I…"

"There's no question about me going. I want to uncover what's happened as bad as you do." Brian stepped away from her and headed toward his car. He turned to look over the roof of his car toward her.

Andrea smiled. "Well, partner. Let's get the stuff done that will allow us to leave as soon as possible. Okay?"

He hung his head, scuffed his toe on the pavement and then looked into her eyes. "I am concerned…I mean…I wouldn't want anything to happen to you. Do you mind?"

"No, I guess...no not at all." Andrea giggled. "Oops." She placed a hand over her mouth.

"I've never heard that from you before. Must be a good sign." Brian grinned and then waved as he sat down on the front seat, closed his door and started the ignition.. He rolled down his window. "Hey, wanna have dinner tonight…to go over what we accomplished today…I mean?"

"Sure. Call me or better yet, I'll call you. I don't know where I'll be staying for the night yet."

"Sounds good to me. See Ya."

Andrea smiled. Brian was not the man she'd thought. He seemed not afraid to have a woman lean on him occasionally. He also appeared to be anything but a womanizer…at least he didn't treat her that way. *I'm probably not his type*. She chuckled. Where did that thought come from? They had just become friends. Sort of. Because of the Michners.

Chapter Ten

What a day. Andrea picked up the phone, dialed and then waited. It rang three times and then, "Hi Brian. I said I'd call when I got settled. I'm at the Beresford."

Brian expressed his approval. "I managed to get most of the things on my to-do list done and I must say, I rather enjoyed myself. Having all that money opened some doors that I'd not been able to afford before."

She listened as Brian teased her about shopping. "Typical woman. Give her some money and the worries of the world go away."

"Yeah, well, I figure I deserved to have a few minutes of 'no worries'. Anyway, I also called Marcia. I wanted her opinion on the money. Having a lawyer for a friend helps in times like these."

"What did she say?"

"Well, since my name is on the bonds, they're legally mine to do with as I please. She says that there's nothing anyone can do. Have you met Marcia and her fiancé Jonathan?"

"I did. In fact, Trent and I have been talking about a bachelor party for Jonathan. How are the plans coming? I understand they've decided to get married in Hawaii...kind of elope."

"Today she asked me to be one of the bridesmaids. I told her that would depend on when the wedding was since we were headed for Haiti. I also told her about my house."

"Changing the subject...wanna go out for dinner tonight?" Brian seemed to want to keep their conversation light this time.

Andrea looked toward the bedroom closet. "I'd like that. It'll give me a chance to show off one of my new purchases."

"Is there any place special you'd like to go?"

"Why not right here. I peeked into the dining room when I arrived and it looks pretty elegant."

"That's right. Some of the guys at work have talked about the Beresford's dinner menu. It's supposed to be really good. How about I come by about 7. That way you can relax and I can take the time to get spiffed up too."

"Sounds great. I'll see you later." Andrea hung up and then picked up the phone again to call the dining room for reservations. That task done, she walked toward the bedroom. *A good long soak in that great tub is just what I need. As long as I don't mess up my new hairdo.*

****

Promptly at ten to seven, Brian pulled up in front of the Beresford Inn, a large twelve story building with penthouse suites on the top floor. He stepped out of the car to enter enormous glass doors that were opened by a doorman. "Welcome to the Beresford," the uniformed man said. Brian smiled in return. He looked around the lobby and noticed that several people were heading toward the dining room. *I'm glad I decided to wear a suit and tie.*

"What room is Miss Wilton in please?" The desk clerk asked for his name and then dialed Andrea's room to announce him. Brian smiled thinking about her being in a secure place for a change.

"Miss Wilton will be right down." Brian walked over to an overstuffed chair that faced the elevator to wait.

Before long, the doors opened and he gasped. *She's beautiful and what has she done to her hair.* Brian watched as Andrea walked slowly toward him. Her hair was shorter and she'd had some highlights added. The dress was spectacular... made her legs look longer somehow. "You look fabulous." He took her hand and held it a fraction longer than he'd ever done before.

"Do you like my new dress. I thought I'd splurge." Then she lowered her voice a smidge. "Max's money helped a lot. It was fun, not having to worry about how much something cost for a change." She giggled.

"Like I said earlier...just like a woman."

She batted her lashes at him and turned for the short walk toward the dining room. "We've already discussed how men shop so I'm not going there." She was actually flirting with him. Brian took her arm to walk beside her. *I didn't think she knew how.*

****

Andrea was feeling a little like Cinderella. "You look pretty debonair too."

Brian chuckled. "I love dressing up once in a while. It gives me an excuse to use my manners." He opened the door to the restaurant. Dimly lit interior was swathed in mood lighting. Small intimate tables surrounded a dance floor. The maître d showed them to their table.

"Andrea, I'm beginning to look forward to our trip. How about you?" A waiter by the name of Peter interrupted before she could answer. "Can I get you something to drink?".

"I'll have a diet cherry coke." Andrea's favorite.

Peter looked at Brian. "Just water for me, thank you."

"I'll be right back." Peter walked away leaving menus for them to check out.

While she looked over the selections, Andrea responded to Brian's earlier question. "I am looking forward to the trip too. I have always loved to travel. Just haven't had much opportunity."

"Me neither. Uh, Andrea. Do you trust me?"

"Yes, I think I do. Why?" Andrea cocked her head to one side wondering what next.

"Well…I just wanted to tell you that I think you look beautiful but you are also smart. I want you to believe that I have no ulterior motives here. I know my reputation. It's mostly exaggerated but…"

"Yes, I know. You've been nothing but a perfect gentleman. I know we're traveling to a foreign country together and I wouldn't have asked you to come if I thought…"

"That I'm a letch?" Brian wiggled his eyebrows up and down.

"Well, no…but…I know I'm not your type so…"

"Oh, and what is my type?" Brian chuckled.

A dark red coursed its way up Andrea's neck. She knew she must be beaming like a neon sign that said unsophisticated in capitol letters. Just then Peter returned. She breathed a sigh of relief.

For the next few minutes, choosing their entrée took up the space vacated by the unanswered question. Andrea focused on the menu and while Brian's eyes seemed turned in that direction also, she wondered what he could be thinking.

"I'll have the poached salmon." Andrea loved seafood of any kind. She handed her menu to Peter.

Brian selected rib-eye steak cooked medium rare. Peter invited them to make a trip to the sumptuous salad bar so Andrea stood. The salad bar, located in a smaller room to the right side of the dining room, contained three salad buffets with enough selections to make a meal.

"Wow. We didn't need to order anything else." Brian perused the assortment of cold meats, crackers, cheeses, soups, and salads. He grabbed an ice cold plate from the container and began filling it.

"You'd better take it easy. You have a steak coming, remember." Andrea's mouth watered. "If I'd had any idea the salad bar included this large a feast, I'd have ordered just that."

Once they returned to their table and said a short prayer for the meal, their conversation resumed between mouthfuls.

"I checked with my cellular provider. My plan enables me to connect to anyone, from any country, at anytime. What about yours?"

"Great minds think alike. I checked on mine today too. They assure me that it's good to go anywhere in the world. I guess we'll see, won't we?" He set his fork down and took a long drink of water. "You know…I can't wait to get started. Not that I have ever pictured myself in the role of detective, but it is kind of exciting to know we could be the ones to uncover whatever is going on here." Peter arrived with their main course.

Andrea took a bite of her salmon. "It is, but it's also a kind of scary exciting, don't you agree?"

"I do. Considering the murder and your fire…well, it does cause one to think about the consequences of our decision. But I haven't changed my mind and I know you haven't either. Whoever these people are, they aren't going to succeed with Strait and Wilton on the case." Brian chortled and then continued shoveling food into his mouth. "Yum. This is so good. The steak is done exactly as I like it."

"What do you mean, Strait and Wilton?" Andrea joined his playful mood. "What about Wilton and Strait?" She broke off another piece of salmon with her fork.

"Eat your food, woman." He winked. "Maybe after dinner, you'll feel like doing a little dancing."

As the meal progressed, they formulated plans for their trip. Brian concurred with Andrea's decision to visit a travel agent and have them make all the arrangements. "Have you had a chance to check on the internet to see what a flight might cost?"

"No...my computer was in the house...remember?" Andrea's smile vanished.

"I'm sure the hotel has one." Brian turned toward their waiter as he poured two very aromatic cups of coffee. Peter cleared away the dirty dishes then returned to take their dessert order.

While they waited, Brian steered the conversation away from recent events. "Did you know that Trent and I were both football players in high school? He was a line backer and I played quarter back. We actually won the state championship our senior year but we had a great team."

"I guess I never knew you both played so much sports. You seem not to do much of that these days. You just watch."

"Yah, well...us armchair quarterbacks have a lot of fun watching too but playing was..."

"Painful?"

"That too."

Peter arrived with dessert.

"Oh my." Brian rubbed his stomach. "Maybe we should have shared."

Andrea blushed. That was too personal. "I think I'll just eat this slowly and enjoy every bite. I haven't enjoyed a meal so much in days."

Thirty minutes later, Andrea sat back to sip her coffee. She sighed in contentment as the flavored brew coursed down her throat cooled by the icy confection. "This is good."

"We'll have to bring Trent and Diane here to celebrate once we're all home again."

"So much has changed in less than a week." Andrea stared toward the dance floor. "Life has certainly not been dull, but some of the excitement I could do without. Do you know that I'm working on a novel? It's gone now, ashes amidst the rubble of my life," she said melodramatically.

"Your life is not a rubble. I didn't know you were a writer. Like Diane, huh?"
"Not exactly. Diane is a journalist. I dabble."

"I'll bet you'll find all kinds of things to write about after this is over. Are you finished with your coffee? Do you want more?" Brian searched for their waiter.

"No, I think I've had enough. I'll never get to sleep tonight. After the workout I got last night, tossing and turning like a gymnast, I need a good night's sleep. Besides, I have a lot of details to get worked out tomorrow."

"Do you want me to come with you … err… I mean, if you need me that is?"

"No, I think I can handle everything myself. Shall we call it a night then?"

"Not yet." Brian stood. He reached out to take her hand in his. "Will you join me in this waltz? I think this is the perfect way to end an evening with a beautiful woman." His eyebrows danced up and down in his best imitation of the worse cartoon villain.

"Why certainly, monsieur." Andrea stood and walked with Brian to the center of the near empty dance floor. The band played softly as they circled. Brian's arms propelled her in the slow sensuous movements. Andrea' heart began to pound.

Stepping back a little, she said, "I think we should travel first class, don't you? When are we going to get another chance to do that?"

Brian looked at Andrea for a moment or two before answering. "First class is okay by me. Should make the trip more comfortable." He drew her back into his arms, masterfully and yet with gentleness. "Relax Andrea. Let the song work its magic. Forget about the trip for a few seconds, okay?"

Andrea could feel herself beginning to like this man, maybe more than she should. She followed Brian's lead and swayed to the beat. Her heart picked up the rhythm. *I think I could grow to like this.* Then the dance ended. Brushing her hands down over the skirt of her dress as if to clear her head, she smiled. "It's been a long time since I danced. I hope I wasn't too rusty."

"On the contrary. I hope we have another opportunity." He placed his hand in the middle of her back to steer her through the tables.

"I am looking forward to a good soak, and then a long night under those soft sheets," Andrea said, stifling a yawn behind well-manicured hands. "The suite is just perfect. I may get to like this lifestyle."

Brian nodded his head in agreement but said nothing. They walked through the lobby to the front door. Brian handed the parking attendant the key to his car.

"Thanks Brian…for coming tonight I mean. The food was spectacular, and I loved the elegant atmosphere in the dining room. It sure took my mind off the stuff, you know?"

Brian whistled a bar or two of the waltz softly, almost to himself, and then launched a smile of pure satisfaction in Andrea's direction just before he walked out of the building. Andrea's heart skipped a beat, taking her breath with it.

Interesting. She walked toward the elevator and another sleepless night.

Chapter Eleven

The hair on the back of Andrea's neck stood on end and goose bumps dotted the skin on her arms. "You mean, someone actually tried to kill me?" She stared out the hotel window at the blue sky and wispy clouds in an attempt to calm her heart. Her backbone tightened and her breaths came in short gasps. She would not let them scare her.

"The perpetrator may have thought you were in the house or he may also have known you were not. However, all indications point to arson." Andrea had left her information with the fire marshal's office the day before. Brent Morrison phoned early, waking her.

"But..."

"That's all I can tell you for now, Miss Wilton. I'll fax

my report to the hotel, if you'd like. Your insurance company may need a copy of this."

"Will you be able to discover who burned my house to the ground or do the police handle that?" Catching this person would not save her house but...*Revenge is mine saith the Lord*...The Holy Spirit spoke loud and clear. Andrea sighed. *Okay Holy Spirit. I'll submit.*

"The police will track down the arsonist although we'll continue to look for clues to help them out. As for the insurance company, we'll be happy to give them any details they want. This investigation is just beginning, so they may not want to settle just yet."

The fire marshal's fatherly, compassionate voice comforted Andrea. She believed he would do his best for her. "Thank you for calling me so soon. I appreciate this."

"I just wish we could tell you more. Will your insurance cover your losses?"

"I don't know." Andrea exhaled noisily and then took a slow, deep breath. "I guess I'll find out after I contact my agent. By the way, why don't you take down my cell number? I won't be here much longer." Andrea proceeded to rhyme off the numbers, then said good-bye. She checked her watch. Eight o'clock. Time for a shower.

After a hurried breakfast in the hotel coffee shop, Andrea picked up the fax report from the fire marshal at the front desk and walked out into the sunshine, toward the parking garage entrance. Confident that God would look after finding out who torched her house, she tried to think of all the things she needed to be grateful for this morning. She drank in the beauty of His creation in the trees and plantings lining the driveway to the hotel. She was grateful He had protected her yesterday. As she thanked her Lord, she wondered why she'd not felt appreciation for life before. Something she'd taken for granted. Not anymore.

Taking the keys from her purse, she walked to the driver's side of her car. *Musk.* A hand, encased in a scratchy fabric glove, clamped her mouth shut. Another arm surrounded her and roughly pulled her body into a hard embrace.

"Forget the Michners." The voice sounded male. "You could be next." He pushed her toward the car. Andrea reached out to catch her balance and heard a loud thump as the man jumped over the barricade to the lower level. By the time she turned around, all she could hear were footsteps running over concrete floors. A scream erupted from her bruised lips but she quickly squelched the urge to call for help. She'd had enough of the police. Besides, what could they do to help her anyway? The guy was gone. She shuddered and her knees felt as if they wanted to buckle beneath her. Holding on to the car for support, she wiped her hand across her mouth. Her face ached from the crushing glove that had almost suffocated her. Andrea brushed the car's dust from her coat, straightened up and opened the door. She sat down hard and then quickly locked the doors again.

She swiped pesky tears from her eyes and put the car in gear. Andrea planned to visit a travel agent this morning. She'd found one particularly helpful when she'd arranged a trip for her boss so she drove to this agency but in a rather roundabout way to give herself time to gain control of her emotions. Thirty minutes later, she parked in front of a little red brick building that housed two agents well prepared to make dreams come true.

Chimes announced her entrance through the front door. The woman closest to the door smiled a greeting and then invited her to sit in a comfortable chair located to the side of her desk.

"Good morning. I'm Betsy Parker. What can I do for you?" Betsy leaned back in her chair as if preparing to give Andrea her full attention. She smiled, a friendly grin with a business like interest.

"A friend and I want two first class round trip tickets to Haiti. We'd like to use American Airlines if possible." Andrea fiddled with the clasp on her purse. "The return dates need to be open since we're not sure how long we'll stay. We'd like to leave tomorrow."

Betsy turned to her computer screen. "No availability on American but there are others." She found a flight that would leave early the next morning.

Andrea had not expected her wishes to be that easily fulfilled. "That's great, I think."

"You'll have to change planes in Miami but the wait between flights is only two hours. Sometimes, we're unable to get these connections the same day, but you're in luck."

"Thanks, we'll take them." Andrea began to fill out the forms.

"Haiti is not the usual place for people to vacation. But today, you are the second person to book a flight to Port Au Prince." Betsy watched her with a look of speculation in her eyes.

"Really? Interesting. Are they on the same flight then?" Andrea wondered who the other people were but she was too busy counting out the cash to consider the implications.

"No, he took the last seat on a flight that went directly there."

"Lucky him. But I've never visited Miami so that

should be fun."

"You won't have time to do more than explore the airport, I'm afraid." Betsy reached for the money but then said, "By the way, it probably would be best if you booked a hotel room in Port Au Prince now too."

"Of course. Let's do that. Do you have any recommendations?" Betsy led Andrea through a few brochures that listed hotels and hostels for the traveler. The photos displayed a tropical country with palm trees and coconuts with clear blue skies and azure seas. Hotels were numerous with a variety of amenities. Andrea picked the one that seemed to be best suited for Brian and herself. While Betsy added the cost of two rooms for a weeks stay to the voucher, she looked at the other pictures in the brochures. Haiti looked like paradise.

Andrea paid for the trip. One task crossed off her list of things to do today. She tucked the tickets inside her handbag, and then walked out of the building. She looked cautiously in all directions. No one lurked nearby.

Relaxing against the seat cushions of her locked car again, Andrea placed a hasty call to Brian.

"I-I've g-got our tickets. We leave tomorrow at 8 a.m." Andrea tried hard to keep the apprehension from her morning's experience out of her voice. It wasn't working.

"Wow. I know we said tomorrow or the next day but…"

"I-I know. It seems hurried but the sooner we go the sooner we…"

"Find the Michners. I know. What's wrong Andrea?" Brian's voice softened. "Still bothered about loosing your house?"

"N-no but the fire marshal did confirm this morning that it was arson." Andrea's voice broke.

"He did. How do they... oh never mind...of course they have ways to find that out. How are you doing?" Andrea could hear a semblance of his protective spirit coming through the phone lines.

"I was fine until some man threatened me in the parking garage at the hotel." Andrea could hear Brian's gasp but then spoke before he could say anything. "That scared the daylights out of me for a second or two but...there's no way they're going to..."

"Andrea, a man accosted you? Did you call for help?"

"His hand was clamped over my mouth so I couldn't. He warned me to forget the Michner's. I have no intention of forgetting them, not ever."

"Andrea, you need to carry..."

"No guns. If I'd had a gun, he might have shot me. Besides, do you remember what the pastor said yesterday about asking what Jesus would do? I think we should rely on the Lord, not guns."

"But, Andrea. Those guys mean business."

"All that thug wanted to do this morning was scare me. If he'd wanted to hurt me, he could have but he didn't. As far as my house, the fire marshal pointed out that the arsonist may have set the fire knowing I wasn't at home."

"Things could get a lot more dangerous once we're in Haiti. Don't you think?"

"Maybe. But if we walk with the Lord, He'll show us

how to find Trent and Diane and keep safe too. Won't He?" Andrea bit her lower lip.

"Of course. You're right. If this trip is God's plan then...OK, I won't mention guns again."

"Great. How's your packing coming?"

"I'm almost done. Don't have anything really summery though. And you?"

"I'll be ready when it's time to leave tomorrow. Right now I'm on my way to the insurance company. I need to get them started on replacing my house." Andrea assured Brian that whatever he needed in the way of clothing could be purchased in Haiti. "Besides, I'm sure that in Port Au Prince you'll be able to find all the nice flowery, tropical print shirts you'll need." She giggled for the first time all morning as she pictured Brian in flowers. She quickly hung up before he could comment.

Andrea started the ignition and drove the short distance to her insurance agent. With the fire marshal's faxed report in tow, she convinced them to release a settlement into her bank account directly. Since she was not at fault, they were happy to settle for the insured amount of her house and its contents.

Next, Andrea went to a Century 21 real estate office. The agent had been very helpful in the selection of a home for Andrea when she'd moved to the area.

"I want a three bedroom home this time, with about 1 acre of land in the country but not too far from the city." Andrea began to enjoy the idea of a new home, one not restricted by budget. "I'd like a fenced yard for my dogs, but that's something I can add if the rest of the house is what I want.

"How soon would you like to visit some of the homes

we have listed?" The real estate agent eagerly anticipated another sale that month.

"I will be away for the next two or three weeks, but I will get in touch by phone a few times while I'm gone. Can you just go ahead and find something for me. You already know my taste since we spent so much time looking the last time."

"I could. I also have done some by videotape so you can review your choices long distance. Would that help?"

"Not really. Just have several ready for me to see when I get back." Andrea picked up her purse, ready to leave. The agent said she would get to work finding just the right place for her.

Her last stop for the day was the police station. A quick visit with Lieutenant Kurshner revealed that nothing new had happened. "We only have so many people that we can place on a missing person detail," he said. "We're doing the best we can."

Andrea drove back to her hotel with mixed feelings. She felt disgusted with the slow pace of the investigation but not surprised since Max had warned her that they could be involved. Her lack of trust cemented her resolve to leave the next morning and do the legwork herself.

She parked her car, outside the garage this time, and entered the plush lobby. The clerk at the front desk smiled a greeting as she made her way toward the elevator. The door slowly opened. Andrea stepped in but just as the door was about to close, a man, large in stature and wearing musk cologne entered. Andrea moved as far back into the elevator as she could. The man pressed a button for the 12th floor and stood facing the door. Andrea let out a sigh of relief. She got out on her floor, hurried to her door and then stopped. She looked toward the elevator. It had continued on its way.

She ducked inside her room and locked her door, adding the night latch for extra security. Throwing her suitcases on the bed, Andrea began to remove items from her closet and drawers, folding them neatly as she placed each item into the bags. *New wardrobe, new luggage. Sometimes new is not all it's cracked up to be.* She missed the familiar. Photos. Memorabilia from her life. She felt like a person transplanted from another era, with no connections to the past.

At a little before seven that evening, Andrea met Brian for a hasty bite in the little coffee shop.

"This is nice." Brian spoke as soon as he sat down across from Andrea.

"Yes, the food is great here too. I had breakfast here this morning. Are you all ready for tomorrow? Do you want me to pick you up, or shall we meet at the airport?" Andrea spoke in a nervous tone, tickled with the thought that her heart beat a little faster when she saw him.

"Why don't I pick you up since your hotel is between my place and the airport?" His dimples peeked out the side of his cheeks.

"Sounds good to me." Long spurts of silence allowed each to concentrate on their food.

"Will the dogs be okay until you can return. I'm sure they miss seeing you every day."

"I have been visiting them as often as I can, but while we are away, they will miss me. It's funny how attached we become to pets isn't it? I wonder if God had pets in mind when he commissioned man to govern the earth?"

"I don't know the answer to that, but they certainly are a comfort when we're lonely, aren't they? I used to have a dog.

Since moving here I've not gotten myself another one. I felt so bad when that bus hit Barney that I just never had the heart to replace him."

"Oh, that would be hard. I can't imagine what I would do without Patches and Pokey. My house in flames scared me. Not for my stuff as much as the dogs." Andrea yawned as they made their way through the lobby toward the front door. "I'll see you here at six then, okay?"

Chapter Twelve

Andrea's luggage sat by the hotel's main entrance at 6 a.m. the next morning. She'd arranged to store her car in a garage near the hotel and, since she didn't know how long it would be before she had a house to move into, she also kept the hotel room in her name. A costly extravagance, but that suite served as the closest thing she had to a home for now.

Brian arrived on time. "Good morning. Ready for an adventure?" He packed Andrea's luggage into his trunk alongside his own and ushered her into the passenger seat of his car. He exited the driveway and turned toward the west side of town where the airport was located. Andrea continued to peer out the window as the sun began to peek over the tall buildings along the way. "It's funny but if this hadn't happened to the Michners we may have never become friends."

Brian shook his head in agreement. "Not that I would wish anything bad to happen to the Michners. But it's kind of nice having a friend who is also a beautiful woman."

"Stop that. You're embarrassing me. I can't remember having a friendship with a man before. No complications. I like that. Don't you?" Andrea hoped Brian would refute the idea, but he just smiled. Comfortable silence filled the car for the rest of the short trip.

The airport bustled. People arriving and departing. Taxis unloading passengers and picking them up. Luggage strewn everywhere. Handlers hustled bags through revolving doors after harried commuters. Andrea and Brian fit in with the vacation crowd, according to plan.

After they checked their luggage in at the ticket counter, they walked toward their assigned gate. "The travel agent said there was another person going to Haiti. A Man. She seemed to think that was unusual. Haiti is not the usual place for vacationers, she said."

"I wonder…" Brian decided to leave the question of the man's identity alone for now. They passed several people sitting close by but never noticed two men leaning against a rail by the escalator with a camera focused on them, clicking away.

****

Trent trudged over the rocky ground as slowly as he could. His escort seemed not to be in any hurry this morning. The sky was a vivid blue with a few contrasting clouds, white wisps of fluff that were strung over the distant horizon. If the circumstances were different…Trent allowed himself to hope for a short second but the gun butt poking him in the rib cage brought him back to reality.

As had happened for almost a week, they entered a

roughly constructed building just a tad larger than the one presently housing Diane and Jeffrey. His keepers watched every movement. Everything else was modern and up-to-date from the lab equipment to the chemicals they gave him to work with.

"This batch is the wrong color." He lifted a tray of vials from the refrigerator. "I'll have to start over."

"The boss ain't gonna like that." A large muscular man with a smooth shaven head spoke from his seat by a table in the corner. "Things are taking too long. Remember, you don't do as we tell you and your boy suffers." He roared as if he'd told a particularly funny anecdote.

Trent choked back a retort. It didn't do any good for him to protest. They had his wife and child to threaten him with.

"Butch…" Another man, smaller in stature but bald as well spoke from a cot where he was reading a book.

"No names." The first man growled. He threw a stick of wood toward the offender but then relaxed into his own chair.

"I just wanted to know how long we was going to be holed up here." The short man spoke in a whiny, defensive tone from his corner.

"As long as it takes. Now shut up and go get some more wood. You," He pointed to the man who had escorted Trent into the room that morning. "Go get us a guinea pig. We'll see if that stuff is spoilt."

"It's not ready. I'll have some more by tomorrow morning. Just wait." Trent spoke around the fear that had been a constant companion since they'd been taken. "You *don't need to waste it. It's fixable."*

"Oh yeah." The large one waved for the third man to sit down. "Then fix it."

Trent bent over the flasks and beakers.

****

Andrea placed her carry-on luggage in the overhead rack. Brian was already settled in for the two hour flight. His seat belt was buckled. A magazine lay open on his lap. Andrea sat down in the window seat. She fastened her seat belt. "I picked up this mystery when we stopped at that book kiosk." She removed the novel from her purse.

A flight attendant, dressed in colorful summer garb, offered them something to drink as soon as their flight leveled off. The airline personnel were able to walk the aisles but the seatbelt sign was still on.

Brian put his magazine down. "I'll have a soda."

"Oh yuck, so early in the morning." Andrea made a face at him. "I'll have some of that great coffee I smell."

The flight attendant brought their drinks, continued down the wide aisle to serve the other passengers and then stopped by again to see if they wanted a pillow. "Might as well." Andrea yawned. "It was an early start today."

Before long, her eyes closed. Brian watched as her eyelids flickered. A short 20 minutes later, her eyes popped open. She looked at Brian seated next to her. A sigh of relief escaped from her open mouth.

"Are you okay?" Brian looked at her with concern. "You seemed restless even though you slept."

"How long did I sleep?" Andrea brushed her hair out of her eyes.

"About twenty minutes. Not long."

"Boy, this stuff is on my mind even when I'm sleeping. I dreamt…" She looked around. People were sitting too close for them to discuss their reasons for being on this flight. She lowered her voice to a whisper. "Trent was holding a smoking gun in his left hand after shooting Max. Diane was laughing at the look of complete surprise on my face, and then she pulled a gun of her own! Can you imagine?"

"Dreams can certainly be unnerving. I know. I've had a lot of them lately too."

"You have? It must the circumstances we're in." Andrea chuckled. "I'd love to just enjoy this trip as a holiday but…"

"I know. We'll still have lots of opportunity to explore, don't you think?" Brian smiled, and then resumed his reading. Andrea looked out the plane's window and marveled, as she'd always done whenever she flew anywhere, at the beauty of the clouds and the blue sky, bluer than could be seen on terra firma. God certainly loved color.

She looked over at Brian. His eyes were closed. She leaned her head against the seat cushion. *When we get there, we'll get to the hotel, check in, and then begin to look for something, anything that will lead to Trent and Diane. If they're there. What if they're not and this is a wild goose chase? We're wasting time. Maybe we should visit the local police. No, Max said the police could be involved. Did he mean at home or in Haiti?* Then she thought about her faith in Jesus Christ. *Would Jesus sanction what we're doing? Maybe we should have left this whole mess in the hands of the police.*

Slowly she leaned forward. She reached under her seat and pulled her carry-on bag out.. Her Bible went everywhere she did, so she opened it to see if she could find the answer to her dilemma.

Deuteronomy 33:29 said just what Andrea thought the Bible would say on the subject. "He is your shield and your helper and your glorious sword. Your enemies will cower before you…." She knew that they needed to seek the Father's answers for finding Max's murderer and their missing friends.

****

Brian stirred. He watched Andrea through shuttered eyelids. She was reading her Bible. God had spoken to him as well while he was resting his eyes. He knew they would have to figure out ways to protect themselves. They needed a plan of action. He watched Andrea close her eyes again. He guessed that she was praying. *I know that we need the Lord's protection.*

Lord, Brian closed his eyes and prayed quietly in his mind. *Help us to know how you want us to handle this situation. Point us to your answers and help us in our search for the one who murdered Max. And Lord, help us to locate the Michner family unharmed. In Jesus' name I pray. Amen.*

****

"Sir, would you like something to snack on?" A pretty blond stood next to his seat. Brian opened his eyes.

"Uh, sure. I guess." He looked through the assortment of packages on the flight attendant's cart. He chose a bag of mixed nuts and a chocolate bar. The attendant smiled toward Andrea who also took some mixed nuts. Brian rubbed his hands together in anticipation "This will hit the spot. It may be a while before we are can find a restaurant to get some lunch after we land in Miami."

****

The seatbelt sign came on. The flight attendants made sure that all trays were in their upright positions. They'd reached Miami for a two hour layover. Andrea looked out the window. As the plane descended through the cloud covered sky, she could see palm trees waving in the breeze. Just off shore were some islands, accessible by bridges but densely populated with large pink, beige or white houses. *Pretty tropical looking.*

"Brian, have you ever been to Miami before?"

"No, but I've always wanted to. I'd like to come back when I have more time to explore. Today, we won't have any time to even leave the airport."

"I guess I could have booked us an extra day but…"

"Oh. No, Andrea. This is perfect. This isn't a vacation. We need to get to Haiti. I know that." Brian unfastened his seatbelt and Andrea did the same. They gathered their carry-on luggage from the overhead rack and then waited their turn to disembark. The line moved slowly until at last they were inside the airport. Their connecting flight left from another gate so they moved in that general direction.

"Brian, let's step outside for a few minutes anyway. Then we can get some lunch. I saw a restaurant on the other side of the building."

The air smelled spicy with a definite odor of jalapenos or something close to it. Warm breezes wafted in from the ocean lending coolness to the tropical climate. Andrea took in a long breath of fresh air. Even though the skies were overcast, the day was already warm.

"I can't wait to see you looking like a tropical babe."

Brian winked. "I may enjoy wearing some of those flowered shirts but you'll look yummy in a muumuu."

"Oh please…"

"Well…I think you'll look delicious…all flowery like that."

Andrea punched him on the arm and moved toward the entrance. "Let's go eat."

Brian wiped newly formed sweat off his brow as he followed her inside. "That humidity sure causes me to sweat in a hurry. I wonder if Haiti is humid."

Her heels clacked on the tiled floor. "Probably. After all it is an island in the Caribbean.".

The inside of the restaurant looked as if it was outdoors among the palm trees. It had a large veranda stretching across the entryway. Brian and Andrea walked down the two steps separating the entrance from the seating area. Its air-conditioned elegance offered them a comfortable place to sit for the next hour.

A tall good-looking waiter brought them the menu, made his recommendations and then left to get their drinks. They'd explained they were in a hurry but the waiter seemed used to that. Real lemonade in frosty glasses were set before them. "I think I'll order the catch of the day." Andrea loved seafood.

"I just want a salad." Brian settled back in his chair to watch the comings and goings as they waited for their food.

"The place is full of tourists." Andrea grinned.

"Gee, ya think." Waiters bustled about with food on

trays decorated with palm fronds. It took only minutes before their meal arrived. "Boy that was quick. I guess it pays to eat at an airport when you're in a hurry."

Just a short thirty minutes later, they were on their way to their departure gate. Andrea skipped to keep up with Brian's long stride. "I hope our luggage got put on the right plane. You know…all those stories about lost luggage you hear." Brian just kept on walking. They were cleared through security again and then seated in the first class compartment. *M-m-m empty… except for the Wilton Strait party.* At least, that's what the flight attendants called them.

"See?" Andrea nudged Brian with her elbow. "Wilton Strait – just like I said."

Brian looked at her with his eyes crossed in the most unattractive way and then stuck out his tongue, a gesture meant to cause laughter, and he succeeded.

The plane took off over the water shortly after they were buckled in and it seemed only a short time before they were in sight of land again. The flight attendant gave them the standard pre-landing instructions.

"Oh Brian. Look at that water. Have you ever seen water so blue?"

"That island hardly looks bigger than a cruise ship." As they descended to 10,000 feet, they could see some of the different towns scattered amongst lush foliage. Beaches framed the island. Palm trees and flowers were everywhere.

They approached the landing strip. "Andrea, there's an island out there, just west of the harbor entrance."

Andrea watched as they quickly passed a smaller, green covered island surrounded by blue, shimmering water. "It's so beautiful."

The city of Port Au Prince was soon framed in the windows of the airplane, a much larger city than either of them had expected. From this distance, the beauty of this tropical paradise was astounding. The thump of the landing gear, a smooth rolling arrival and then the fasten seatbelt sign went off. They had arrived in Haiti.

Chapter Thirteen

The airport loudspeakers had informed arriving passengers that the temperature outside was about 85^0, but neither Brian nor Andrea expected the wall of humidity to reach out and envelope them as it did. "Brian, did you notice that strange scent in the air?'

"No, I can't say that I did. By the way, do you think that we should develop a story in case anyone should ask us what we are doing here? I mean, what explanation do we offer, should the subject come up?" Brian began to whisper. They moved toward the customs agent.

"I guess I hadn't thought about that. Why couldn't we just say that we are looking for our friends?" Andrea looked at the people-milling around them. The airport, not a large one by American standards, had a couple of planes on the tarmac with people disembarking to enter the building for inspection by customs officials.

"I'm just thinking that maybe we don't want to give away our reason for being here until we're sure who we can trust and who we have to be careful with," Brian went on. "After all, if what Max said in his note is true, then we are dealing with some pretty dangerous people. If what they are doing is illegal, and most likely it is, then they won't take kindly to someone snooping around."

The customs agent finally waived Andrea over. "Mam'selle, please to open your suitcase," he asked in a halting French dialect. Andrea complied and then it was Brian's turn. They walked toward the entrance.

"Brian, I read in one of the brochures that the travel agent gave me that there are two official languages spoken here; French for the educated people and Creole for the illiterate. And...snobbery exists between the two classes. The upper and middle class consider themselves better than the people who don't speak French. Creole isn't taught but somehow the language seems to perpetuate itself."

"Do they also speak engl..." Brian noticed someone watching them. "Do you see that man near the water fountain?" He opened the door to the exit.

"No, what about him?" She swiveled her head around. "I don't see anyone."

"I guess he left. His face seemed familiar to me but I can't remember where I've seen him before or even if I have." Brian began to feel a little paranoid. "I'm just a little jumpy."

The sunshine was hot and very bright as they moved toward a large van marked Al-B-Oloffson Hotel. People spoke in rapid French all around them. "There, can you smell that?" Andrea hastened. "There's our ride. Let's go."

Stowing their bags in the back, Brian took a deep

breath. "The air just smells so different than at home."

"Look, Brian. There are flowers everywhere." Andrea gripped the arm rest as she gazed out the window. Their driver ignored the pedestrians as they jumped out of his way. "I never expected to see so many people here. I guess I thought…"

"I know…you'd think that so small an island would only house a small population but…it's almost crowded."

"From the look of some of them they probably have never been anywhere else." Poverty was evident not only in the well-worn clothes that some wore but also in the rundown condition of many of the buildings they passed. "Their clothes are certainly colorful. But look, there are also men dressed in suits." Passing an open air market, they heard people bartering over animals being sold.

"Oh Brian, look. Isn't this just the most picturesque building you've ever seen?" The hotel looked like it could have been built in the last century. A long wrap-around veranda or deck was accessed by a wide flight of stairs with handrails on both sides.

"I can't wait to sit out here and watch the sights and sounds of this city." Brian looked toward the people sitting on wicker chairs all along the deck, relaxing under the shaded awning.

"Maybe they have a siesta time during the hottest part of the day." Although it was mid afternoon, the heat was tolerable and then just as Andrea entered the hotel, she felt a breeze. "O-o-o-h, did you feel that. We must be close to the ocean."

The clerk or concierge behind the desk greeted them with a strong French accent. "Bonjour, Monsieur et Madame." They gave him their names and he handed them each a room key. Two small boys worked hard to take their luggage toward and antiquated elevator. The couple silently walked behind the boys down the narrow hallway to their rooms, located on the second floor.

"I'll give you a half hour to get settled in, and then we can go get something to eat. I don't know about you but I'm starved. I can't wait to go sight-seeing." Brian sounded almost excited. His room was located a couple of doors from Andrea's.

"See you later," she called after him and then entered another world again. Her rather large room was decorated in a quaint manor reflective of plantation owners and mint juleps. Its grandeur was displayed in the small settee that was located off to one side. Andrea stepped through the French doors onto a small balcony with a view of the ocean in the near distance. She took a deep breath of salt air.

She returned to the room to run her hand over the large bed. Colorful pillows adorned the white coverlet. A dressing area with a tiny closet led into a small but functional restroom. Excitement warred with dread inside her. Andrea liked to travel but the circumstances weren't what she would have chosen for this trip.

Unpacking as quickly as she could, Andrea stepped onto the balcony once more. Just as she was beginning to get her bearings, a knock sounded on her door. "Come in, Brian. How do you like your room?" Brian stepped inside the door. "You sure seem in a hurry to see the sights."

"It's my stomach that's in a hurry. It hasn't stopped gurgling since we arrived." They took the elevator down to the lobby. As they stepped onto the veranda, they could hear car horns loudly discouraging people from walking in the street. The horns were ignored by pedestrians with shaking fists and unusual epitaphs.

"There's a restaurant. Let's go." Brian led the way.

Soon they were seated at a corner table. They looked around. "This place seems to have been built about the same time as the hotel." Andrea noticed the vintage grandeur and the faded wallpaper everywhere. "Let's try some authentic pastries." Andrea couldn't wait to immerse herself in the culture.

"You can try all the pastries you want, but I need something more substantial. This meat pie thing sounds interesting." Brian continued to peruse the menu. "They have a pretty good selection of French food."

"French would be fine and in fact, probably better than Creole since that cuisine would be more peppery." Andrea's mouth began to water as she read over the different selections and their descriptions.

Once the waiter brought their selections, they ate quickly. "M-m-m." Andrea's voice hummed with satisfaction.

"Me too." Brian stuffed another piece of the meat pie into his mouth. "This is great." Wiping the remains of their hurried meal from their faces, they paid the bill and strolled toward the door

"Let's walk some of that rich food off," Brian suggested. "We might as well get our bearings before we start hunting for the Michners."

"Boy, until you mentioned Trent and Diane, I had almost forgotten why we were here. You're right, we need to get the lay of the land so we can better decide which direction to go." Andrea pulled out a travel guide from her purse and their foray into Haitian culture began in the direction of the port.

"I love all those quaint shops. I wish I had more time to explore them." There were lots of native stores that allowed visitors to experience some of the local arts and crafts, but there were also shops catering to the rich and famous, or so it seemed to Andrea as she noticed the prices of window merchandise.

Brian chuckled. "Just like…"

"Ne-ver mind." She made a face at him. "I suppose this city hasn't changed a lot in the last 50 years. I read in the guide that a section just east of our hotel was rebuilt for their bicentennial in 1949 but not much has been done since. That's where the American Embassy is as well." The crowds never seemed to thin out as they continued to walk east of the port through the business section of this highly populated city. People continued to battle for road space with automobiles and drivers who never ceased to honk their horns as loud as they could.

"Let's go to that Welcome Center." Brian steered Andrea in that direction. There they selected a number of brochures describing various areas of interest to them both.

"People come to dis place all the time to scuba-dive," the man behind the desk stated. "Are you divers as well, peut-etre…er…maybe?"

"Not yet, but we want some lessons." Brian noticed Andrea's look of surprise. "Well it's something I've always wanted to do so…"

"Yeah, I guess so…while we're here anyway, but…" Andrea frowned at the thought of relying on a scuba tank to breath.

The helpful volunteer behind the counter continued. "There are several excursion companies located just quinze...huh…fifteen minutes from here by l'auto." He was clearly more comfortable speaking in French as he lapsed into the French term for car. "Do you have a vehicle, monsieur?"

"No, can you tell us where we can rent one?"

"But not a car, monsieur. You need a four-wheel drive to get to most places on this island. Those you can get at Jean-Pierre's, just around the corner." The clerk was most helpful.

"Thank you, monsieur." Andrea tried out the little French she was familiar with.

"About that excursion company... where can we find one that will teach us how to scuba-dive?" Brian leaned on the desk while Andrea moved toward the door.

"As I said before, dere are several just a few miles west of the water front along the coastal road. It is rough to ride on that road but with a four-wheel drive, it is easy, non? Au revoir, mam'selle et monsieur. Have a good time in our country." The clerk waved to them as they made their exit and proceeded around the corner where Jean-Pierre's Rental Service was clearly visible.

"We need a four-wheel drive and want it for an indefinite length of time," Brian began. "Can you supply us with one?"

"We also need to rent some scuba equipment, since we plan to learn while we are here," Andrea added.

This time Brian yanked on Andrea's sleeve to pull her away from the prying ears of the rental agent. "I thought you weren't all that keen about diving. I'm already certified, but I've only had about 3 dives since then."

"I thought about this and since our cover is tourist... this is what tourists do here. Learn to scuba-dive. Besides the skill may come in handy someday, who knows?" Andrea nodded towards the rental agent.

"While you get some lessons then, I'll stick to boating." Brian whispered. "That way I can get the lay of the land, if you will, over the water."

"Oh, why not join me. A refresher can't hurt. Besides this was your idea." Andrea was adamant. She led the way toward the agent.

Brian handed him a fifty dollar bill. "This should cover the deposit for the vehicle." He followed the man to the back of the building where the parking lot was.

"We 'ave some scuba gear over 'ere but if you go to take lessons, the excursion company will provide de gear," that man explained. "Dis is your vehicle."

He had pointed them to a dusty looking jeep that had certainly seen better days. It had the remains of a green paint job, but rust covered most of it and where there was no rust, there were holes. "Will this hold together over these roads?" Brian asked. "We were told that the roads are pretty rough."

"Oh, oui monsieur, it will hold." Clearly he didn't have anything better to offer either as Brian and Andrea looked at the other vehicles in the lot.

"I hope you're right," Andrea added. "We certainly don't want to get stranded somewhere along some deserted road."

"Deserted, Non…not in Haiti. Wherever you go there are people and most are willing to help a stranded tourist. Just smile a lot, mes amis and make sure that you say hello before asking directions or for help…. which you won't need, I am sure." The agent handed over the keys and proceeded to return to his shop leaving Brian and Andrea looking at his back as he retreated inside.

"Oh, well, I guess we might as well give it a try. After all, we may waste all day looking for another rental agent. Hop in, Andrea. I'll drive for now, but if you ever want to take over, just let me know." As they pulled out into the traffic flow, Brian decided that a horn blasting in their ears was a better choice than running over someone. Leaning heavily on the decrepit apparatus in the middle of the steering wheel, they proceeded in the direction that the travel agent had suggested.

Before long they were in less populated surroundings, and the scent of ocean breezes was everywhere. "I'm not sure I'm ready to scuba dive so soon. We know nothing about these waters." Andrea started to backpedal.

"Oh, you'll do fine and the instructors won't let anything happen to you." Now Brian had begun to look forward to the experience.

"Maybe we need to get on the same page. I want to, you don't. You do, I don't." Andrea screwed her face into a grimace. "Of course, there's always the possibility they won't take me." She actually sounded hopeful.

Brian laughed. "Let's find them first."

A junction in the road caused the two to pause momentarily to decide which way to go. They chose to head towards the harbor. "I can't believe all the potholes. I'm glad this is a four wheel drive." Brian's body jumped in the seat as they hit a particularly deep hole. The car shuddered.

Soon they were in front of an excursion company, the first listed in the guidebook. "We would like to take some diving lessons. How much do they cost?" Andrea entered the only door just ahead of Brian.

"We have an excursion boat going out daily. What you need is some short lessons in a pool first so we should schedule some for you as soon as possible." The guide, speaking perfect English, was quick to place the two novices on the schedule.

"See you then." He waved as they left.

Brian returned to his position behind the wheel. Just as she was opening the car door, Andrea saw someone who looked very familiar to her. Her jaw dropped in utter and complete surprise. Jason! He was talking to a man across the street. "Brian, that's Jason over there talking to that man!" she exclaimed.

"Who's Jason?"

"You know that guy I told you about from work."

"Are you sure?" Brian turned in his seat to get a better view. "Maybe it's just someone who looks…wait a minute. He looks like one of the men I saw when we went to the bank. Remember I told you that I thought we were being followed, but I never saw them again." Brian added. Andrea slid into the passenger seat, but then began to slide out of the rickety old car again until Brian placed a hand on her arm to stop her.

"Andrea, don't go over there. He may be one of the men who kidnapped the Michners!" Brian held onto her arm so she couldn't run across the street. "Just think for a minute…why would he be here? Did you tell him we were going to Haiti?"

"The day I left work, I told him about the murder; all of it. I wonder now why I trusted that information to him. I guess I just needed to get another opinion. Anyway, all he wanted was for me to go to the police. Max felt that I shouldn't trust anyone…so I just ignored him. I'm sorry I didn't tell you sooner. Jason asked me to go out with him the day I went over to see Diane…the day we found them missing."

"Oh, ho…"

"Never mind. I told him I wasn't interested Anyway think about this for a second. I wondered then why Jason was interested in me. Now it looks like it could be because of the

Michners…"

"Andrea, we don't know that for sure. And besides why wouldn't he be interested in someone like you?" Brian sucked in a deep breath as he realized what he'd just said. Andrea was worth his interest too. *M-m-m-m*

Andrea tugged at Brian's sleeve. "Let's get out of here before he sees us."

"He probably followed us, Andrea. He knows we're here already, I think. Why not keep the fact that we know he's here to ourselves for the time being. If he doesn't think we know he's here, maybe he'll slip up, lead us to someone who knows what's going on." Brian steered the car back toward Port-au-Prince.

Feeling as if her heart wasn't in it, Andrea followed Brian's lead as they headed towards the Iron Market, a large outdoor bazaar where many of the locals shopped, according to the brochure. "Let's get some fresh fruits and vegetables as well as some cheese and French bread. That way we can eat in our room tonight and get to bed early so we'll be fresh to begin our search tomorrow." Brian tried to distract Andrea.

"That sounds like a plan. All of a sudden I'm really tired." Andrea yawned as she picked out some particularly tempting pieces of fruit.

Chapter Fourteen

As her eyes opened, Andrea could see the remains of her short meal from the night before. Her stomach rumbled now. She decided it must be time for breakfast. Quickly she threw back the covers on the large bed. She'd just experienced the best rest she'd had in a week. Andrea turned on the shower to wash away the sleep from her eyes. She wanted to be fresh and fully awake for the search for answers that would begin today.

As she toweled her body dry, Andrea thought about the heat yesterday and the sparse wardrobe she'd brought with her. *The shorts I bought in the US won't be enough. I need to find time to add to my wardrobe today.* Before she had her hair dry, the phone rang.

"Hi Brian. Yes I'm starved. I'll be ready. "He promised to pick her up for breakfast in thirty minutes. Thank goodness for her simple hairstyle. She would be able to have her devotions before leaving.

Exactly thirty minutes later, Brian was at her door. "I don't know whether it's the sea air or what, but I'm famished… again." He led the way downstairs. "I've hired a guide for us today. That way we have a local who can tell us all the right places to go so we can begin gathering the necessary information to find Trent and Diane, if they're here."

" Do you have some doubts? I mean…I thought that we were both feeling pretty sure that this trip would lead us to them." Andrea matched her stride to his as they made their way to the restaurant next door.

"I know we hoped it would but really we have no proof they are tied to Max's murder, do we? I mean…. other than Max's note. This could all be coincidence. All of these bizarre events could be separate incidences. I spent a restless night, thinking about how we don't know if all this is tied together. It's already been a week since we reported the Michner's disappearance. I called Lieutenant Kurshner early this morning and he doesn't know anything more than what we've already told him. Some help the police are. I hope we'll find some answers today, though, don't you?"

"Yes I do. I want to enjoy the day, but until we find out what happened to Trent and Diane, we won't be able to concentrate on anything else, even scuba diving," she added. "Should we postpone those lessons…until we've had a chance to find out something, anything that will lead us to our friends." They were seated at the same corner table as before.

"No, I don't think so. We need to act the part of tourists and that's what tourists do. Besides, the guide might have some useful information, who knows? Maybe we should be praying through each step of the way, like you said on the plane, instead of leaving discovery to chance. God knows where they are and why they are there." With that Brian bowed his head and silently petitioned God to show them the way. While he was talking to the Father, their waiter brought some menus.

"I'd just like some fruit and biscuits, please." Andrea had enjoyed the fruit so much the night before, she decided to have more.

"How about some coffee, mam'selle?" The young man wrote her choices on a pad of paper.

"Oh, yes. I need some coffee. See anything appetizing, Brian?"

"I need something more substantial than fruit this morning. How about steak and eggs with a side order of potatoes and toast?" Brian smacked his lips in anticipation. "Add some juice to that, would you please?"

"I'd say you have a very hardy appetite. Where do you put it all?" Andrea chuckled when he looked rather sheepishly towards the door.

"Never you mind, Miss Andrea…I am hungry, and I love to eat a good breakfast. Besides…I…ah…isn't that Jason again across the street? He seems to be waiting for someone this time or something."

"Where…oh…there. Yes…that is Jason. I still can't believe he's here." Andrea's appetite suddenly left her as she remembered the argument they'd had the last time she'd seen him. She decided to fill Brian in. "He couldn't believe that I wasn't interested. He made it seem as if I was missing what every girl dreamed about. Yuck…so egotistical."

"Obviously he was covering his tracks and had every intention of coming here anyway." Brian mumbled around a mouthful of food. "I think we're going to find that he's up to his ears in this case."

The whole time they ate, Andrea and Brian could see Jason standing next to the building across the street. He appeared to be watching the hotel entrance.

"I think we should sneak out of here and see what happens," Brian suggested. "We can pretend that we just decided to go out the back way to hook up with our guide. If Jason follows us, then we know that he's with the wrong side, won't we?"

"But if we sneak out, he may lose us and we'll never know. Why not just spend the day as we had planned… sightseeing…see if we're followed. After all, Jason knows what we're here for anyway. We just need to confirm why he's here."

Brian agreed and then asked the waiter how they could get to Robichaud from there. "Ah.. I see you have engaged the guide...non. Robichaud, he is good, but he costs a lot of money. I think that you will have a good time visiting the island today. He is located across the alley at the back of the 'otel, monsieur."

"Thank you, sir. I know we will," Andrea stated. "Brian, let's get going. We have a lot of ground to cover today. Oh, wait a minute. Why don't we get the restaurant to pack a lunch for us and pretend to be real tourists? We could even buy some swimsuits along the way. Maybe Robichaud knows of a great beach where we could have a picnic lunch."

Brian quickly got in the mood for a great day of sunning and swimming as well. He chuckled at her. "I'll bet Jason will be extremely hot in that suit of his if he does follow us all day."

It took less than fifteen minutes for the restaurant to pack them a substantial meal. They walked, in plain sight, around to the back of the hotel to find their guide. The man Robichaud joined them beside their jeep, also parked behind the hotel in a spot designated for hotel guests. He climbed into the driver's seat leaving the back doors open for Brian and Andrea to hop in.

The trip began with a tour of Port-au-Prince. Robie, as he preferred to be called, showed them all the regular sights as well as those that were usually seen only by the locals. "There seems to be so much poverty…everywhere." Andrea pointed toward a particularly decrepit house with dirty children playing in the front yard.

"Oui. People are not so rich as you Americans." Robie pointed toward another example of the poor living conditions that his people languished in. Everywhere they went the poverty of the majority of the population was evident.

"Let's head out of the city." Brian looked at his watch. "We can look at more in Port Au Prince later, if we have time." The next town on their route was Bidonville or Shantytown. They couldn't believe the living conditions here was even worse.

"Some of these people have only tin shacks to live in." Andrea soft heart yearned to stop…to see if they could help some way.

"Some of them are lucky to have tin shacks to call 'ome. Others are not so lucky, non? Cardboard is a article of trade 'ere." Robie continued down the road to a barren stretch of land before ascending into the mountains. At the top of the climb, he pointed out the city behind them.

"Oh, what a wonderful view. The city looks so beautiful from here with the ocean just beyond." Andrea snapped a picture and then pointed. A car, one that they'd seen a few times already, was stopped where the mountain road curved toward their lookout. Brian nodded his head in acknowledgment. They returned to the car and drove another few miles to the village of Mirebalais.

"Dis," said Robie, "is de wettest town in Haiti." Poverty was everywhere, but for some reason, the lush, green landscape seemed to cushion the extent of it.

Since Robie was driving a vehicle they had rented and not his own, the charge for his services had been reduced. Brian and Andrea were enjoying their time with him to the fullest, and making mental notes of all the information for discussion later. They knew that they would have to gain the confidence of someone in order to get the exact information they needed but this would suffice for now.

In the charming village of Ville-Bonheur, their excursion took them by a church that was built on the spot where the Virgin Mary was once seen. "Every July 15, pilgrims come to dis spot to pray." Robie stopped the car to let his guests walk around a little.

Andrea stretched and Brian stooped down pretending to tie a shoelace. Andrea scrunched down beside him. "If that's Jason, he's still following us." Brian stood again and the couple returned to their warm mode of transportation. Even with the windows open, it was stifling in the car and it was only eleven o'clock in the morning.

Four kilometers away, at Saut D'eau, Robie pointed out a voodoo shrine. "De waterfall is magical with special powers. Voodoo pilgrims like to hike up to eet and swim in de healing waters. Dey light candles to ask de ancient spirits who live dere for help." Robie stopped by the side of the road for them to take in this new sight. The waterfall was beautiful. Its beauty was displayed in hanging creepers, which decorated the more than thirty-meter waterfall. Limestone shelves separated shallow pools and the sight did indeed seem enchanted.

Brian and Andrea couldn't help but feel sorry for these

people who had such emptiness. Simultaneously, they mouthed the words "People need the Lord" so that Robie couldn't hear them.

His commentary continued. "Many of my people are practicing voodoo because dey need to believe in something. Me, I believe in me." Robie was proud that he had worked most of his life when others had to rely on their wits to survive.

RN3, the roadway they were on, headed north out of Mirebalais on to the Central Plateau where the military crack-down was especially harsh after the 1991 coup. "Peasant move-ments 'ad been pressing for change for a long time before that."

The travelers skirted the Peligre Hydroelectric Dam, once a powerful producer of electricity but now silted over and almost useless. The region's Capital, Hinche, was the next town they passed through. There they noticed a couple of hotels that had seen better days. In fact, most of the houses were in a state of disrepair.

"Robie, do tourists come to stay here when they travel to Haiti, or are these hotels used primarily by the local people?" Andrea asked.

"Mostly, dey're used by de locals, non, but mam'selle, dey are sometimes visited by some businessmen who are 'ere to 'ire some of de local people," Robie supplied. "What is so strange about dat place is dat people who come to look for work seldom come back again."

"Why is that so strange?" Brian's curiosity was aroused.

"Well, dey are never seen again by family who live round 'ere. No money is ever sent for dere support which is de custom hereabouts."

"Hm-m-m-m." Andrea looked at Brian. "Disappearances…here. I wonder?"

"We'll talk about this later." Brian whispered and then shrugged. They continued to look out the window. The car continued along a road that ran east of Hinche towards Bassin Zim. The interesting sight that met their eyes this time was a 20-meter waterfall set in a lush jungle-like atmosphere.

Andrea whipped her sweaty brow. "Robie, stop." She looked toward the cascade of water as it fanned out into a 60-meter wide natural pool. She could see the deep blue water as soon as she stepped out of the hot vehicle. "Let's have our picnic lunch here."

Many people were taking advantage of the time of day to refresh themselves in its depths. Andrea and Brian walked toward a hut to the right of the beach which offered bathing suits for sale. They each purchased one, changed in the restrooms at the back of the hut, and then joined Robie, who'd already jumped in.

"Oooh, this water is wonderful and so warm," Andrea was quick to say after surfacing from her dive. "This is a little bit of heaven, I think."

"I don't know about your heaven mam'selle, but de people 'ere use dis pool all de time when de day is at it's 'ottest," Robie stated. "Dis is the beginning of siesta, and after swim, people eat slow lunch and rest until about four or five o'clock when de shops open for business again."

Brian floated nearby. "I could use a nap, too."

The trio spent about an hour in the water, its cooling effect relaxing them. After they towel dried their bodies, they spread a blanket on the banks of the pool and sat down. Andrea pulled out the basket of food.

"How often do the voodoo practitioners get together for a service or whatever they call it?" Andrea asked Robie. "Are their services open to the public?"

"No, not really, and dey are called ceremonies. Why are you interested anyway? Sometimes dese 'services', as you call them, are dangerous."

"Why would they be dangerous?" Andrea bit into another fresh piece of fruit. She couldn't seem to get enough.

Robie swallowed the food that was in his mouth. "Well, it is rumor, but some people do not come back from dese ceremonies." He looked around to see if anyone was listening. He noticed a man, standing by a tree, with a suit on. He seemed so out of place in this location. The man was mopping his brow. "Do you see dat man over dere?"

"Yes." Brian glanced where Robie was pointing and then pulled Robie's hand to the ground. "He followed us from Port-au-Prince this morning. Andrea, don't look now but it's Jason again. You were right. He looks very hot."

"Well, I hope he roasts in that stupid suit." She spit the words out before considering Robie's reaction. "Oh, I'm sorry, that was so unkind."

Robie picked up the mysterious tone of her voice. "You know dis man?"

Brian worked hard to cover Andrea's blunder. "Why not tell us more about the voodoo ceremonies, Robie. Can we see one?"

Chapter Fifteen

Before Robie could answer Brian and Andrea's query about Voodoo ceremonies, a low rumbling voice spoke from a location near the trio. "I couldn't help but overhear." Andrea had noticed the man earlier, sitting on a chair that leaned against the hut where they'd purchased their swimsuits. "You sound interested in voodoo ceremonies and I happen to be the local Houngan."

"What's a Hungan." Andrea peered up at him with one eye closed against the glaring sun at his back.

"No, Houngan. I am the high priest of this temple." He pointed to the hut. "In the back room, I council anyone who is part of the local congregation. I would be happy to explain voodoo to you."

"No, monsieur," Robie piped up. "We are ready to leave and 'ave to be in de city in a half hour. Maybe another time." He rushed about, quickly gathering up all of the leftovers from their lunch. Brian and Andrea could only look on in surprise. They watched this happy go lucky individual all of a sudden become tense and fearful. He ushered them to the jeep looking over his shoulder often.

"What's w-w-w-wrong,' Andrea's teeth chattered. All of a sudden, she was cold to the bone. "We wanted to talk to that man. Besides we thought that this was siesta time. We could both use a nap."

"Dat man is evil." Robie looked over his shoulder. The man was still standing on the grass by the pool of water. After they'd left the parking spot, Robie continued. "He is de one who holds those ceremonies where people go poof in de night and are never seen again. De locals say he is possessed, and dat Satan himself uses his body to live in some of de time."

Andrea looked at Brian. "Well, I guess we don't want to be seen with someone like that then. Robie, I thought you didn't believe in voodoo? How can you be frightened of something you don't believe has any power?"

"I may not believe dat dere is any worth in lighting de candles and dancing around de open fire, but I have respect for de fools who do believe. Me, I stay as far away from dem as I can." He crossed himself as a catholic believer would. "I advise you bote, mam'selle et monsieur, to do exactly like me, non?"

The trip home, as they had begun to call their hotel, was faster than their trip out, but still as fascinating once Robie calmed down. He continued to inform them about the views and vistas they were passing. Brian and Andrea glanced behind them once to supposedly view a rambling plantation, but in reality to check on their pursuer. At the next turn in the road, they noticed that the same car was not far behind and now they knew that Jason was driving.

"I'll bet Jason is happy to be sitting in air-conditioned comfort," whispered Andrea, in order not to arouse Robie to the existence of the car following them. Their cover as tourists had to be kept intact.

"It is going to be nice to have all this cloak and dagger figured out." Brian settled deeper into the seat and laid his head back. He closed his eyes for a moment.

Andrea looked toward him. "I can't for the life of me figure out how Jason could know the Michners or how the Michners could be mixed up with someone like Jason." She shook her head and also leaned back into the cushions.

"We'll figure it out, Andrea. Let's just enjoy today and gather as much information about this place as we can. I think the voodoo disappearances need further investigation, don't you?"

"Maybe." Andrea opened an eye to peer out the window again. "Robie, where are we now?"

"We are passin' another landmark dat touristas like to viseet." Robie looked at the couple in the back seat and snickered. *Dey whisper together like lovers, non.* "We are now on de south side of de island, and we will be in Cap-Haitien in a few minutes. Cap-Haitien is de second largest city and de place where de sugar plantation owners send deir products to market, eh? It once was a wealthy place, but not so now. Government is lazy." He said this as they entered a city with run-down buildings, sewage running down the center of the streets, and garbage piled beside the roadway.

"De city was burned to de ground three times and was destroyed another time when an earthquake killed almost half the people." They traveled through the interior and into the outskirts, where lush sugar cane grew in field after field. The plantation homes they saw were better cared for than the homes in

146

the downtown area of the city, but not by much. So far, Brian and Andrea's sense of Haiti was intense poverty with little government involvement to change things.

By the time they arrived back in Port au Prince, it was three o'clock in the afternoon. Their first day had been pretty productive as far as learning a little about the culture, but so far they had not seen anything that could tie in with Trent and Diane's disappearances or Max's murder, except for their constant companion in his business suit and the voodoo disappearances.

****

Brian continued to rest all the way back to the hotel. It felt good to just reflect on what they did know. First, Trent and Diane had disappeared, and Max had been murdered, an act that Max had anticipated, it seemed. Also, someone had deliberately tried to run him down and had burned down Andrea's house.

How someone as sweet as Andrea could be the target of foul play is beyond me. He rubbed his forehead to remove the sweat collecting and running down his face. *Do I really think Andrea is* sweet? *Do I find her attractive?* Maybe he was a womanizer after all. *Oh, get off it, Brian. There's nothing wrong with finding her attractive. After all, we have been spending a lot of time together lately, and we've also been through a lot together. Besides, she is a good looking woman.* He concluded his thoughtful analysis of his relationship with the woman beside him then returned to thinking about their predicament. Jason was on the island and had followed them all day. That was no coincidence! He was somehow mixed up in all this, and Brian intended to find out how.

****

The jeep jerked to a stop in the familiar parking lot behind the hotel. Robie turned in his seat to look at the two who had shared their day with him. "Do you want me to pick you up tomorrow morning?"

"No, I think we'll just spend some time exploring the city on our own." Brian was quick to answer. "At least, if that's alright with you, Andrea?"

"Sure, that sounds fine to me." She handed Robie the money they had agreed to pay him. "We have your number if we need you for another trip."

Robie reluctantly got out of the jeep and handed the keys to Brian. "Thank you for allowing me to guide you around my country." He immediately walked away.

Brian and Andrea almost felt sorry for him but not enough to change their mind. "I take it you have a plan." Andrea hopped out of the jeep. "Why not tell me about it as we walk inside. Or would you like to talk about it over dinner?"

"Over dinner sounds fine to me. My body seems to think it has jet lag or something. I am so-o tired all of a sudden. A nice nap sounds like just what this old boy needs."

As they moved towards the front entrance of the Al-B-Oloffson, a large black man ran out and nearly collided with them. Shouts could be heard from inside the establishment and another large dark brown man dressed in a suit erupted from the door onto the veranda. "Ooh, Monsieur, et Mam'selle, I am so-o-o sorry. It has never 'appened in this 'otel before. I am so-o-o-o sorry." The man appeared to be very distraught.

"What are you sorry about?" asked Brian as they rushed inside. "What's going on here?"

"It seems that the man," he pointed toward the doorway they had just come through, "whom you saw just as you came in, 'as broken into your room and was looking for something when my wife, the maid, noticed him. I am Le concierge, Nicolas Benedict. We chased him away, but not before he made such a mess. We will clean it up as soon as you see what he 'as taken. We are insured for these kinds of things, but they 'aven't ever 'appened before as I 'ave said."

Brian and Andrea rushed up the stairs to their rooms to discover that both had been ransacked. Clothes were strewn everywhere and dresser drawers were torn from their slides to lie upside down on the floor. The closet door was torn off its hinges. Attached to the mirror with some type of rope was a bunch of feathers tied together with another rope. The Concierge took one look at this strange decoration and screamed for his wife.

"Marie, what is this? 'ave your friends been up to their old tricks again in this 'otel?" Mr. Benedict was almost beside himself.

"That is not from us. But it is a message nonetheless. They say you must leave, monsieur, for this is your room, non?" Marie was dead serious as she told them the meaning of the feathers.

"Come, let us see what damage has 'appened in your room, mam'selle." She guided them down the hall. It was evident that the same destructive force had been in action there too. "It seems that they have meant de message for you too," she exclaimed as she pointed to an identical clasp of feathers tied to the bedpost of Andrea's bed.

"What is missing do you think?" asked Nicolas. Andrea took a cursory glance around the room but could not see anything that should have been there, but was not. Brian concurred when the trio returned to his room.

"I think there was nothing worth taking here, and anyway, this doesn't frighten us." Andrea was very quick to reply.

"We don't believe in voodoo or magic or whatever cult placed this in our rooms."

"That's right," Brian chimed in. "Why not get this mess cleaned up, and then we can get dressed for dinner. I understand you have entertainment here this evening?" The concierge was quick to apologize once again. He directed his wife to get some help to clean up the two rooms.

"We 'ave a local who comes in and sings some of the islands favorites. 'e also brings in a band to accompany heem and dey play some of the instruments native to dis city." Nicolas forced a smile. "We would be 'onored to 'ave you join us. Dere will be no charge."

Andrea and Brian decided to go for a walk while their rooms were being cleaned up. "I think this is just the beginning." Brian steered Andrea down the steps of the veranda as they left the hotel. They headed toward the main street and the shopping area. "We knew when we left for this trip there were people who didn't want us to stick our noses into whatever this is. Now we've become conscious of the fact they aren't afraid to let us know they are onto us."

"I wonder if our encounter with the priest has anything to do with this?" Andrea was thinking about all the voodoo signs that had been left by the intruder.

"I don't think so. Whatever they were looking for, they were unsuccessful. That means they could be back. We've decided not to use guns to defend ourselves. WWJD...what would Jesus do?"

"I think that he would place some form of warning device near the doors and windows and keep a club handy." Andrea knew that planning a course of action without praying first was not a good idea. "Tomorrow, I would like to go back to meet with that priest, Houngan he called himself, and find out more about this voodoo stuff. It could be tied to the Michner's disappearances, since it seems that voodoo practitioners seem to disappear too. What do you think?"

"I think maybe you're right. By the way, where did you hide your money? Mine was in my back pocket all the time." Brian grinned at the idea of carrying so much money with them all day.

"I did the same thing. I didn't know what else to do." Both Americans laughed at the idea of someone trying to rob them when they had all their valuables with them. Soon their laughter stopped, however, when they spotted a little girl crying and calling for her Mama et Papa.

Chapter Sixteen

Andrea's heart ached at the sight of her thin little body perched on a rock by the side of the road. Arms and legs with little extra flesh emerged from tattered garments. Her dress seemed to be pieced together from different fabrics, well worn with holes in the hem and the edge of the sleeves.

As Andrea moved closer, ever so slowly so as not to scare her, she noticed sores all over the little girl's legs. Her fingernails looked as if she'd been digging in dirt for days. Her hair was tattered as if it hadn't seen a comb since she was born. She couldn't have been more than three years of age but Andrea and Brian didn't know for sure since she was also talking or, at least, crying the words, Mama et Papa.

"Hi sweetie. Where're your parents?" Andrea took a clean hanky from her purse to wipe away the tears and dry her runny nose.

The little girl, eyes big as saucers, leaned away from Andrea's touch but then scooted closer when she saw Brian. "Do you know where my mama went?" she asked in a hesitant way.

"No I don't, but maybe we can help you find her. What is your name and how old are you?" Andrea sat on the curb beside her. Brian stood watch.

"I am named Camilla and I 'ave five years old." Her tiny voice quivered. She sniffed. "My mama et papa left me alone three day ago and I 'ave no food. I am 'ungry."

"Well, let's get you something to eat before we go in search of your parents." Brian held out his hand but Camilla folded them behind her back.

"He come?" She looked to Andrea for an answer.

"He's a friend." Andrea took her hand and followed as Brian led the way towards the restaurant they'd just left. The trio walked back inside just as the waiter was clearing the dishes from the table they'd vacated.

"You cannot bring that dirty child in here." The manager quickly ran toward them. "She is a child of the street. We do not feed child of the street."

Andrea moved to block the woman's view of Camilla. "But she is hungry, and her parents are missing."

"Parents go missing all the time in Haiti. We cannot feed all the children who are left behind. If their parents do not care what becomes of them, why should I?" The irate woman placed indignant hands on her hips.

"We'll order some food to take with us then." Brian took his wallet out of his pants pocket.

"Humpf. As you wish, but you can not feed all of them." She walked toward the kitchen and beckoned the waiter to take their order.

While Andrea and Brian waited for their food, the little girl spent her time looking in all directions as if she had never been inside a restaurant before. "I wonder what he meant by 'all of them'?" Andrea spoke quietly so only Brian could hear.

"I'm sure I don't know. I'll ask the waiter when he returns with the food. Her parents have vanished, so maybe this ties in with Trent and Diane's disappearance."

****

The waiter returned shortly with the few morsels of food that Brian and Andrea had ordered. There were few things on the menu for a starving child. Brian drew him aside while Andrea took Camilla outside to eat across the street where they'd found her.

"What did your manager mean by all of them? Are there a lot of street children?"

"There are many hundreds of children in Haiti who have no parents." He placed the wet towel over his arm and crossed his legs in a relaxed pose. "Some parents sell their children to people who put them to work because they cannot afford to keep them. Some are stolen from the village they live in to work for their captors."

"Aren't there any laws to prevent this type of thing?" Brian's voice moved from shocked to indignant.

"Yes, there are laws, but for the most part people ignore them. The children eventually run away and end up on the streets where they are used for their body, or they become slaves to someone else. They know there is no place to run and since they are uneducated, they don't have any way to earn a living except to work for someone who will feed them a little and let them sleep somewhere protected from the weather. She is probably one of them." He nodded his head in the direction he'd seen Andrea and Camilla go.

Brian has a hard time digesting this piece of information as he walked slowly back to Andrea. He watched Camilla wolf down another bite of food. To imagine her little body being used for someone's perverse pleasure was incomprehensible. He reached Andrea and pulled her aside.

"Well?" He saw a tear begin to appear at the corner of her eye.

Brian hardly knew where to begin. "The children are sold or stolen for manual labor or worse. We need to do something…for this one at least. Maybe there are some Christian organizations where children could receive better care and love. Suffice it to say, we can't leave her alone until we find out where her parents are, if she even has parents anymore."

****

The trio moved to a bench located in a little park nearby. Camilla stuffed the second half of her sandwich into her mouth but then sat back and patted her stomach. "I am full." She hiccupped.

"You have not eaten very much." Andrea gave her a drink from the bottle of water they'd purchased at the restaurant. "You can take the rest with you to eat later if you wish. This sandwich is yours. Camilla, where do you think your parents went?"

"Dey always go to the ceremonies at night after I am supposed to be asleep. Sometimes I 'ave follow them though. Tree days ago, they left like the time before and the time before that, but dey don't come back the next morning. I went to the place of de ceremony. No one was dere, so I return home. I wait but no one come." Camilla yawned.

"So Camilla, you don't work for someone then?" Brian wanted to be clear about her situation.

"No, I am not restavec. But maybe I will have to sell myself to live, non?" Her eyes watered, clearly not looking forward to this choice either.

"What's restavec?" Andrea rubbed the little girl's legs and arms in an attempt to find any invisible injuries. "Why would you have to sell yourself? Do you mean to sell your body for…for… " Her voice had risen to a high pitch by this time.

"Andrea, calm down. I'll tell you later. Camilla, we are not going to let you sell yourself. We're going to find someone to look after you until we can find your parents." Brian stood, trying to decide where they would go with their new friend.

Andrea nodded her head in agreement but looked toward Brian.

"We are?" Her voice almost hissed. Only Brian could hear. "How are we going to do that do you think?"

Brian gave her a look that Andrea had a hard time interpreting, but she was willing to let him lead the way if he had a plan. "Why not take us to your house so we can begin the search for your parents." Camilla smiled for the first time as she took off for the east side of town.

"Come, come." She waved them along excitedly. "You help, non?"

The walk took them past the harbor and along the seashore for about a mile. Andrea pointed out the blue-green ocean washing up on the white sandy beach. Camilla seemed oblivious to her surroundings. She continued to skip towards her home.

"Oh, Brian look." The trio walked up an embankment. "Those houses look no better than wood boxes."

Even though larger than any box either Andrea or Brian had seen, these hovels were made of very flimsy wood with holes cut for a door and a couple of windows. Camilla led them to one and stepped through the door. Andrea stifled a gasp. The floor was only hard dirt. The furniture consisted of one chair-less table and there did not appear to be any beds in the one-room home. "How many of you live here?" she asked the little girl.

"Just ma mère et papa." Camilla lapsed into her native dialect. "I also 'ave two sisters but dey are younger. I 'aven't seen dem in a while. I tink dey are restavec." This last statement was made without any emotion to the surprise of both adults. "Ma pere 'ave been out of work for a long time. Dere is no money."

"I can't imagine what this restavec is." Andrea led Brian outside behind Camilla.

Camilla responded to her question at last. "Restavics are slaves. Parents sell de children. Dey can't afford to keep them."

Brian grabbed Andrea's arm and led her away from Camilla's hearing. "The owners of these little ones use them physically or for manual labor. I think there are a lot of these kids. In fact the restaurant manager said there were hundreds. Sometimes the children are stolen and, as you can see by Camilla's attitude, it's an excepted way of life here, although there is a law protecting the children from all this."

"Why that's horrible." Andrea's eyes filled up with tears as she thought of this little girl living that way. "What kind of people are they anyway?"

"Very poor people, with no welfare system to feed them when 'papa' is out of work. Did you notice anything inside that could tell us what happened to her parents?"

"There was so little to see. What a way to live! Maybe we ought to go to the sight of the ceremony and see what we can find out there." Andrea looked around at all the other wood box homes. There were no people in sight.

"I am assuming that the ceremony is Voodoo. But you're right. Maybe someone will tell us something."

Brian spoke to the little girl first. "Camilla, will you take us to the place of the ceremony?"

Camilla cringed. "I am not supposed to go dere. It is for the grown people."

"This is daylight and you can stay hidden once you show us where they are held." Brian crouched down to her level.

"Okay." There was no smile for Camilla's protectors. She began to walk in the opposite direction they'd come from. As they passed the next hut, a smallish woman appeared in the doorway.

"Do you know this little girl?" Andrea and Brian spoke in unison.

He looked in her direction. "We seem to do that a lot."

The woman ignored their interchange. "Oui, she is of the Demer family. They 'ave not been seen here for a while."

Three children wrapped themselves around her legs. "Who are you?"

Brian looked at Andrea before he spoke. "We are tourists. While we were walking, we noticed Camilla crying by the side of the street. We told her we would try to find her parents. Do you know where they went?"

"Fuf-f-f-f, no one knows nothing here. We mind our business. People disappear a lot lately. How can you find her parents when no one knows anything?"

"When you say people have been disappearing a lot lately, what do you mean by lately?" asked Andrea.

"Well, maybe for the last year or so. People have not come back from the ceremonies. They just disappear and even the Mambo does not know where they have gone to."

Andrea's ears picked up the new name. "Mambo? Who is that?"

"Why the high priestess, of course!"

"But I thought they were called Houngan."

"The priest…he is Houngan. De Mambo is a woman. Dey take turns visiting de people.." The woman turned to go back into her hut.

"Wait, please. The Mambo doesn't know but does the Houngan?" Brian reached out to grab her shoulder and then pulled his hand back. "Can anyone else tell us what has happened to these people? How many are we talking about anyway?"

"No one knows, I tink. We just hear about people disappearing."

"Thank you for you time, Mrs.???"

"I am Mrs. Benedictan. But no one must know dat I talk to you." She seemed to shrink in size as they looked at her. "I am afraid they will come for me next."

"We won't tell anyone," promised Andrea. "What will happen to Camilla if her parents are not found?"

"She will be a street child until someone makes her restavec." The woman sighed. "Dat is the way 'ere." She returned to her hovel. Her children giggled at the silly tourists and then followed her inside.

"Not if we can help it." Brian stalked off after the child. Taking her hand, they proceeded towards the tree line. Before they had gone three feet inside the wooded area surrounding a large meadow, another figure appeared from a different direction. He stalked toward them appearing to have a purpose. Brian and Andrea placed their bodies in front of Camilla and waited until this large, black man was close enough to talk to.

"Can you tell us where the parents of Camilla Demer are? They seem to have disappeared from a ceremony held somewhere around here three nights ago." Brian was not above asking anyone for the information they required to get to the bottom of this latest twist in their mystery. This new development was somehow connected to the disappearance of his friends, he was sure, since everything seemed to point to this island and the strange goings-on here.

"I know nothing of any Demers or of any disappearing people. I am Houngan here. Do you want to know about our ceremony, maybe?"

"Since we are new to your island, I was not sure that we could know about your ceremony." Andrea pulled Brian out of earshot of the priest and asked "Brian, do we want to get involved in this Voodoo thing? Does this not fall into the category of astrologers and psychics, things that the Bible warns us about?"

"I will do anything to find out what happened to Trent and Diane. What about you? This thing is leading us in the direction of the ceremonies. Maybe we can be really careful and not actually get involved."

"Okay, Mr... we would really like to know more about Voodoo. Do you have the time now or would you like us to come back another time?"

"It is getting dark, and I think that the little one needs to be in bed. Why not come back tomorrow night about this time, with no one else, eh? And then we will teach you about Voodoo." The Houngan actually made a lot of sense, so Andrea and Brian began the slow journey back to the hotel. Andrea had thoughts questioning the appropriateness of this course of action, but neither she nor Brian could see any other way to find out the answers they felt they needed to find the Michners.

Chapter Seventeen

Brian lifted Camilla to his shoulders. He sniffed the air, smelling the absence of soap and water. There was not a stitch under her dress either. Before long, her exhausted, little body slumped in sleep. Brian shifted her to his arms. "I'm glad we don't have too far to go. She may be tiny but she's dead weight now." He grunted and shifted her in his arms again.

"A nice hot shower will fix the smell but what about her clothes? She needs something to sleep in at least." Andrea fingered the thin fabric covering the emaciated body. When they arrived on the street that led to the Al-B Oloffson, she spotted a store located next to the restaurant. "Look. Children's clothing. Let's take a detour before heading to our room for the night." She tickled Camilla's arm. "Wake up sweetie. Let's get you some clothes."

Camilla stirred and opened weary eyes just as they

reached the sidewalk in front of the shop. Brian deposited her on her feet. She weaved a little from side to side and then rubbed sleep deprived eyes with her dirty hands. "Clothes? New ones? I've never 'ad new ones."

The store looked like many of the boutiques back home. As the trio walked in, Andrea noticed that the clothing in stock was not the same as the items worn by locals. Camilla was wedged between the two adults. "I like dis one. O-o-h and this one." She reached for one outfit after another. "Oh mam'selle, dis is too expenseeve." She picked up the price tag on the first dress she'd admired. "My mama et papa would never bring me 'ere for clothes. Dey make from rags dey find around town. Much cheaper."

Andrea smiled and then cast sad eyes toward Brian. "Well we can afford better." Andrea marched toward another rack. "These are more your size I think."

Brian walked to stand beside her. "These prices are ridiculous," he whispered to Andrea. "If this store was any-where else on this island, they'd have gone out of business a long time ago. This must be for the tourist trade, such as it is." Brian fingered the fabric on the cutest little dress and he knew that Camilla would look really pretty in it.

Andrea looked towards the little girl standing beside her, hope sparkling in her eyes."We'll try on a few and when you have found some outfits that you like, we will buy them for you. Right Brian?" Andrea turned towards her companion. Brian was staring out the window. "Right? Brian?"

****

Brian was focused elsewhere. He'd spotted Jason out-side. The man was leaning against a fence post just down the street. From his vantage point, Brian guessed he could see eve-rything that happened from any building along the street. Brian watched as he removed his jacket, rolled up his shirt sleeves that, even from this distance, looked a little rumpled. *I've had enough of this. I'm going to have a word with that lout. See if he'll slip up, provide us with another piece of the puzzle.*

"You ladies go ahead. Have fun shopping for new clothes. Make sure to get something for play, Andrea. After all, little girls can't be clothed in dresses all the time. I see someone outside that I want to talk to." He pointed outside for Andrea's benefit, but as soon as she saw who he was indicating, she panicked.

"Brian no, he could be dangerous. Besides, what do you hope to get out of him? He's already proved to be a liar."

"He may slip when I confront him since he doesn't think we're on to him. I'll be only a few minutes, and then we can go to the hotel, okay? I'll be alright." He saw the look of fear sweep across Andrea's face. He touched her arm. "I'll be alright." He walked out the door. He felt Andrea's eyes follow him as he sauntered across the street.

****

Camilla tugged on her sleeve. "Mam'selle, mam'selle, are we shopping now?" Her large dark eyes were bright with anticipation.

"Sure, let's shop." Andrea and Camilla searched some more and continued to add articles of clothing to their pile of choices. "We have four or five dresses, a few play outfits, some pj's and underwear, and I love those shiny patent leather shoes, don't you?"

"What ees patent leder?" Camilla looked toward the biggest pile of clothing she'd ever seen in her life.

"That's just the name of the shoes. Let's get some san-

164

dals, too." Andrea took her little charge in tow, moved towards the change room with several items of clothing over her arm.

The sales clerk stepped in her way. "Mam'selle, we cannot let you try these things on that dirty child!" Her arms crossed. A frown furrowed her brow as her lip curled in disgust.

Andrea glared right back at her. "Fine, I'll just hold them next to her then. Camilla, you look in the mirror and tell me which ones you would like to keep, okay?"

"Oh, mam'selle, I like dem all, but so-o much money."

"Let me worry about the money. Tell me which outfits you really would like to have?" Andrea began holding first one then another in front of the child. Camilla peered at herself in the mirror. They had guessed her size pretty accurately but Camilla had a hard time deciding.

"Oh well," sighed Andrea. "Let's take all of them."

"Dese are for me?" squealed Camilla. "I 'ave never 'ad so many new clothes before. Can I put dem on?"

"Not until you have had a chance to wash away some of that street dust." Andrea heard a rustle behind her. Brian was back. She breathed a sigh of relief. "Let's pay for these and go home."

"Home, where is home?" Camilla stopped in her tracks, a puzzled expression on her face. "I go to America wit you?"

"No, no, I mean the hotel…just down the street. You can stay with us tonight."

"Oh, oui. I 'ave never stayed in 'otel before." Camilla grabbed Brian's hand as Andrea paid the salesclerk.

"Next door is an apothecary…you know pharmacy. They will have some soap." Her face clearly showed her distain for the child." Happily though she grabbed the bundle of cash Andrea handed her.

That look of joy on Camilla's face is worth it. Andrea led Camilla toward Brian who was already standing outside. The adults looked across the street where Jason stood.

"Later." Brian looked toward Camilla. The child's excitement was almost contagious. She skipped behind her new friends. The trio made their way to the pharmacy next door. "I'll bet she's never sat in a bathtub or seen clean fingernails in her life." Brian nodded toward Camilla who was oblivious to her filthy condition it appeared.

"Maybe but that's going to change." Andrea approached the sales clerk. "We need some nice smelling bubble bath, detangling conditioner for a little girl's hair, and some," she whispered, "lice repellent shampoo."

"But, of course." The clerk gathered the items requested and rang up the sale. "Will that be all?"

"Thanks." Andrea placed the purchases in her handbag. Once outside, Jason was still there they noticed, they moved to the hotel. Camilla rushed up the front steps ahead of them, full of energy in contrast to her earlier demeanor.

The Concierge hurried toward them as soon as they entered the lobby. "Mam'selle et Monsieur, your rooms are as before." He looked at Camilla with distaste. "But monsieur, you cannot bring a street child in here!" His alarm over the idea of such a dirty child mixing with his patrons was clearly etched all over his face. "She is not welcome here."

"Well then, neither are we." Brian face held a look of resolve. "Either she stays or we go!"

"Okay, okay, monsieur. But please see dat she takes a bath before sleeping on our bed, non. The lice, eh, we don't want to have to fumigate de entire hotel."

"We have the right stuff for just that, and we have some new clothes. When we come down for dinner, you won't recognize her." Brian led the way to the elevator.

He left Andrea and Camilla at their door. Andrea watched as he moved down the hall toward his own room. "Camilla, let's go have that bath now." She opened her door.

Camilla followed. "Bath, what ess bath?"

"Come, I'll show you," Andrea responded as she led the dirty little waif into the adjoining bathroom. "See that thing over there? That is called a tub and I am going to fill it with a little water and some bubbles. You will get in and use that cloth to wash yourself all over."

"I do not know 'ow to sweem." The little tyke's eyes were round as saucers. "Do I get in with all my clothes on?"

"No, you need to take them off and. . ...."

"But..but…"

"I will only put a little water in until you get used to it." Andrea turned on the tap.

"Oh oui, bien sur. Let's 'ave my bath, den." Camilla proceeded to strip. Warm water flowed into the tub. Andrea added some of the bubble bath she'd purchased and then watched the child's look of pleasure.

Camilla gingerly stepped in with Andrea's help. "It feels good on de skin." She wiggled her arms and legs in the soapy water. "More water, please." Camilla picked up and handful of soapy bubbles and blew into them. She giggled.

Andrea handed her a washcloth. "Take your time but I want you to wash everywhere, behind your ears, between your toes, everywhere. Understand?" A short while later, the little girl was as clean as one well cared for. Andrea noticed that her ribs were more evident, however, and the sticks that she used for arms and legs drew attention to her malnourished condition. *We'll feed her well as long as we have her with us.*

Andrea poured a liberal amount of the special shampoo on Camilla's hair, rinsed it well and then added the conditioner. She helped Camilla hop out of the tub, wrapped a warm towel around the little body. She selected some undergarments. "Which dress would you like to wear? We're going downstairs to eat."

"O-o-h this one," Camilla held up a pink frilly dress that suited her coloring perfectly. She turned and strutted before the long mirror on the back of the bathroom door. "Ooh, Mam'selle. I 'ave never been dressed so before. Always it is from other people who don't need any more." She was as overcome as a small child could be.

Andrea blow-dried and then combed Camilla's hair. Soon long, shiny, black curls cascaded down the child's back. The transformation was everything she'd imagined and more. "You wait right here, and I'll have my shower. Then we can go down to dinner. Brian is going to be so surprised when he sees how pretty you are."

The shower felt so good. The day had taken it's toll but standing under the hot spray, washed away all tiredness. She quickly dressed, dried and styled her hair and was ready long before the appointed time to meet Brian. "Camilla, since we are both ready and don't have to be downstairs for 15 minutes or so, why not play a little game with me. I'll ask you a question. If you can answer it, you can ask me a question, okay? The first one to ask the most questions wins."

Camilla had never had anyone pay so much attention to her before "Oh oui, okay, I'll first go. Where did you come from?"

"Brian and I are from the United States. Now it's my turn. What grade are you in school?"

"Oh, Mam'selle." The little girl dropped her eyes. "I 'ave never been to school."

"Oh, that's okay. Now you ask me a question." Andrea was quick to change the subject.

"Are you and Brian, how you say, the lovers?" The child grinned, a mischievous smirk slanting the corners of her mouth ever upwards.

"No, we are just friends? How long ago did your parents move to this place?"

"I don't know Mam'selle. I was not born den."

"Okay," Andrea said, "you couldn't answer that question so here's another. How did you find out where those voodoo ceremonies were if you are not allowed to attend?"

"I followed my mother de last time when she went to find my father who 'ad not come 'ome from de time before. I fell asleep before de ceremony was over. No one saw me, and I never saw my mother again." Big, sad eyes looked on her inquisitor.

Andrea gave her the go ahead to ask another question. Each time one was asked, Andrea gave a point to the questioner.

"Am I winning? Am I winning?" Camilla perked up in anticipation.

"Not yet, little one. Ask your next question."

"What is like…to fly in a big airplane?"

"Why it is nothing you can imagine. You feel the plane leave the ground but then it is so smooth. Soon you can see the tops of the clouds, and they are all fluffy and white with the sun's rays gleaming off of them. The stewardess…that's the person who works for the airline to make sure everyone is comfortable…she brings us something to drink, and we can walk around if we want."

"Oh Mam'selle, dat sounds so wonderful. Can I fly to your 'ome someday?"

"Wait a minute, Camilla. It's my turn to ask a question," laughed Andrea. "When will the next ceremony be held?"

"I tink tonight. Does dat count, Mam'selle? I'm pretty sure."

"That certainly does. Now I will answer your last question. I don't know if we would be allowed to take you with us, but we will check into it, okay."

"Dat's an 'I don't know' answer just like mine, yes? Now I get to ask again, non? I'm winning! I'm winning! How long did it take Mam'selle et monsieur to get 'ere?"

"It took us quite a few hours but we slept through some of the trip."

"Oh, I could not sleep a wink on de airplane," interjected the little voice. "Now you ask, eh?"

"I would like to know when the ceremony starts?"

"After de moon is overhead in the sky. Mama always waited until she tot we were asleep, so it was very late."

"Yips!" Andrea jumped to her feet. "Speaking of late. We were having so much fun that I forgot to keep track. You win so you can choose anything you want from the menu when we go for dinner, okay?"

"Okay! I win. I win. I never win before Mam'selle." Camilla was excitedly hopping up and down as they made their way to the elevator. "I tink I am 'ungry enough to eat a goat."

"Oh baaaaaa." Andrea made a face that sent the child into a fit of giggles. She enjoyed the look of pleasure on the little face. "Goat does not sound too tempting to me. What about chicken?"

The elevator stopped on the first floor. There they found Brian pacing, impatient to sit down to a real meal. "Where have you two been? I'm starved. Camilla." He placed his hands on both sides of his face in a look of utter surprise. The girl giggled again. "You look just like a princess."

"I'll tell you later." Andrea answered his question about where they'd been. The dining room was full of people, many obviously not from the hotel. The food was delicious, everything the concierge had promised. Energizing music with plenty of island rhythm kept the evening lively but it wasn't long before Camilla's head was nodding, not in time to the music either. Brian and Andrea looked at each other in agreement as they signaled the waiter to bring their check.

At her door, Andrea spoke in a whisper. "When I put her to bed, I have something to tell you. I'll meet you in your room after I change into something more comfortable."

Chapter Eighteen

Andrea knocked quietly on Brian's door a half hour later. "It sure didn't take any convincing to get Camilla to bed." She walked into the room assessing its beauty and admiring the tidy bed. "Her eyes were almost closed by the time she was in her pajamas. She didn't even notice how soft and new they were."

"Do you think she'll be all right for a little while? I wish we had adjoining rooms. It would make looking after her so much easier."

"She'll be fine. I locked the door and asked the woman next door to listen for any disturbance. After what happened this afternoon, she was more than willing."

"What is it you have to tell me?" Brian sat on the edge

of the bed leaving the only chair available for Andrea.

"I managed to get some more information out of Camilla by playing a game with her before dinner. That's why we were so late." Andrea crossed her legs. "The voodoo ceremony will probably happen tonight at midnight or thereabouts. Camilla said that they happen when the moon is high in the sky. She managed to follow her mother one night without being seen, and I think we should do the same thing…follow someone, I mean."

"Do you mean tonight?" Brian sat forward, his intense stare making Andrea a little nervous.

"Yes, tonight. We've already been a whole day. We're no closer to solving Max's murder or the disappearance of the Michners than we were when at home. This is the only solid lead we have. We need to find out if these events are tied to the disappearance of the Michners. If the voodoo ceremonies have something to do with all of them, we need to find out. Don't you think?"

"Yes, I certainly agree there. What will we do when we get there?"

"Just watch, I think, but we can play it by ear. Then tomorrow we can decide what to do as far as bringing the police into this."

"Is it your plan to leave Camilla all alone then?"

"No, I was thinking we could move her into the room of our neighbor if she will allow us. Then we won't have to worry about hurrying back in case we see something we want to follow up on."

"Andrea, are you curious at all about what Jason had to tell me this afternoon?"

"Oh that's right. I got so involved with finding Camilla under all that dirt that I completely forgot about Jason. What did you find out?"

"Well, if he could have crawled into a hole to hide from me, he would have, I think. He was shaken when I told him that I knew who he was and that he had been following us all day. He tried to tell me he was only concerned about you, but…"

"Yeah, right." Andrea huffed and then waited for Brian to continue.

"Of course, when I told him I knew that he was also following us in the states, that he tried to run me down, he became uncomfortable and then defensive. He told me we'd better leave the island. He said his friends didn't want us here, that we didn't know what we'd gotten ourselves involved with." Brian poured each of them a glass of water. "Do you know, his face changed right in front of me? Lots of anger and full of evil. I'm sure glad you no longer work with that man."

Andrea swallowed. "Did he know that his warning fell on deaf ears?"

"I think so. He made the remark that you're bullheaded, that you were not one to let go of something once you got hold of it. Is that true about you?" His eyes twinkled in the now familiar teasing manner that had become so recognizable to Andrea.

"Never mind that. Did he say who his friends were?"

"No, only they were powerful men who plan to change the world. A magnanimous statement if I ever heard one. His mannerisms suggested that he felt he was above the law and so are his friends. He said the world would thank them someday, that what they were doing was important. No one would or could do anything to stop them. Just one more part of the puzzle that keeps getting more complicated every day." Brian walked over toward the window and looked outside. "Anyway, let's make plans for tonight. When do you want to leave?"

"It's already 11 p.m. Meet me at the top of the stairs in fifteen minutes. I'll put on some dark clothes, if I can find some, and see you then." Andrea left, returned to her room and then retraced her steps to knock on the door of her next door neighbor.

****

Trent slowly placed one foot in front of the other. The whistler behind him pushed. "Hurry along. I want to get something to eat." Trent took a quick step closer to the rundown cabin where Jeffrey and Diane waited. He stole a furtive glance toward the wharf where a small boat lay at anchor.

"Doing any fishing while you're here?" He hoped his captor hated being here as much as he did.

The man pushed him again. "None of your business, Michner. Keep moving."

Trent felt the warmth of the sun on his back. If only Jeffrey and Diane could get out for part of the day. He decided to risk another back hand. "Tomorrow, couldn't my wife and son get some sunshine for a couple of hours? They'll be good…er…they won't try anything. You have my word."

"We'll see. Maybe we have some fun with them, eh?" The thug chortled as if he was making a joke.

"You harm them and you'll never get me to do what you want." Trent spun around and raised a fist only to be knocked to the ground and kicked…again.

"Keep your distance. You'll do what we want or your wife and son will pay." He pulled Trent to his feet, dragged him toward the cabin, and slammed his body into the door.

Trent winced in pain. He rubbed his rib cage, then quickly wiped the grimace from his face as the man unlocked the door. He fell inside.

"Trent." Diane was by his side the instant he arrived. She glared at the brute as he shut the door again. Trent's eyes became accustomed to the dark interior.

"Daddy." Jeffrey raced toward him but Diane stopped his headlong tumble into his father's body.

"Hi there buddy. Let daddy get up first." Trent stood painstakingly and brushed a trembling hand over his eyes. He plastered a smile on his face for his son's benefit. "How's your day been?"

"I want to go outside, Daddy. Why can't we go outside?" Trent stooped down to hug his son. "I know, son, I know. These men won't let us walk around outside, at least not yet. I've asked them and I'll ask again, okay?" Trent looked toward Diane. She quickly averted her eyes. His guilt rose to the surface. "Diane."

"I have some food for you. Eat. We'll talk later." Trent ate the meager fare that Diane set in front of him on the metal plates that these people provided. Everything tasted like sawdust to him these days, dry, tasteless, hard to swallow. He pushed his plate aside after only a few bites.

"Look, Trent, Jeffrey and I ate less so you could have something to eat. The least you can do is eat it. You need to keep up your strength. We're counting on you to get us out of here." Diane left the rest of the sentence unspoken. This is your fault.

"Diane, I'm sor…I guess I've said that so many times, You don't think I mean it. Well, I do. I told Max 'no' but…he passed my name along. I can't help that. Now…" He stood, turned his back on his wife and walked toward the bed. He hung his head. Tears coursed down his cheek. He was so scared…not so much for himself but for his family. These men were without conscience.

Diane walked over and sat beside him. She placed her hand on his arm. *"No, this time I'm sorry, Trent. I am just so scared and I need to blame someone for this. You're handy, that's all."*

"There's a boat." Trent swiped at his face. Jeffrey didn't need to see him this way. The little boy was coloring at the table near the half eaten plate of food.

"What do you mean…there's a boat?" Diane sat up straighter. She looked into her husband's anguished features.

"There's a small boat tied to the wharf. If we could just…"

"…get out of here." Diane looked toward the closed door. *"We'll have to find another way out of here and then…"*

…get to that boat."

****

Brian met Andrea just as she closed the door to her room. "Hi, Brian, could you take her?" She had Camilla in her arms.

He moved closer and took the light bundle from her just as Andrea reached the door of her next-door neighbor. She knocked lightly so as not to wake the sleeping child. Her new friend opened the door. "Thank you so much for keeping her for us tonight." Andrea spoke in a whisper as she gently placed Camilla on the room's sofa. Giving the woman a smile of gratitude, the two left confident that the little child was in good hands.

"How did you manage to talk that woman into keeping Camilla?" Brian pressed the down arrow for the elevator.

"Mrs. Gevin was very accommodating. She even said she would look after the child's breakfast. It seems she has also been touched by the plight of these little ones on the street and is more than happy to help this one."

"There are some good people in this world, aren't there? I think, before we start out, we should protect ourselves by praying for God's provision in all this, don't you?" After Andrea's nod of agreement, Brian bowed his head. "Lord, we are entering into unknown territory and there could be danger. We are also entering into Satan's realm so we ask your protection over us with a hedge of your angels. Keep us safe and help us to find out something that will tell us what happened to Trent and Diane. Amen."

The lobby of the hotel was deserted as they walked out into the night air. Some distance away, music was playing but for the most part all was quiet and peaceful.

The moon was shining brightly through the gaps in the buildings along the street. From the lobby of the hotel, a man walked out onto the wide veranda with a newspaper in his hand and his eyes on the couple but the two sleuths were fully aware that someone else was on the street with them.

"What if that man is trailing us? I think we should go back up to our floor and then down the other set of stairs through the kitchen."

"He does look suspicious," agreed Andrea. "But if he saw us leave the hotel, he'll get suspicious if we just turn around and go back in. Let's get a coffee from that vendor over there. Since the hotel restaurant is closed it will appear perfectly normal. Come on. Let's hurry."

The two made their way over to a kiosk where cappuccinos were sold and ordered a tall cup of the hot beverage with frothy whipped cream drizzled with chocolate syrup. They chattered companionably, laughing occasionally to keep their watcher from getting suspicious. Andrea was almost in a giddy mood, excitement chasing a string of bubbles through her stomach. "We're getting good at pretending not to know we're being watched." She took another sip of the frothy concoction as they retraced their steps. The lobby was completely dark.

Upstairs again, they tiptoed down the hall to the alternate stairway used only by the hotel staff. Andrea was careful to place her foot gingerly on each tread so as not to alert anyone of their escape route. Soon they were outside in the cool night air again, although the air was not nearly as cool as the couple was used to back home. In fact the humidity was still very high, eliminating the need for a jacket.

Drinking the last of their beverage, they made their way toward the edge of town, down the small country road Camilla had pointed out to them earlier. Choosing to keep in the shadows, Brian and Andrea slithered from tree to tree toward the meadow where the ceremony was supposed to be held. They could see others, many others, moving in that direction.

"These ceremonies are well attended." Andrea watched from behind their current hiding place, her gaze sweeping the road near the tree they'd crept to.

"Sh-h-h-h," hushed Brian. "We don't want to give ourselves away."

The sound of drums could be heard now in the near distance. "We're n-not t-too far a-away, it s-seems." Andrea's nervousness caused a catch in her voice. People moved faster as if a voice had called them. Andrea and Brian remained hidden in the trees.

Clandestinely they approached the clearing where a large bonfire in the center displayed several figures dancing around in wild abandon. The Houngan wore a large headdress of feathers of some kind. He held several sticks also adorned with chicken feathers. One, longer than the others, was used to beat the backs of the dancers in a not too gentle manner.

The uninvited guests watched in fascination. They could feel the satanic nature of this ceremony. Their spirits crawled with revulsion. Dancers were given a drink that made them appear to be drunk or in a trance. The drums grew louder. The beat more frenzied. The priest called to some demon to leave this person or that person. He beat the drums some more. Some words were in English, but most in a dialect unknown to the watchers.

It seemed like hours later, three men, dressed entirely in black, appeared like specters from the bushes on the right side of the clearing, twenty yards or so from where they stood. "It's a good thing we're wearing black and have been so quiet." Brian whispered as they hunkered down even further in the tall underbrush. The men were waving their arms and seemed to be in control of the Houngan. The dancers gave them no heed, just kept gyrating and jumping around the fire to the frenzied beat of the drums.

Each of the menacing figures grabbed a dancer by the arm. They led them cautiously toward the far side of the clearing , opposite Brian and Andrea's location. No one protested or seemed to care. In fact, everyone just went on with their twirling and chanting, oblivious to the Houngan's downcast face.

"We've got to see where they are going." Andrea spoke a little louder than necessary. She covered her mouth but no one seemed to hear. She lowered her voice. "This may be what happened to Camilla's parents and all the others who have disappeared from this village."

Brian led the way around the clearing being careful to remain hidden. The Houngan wasn't in a trance but was clearly under the influence of the strangers. He was afraid of them, it seemed to Andrea. She stepped on a twig. Let's pray." Andrea sent Brian a look that pleaded for him to agree. She began, "Lord, watch over us tonight and help us discover without being discovered ourselves."

"Yes, Lord, keep us safe and watch over little Camilla at the hotel," added Brian. "Amen. We've got to move quickly now, or we may lose them."

Andrea's muscles were tighter than a drum as she moved stealthily through the underbrush. Usually described as a bull in a china shop, she was terrified that she was going to stumble and give them away. The drums were a definite asset. They broke out of the brush to find themselves on a path of sorts.

****

Brian's hands shook. His insides felt like jelly. He didn't want Andrea to know how scared he was. *What are we doing here? We're not sleuths or private eyes. Why are we playing these games with such ruthless people?* He followed Andrea down the path but then straightened his back and walked quickly in front of her. Without words he pointed ahead. He placed one foot in front of the other, stepping where he couldn't see but praying there were no more twigs here to snap in the still of the night. His eyes watched carefully in case the path ended sooner than they expected. He had no idea how far it went or if it ended at the water's edge. After all this was an island.

****

Voices. Up ahead. Water lapping on some rocks. Andrea grabbed Brian's arm for support. It was so dark. The moon had gone behind some clouds. Brian and Andrea slowed their pace even more, keeping trees between themselves and the men ahead, they hoped.

"Use the chloroform before we put them into the boat, you dumpkopf." A deep menacing voice delivered the order. "Do you want them to come out of their trance and make a racket?"

"Ah-h-h Heine, I know what to do." Another man's voice whined giving away a heavily accented brogue.

"You are stupid, Yah!" replied the one called Heine. "Do as I say."

"Ya vol mien heir." This man had an American or at least English speaking voice. "Who died and made you boss?"

"I was just trying to push the idiot, that's all Werner." The menacing voice seemed not so menacing this time.

"I will do the pushing. I want you to leave my brother alone. You will end up dead like the others if you don't watch yourself." Werner threatened deadly force, obviously used many times.

"Let's get going with these guinea pigs, yah?"

As Andrea and Brian watched from the shadows, the three men pushed their three captives into a boat beached on the shoreline. They each grabbed a spot on the hull and began to push the craft into deeper water before climbing aboard. Once everyone was in the boat, one man started a small motor attached to the back of the boat, and off they went out to sea, very slowly and very quietly.

"We have to see what is off shore from this side of the island." Andrea's spoke with an urgency she didn't quite understand but felt with every fiber of her being. "Next time we need to be prepared to follow them, wherever they are going. Do you think we could hire a boat somewhere?"

"I have a better idea," said Brian. "Let's get back to the hotel, and when we get up in the morning, we need to take some scuba lessons."

Chapter Nineteen

"I can't believe you expect me to learn how to do this in one easy lesson." Andrea's indignation came across loud and clear.

Brian turned thunderous eyes toward her. "This was your suggestion in the first place, remember? Now quit belly aching and get suited up." He motioned her to follow his lead. He faced Camilla and grinned. He was clearly enjoying the woman's temper.

Andrea grabbed her wetsuit and began to squiggle one leg into the rubbery fabric. "I'll never fit in this tight thing. Haven't you got one that fits?"

Camilla giggled from her seat on a bench along the dock. "You look funny, Mam'selle Andrea. You too, Monsieur

Brian."

"Never mind, smarty pants. If you don't behave, we'll make you go to bed before eleven tonight." Andrea had considered the idea of swimming with forty feet of water over her head for a long time, but now that the moment was soon to be experienced, she doubted she was where she wanted to be. *It's easy for him. He's already done this before.* She turned a murderous look in Brian's direction.

"Scuba diving is easy to learn, easier than learning how to snorkel in fact." He lowered his voice. "Andrea, this will be the best way to follow those men without being detected, and you know it. Behave yourself and this afternoon, we'll rent a boat. Maybe we can check out that island out there or if they came around this island to land."

Andrea struggled to push her arm into the short sleeve. She pulled the suit over her shoulders and then sucked her stomach in so she could close the zipper. "Ugh, this is tight. I must look like a sausage in this thing. Boat ride, huh? Sounds like a good idea but, Brian, there is no way I can learn all this in one day. I'm telling you. Just the thought of putting my head under water for any length of time scares me to death."

"You'll be fine. Just breathe slowly." He finished zippering his suit and then grabbed his flippers, BC, mask and tank."This buoyancy compensator vest will float you to the surface if you need to get there."

"Brian, it will be a few days before the Houngan has another ceremony according to the wife of the concierge. I spoke with her this morning while you and Camilla were getting dressed." Andrea's eyes pleaded with him to listen to her. "We'd have time to find where they went by boat and then just meet them there. We don't need to do this."

"No, now get over this. We'll have time to practice

some more, so …no…we don't have to do this all in one day. Now be a good girl and listen to what the instructor tells you." Brian put his gear at his feet and turned his attention to the young man before them. Every now and then he'd glance in Andrea's direction. She was listening…finally.

The man was evidently experienced in the art of scuba, if art it could be called. He began to demonstrate the correct use of the equipment they had in front of them. "This gear is designed to make swimming underwater as safe as it can be. The buoyancy compensator, or BC as most call it, is attached to your air tanks by this hose and will inflate if you pull this valve. It will bring you to the surface as slowly or as quickly as you want it to, in case of emergency." The piece of apparatus he was pointing to was a vest with a couple of hoses attached to it.

"In case of emergency. I can't do this. I just can't." Andrea's whiny voice could be heard over the water sloshing against the wood pilings and the boats moored nearby.

Brian took her for a short walk down the pier. "Andrea, you've survived a murder, your house burnt to the ground and threats on your life. Are you telling me this is beyond your capability now?"

"We don't even know if those disappearances are connected to the Michners!"

"No we don't. But we will never find out if we don't go after those men. Just how do you think we could ever follow them in a boat and not be seen?"

"Alright, alright. You win. Let's get on with this, but you had better be by my side every step … or should I say… stroke of the way." Andrea stomped back to the instructor.

The instructor went on to tell them how to assemble their gear and how to make sure their tank was attached securely to their BC. He also demonstrated the use of a regulator and how to clear a mask underwater. He showed them how to take off their vest and put it back on underwater.

"What do we have to know that for?" Andrea's voice gave away her attempts to hide her fear every time she spoke. *This is so out of my comfort zone.*

"You never know what might occur when you scuba dive, so it is best to know survival techniques. We will practice these things when we are in the water." The instructor proceeded to explain the method to obtain neutral buoyancy and how to read the gauges telling them how much air they had in their tanks..

After a couple more hours in his pier classroom, the instructor motioned for them to follow him with their gear. They'd learned a lot of stuff…like the calculations needed to assess how long they could be at a certain depth and still have enough air to surface. There was a lot to learn.

They hopped into the instructor's jeep with Camilla along for the ride. The drive was a short one but easier than carrying all their equipment by foot. They arrived at one of the better hotels in Port Au Prince. The instructor led the way to the back deck, overlooking the ocean. "We are allowed to use their pool."

They seated Camilla on one of the lounge chairs. "You stay right here. We'll get some lunch when we're done, Okay?"

"Okay." The little girl was already looking with interest at all the new things around her, sights she'd never seen before. Andrea and Brian watched as the instructor taught them how to attach their tank, filled with one hour of air, to their vest, making sure that their regulator and inflation hose for the vest were connected in the right places. They pulled on booties and then swim fins. Next, the mask and snorkel. These were purchased items, not rented. More hygienic.

Once they were outfitted, the trio descended into the pool. Camilla scooted to the side of the pool. She dangled her feet. Andrea knew she'd never been to a pool before, so this was a new experience for her as well. She decided to let the little girl enjoy the experience from her watery vantage point.

Before they went completely under, the couple's instructor explained several different hand signals and told them to clear their mask. "Now walk to the deep end and we will begin."

Brian and Andrea began slowly to walk toward the other end of the pool, feeling the water rise higher and higher on their bodies. The water came up to Andrea's neck first since she was shorter than Brian. Soon she could feel the water flow over her head.

Almost like the rising tide, panic filled her brain. She wanted to breathe through her nose, a function she was accustomed to performing without giving it a second thought. However, her mask blocked any air from entering her nostrils. She had her mouth full of breathing apparatus that made any mouthful of food she'd ever eaten pale in comparison.

All sense of what her instructor told her fled. She did the only thing her instincts told her she could do. She ripped the regulator out of her mouth, but when she tried to swim to the surface, she did not have the strength, even though the surface was only a few inches over her head. With a weight belt, full tank and her BC, she did not have enough strength to swim those few inches. In her panic, she forgot all about the inflatable vest she was wearing.

She wanted to scream for help. She couldn't. She was underwater. Andrea's depth of fear was greater than anything she had ever experienced in her life. She knew death was close beside her if … if only … but then her instructor was beside her, inflating her vest, lifting her to the surface. She gasped quick breaths into her air starved lungs.

"What happened? Your eyes are almost the size of your mask. Did something frighten you?" His face had concern written all over it.

She was breathing normally again, something that took quite a few minutes to achieve. "I only know that as soon as the water was over my head, I panicked…forgot everything you told me." She sucked in another deep breath.

Brian was beside her by this time, watching her for any sign that she had been injured. She looked into his eyes. "I can't do this. I really can't do this," They now stood in water chest high. "I never knew I was claustrophobic until that water was over my head. What a feeling!"

Brian moved close to her and held her shoulders while she trembled and started to cry. "Brian, I am such a wimp. I can't even do this in a pool. How am I ever going to do this in the ocean?"

"Now that we know you panic, we can compensate with some breathing exercises." The instructor told her that she wasn't the first person to feel this way. "When we go under water the next time, I will be right by your side. We will breathe together, okay. You can even hold my hand." He wiggled his eyebrows adding a lighter tone to the day.

"Please Andrea, try it again. I know how much you want to help…" He whispered. "…Diane and Trent. We'll just take it a little slower, that's all."

"I feel like such a fool. All those people are watching us, and Camilla is as well. I'm a baby, and I can't do anything right." The hotel pool had several patrons lounging beside it soaking up the sun's rays. Some were in the pool swimming. Everyone was curious about the scuba lesson in progress.

"Andrea, listen to me, not everyone learns to scuba dive as if they were born to it. Some people have to concentrate on breathing slowly so panic doesn't set in. Know though, panic can be deadly in the water, so it's important that you overcome it, take control over it. My instructor told us a few stories about divers, good divers, who lost their lives because they forgot the basics of diving during a panic attack. Now with that all considered, will you give it another try ... for the Michners...please? I really believe this is the best way to follow that boat."

"Okay, I'll try again but that scared the daylights out of me. I may panic even more now."

The instructor held some rings about the size of a dinner plate in his hands. Each was colorfully decorated and sturdy. "With these, we'll make a game out of the water and you'll see how enjoyable it is to be down there." He threw all six into the deep end.

Still sitting in the shallow water, Andrea grabbed the hand of the instructor. They stood and began to walk toward the deep end. Water closed over their heads. Brian watched Andrea's eyes grow as large as saucers inside her mask again. Then she began to take slow, even breaths, inhaling and exhaling through her regulator in unison with their instructor. She focused on the young man's face. Before long, he saw her look around, her body relaxed. She bent her head back to look up. She gave Brian the all clear sign, a circle made with her thumb and forefinger, as the instructor had told them.

Both men signaled their approval back to her. The instructor signaled for them to roll over on their stomachs. Now Andrea and Brian were horizontal. They had room to move their feet. They kicked their fins, propelling their bodies toward the deeper part of the pool. Every movement was done slowly at first but then they were swimming as if they'd done this many times before. Andrea grabbed one ring, then another, forgetting that she had about twelve feet of water over her head by now.

Their instructor corralled them once more and, with hand signals, told them to remove their vests and put them back on. For Andrea's benefit, he knelt directly in front of her. He motioned for her to focus on his eyes and they inhaled and exhaled slowly. Then he demonstrated for both how to do this task again. Once his vest was back on, he motioned for his students to do likewise. Andrea looked at him. He nodded his head and she began, slowly, to undo the clasp.

This procedure was completed a couple more times and then the instructor indicated he would time them. Andrea moved through her paces easily now. She lithely slipped out of her vest and then into it again.

The next step of their instruction was buddy breathing. Since every BC comes with a second regulator, Andrea and Brian could assist each other…if one of their tanks ran out of air or if the hose, connecting the air supply to the regulator, was damaged. The novices proved to be apt pupils. They could see their instructor was pleased as he began to teach them how to use a compass..

The time to surface came all too quickly. The instructor signaled them to check their gauges. Since Andrea had panicked in the beginning, her gauge showed less air in the tank than the men's.

They rose out of the water like the mythical Neptune and pulled the regulators out of their mouths as they walked to the stairs leading to the pool deck. Their instructor continued to give them vital information. "Each dive will be recorded in a log once you are both certified. In it you will record how deep you went and how long you were at that depth. Remember, each tank only holds one hour of air supply. The dive down and back has to be calculated in that hour. It is never a good idea to leave yourselves short for the return trip to the surface. The deeper the dive, the faster the air supply is used up. That's what these calculations are all about."

"Our next lesson will be in the ocean." They began to remove all gear. "We will meet at the dive shop the same time tomorrow. There's a very picturesque reef nearby that you'll enjoy. We will dive a little deeper, see some fish and coral, and learn to get comfortable under the surface of the ocean. This could also be your certification dive. You will need to pass all the tests I'll give you. We can decide that tomorrow before we dive the second time."

The stowed their gear in the back of the jeep. "The second time? Are we doing two dives tomorrow? How long will we be on the boat? Should we get someone to look after the little girl?" Andrea's questions rolled off her tongue staccato fashion.

"Your little one is welcome to come, but she may get bored. We wouldn't want her to attempt to go into the water alone." The young man drove the few blocks to the dive shop. "The boat will have a captain and a first mate, but they usually do not like to be considered babysitters."

"Does the boat crew ever take anyone out to snorkel?" asked Brian.

"But of course." They parked and exited the jeep. "I'll take care of the gear."

As Brian and Andrea prepared to say good-bye, they looked toward the pier. "Do you think they would supervise Camilla if we paid them for a snorkeling trip as well as diving?"

"Maybe. Why don't you ask them? That's their boat, docked over there by that catamaran."

Andrea and Brian, with Camilla skipping along behind, walked quickly down the pier. They noticed that the boat was being outfitted for another trip to sea. Several people, dressed in swim suits and lugging diving gear were standing around waiting for the captain to tell them it was time to board.

In the Haitian dialect, the captain and the first mate considered Brian's request. The captain shook his head in agreement. Brian knelt beside Camilla. "Would you like to snorkel tomorrow while Andrea and I dive?"

"Snorkel, what is dat?"

"You put on a mask to keep the water out of your eyes, and you breathe through a tube like the one that Andrea and I have attached to our masks. That's called a snorkel. Here try this one." Brian held his towards the child's mouth. She placed her lips and teeth around the nozzle and took a deep breath.

"Oh, dat is easy. How you do dat in the water." Camilla hung her head. "I can't swim yet?"

"You'll wear an inflatable vest…you know…one that blows up to keep you floating. The first mate will be right beside you. Okay with you Camilla?" Brian smiled trying to look confident in their arrangements.

"Okay with me," Camilla's smile revealed her missing teeth..

Andrea watched the two smile at each other. *I'm actually looking forward to tomorrow.*

Chapter Twenty

Back in their hotel room, Andrea bent down, placed her hands on Camilla's shoulders and jostled her. "Would you like to go on a picnic?" She grabbed some dry clothes and then headed for the bathroom to change leaving the door open a crack. "Brian and I have decided to rent a boat for the afternoon. So we thought…" Andrea stepped out of her wet swim suit.

Camilla had decided she wanted to wear her new shorts. "Oh Mam'selle Andrea could we? I 'ave never 'ad a picinic. What is a picinic?"

"Picnic, not pic-i-nic. A picnic is when we get the hotel to pack us a scrumptious lunch with lots of good things to eat; we boat to a beach somewhere, spread a blanket on the sand and eat, swim, and laugh a lot."

"Oh mais oui." Camilla squealed with delight, a sound that Andrea never tired of hearing. "Can we take my new swimsuit, can we?" Camilla jumped up and down in excitement. She steadied herself and then slipped her head into the t-shirt part of her ensemble.

"Yes, you certainly may. The suits will be wet but maybe by the time we decide on a beach, they'll at least be warm from the sunshine." Andrea exited the bathroom just as Camilla grabbed her swim suit. "Here let's put these into this plastic tote. We'll put some dry towels in as well."

"Mam'selle, why you bring Camilla wit you? Nobody care about Camilla…till you come…except for ma mama et papa." Camilla looked intently toward her benefactor, clearly wanting to understand.

Andrea sat on the bed and gathered the little girl to her. Her voice cracked. "Camilla, where we come from, people take care of children. They are not left to wander the streets alone."

"Oh…but..Mam'selle Andrea…"

"No buts. We, both Brian and I, care about what happens to you and we will not let anyone hurt you ever again, if we can in any way help it. Now let's go meet Brian. He was going to order our lunch and meet us downstairs." Andrea swiped a tear from her eyes before it trickled down her cheek. *How could anyone abandon such a sweet child?*

She locked the room door and walked toward the elevator. "I'm looking forward to another boat ride, aren't you? Let's hurry."

The elevator door opened. Camilla skipped out first and ran headlong into Brian. He laughed and wrapped one hand around her thin shoulders. He held a bulging basket of food in the other. "They are still apologetic over the break-in." He lifted the basket indicating this was the hotel's way of making up for it.

Andrea looked inside. A scream erupted from her lips. Lying on top of the food, with blood dripping over the sandwiches, was a dead chicken still attached to its feathers this time.

Brian swung the basket away from her line of vision and marched back to the front desk. "Look at this." He held the basket toward the concierge. "Someone in your hotel is responsible for this and probably the other creepy stuff that's been going on. I want an explanation."

"Oh monsieur. Not my staff. Someone must have come into the kitchen when ma wife was not looking, non?" The man was beside himself. "We will make another basket, only this time you do not pay for anything,"

"Somebody sure buys into this voodoo stuff here. Do you know anyone who works here that goes to the ceremonies?" Brian handed over the basket.

"Non, monsieur but then I do not ask what they do when they are not 'ere. I am not responsible. But ma wife? Huh. When she want to go, I say NON." He stomped his foot.

"I'm sure glad we discovered that before we left. Can you imagine what our lunch would have looked like if we'd waited till after a long hot boat ride? What does this mean?" Andrea stood beside Brian at the desk as the concierge took the basket back to the kitchen.

"Who cares what it means, It's not going to scare us away from doing what we know is right. Besides we have Christ to protect us."

A tiny voice spoke beside them. "What is this Christ?

Why feathers not scare you?" Camilla was obviously curious about why her new friends didn't believe what she'd grown up believing was normal. "I hear you talk much about heem, but I never hear about heem before."

"Let's go outside while we wait for our lunch." Andrea and Brian walked toward a swing on the veranda, lifted Camilla into the seat and then sat on either side of her.

Andrea was the first to speak. "Christ is the Son of God. Do you understand who God is?"

Camilla shook her head. "He punish us if we are bad. The ceremonies…"

Brian sighed. "The ceremonies have nothing to do with Him, Camilla. They are the people's way of trying to reach God but He doesn't want anyone to do that stuff."

"God's Son, Jesus, came to earth a long time ago to die on a cross for the things we do wrong. We don't have to dance in the moonlight or any of that." Andrea tried to form the words from the Gospels into language this child could understand. "God tells us how to behave in His Bible."

"Oh oui. Bible. Ma mere, she 'as one but…she don't know how to read so…" Camilla shrugged her shoulders. She hung her head again as if ashamed that her parents were members of the uneducated.

This society sure has people fooled about what's important. Andrea continued. "After Jesus died on the cross, He came alive again, and then went back to heaven to talk to His Father about us and for us. That's like a present for us. All we have to do is take it. Do you remember all those nice clothes we bought for you? Those are presents from us to you. You had to take the presents didn't you and then they were yours. God wants us to

197

take His present too so when we pray, He can hear us. Oh it's too complicated for someone as young as you to understand, I think." Andrea scratched her forehead.

Camilla shook her head. She spoke clearly. "You tell me dat dis Jesus is de Son of God. 'e died. Why 'e 'ave to die?"

"A long time ago, before Jesus came, a man named Adam sinned, did some bad things. God told him that now he would die. Before that people did not have to die. Anyway, God allowed people from then on to be forgiven of their sins when they put a new lamb to death as an offering. Jesus became that offering once and for all."

"Ah-h-h…and is now in heaven speaking for us. Dat is a gift. I accept, non?"

Brian sat back on the swing and looked at Andrea before answering. "We just have to tell Him that we know we do wrong things."

"Ah oui. I steal when I am 'ongry." Camilla shook her head again.

Brian continued, smiling at the little girl's understanding. "Then we ask Jesus to live inside us ….."

"You mean like a ghost …" interrupted the little girl.

"No …. Like the God He is, the One that made us, the One who loves you even more than your mama or papa. Then He helps us through the good times and the bad times when we ask and He changes us so we become more loving…"

"Like you are to me?"

"Yes Camilla. But even if you weren't the nicest person we know here, we'd still love you. That's the way God wants us to love…all people, all the time."

"Oh, I want that," she said in her tiniest voice. "Can I ask Heem now?"

"Sure you can." Andrea glanced up just as the concierge brought their basket of food to them. She thanked him and then turned back to Camilla. "Just say this prayer with me. Lord Jesus, I am a bad girl sometimes. Please forgive me and come into my heart. Amen." Camilla repeated the words in her broken English. When she'd finished, tears ran down her face, her happy smile contradicting the watery evidence.

Andrea hugged her first and then Brian, also teary eyed, gathered her to sit on his knee. "You are now God's child. Even if your parents are never found, God will always be your parent. Do you understand?"

"I do, I do. Will Jesus come with us when we go for our pic-nic?" She said the word slowly.

"Yes, He will, if we ask Him to."

Camilla immediately bowed her head. "Jesus, please come with us today. Amen"

Brian grabbed the basket. "If we don't get going there won't be much of the day left. I'm already hungry enough to eat a horse."

Camilla giggled. "That's a tough thing to eat, a horse. Too big to bring in a boat, non?" She skipped along beside them all the way to the pier. "I 'ave Jesus now." She slid her hand into Brian's, a gesture of total trust for the first time since they'd met her.

The man looking after the boat rentals pointed out an aluminum craft about 16 feet long. "You cannot take this boat out in the ocean. This is only for traveling along the shore." He took their money and went on to explain the workings of the little craft. "Stick close to shore. Watch out for rocks and if you want to land it on a beach, cut the engine just before you hit the sand."

Camilla jumped into the boat and then sat quickly as the boat rocked with her movement. Andrea stepped in next. She had mixed feelings about their afternoon. She knew they'd be looking for any sign of habitation off shore, a place where those thugs had taken the people last night. But she was also in a celebratory mood. Camilla, just yesterday, had nothing to call her own, not even a family. Her life held no hope, and now she had the assurance of heaven to look forward to. *God is so good.*

"Let's get this new adventure underway." Brian sat at the stern where the motor was. He started it and then steered them out of the harbor.

"Aye, Aye, me capitan." Andrea spoke in a grizzled sort of way. "We're pirates looking for buried treasure. Aye me hearties." Her voice rumbled in her throat.

Camilla giggled and then her face turned serious. "Pirates are bad, non? God doesn't want me to be bad anymore."

"Oh, we're not going to do anything bad. We're just pretending. It's fun to pretend. We'll just look for treasure, okay?" Andrea hugged the little one seated on the bench seat beside her. "Look at all the water out there."

Brian and Andrea scoured the shoreline, trying hard to determine where the men had landed their boat last night. They traveled for about an hour, doubling back as they guessed the distance they'd walked to the ceremony and in what direction. Camilla sang a little French song to herself and dangled her hand over the side of the boat. Water splashed up her arm.

"Andrea, do you think that might be the spot? If it is, look." Brian pointed just off shore where a stretch of land could be seen just off the horizon. "It's probably only a mile from shore. It might not be the same place but at least we have an idea where the boat might go when they leave this island." He tried to speak so Camilla couldn't hear. The child seemed in her own world at the moment.

"I guess we won't know that until…" She looked toward the child. "Camilla, look. Do you think that might be a good spot to look for buried treasure?" Andrea pointed toward the shore where they thought they had been the night before. "I'm hungry too. Brian, let's go ashore. We can explore for buried treasure and eat." She winked at him. "Don't run the boat all the way in though until we've had a chance to see if this is where they beached their boat last night. We don't want to mess up any telltale signs."

Brian steered toward shore, rubbed his tummy for Camilla's benefit, and then turned serious eyes toward the beach. He stopped in three feet of water." Andrea, my shorts are all I brought. I planned on swimming in them anyway so I'll walk the boat in from here." He slid into the water, felt around with his feet for any rocks that might be in the way and then pulled the boat with the rope attached to the anchor at the bow. He looked for any signs of another craft landing. *There, just to the right. A ridge in the sand.*

Andrea looked toward the spot Brian pointed out. She could almost see the path leading to the water's edge as well. She shivered. "Let's pull in over there." She indicated a spot well away from the previous night's activities. "I see a perfect spot to spread our blanket."

After they had all stepped onto dry land, Andrea spread the blanket and opened the basket of food, carefully this time. Nothing there. A whoosh of breath escaped her pursed lips. *Thank You Lord.* "Wow, look at all this food." She began pulling plates, napkins, and forks out of the hamper.

Brian tethered the boat's rope to a tree after taking the anchor off. Camilla was busy throwing stones into the water. She was soon chasing a crab across the sand. Andrea decided to reel her in. "Camilla, that's far enough. It's time to eat."

The child ran back toward their picnic. "Can we swim as soon as we eat, huh, can we?" Her excitement was spilling over.

"We'll see. Maybe we'll go look for some treasure for a while…to let our food settle. What do you think?" Andrea dished up some of the salad that the hotel had added to their sandwiches.

"Oh-h-h, the sandwiches, they look so good." Camilla stuffed a big bite into her mouth.

"Wait until we have asked God for his blessings." Andrea looked toward Brian. "Could you pray for the meal?"

"Certainly. Dear Lord, thank you for the food you have provided. Thank you also for a successful lesson and for protecting Andrea when she needed it. Place your hedge of angels around us now as we swim and enjoy some of your creation. Amen"

"What is creation?" Camilla spoke as soon as Brian had finished his short prayer.

Andrea swept her hand in a half circle around them. "That's all the things that we see here. God made or created everything on the earth, so we are thankful that he made many beautiful places for us to enjoy. We believe that God made you and me and Brian and all the other people here and elsewhere in the world. As His creation, we can be thankful every day for His provision."

"What is provision?" asked the little girl between mouth-fuls.

"Provision …. Um-m-m-m …. Did your Papa go to work?" asked Brian. He scooped some of the salad onto his plate. "This looks so good."

"Oui, he work at plantation."

Brian lifted a forkful. "When he got paid, he bought you and your family food, didn't he?"

"Oui, just a little. Not like we have here. Nothing like this." Camilla swept her hand across the items lying on the blanket.

"Well that is called providing or provision," said Brian. "Your father worked to provide you with food and God has helped the planters grow food, so we can eat such tasty things. He has provided." Brian took a large mouthful of fresh pineapple and smiled at the wonderful flavor he was enjoying.

The rest of the meal went very quickly. Camilla was so anxious to look for buried treasure; she had a hard time eating. Andrea packed away the leftovers. "There's enough here for another meal at least. Maybe we can eat the rest in our room tonight instead of going downstairs to eat."

"Sounds like a plan to me. Speaking of plans, let's check out that path over there; see if it leads to the clearing." Camilla was bouncing from rock to rock. "We can disguise our search as a treasure hunt."

"Good idea. Camilla let's look for treasure." Andrea brushed the sand off her clothes. She walked toward the edge of the trees with Brian right behind. "You have to turn over rocks, dig into the sand with your toes, see if there's anything hidden." She showed Camilla how to look under a rock nearby. Then once the child was happily searching, she and Brian wandered casually down the path. Camilla followed, looking by tree roots, and under anything along the way.

"Andrea, I think this is the path. Look over there. Isn't that the same tree we hid behind last night?"

"You're right Brian it looks the same. But let's continue until we see the clearing, Then we'll know for sure." Andrea walked a little faster while Brian lagged behind Camilla, "Brian, come here." Her voice carried over the birds singing and the crickets chirping.

"We were right. This is the spot. That means that the land we saw is probably the place they took those people and could be the place where they have Trent and Diane. We are so close. Brian, do you think we could go there by boat today?"

"I don't think that's such a good idea. What if they catch us? Then we'd be no good to the Michners or anyone else. We'll wait till the night of the ceremony so we're sure it's the same place, okay? I know you want to find them. So do I but…"

Andrea turned to walk back to the beach. "You're right. We'll wait. I just wish…"

"I don't like this place. The ceremonies 'appen 'ere." Camilla looked around and then ran back down the path ahead of Andrea.

Andrea ran after her. "It's alright Camilla." She stooped to the child's level, wrapped her in her arms. "Let's go swimming, okay?" Andrea's face showed her seriousness to Brian. "I think you were right about following them under water. It shouldn't take too long, if that's the right place."

"I'll make some inquiries in town to see if anyone knows

anything about that place. In the meantime, Camilla has earned her swim, don't you think?" Brian ran toward the water with Camilla close behind.

"Camilla and I'll catch up to you. We need to change into our swim suits first. Camilla, let's get you changed and then I'll change." Andrea and Camilla walked behind some bushes.

****

Brian turned toward the ocean. *That island. Looks close enough to swim to from here. Trent and Diane could be on that island. So close and yet so far. It'll be hard to wait for the next ceremony.* He walked a little further out into the water. *Seems to be pretty close to the harbor as well. I wonder if people have any idea what's going on over there.* He turned toward shore just in time to see Andrea and Camilla lay their clothes on a nearby rock and skip down the beach toward him.

****

Diane looked toward the piece of land in the distance. Do people know we are here? She watched Jeffrey playing at the water's edge. "Keep your shoes dry, Jeffrey. They're the only ones you have." She was thankful her captors had decided to let them walk along the beach a little today. It's good to be outside.

Furtively, Diane looked at the boat tethered to a cement block at the water's edge. It was large enough to take them the short distance to that other island but what if it too was uninhabited like this one. A large chain was padlocked in place. These guys didn't trust even their own people, it seemed.

A small motor was attached to the back of the boat. Every now and then she'd heard a motor put-puting away but then a short while later, it would return. Usually at

night. Diane walked closer to the water's edge. She stood just beside the boat. She glanced back at the man guarding them. His attention seemed elsewhere at the moment. She looked into the boat. It seemed to be sound, no holes or cracks.

"Hey, what you lookin'at?" The large beast of a man grabbed her arm and pulled her up the bank. "Don't go getting any ideas, hear? Your man'll pay if you try anything." He continued hauling her toward the cabin. "Play time's over."

"Jeffrey." Diane screamed her son's name. "Come here…now."

"That's right lady. You keep your kid in line too." He laughed at the fright he was causing her and yanked all the harder on her arm.

"Jeffrey." The little golden haired urchin appeared over the embankment. He raced toward his frantic mother.

****

The rest of the afternoon flew by. Andrea and Brian taught Camilla to dog paddle and then float. *For a child who's not been swimming before, she's sure picked it up fast.* Andrea watched as Brian carried her on his shoulders and then ducked under the water with her head still about the surface. The child's giggles echoed off the shoreline. *Anyone passing by will surely hear us but…so what. We're tourists enjoying the laughter of a little child. Nothing more.*

The water was cool, the sun very hot. Sunscreen was applied liberally but Andrea and Brian were soon a little pinker than they thought was healthy. It was time to leave. Camilla, in typical childlike fashion, wanted to continue to play in the water, but Brian and Andrea were adamant.

"Maybe we'll come here again tomorrow, eh Brian?" Andrea grabbed their clothes while Brian dried off in the sunshine. "Let's get out of these wet sticky swim suits. We'll have a shower to wash off the salt when we get back to our hotel room." Andrea took Camilla back to their changing area, helped the child towel off and dress. "Camilla, go keep Brian company. I'll be out in a minute."

As she dried herself off and changed into her clothes, a thought skittered across her brain. If those men were ruthless enough to kill Max and torch her house, would they use Camilla to get to them? Would they hurt the child? Andrea shuddered and then hurried to the beach where her two companions waited. The girls piled into the boat as Brian untied its tether and then pushed them toward deeper water. He tried not to get his pant legs too wet but still ended up soaked to his waist when he got aboard.

Andrea waited until they were well underway. Camilla was absorbed in making the water spray up her arms again. She lowered her voice and spoke her fears to Brian. "Do you think they would hurt a little girl?"

"Whoa. Where did that come from? I hadn't thought about that but, yes, I think they are capable of almost anything. Whatever it is that they are up to; you can bet they don't intend to let us stand in their way, if they can help it. As long as Camilla is with us, I guess she's in as much danger as we are." Brian eyes betrayed the anguish this thought brought to his mind.

"Then we have to make sure she is some place safe before we go ahead with our plans. I mean, we can't risk her life, can we? But where do we take her?"

"I don't know. It seems most of the people here don't care one way or another if these little ones live or die,. I don't know whether they have a place to care for them or not, but I would guess they do not."

"Maybe we can find some private agency or something. In the meantime, I don't plan to let her out of my sight." Andrea rubbed Camilla's arm. Her brow furrowed, worry causing her stomach acid to flow freely. *How do we find a safe place for her? How do we leave her some place...without us? I'll miss her so much.* The motor chugged, carrying them toward the harbor and the boat landing.

Chapter Twenty One

"Wow, Brian, look at the time. The day went by so fast." Andrea climbed the few steps to the deck in front of their hotel. A slight breeze blew inland from the ocean making the hot summer afternoon very pleasant. Many of the hotel's guests were sitting in large rocking chairs enjoying the shade of the large overhanging roofline of the veranda. "Let's join the folks out here for a little rest. By the way, I think I'll get rid of this basket of food. It won't taste as good later as it did today."

****

"Sure. We can…" Camilla was whiny all of a sudden. "I think she's in need of a nap. Camilla, come climb up on my lap, and I'll tell you a story" Brian sat on a nearby rocker, away from the other folks outside while Andrea went inside to get rid of the basket. He patted his lap. Camilla hesitated and then slowly complied. She sure didn't seem to be as enthusiastic as she was earlier that afternoon. However, Brian began to quietly tell the story of *Goldilocks and the Three Bears*. The little girl rested her head on his shoulder. He rocked slowly as he related this story he remembered reading to Jeffrey Michner a time or two.

****

Andrea stood in the doorway and watched them. She couldn't help but see how comfortable Brian was with the child. *He seems so gentle. He'll make a great father some day. It's nice to be able to share the responsibility for Camilla, too.* She leaned back in the rocker she'd chosen, relaxed after such a strenuous day. She reflected on the diving. A shudder traveled up her spine and back again. *I'm not sure I'll ever find scuba diving comfortable but at least I did do what was required. Now we just have to decide if we're ready to be certified tomorrow.* She closed her eyes. *Oh, this feels so-o-o-o good.* She sighed. Sleep came quickly.

****

Brian was a little sleepy, but not as much, obviously, as his tiny charge. He had only told his story as far as Goldilocks discovering a bed just right for her when he noticed that Camilla was sound asleep. He smiled and laid his head against the back of the chair, closed his eyes, and let his thoughts travel to the events of the day.

All this cloak and dagger stuff. I think I'm actually enjoying the idea of solving this mystery. I sure enjoyed the diving this morning. Not something I'll get to do often back home but...hey... it's another skill well worth exploring. If we could just figure this whole thing out...before anything worse happens to any of us. Camilla, though. That has to be taken care of. She needs to be safe.

He glanced at the woman beside him. *She is one spunky gal. Life around her is not nearly as dull as I'd once thought it would be. Wouldn't Trent laugh? He'd tried to get me to ask Andrea out once. But I told him then I wasn't interested. I knew he'd push for it again though. Maybe...just maybe Andrea is*

210

worth getting to know on a more intimate basis. She's not at all like the other girls I've dated. In fact, Andrea is the most adventurous woman I've ever met. She's never really complained about the bad things that have happened to her.

"Brian, what's the matter? You look a little confused." Andrea whispered.

Brian relaxed his face and smiled toward the woman he'd been thinking about so intently. She was rubbing the sleep from her eyes. "Oh-h, you're awake. Nothing really. I was just thinking about the circumstances that brought us here. You and I have never had much of a chance to get to know each other before. I mean…you were always doing something with Diane and I was with Trent but we've never done anything together with them. Maybe when all this is over, we can remedy that."

"I'd like that" Andrea lowered her eyes, warmth creeping up her neck."I-I-I see that Camilla has dosed off. Do you think you could carry her up to my room? I'd like to take a nap and then get ready for dinner without rushing this time."

"Sure, but I think you already took that nap. You've been sleeping for the last half hour."

"I know, but I still feel very tired. And as long as Camilla is sleeping, I might as well take advantage of some quiet time."

"I think I'll do the same. The scuba lesson and then all the swimming have taken its toll. My body could use a little relaxation." Brian stifled a yawn as they got up. He carried Camilla through the entrance to the lobby and then into the elevator, oblivious to the stranger standing on the far side of the room.

The trio entered the elevator with another couple who were guests of the hotel. Brian pushed the button for their floor. "Is eight okay for dinner tonight?" Andrea stepped through the elevator door when it opened on their floor. She motioned toward the child sleeping soundly in Brian's arms. "Bring her to my bedroom. I'll sleep on the sofa so I won't disturb her."

He lay Camilla gently down and then turned toward Andrea. "Eight o'clock will be fine. That's give me some time to go over the logistics of the trek under that boat." He closed the door behind him and moved farther down the hall to his own room. *I'll have to take it slow with this woman, I think. But she seems interested.*

****

Andrea slipped into a nightgown, pulled a spare blanket over herself and closed her eyes, forgetting to check to see if the door was locked. She drifted from wide awake to semi consciousness and before long, she was dreaming. Brian was kissing her. He was her protector in this nether world. It felt right.

A hand. Over her mouth. Again. Her eyes popped open, as large as they'd been inside that scuba mask, she was sure. She looked up to see a tall man with a large, bushy beard. He looked like the man who'd been seen running from their hotel room yesterday. His hair was black and unkempt and the glove on his hand smelled of cigarette smoke and beer.

The hand shook her head so hard she began to see pinpoints of light before her eyes. His grip was so tight she had a hard time breathing. She kicked the blanket off freeing her legs. The she kicked at the man. He tightened his grip. "Keep quiet or I will kill the little girl."

Andrea immediately relaxed her body. Nothing could happen to Camilla, She had to protect her. The man removed his hand. "Wha-what do you want." Her body trembled as she moved to a sitting position. She pulled the blanket over her nightgown.

"I want you and your boyfriend to go home. His voice

erupted in a quiet menacing snarl. "If you are not gone by to-morrow, we will have to kill you both and the little girl."

"We have every right to be on this island." She glared at the man who's angry countenance glared right back. "We're enjoying our vacation. We'll not be rushed home."

"Well then, you will see your little friend here killed." He moved toward the bed where Camilla continued to sleep soundly.

"No, leave her alone." Andrea rushed to stand in front of the child, placing her body between the ruffian and the little girl. The blanket slipped but she reefed it around her more tightly.

"Take my warning seriously, lady, or you'll be sorry." He turned, walked purposefully toward the door. He closed it firmly behind him as if accenting that he meant business. Andrea sank to the carpet. She was thankful Camilla never moved. *Thank the Lord. Who are these people?* Although black, like many of the people hereabouts, he did not have a native accent. *Interesting.*

She stood, dropping the blanket. She resolutely checked to make sure the door was indeed locked this time. *No one is going to scare me into giving up on the Michners, that's for sure.* She placed her hands on her hips as if accenting her deci-sion. *These people, whoever they were, seem to be threatened by Brian and I being here. We must be near enough to the truth to make them feel uncomfortable.*

Andrea picked up the phone to call Brian and then thought better of it. He was probably sound asleep anyway. She could tell him all about this latest turn of events when they met for dinner. *What's next?* She returned to the sofa, lay down, but knew sleep was no longer an option.

She tossed and turned for about half an hour. *This isn't working. It's time we began asking some questions if we're ever going to solve this thing.* Andrea looked toward Camilla. The child looked angelic as she slept. Andrea changed into a pair of pants and a fresh blouse. *Let's see who's downstairs who might know something.*

She locked the door behind her. *I won't be too long. Camilla will sleep for at least another half hour or so… probably.* Looking over her shoulder to make sure no one was following; she pressed the down arrow on the elevator.

Andrea slipped into the restaurant and approached a waitress just before claiming her seat.. "Can I have a cup of coffee?" She looked around to see who was seated nearby. A native was clearing the table next to hers. "Excuse me. Can I ask you a few questions?"

"Mais Oui." His English was broken just as most natives of Haiti. "I would be 'appy to 'elp you."

"Can you tell me anything about the Voodoo ceremonies held in the clearing north of town?" Andrea took a sip from the cup the waitress had placed in front of her. It was strong.

"Oh-h-h … oui …but they are not for the tourists, non. Only the island people go to them. They are sacred." He continued to wipe the table top.

"Oh, I don't want to go. I am writing a book about some of the customs here and would like to add some information about that part of island life." Andrea hated to lie but then thought maybe some day she would write a book.

"Well then … they are held several times each year, not as many times as your church services but almost. There will be another in three days because the people believe that is the time when we dance for new babies. Some people are beginning to stay away from these dances now because others, they are disappearing." He glanced quickly around, looking, Andrea supposed, to see if someone was close enough to hear.

"What do you mean disappearing?"

"Well they go to the dance and do not come home. The word all over the island is that many are lost and the spirits are adding to their numbers. So I am one who has not gone for some time. I do not want the spirits to have my body. Now miss, I must…"

Andrea continued. "Are any of these people ever seen again?"

"Only when they wash up on the shore some weeks later. Now, I 'ave to…" He wrapped his cloth around his fingers. The questions seemed to make him uncomfortable.

But, people don't do anything about this?" Andrea's voice gave away her astonishment at this situation.

"Mais oui. We bury them but not in a 'oly place. The priest at the Catholic Church calls them un'oly. They are buried in a plot east of 'ere. Now I…" The man clearly wanted to escape.

"Would you take my friend and I to that place?"

"Non. Non, please do not ask this of me. That is an un'oly place. No one goes there except to bury someone." He shivered as if a cold breeze had just blown through the room.

"We'll make it worth your while. You don't have to actually enter the place, just get us near and we will go the rest of the way."

"Okay, I begin work here at 4 p.m. demain…ah…

tomorrow, so we will have to go before dat. How much you pay, eh?"

"Fifty dollars. Is that enough?"

"Yeah, dat be okay."

"Thanks, uh … what is your name?" Andrea wanted to make sure that she knew who to look for if he didn't show up. "Where will we meet? I think we could be ready to go about 1 o'clock just after lunch tomorrow."

"My name is Bernard. I will meet you 'ere, in front of de 'otel about 1 p.m., n'est pas."

"That'll be great." Andrea signed her check as the young man hurried through the kitchen door.

She sauntered casually outside. *We only have three days to become adept at scuba diving.* Andrea looked around to make sure she was not being followed. She continued toward the harbor. As she crossed the street, a young boy who looked to be in his early teens caught her attention. He was standing beside a small vehicle that could have been a car but not one she had ever seen before. The vehicle was a mix of many colors. It also looked as if it could have been put together from a variety of vehicles. "That's an interesting vehicle you have."

"Oh yes, and it gets me to town when I need to be here." This young man spoke perfect English.

"You speak English very well. Are your parents English?"

"Non, I have no parents, but Father Bertrand teaches an English class. I live at the orphanage just over the border in Santo Domingo, east and a little north of here in the Dominican Republic. I have lived there for a long time."

"An orphanage. Really? Do they allow children from here to live there?"

The boy hesitated. He looked around. Finally he spoke again. Why do you want to know that?"

"I'm just curious. I've noticed so many children on the street here who seem to have no home. In fact, the hotel concierge calls them street kids." Andrea spoke quickly hoping not to scare him off.

"Ah, bien. I come to town to seek children who need to have a good place to live. Always there are children. Some have lost their parents. Some are throw away children. Their mama and papa cannot afford to feed them." The boys face contained the sad reminder of his own journey from days gone by. "I bring them to Santo Domingo…when no one notices so much. Besides no one really cares that I take them to another country, since they don't have to look at them. It reduces the crime rate here. With so many starving children, people lose their wallets, their food, and sometimes even their clothing."

"Will you bring us, my friend and I, to this orphanage." Andrea's heart gave an excited leap. *Maybe this is the answer for Camilla.* "We'd like to know more."

"Why do you want to know these things?" The boy looked at her with suspicion. "Father Bertrand is a very busy man and has no time for tourists."

"My friend and I found a little girl whose parents have disappeared.".

"Oh, yes … disappeared. That is a common story among the newest arrivals at our home. That story began about six months ago and more children are telling it every day."

"You sound as if you don't believe the story. Is there a

reason you question its validity?"

"Well some children will make up stories to come to the home because they are being beaten in their own homes or because they were restavec and are now runaways. The story gives them an excuse for being on the streets, I think."

"I have seen people being snatched...er…I mean…well that is the story Camilla told us anyway. I am Andrea Wilton, and I am visiting Port Au Prince with my friend Brian Strait. One day while we were taking a walk, we met Camilla crying by the roadside. She has been with us ever since."

"So you want to get rid of her now." The teenager spoke with derision. "I am Troy Depuiz. I will show you the orphanage."

"No, you don't understand. We don't want to get rid of Camilla. In fact, I think Brian, and I know I have, fallen in love with that little girl. It's just that we're not married, either of us. I don't even have a house to go back to in the United States since it burned in a fire just before I left to come here … for vacation … that is. We just want a good safe home for her."

"Well, I will take you day after tomorrow. That is Sunday. It is a long way through the jungle but my "car" has made it many times. I'll see you here about ten o'clock in the morning, okay."

"No, that won't work. We usually go to church on Sunday morning. Can we meet about 1 o'clock, just after lunch?"

"Ah-h-h, church. Tourists do not usually go to church when they come to this country. They just like to play. Yes 1 p.m. would be fine."

"Okay then, thanks Troy. We'll see you day after tomorrow." Andrea almost skipped on her way back to the hotel. *A place for Camilla ...the day before we have to go for their mid-night dive. What an answer to prayer. Thank you Lord.* She took the stairs to the second floor, too excited to wait for the elevator. *I've been gone longer than I wanted. I hope Camilla is alright. I can't wait to tell Brian what I found out though.*

Andrea pushed the stairwell door open. A small head peeked around the corner in the doorway to her room. "Where you go?" The tiny voice sounded scared.

"Just for a short walk. Are you okay?"

"Oui, just a little scare dat's all. I tot maybe you 'ave dis-appeared too!"

"No, nothing like that. Let's get ready for dinner. Are you hungry? You slept for almost three hours, you know." Andrea led the way back inside her room. She shut and locked the door.

"Oh oui, I am empty inside, I think. Can I wear another of my new dresses, can I?" Camilla had obviously forgotten how scared she was.

"A new dress it is. I want to phone Brian. You go ahead and get in the tub. I'll be right there." Andrea sat on the bed and picked up the phone. She watched Camilla slowly head toward the bathroom.

The child shook her head. "Another bath...so sooon? I am already clean, non?"

Andrea chuckled. "Another bath...yes. You will feel bet-ter and it will make you extra specially clean for tonight. Now scoot."

"Why … What is happening tonight?"

"Well, we are going to the dining room, and I think this

time we will try a little dancing like your people do, maybe."

Camilla grinned at the prospect. "Okay, I take de bath."

"Good, I'll make my phone call and see you in a minute. Do you remember how to turn on the water and add the soap bubbles?"

"Yes I can … err … I mean .. I do," she said as she ran into the other room.

Andrea quickly dialed Brian's room. After the third ring, huffing and puffing, Brian answered. "Hello."

"Hello yourself. Where did I bring you from?"

"I was just in the shower. What can I do for you?"

"Well, I have a lot to tell you, so I thought you should come over here now while Camilla is in the tub. I don't want her to hear what I have to say."

"I'll be right there. It sounds serious."

"It is."

In less time than it took to hang up the phone Brian was at Andrea's door. "What's going on." Andrea let him in, checked to make sure Camilla was okay, and then began to fill him in.

Brian's face clouded when she told him about her latest visitor. "Are you alright?"

"Yes, but I couldn't go back to sleep, so I took a walk" Andrea's smile lit her face as she told him about the information she'd uncovered. "I've arranged for us to go to the burial plot tomorrow at one o'clock. I want to see those grave markers in case there are clues to the identity of some of the people buried there. Maybe we'll find Camilla's parents."

She continued. "I also ran into a young man who collects orphans to take to an orphanage in Santo Domingo, just over the border in the Dominican Republic, northeast of here. Camilla could find a home there, I think."

"When can we see it?"

"I've arranged the day after tomorrow to visit. I want to see it for myself before we consider taking Camilla there. Apparently, the boy comes to town a couple of times a week in search of children with no home. He spoke very good English and said that Father Bertrand, the priest who runs the orphanage, is his English teacher."

"It sounds like you have been busy. Although, I think we need to take Camilla with us to the orphanage. That's the day before the next ceremony. We don't know what will happen after that. She needs to be safe and in light of the latest threat…"

"Of course, you're right. We knew when we flew down here that our lives were at risk but now with Camilla…we need to get her safely away from us. The sooner the better I guess. It's just that I know I am going to miss that little girl. I've come to love her, Brian"

"Yeah I know. Me too." Brian changed the subject. "We have scuba lessons scheduled for the next three days at 9 a.m., so we should be ready for the next voodoo ceremony. In the meantime, once we feel comfortable enough, why don't we think about going to the place that let's you dive with the dolphins? They have people who watch the divers closely, and it will give us more practice to build our confidence."

"That sounds like a plan." Just as she spoke, Camilla appeared in the bathroom doorway. "What's a plan?" she asked.

"We were just saying that we're hungry, and it's time we get ready to eat. How about you?" Andrea rushed to the little girl's side to help with the towel that was slipping from her soapy body. "Let's rinse these bubbles off and get you dry."

"I'll go and finish getting dressed and meet you both in the lobby in…say… a half hour." Brian glanced at his watch.

"Make it 45 minutes and you have yourself a deal." Andrea smiled toward him. Brian walked through the door but not before reminding her with a gesture to lock it after him.

Forty-five minutes was hardly long enough for her to wash her hair and shower before getting dressed, but Andrea knew she would feel a little more rested if she did. She quickly settled Camilla in front of the television with a cartoon and hopped into the shower.

Chapter Twenty Two

Andrea's dinner of fried Yellowtail, rice, and beans was prefaced by deep fried plantain. She and Brian loved the appetizer. "How do you cook this?" Andrea spoke to the waiter when he returned with their main course.

"We peel, then slice the plantain before we fry it in vegetable oil." He set their plates in front of them. "Mam'selle, here is your petite dinner." Camilla giggled at his use of so formal a name for her. He set down a smaller version of Brian's chicken dinner.

As they took their first bite, the music started. It was the same band that had entertained them the last time they ate here. "Do you think we'll be able to dance like those people?" Andrea laughed between mouthfuls imagining their efforts.

Camilla spoke around the food in her mouth. "Papa teach me some of dose dances. When we walk on de street and the music guys play out dere, we dance."

"Well then I guess you'll have to teach us, eh little one?" Brian straightened the napkin on her lap. He poured her another glass of water from the pitcher left by their waiter. "Mam'selle Andrea will just have to follow my lead, I'm afraid."

The dinner was delicious. As soon as they'd finished, Brian led Camilla to the dance floor. She demonstrated the easy steps taught her by her father and he followed amidst plenty of laughter. Then it was Andrea's turn. Brian walked over to the table, seated Camilla again, and then bowed from the waist as he held out his hand. Andrea giggled but then placed her hand over her hot face.

"Let's give it a try, shall we? We can't go home not having tried to at least make a good attempt to learn the dances here." Brian led the way and turned slowly. He opened his arms for Andrea.

"Brian, maybe this is not a good idea. I mean…well… we're not really here to enjoy ourselves, are we? This is business."

Andrea, when we left, we said we were also going to have some fun. Now come on. It's just a dance. I promise I won't bite." Brian made his arms as inviting as he could.

"Oh, alright. But…"

"No buts. Come. Let's have some fun." Brian tugged on her hand until Andrea was encased in the masculine scent of him. He swayed, almost in perfect rhythm to the beat of the steel drums. Andrea felt herself relax.

Lost in their musical surroundings, appearing as if they didn't have a care in the world, Andrea and Brian swayed, twirled, and sashayed through three more numbers. They laughed a lot but the rhythm from the band was definitely not all that beat in time to the music. Andrea caught herself several times wanting to lay her head on his shoulder as Brian's hand cradled her back. She feared looking in his eyes so kept her head down the whole time.

"I think Camilla is getting lonely." She turned toward their table. Brian followed but seemed to lag behind a bit. When they reached Camilla, she looked as if she was having a hard time keeping her eyes open. "Are you tired?"

"Oh, oui. But I tink you want to dance more, non?" Camilla grinned at her two new friends.

"Huh…we've danced enough. Right Brian?" Andrea's face flushed more as her thoughts betrayed her common sense. "That was fun but now we need to get rested up for a busy day tomorrow." She felt like she was escaping a cleverly laid trap.

****

Brian was sorry the night had to end. *There's some-thing about that woman. I wonder why I never noticed before.* "I guess I'm not too tired yet. Andrea, you dance very well. We'll have to do this again." He waltzed another step or two as they left the dining room, his feet clearly not done for the evening.

****

Andrea walked slowly beside Camilla to the elevator. *I'd better not let that happen again. I can't believe I acted that way. I hope he didn't notice. I like Brian. I'd hate to ruin a perfectly good friendship with my nonsensical female emotions.* She turned toward the topic of her thought at the door to her room. "Er…night Brian. See you tomorrow." She turned toward the interior of her room.

"Goodnight Andrea. Sleep well. If you need me, call. Lock that door, okay. Maybe even put a chair in front of it." She watched as Brian pulled the door shut.

Camilla was almost asleep before her head hit the pillow. Her last words before she drifted off were about the "party" they'd just attended. Andrea smiled. She took her time getting undressed. *That child has experienced so little of life. Everything she does is a special event.* The novelty of being in the Caribbean had not worn off for Andrea either. It seemed that when she and Brian had a chance to do something other than detective work, they really had a good time together. *Of course, it was all for Camilla's benefit, wasn't it? I'm going to miss her when we take her to the orphanage.*

Carefully removing the little make-up she wore, Andrea creamed her face. She did a quick step toward her side of the bed and then slipped her bare feet beneath the sheets. Camilla had sprawled across the entire width, but her waif like frame made moving her a simple task. Andrea lay quietly waiting for sleep to come. *Another scuba lesson tomorrow. Ugh. I sure wish I enjoyed it more.* Andrea was determined to get over her fright even if the mere thought of going into the water again caused her to toss and turn.

Lord, I want to trust you with this situation as well as the safety of the Michners. Please give me a good night's sleep and let me not worry about the things I cannot change. If you have another way for us to follow those men without being seen, please let us know. But if this is your plan, please protect both of us and allow us to accomplish the task at hand. Oh, and give Brian a good night's sleep too. In Jesus name, Amen. Andrea felt her body drift into a peaceful sleep as her mind hummed the words to her favorite praise chorus, Awesome God.

****

Morning dawned bright and sunny. While she lay there waiting for Camilla to stir, Andrea thought about the day ahead. *I wonder if there are any days here when the sun doesn't shine.* She stretched. *Maybe the scuba thing will be just fine. Maybe I'll find something to concentrate on once I'm in the ocean instead of my fear.* Andrea looked at the sleeping child. *Maybe Camilla would be safer if she stayed at the hotel today. I'll have to ask Mrs. Gevin if she would consider keeping Camilla for us again.*

Camilla squiggled and then opened her eyes. She smiled. "Bonjour mam'selle. I 'ave a long sleep, non?" She raised herself onto one elbow. "We go eat now?"

"As soon as you can get dressed. After breakfast, though, I want you to stay with Mrs. Gevin again. Brian and I have another scuba lesson and…"

Camilla pounded her fists on the bed. Tears streaked down her cheeks. "I don't want to stay 'ere. I want to come wit you."

"Honey, I know you do but Brian and I will work hard to get done as fast as we can and then…"

The child was inconsolable. She climbed onto Andrea's lap and clung to her as if she'd never let her go. "Please don't leave me. I'll be good. I promise." She sobbed into Andrea's nightgown.

"Camilla, listen. We are not leaving you. If I give you my handbag to keep for me and my passport, will you stay here until I can come back for you. We'll only be gone for the morning and then we'll…well we'll talk about the afternoon later. I can't go anywhere without my handbag pr passport, now can

I?" Andrea hugged the tiny body to her. She rocked her until the sobs subsided.

Camilla looked into her eyes with damp eyelashes sparkling in the sunshine. "I go to Madam Gevin. I will wait, non?" She sniffed. "Can we get dressed to eat now?"

Andrea laughed and mussed her hair. "You sure can change your tune in a hurry can't you? And I'm glad you can." She placed the girl on the bed beside her, stood and began rummaging through the dresser for some fresh clothes. Camilla did the same.

After a short meal in the dining room, Andrea spoke to Mrs. Gevin about looking after Camilla for her. Once that was looked after, she and Brian walked the short distance to the dock where their scuba instructor's shop was located.

The next lesson began as soon as they arrived. "I want you to gather the equipment you will need without my assistance. Assemble your gear by yourselves." He folded his arms to wait for them to begin. When you're ready, we'll go to the pool again for our first dive. I was going to take you straight out to the ocean for both dives but, Andrea, I think another pool lesson is warranted for you. We'll go over the basics again before we try the ocean."

Andrea's stomach lurched. She gave their instructor a look of gratitude for his patience and then began to assemble the equipment she'd need. She remembered her prayer from the night before as she grabbed a tank that had already been filled according to the gauge that was attached to it. She attached a regulator as she'd been taught the day before and then plunked the whole thing through the straps at the back of the vest. Brian, as her buddy, made sure her vest and tank was secure while she checked his.

"Just carry the wet suit with you. We'll suit up at the

pool. Do you have your swim suit on under your clothes?" The instructor was holding the door for them to leave for the pool.

Brian walked beside her. "Andrea, I hope that you feel okay about all this. And about last night…"

"What about last night? We were just having fun. Isn't that what you said?"

"Yes but…" He shifted his load from one hand to the other.

Andrea looked into his face to see if she could detect anything. She decided to change the subject. "I'll do just fine today. I prayed about all this last night."

"Well, here we are. Thank goodness. This stuff is heavy. I don't know how you can carry all that."

"I have more muscles than you might think." Andrea smirked at him with a teasing glint in her eye. "Maybe I work out. You never know, do you?"

"No, you are full of surprises." He opened the door leading to the deck and the pool. They set their equipment on a nearby bench, took off their outer clothing and donned their wetsuits over their swim suits.

Their instructor checked the equipment and then slowly, all three entered the water. Andrea carefully inhaled and exhaled as the water covered her head. Kneeling on the bottom of the pool beside Brian, as relaxed as she had ever been, she actually began to enjoy the clear blue water. With hand signals, their instructor directed them to remove their equipment and then to put it back on again. He asked them to buddy breath while they swam to the deepest part of the pool.

As long as she relaxed, Andrea swam with ease. The

panic attack from the day before was non-existent. The water was cool, clear, and an azure blue. Other people were swimming at the shallow end. Andrea enjoyed watching their antics from under the water instead of always on top. She saw Brian's eyebrows lift a little as he gave her the approval sign. All too soon their instructor signaled them to check their gauges. It was time to surface.

"Wow," Andrea exclaimed when she had taken off her mask and spit the regulator out of her mouth. "That was fun. In fact I found it downright exhilarating. Now I know why people do this and I - I haven't even been in the ocean yet ... Gosh .... all the fish and other sea life." Her excitement caused her words to jumble and her eyes sparkled. Brian smiled as he watched this otherwise quiet woman become boisterous and even a little loud. She seemed to be almost beside herself.

"Now we go to the real water?" At the dive center, they were told to disconnect their tank from their BC in order to replace it with a full one. They loaded their equipment into the boat docked alongside the dive shop. Soon they'd left the harbor behind. "We'll go out about three miles. There's a reef made of coral, home of many fish with a variety of colorful markings." The proverbial teacher, their instructor went over some added information for a sea dive. "We will have a good dive, I think. All is calm today."

Brian and Andrea sat towards the back of the boat watching the seagulls fly alongside. At almost the same speed, they skimmed over the water. "Those birds are so graceful." Andrea pointed to one that seemed to fly sideways.

"He's hoping we'll throw him some food, I think. This boat looks about the same size as those fishing boats we noticed in the harbor yesterday." Brian looked from front to back.

"I wonder what kind of fish they catch here. I'll bet you'd like to go deep sea fishing here sometime. Maybe when this is all over, we can spend an extra day or two." Andrea leaned her head back over the railing, letting the salt water spray her warm face. The air was warm with the sun blazing to the east.

The sky was completely cloudless and the bluest blue either of them had ever seen. "If it wasn't for our ultimate mission here," whispered Brian, "I could really get to like Caribbean life."

"Oh, me too. Everyone seems so relaxed and in no hurry to go anywhere. I love being so close to the water and the sandy beaches." Andrea had already acquired a modest tan.

****

Brian took a deep breath. It felt as if they had been here much longer than just a few days. *I'll bet Trent and Diane think they've been here a lot longer too. I miss them. I miss Trent's humor and Diane's cooking.* He sighed, feeling a little guilty that he was enjoying himself so much when they probably weren't. Of course, the look on the face of the woman across from him was a good reason to go on enjoying what time they had left before the real work of finding the Michners began. Andrea looked radiant.

****

No one noticed the other boat, just off to their right heading in the same direction. At least not at first. When they did see the sleek craft skimming on top of the waves, Brian and Andrea thought it was just another tourist, one of the many deep sea fishing craft or pleasure boats anchored in the harbor. After all, the native people made their living on the water.

The ocean rolled gently as the boat cut through each crest. Spray hit the dive team giving their skin a slightly sticky feel. It still cooled them from the hot rays of the sun. Andrea's skin glistened. She remained relaxed while the boat captain took them to their destination.

Emerging from below decks, their instructor offered them a cool drink of bottled water. He sat beside his clients. "Why do you want to learn to dive, Brian."

"We – uh - we are doing – uh – research … for a - a book that we are collaborating on." The lie stumbled over his lips. "Andrea and I are writers." He nodded his head in an attempt to confirm his story and then adroitly changed the subject. "How much farther are we going out?"

"We will go about another ten minutes or so, and then we will dive."

"Do you take very many novices like us to this place?" Brian asked.

"Oh yes. I have enough clients each year to feed my family. Last month, I took some men, also from your country, who wished to dive for treasure, they said, but I never saw them take a boat out again after they learned to dive. Once in a while, I see one or another of them around town, but I don't think they are doing any diving."

"Can you tell us what they look like?" Brian's interest was piqued.

"No, they just look like Americans. One has a thin face. The other has a large nose, but that's all. I recognize them when I see them though. Here we are. Time to make a real dive."

Andrea's eyes opened just as the boat's engines reversed to keep them steady in the water. They were faced with calm seas. There was nothing visible for miles around except a few other boats. One was just to their right but far enough away that no one on board was recognizable. "I guess we are going to have some diving buddies." She nodded her head in the direction of the other boat."Look over there." Two men could be seen equipping themselves for a dive. They were still too far away, though, for facial features to be seen.

"We have many other excursion boats here." Their instructor gathered the equipment for his students. They proceeded to suit up once again. "Now, when you have your equipment in place, put the regulator in your mouth before you enter the water. Stand on this little deck at the back of the boat. With your hand over your mask and regulator, jump into the water feet first and well away from the boat. Come to the surface, but keep your regulator in your mouth. You'll not like the taste of the salt water. When we are all in the water, we will descend together. The water here is only 25 feet, so not too deep, eh?"

Andrea and Brian completed the task of putting on all their gear, making sure they checked each other's equipment. With swim fins on and the regulators in their mouths, first Brian and then Andrea jumped into the water. Their instructor followed closely behind.

As Andrea hit the water, it closed over her head. Panic enveloped her in its bile wrenching grip. Sucking all knowledge of scuba training from her brain, the panic scattered her senses to the wind. She kicked for the surface as if her life depended on it. At that moment she was convinced it did. Once she reached fresh air, she yanked the regulator out of her mouth. In her panic, she gasped in salt water with the air she so desperately wanted and choked immediately on the briny taste.

Almost instantaneously Brian and their instructor were by her side. The instructor shoved the regulator back in her mouth, grabbed her head between both of his hands as best he could while bobbing on the water's surface. He pointed to his eyes and signaled for her to take slow even breaths. Andrea did as instructed. Before long the feeling of terror left her. She was able to slowly descend with one man on either side of her. She grasped their hands with the strength of a wrestler until they stopped at the ten foot level. There Andrea calmly let go of Brian's hand and then that of their instructor. While both men flexed their fingers where her grip had almost cut off the blood supply, she became engrossed in the water world surrounding them.

Andrea saw the most incredible sight. Fish were everywhere. A small school of silvery bodies swam close by. It was an awesome experience. The trio stayed at this level for a couple of minutes until Andrea felt as comfortable as she had in the pool, then proceeded to the bottom. In the lower depths, she could see sea fans waving gently in the slight current. Off in the distance, a stingray presented its tail end as it swam toward a far off place. White sand, or at least it looked as white as anything the novices had ever seen, decorated the bottom. They swam toward small sandy hills accented with sharp coral, the home of hundreds of tiny animals.

Andrea vowed not to forget the lesson she had just learned again as she continued to take slow, even breathes. Brightly colored angel fish arrayed in blues and yellows swam by, as did a small version of Jaws. Their instructor had warned them about nurse sharks so neither grew alarmed at the sight of their first one. A giddy feeling of pure pleasure erupted inside Andrea. *Who would have thought that I, little mousy office girl, would be swimming with the fish in Haiti? Boy, is God stretching my boundaries or what!*

The duo swam slowly around the bottom exploring their territory while their instructor hunted for treasure. He picked up this object and then another, this one valuable enough to place in the pouch similar to the one each of them carried. Andrea noticed a large school of tiny gray fish that glistened as they swam towards her. She knelt on the bottom, staying very still to see if they would swim around her. She held out her hand slowly. Fish seemed to be everywhere within her line of sight.

****

Brian, seeing how relaxed Andrea appeared, decided to explore further. Visibility was about twenty feet, so he felt she would be in no danger. They could see each other wherever they went. Brian turned his attention to another large creature of the deep, a lobster this time. The native Haitian explored for treasure dropped to the bottom decades ago. This part of the Caribbean had been inhabited by pirates who accosted ships for their precious cargos, much of which was lost to the ocean. A lot of divers spend their time looking for treasure in these waters.

****

Andrea slowly passed by a sand outcropping with several sea fans growing beside it. No one noticed the black garbed stranger, or his gloved hand as it grabbed Andrea's air hose from behind. With the knife he carried, he cut her air hose in two, careful not to tug or let her know of his presence. He then swam off completely unnoticed.

Andrea, caught up in her surroundings, was totally unaware of what happened until she gasped for her next breath. There wasn't any air. Frantically searching for her dive partners, she signaled them for assistance. She carefully continued to maintain her calm since the instructor had warned them that panic could kill. In a few seconds, they were beside her. She signaled she was out of air as previously instructed so Brian offered her his spare regulator. She inhaled slowly, thankful they'd been close by. The trio slowly ascended to the surface.

"What happened?" Brian asked as soon as they were safely aboard the boat and their regulators and masks were removed.

"I don't know! One minute I had air, the next I didn't." Andrea grabbed her sir hose. "I think it's been cut or maybe I cut it on some coral."

"It looks to me as if it was cut on purpose." The instructor looked closely at her air hose. "Someone want to scare you, maybe?"

"Well, they succeeded. I thought I was going to die. It was lucky you guys were not too far off."

****

"Not lucky. That's why we swim with a partner, someone to help when we need it. I think we're finished for today." He slowly looked around at the other boats nearby wondering where the unseen assailant had come from. The boat anchored closest to them, the one they had seen earlier, had no distinctive markings as a means to identify whose boat it was. Curious, he thought, as he proceeded to ready his diving equipment for unloading once they'd reached the dock and the dive center.

****

"When do you think we can make another dive?" Brian, more confident than ever before that someone wanted to stop them from finding the Michners, was anxious to become certified so they could be prepared before the next ceremony. *We must be on the right track..* If diving was the only means to locating their dear friends and discovering why Andrea's neighbor was killed, then so be it. He looked attentively towards Andrea. *Somehow, everything seems to happen to her.* The guys they were up against, were obviously cowards, afraid to tackle him, but willing to terrorize a defenseless woman. He began to feel angry, so much so that he almost choked. *What would Jesus do?* He knew immediately. Jesus would protect this woman from any more harm, one way or another.

****

The boat took them back to Port Au Prince following the same route they had taken to get to the reef. Instructing his students to meet him the next morning at the same time, he bid them good-bye and watched as they walked back to their hotel. He removed his equipment from the boat, and began hauling it into the dive shop for cleaning. Before the job was complete, he dialed the number for the local police.

"Hey Sergeant, put me through to the Captain, will ya?" He scratched his nail across the well worn counter top. "Good morning Captain. I wanted to report an incident that seems mighty suspicious. Someone cut the air tank hose of one of my students today. I saw a boat, unmarked, not far from where we were diving. I saw that same boat tied to the pier just down from my shop. Maybe you should check it out."

He listened while the Captain tried to explain the incident away. *That man is so lazy.* "Well, I reported it anyway. If you choose not to do anything about it, that's your business now." He slammed the phone down, agitated that the police were so inept. He continued the job of unloading his equipment.

When his task was done, he left the shop, and headed for his truck and a trip home for a hot lunch. Just as he was getting in the vehicle, two men approached him with a look of purpose about them. It didn't take him long to recognize his students from a month ago. He smiled a greeting. "Good morning gentlemen. Back for some more diving?"

They did not return his smile. Continuing to walk purposefully toward the native, they both reached into their jacket pocket. "You called the police on us." The larger man growled. He pulled a knife from his pocket. The dive instructor started to back away from them. They were not there for a friendly visit. "What do you want?"

They shoved. The native backed towards some fishing nets located along the edge of the dock.

"What do you want," he asked again. Fear seeped from

his eyes. *Maybe these men did cut Andrea's hose.* "I have done nothing to you. Leave me alone."

The men never said another word. They looked around but no one was watching. They pushed him over the side into the water. He grabbed onto a net. It collapsed on his head as he hit the water's surface. The weighted net dragged him under, entangling him in its folds. He struggled frantically to free himself. Within a minute or two, he was dead. No one along that side of the dock saw a thing, or so they told the police who arrived later.

****

Andrea and Brian were totally unaware of the nearby drama. They sauntered towards their hotel, anticipating a tasty lunch with Camilla. "That was scary this morning. Are you sure you're alright?" Brian took Andrea's elbow and stopped her in the middle of the street. He watched for any sign that she might be faltering in her resolve to find the Michners.

"I don't care what they try to do to me. I know I'd never forgive myself if I gave up now. We need to know what they do with those people and where they take them."

They continued toward the hotel. "It won't be any fault of yours if you decide to end this search and hand it over to the police. I want to find the Michners as much as you do but somehow you seem to be the target all the time. They're cowards. They know I'd fight back."

The conversation ended just in front of the hotel. Camilla was reading a book on the veranda with Mrs. Gevin. She danced with glee when they approached. "Can we eat now? I am very 'ongry, non?"

"We can eat, and then we want to visit the graveyard where people who are washed ashore are buried." Andrea held the little girl's hand. "You can stay with Mrs...."

"Non, non, let me come with you, pleeease," begged the waif, looking every bit the little girl in one of her new shorts and top sets. "I be good, I promise."

"It's a graveyard," explained Andrea, "not a place for little girls." She hugged Camilla close to her heart. Her desire to protect the little girl from any more unpleasantness in her life was overwhelming. Andrea knew that could very well be the place where they would find Camilla's parents.

Brian led his female companions into the dining room while they continued to argue about the trip to the cemetery. Camilla was adamant she not be left alone again that afternoon. Andrea was just as convinced that it would not be a good place to take her.

"Why not let her stay outside the graveyard while we explore the markers for the names of anyone we might know?" Brian hoped to appease the two females before the argument ended in a tantrum.

Andrea grinned with a twinkle in her eye. "Now, why didn't I think of that?" It was the perfect solution.

****

When Camilla was asked what she thought, she acquiesced almost immediately. Lunch proceeded with the laughter and fun that had become commonplace when Camilla was with her new friends.

Camilla had never before known people like these two. Now they had introduced her to a friend who would never leave her, even if they had to someday. *Jesus love me, care about me.* She hugged the knowledge to her chest. This she believed with all her heart. Andrea and Brian had told her over breakfast that morning that she was going to go to the orphanage in Santo Domingo. *I 'ear good rumors 'bout dat place. I can take my Je-*

sus dere, dey tell me. At least, Brian said dey would see if that be a good place pour moi. Dey are family now, but the Padre would soon become my family, non? Her insides wanted to cry. *I will miss de Americans very much.*

Chapter Twenty Three

The adults laid their napkins on the table. Lunch had been satisfying but not as much fun as their picnic the day before. "Let's get some sunscreen on before we go. I don't want to spoil our time here by getting burned. You look a little red already, Brian, just from this morning." Andrea led the way to her room up the flight of stairs. After liberally applying the sun protection, they left for their trek to the cemetery.

Bernard met them on the front steps of the hotel. "Bonjour, monsieur, mam'selle. We go now, non? I 'ave to be back for my shift soon." Andrea nodded her head and took hold of Camilla's hand. The trio fell into a steady pace close behind their silent guide.

After a short distance, Camilla complained of sore legs. "Hop up then, little one. I'll give you a ride." Brian tossed the child up on his shoulders as if she weighed nothing. It wasn't long however before her weight began to feel like a lot more than the pint sized girl that she was. "Don't bounce so much, Camilla. You're getting heavy. It must be all that food you've been eating lately."

"Oh, Monsieur Brian. I eat too much, non? I eat only a little from now on." Camilla turned serious eyes toward Andrea.

"Oh, please. Camilla. You eat like a bird. Brian's only teasing." She punched him on the arms. "Stop that. I'm trying to put some meat on her bones."

"You want me to put meat on my bones. I like to put it in my mouth, non?" Camilla looked confused.

"Honey, that's the right thing to do. It goes in your mouth." Andrea decided not to try to explain the colloquialism. She chuckled. *It's strange how we take some of those phrases so much for granted until we cross paths with someone who has no idea what they mean.* "This walk should give us some exercise, don't you think, Brian? I mean, we did put away a sizable lunch. The weather's so nice, no winds. . . well .."

★★★★

"Andrea, do you want to talk about this morning's events?" Brian could sense that Andrea had something on her mind besides Camilla's eating habits. They'd have to talk in circles. Camilla's little ears didn't need to hear any more scary stuff. However, he felt Andrea needed to talk through the implications of their morning.

"I just seem to a-t-t-r-a-c-t the wrong kind of a-t-t-e-n-t-i-o-n," she began. "Why is it that I seem to be the one they are a-f-t-e-r? They leave you totally alone? I mean…I don't know what I mean…" She sighed in frustration.

"Are you thinking that I may be involved with the people who are d-o-i-n-g this to you?" Brian face conveyed his worry over that possibility.

Andrea looked toward Camilla to see if she was paying attention to their cryptic words. Camilla was happily watching the birds flying through the trees. "N-no…" She seemed unsure at first but then spoke with more conviction. "No, of course not. That's preposterous. But they do seem to leave you alone."

"Yah, well you already know my take on that. Only c-o-w-a-r-d-s would come a-f-t-e-r a woman. They l-e-a-v-e me a-l-o-n-e because they're afraid I might be able to defend myself."

"Well, I wish they would l-e-a-v-e us all a-l-o-n-e."

"You know they're not going to do that. These are people who k-i-l-l-e-d Max. And they didn't hesitate to t-a-k-e a young family with a three-year-old boy. I believe they would stoop to almost anything to s-t-o-p us from finding out what is going on, don't you?" Brian turned his head to the child on his shoulders. She seemed oblivious to their conversation. *Thank You Lord.*

"I guess we should have expected this but when reality hits, we're just not cut from the same cloth as these people. Their thinking is warped. How could they think that no one would come looking for the Michners. I wonder if the   p-o-l-i-c-e back home have discovered anything yet? I also wonder why Max said not to involve them? Boy there are still so many unanswered questions."

Their walk took them through a wooded area where large sections of trees were covered by moss. The smell was a little musty but could not overpower the strong scent of flowers close by. Everywhere they traveled, a preponderance of blossoms greeted their eyes and their sense of smell, making this trip in Haiti enjoyable in spite of the circumstances. Bernard's pace kept him just in sight of the couple as if he didn't want anyone to know he was guiding them.

"The closer we get to some of those answers, the harder those thugs will work to keep us from finding them out. You need to stay close to me at all times. I intend to ask the concierge to place us in adjoining rooms from now on and we need to get C-a-m-i-l-l-a to some place safe. When did you say your friend from the o-r-p-h-a-n-a-g-e would be back?"

"Tomorrow afternoon, about 1 p.m. We'll meet him by the dock. Speaking of tomorrow, the reason I told him we couldn't meet him in the morning was church. Now we're scheduled for another dive. Aren't we going to find a church?"

"Have you seen any church that you think would teach from the Bible? I haven't, so I thought that we would have our own service in either my room or yours. Maybe I should have discussed this with you earlier. We both have our Bibles with us. We could have a praise and worship time about 8 a.m. and then meet at the scuba shop for another lesson. We'll need to get back before noon if we are to be ready by 1 o'clock, though."

"That sounds like a good plan. I'm glad you thought of it. Camilla, how are ... Look, Brian, she's sound asleep on you shoulders."

"I know. For a small child, she can sure get heavy when she is dead weight like she is now. I hope we don't have too much farther to go." Just as he spoke, a clearing appeared, and they saw the fence surrounding the graveyard they were looking for. Bernard waved toward the site and then disappeared into another grove of trees.

The metal fence was coated entirely with rust and the grave markers inside were simple wooden crosses even though many of the native Haitians believed this was unholy ground. Brian gently laid Camilla on a mound of grass under a tree and out of sight of anyone who might happen by. "We'll still be able to keep an eye on her from here." *I hope. I hate having to worry about someone hurting a little child.* He led the way toward the first marker.

"Brian, these look fresh." Andrea pointed to several near the fence on the right side of the graveyard. Brian joined her. The first one seemed to be of a woman close to Andrea's age, according to the dates on the marker. The next wood cross marked the resting place of a couple.

Brian looked closer. The name was the same as Camilla's last name. "Oh, I'd hoped we'd not find this. It's easier thinking of them as bad parents who abandoned their daughter than dead somehow. We need to bring the neighbor here to confirm they are Camilla's parents. She deserves to know someday where her parents are. We can tell the priest who runs the orphanage, so he can tell her when she is old enough. At least she won't be wondering where they are for the rest of her life."

"I agree. I feel so sorry for that little girl. Imagine, losing both parents at once. Oh, Brian, what's going on here? Why are people disappearing and then washing up on the beaches dead?"

"I don't know but I think we are going to find out." They passed more graves. "These are all young men and women. And the fellow you talked to said they had all washed up on the beach?"

"Well... no, I guess he didn't say all but...this is where they bury the ones who are considered unholy for whatever reason. Maybe there are other reasons for someone to be unholy... according to the priest anyway. There seems to be so many of them." Andrea looked toward Brian and then moved toward the other side of the graveyard. "These dates are a lot older so maybe..."

"...other people are buried here too. Brian finished the sentence for her. "We know God does not consider anyone unholy, just unsaved." He watched as Andrea bowed her head. He decided to pray silently as well. *Father, we know you know all these people. Please comfort their families and bring closure to them. Amen.*

Camilla stared at them through the rusted iron fence. Brian looked at his watch. They'd been there for almost an hour. *Poor kid. She has no idea that she no longer has any parents. At least it looks that way.* "Hi there." Brian peered at the child through the fence. "We want to go visit your neighbors again. Would you like that?"

"I would, but I always miss my mama et my papa when I go see them." The tiny face displayed the sadness the child felt inside. "But it will be good to see the girls again." Her spirits, apparently revived at that though, sent her hopping and skipping through the grass. She traversed the wooded areas as if she made this trip every day of her life.

Maybe she had. Brian couldn't imagine why her parents would have brought her so often to this graveyard but the child really did know her way back to the place where their hut stood. *Little children should not have to face such a horrific childhood.* For as long as he could, Brian vowed to keep Camilla safe. *She needs to know she's loved.*

As soon as Camilla saw the neighbor lady, she ran toward her. At first the woman appeared to be angry but her face soon softened when she realized that this child, dressed in finer clothing then her children would ever wear, was Camilla.

"Come child, let me look at you. You look so grand. These people are taking good care of you, non?" She patted the child on the head. Then she looked toward the adults following.

"These are my friends. They 'ave introduced me to Jesus.

'e will be my friend when dey go back to America, non?"
Camilla smiled at the other woman, whose wrinkled face told
of the hardships she'd endured. By the age of the kids, Brian
supposed she was not as old as she appeared.

"Humpff, Jesus … just another religion, non." With that
said, she looked into the eyes of Camilla's benefactors. Although she didn't thank them for caring for the little girl, her
expression was far softer than it had been the last time they'd
seen her. "She look well."

****

Andrea looked to the woman for approval. "We've come to
love her very much. Now, however, we need your help, Mrs.
Benedictin. We visited the graveyard by the swamp with the
rusted fence surrounding it. Do you know anyone who is buried
there?"

The woman looked at Camilla and then nodded her head.
"Dey are dere. We brought dem up to dat spot two days ago,
just after you were 'ere. We, my husband and I, figure you
would someday come back. We would tell you den."

"Are you not afraid that someone will know you are bury-
ing those people when they wash ashore. During our last visit,
you seemed not to want to get involved." added Brian.

"Dese were neighbors, the Demers." She looked toward the
children playing in the grass to make sure Camilla was not
within earshot. "To bury means that no one smells, de bosses
say."

"So they let you bury your friends, how awful. Can you tell
us how long from the time the Demers were taken, or disappeared, to the time they washed ashore?"

"Maybe two week, maybe three. I don't know 'xactly."

"Okay, well thank you for all your help. We're planning to take Camilla someplace where she will be well looked after."

"You take her to America, den?" The tired woman tilted her chin toward the children. "She is better off now that her parents are no more, non?"

Andrea's heart hurt at the obvious misstatement made from a mother wanting only the best for her own children too. "No, we can't take her back to America with us, but she will have a good home and clean clothes as well as food three times a day. They will also teach her to read and provide her with an education."

"Well den, good for 'er." The woman returned to her seat by the door of her hovel. She sat down wearily, shoulders sagging in her worn dress. *Her children were not so lucky she's thinking but they have two parents who love them.* Andrea turned away from the pitiful sight wishing they could help more people.

Completely oblivious to the adults' distress, Camilla skipped happily beside her two friends. "Did you find someone you know at the graveyard."

"Yes, we did." Andrea eyes unveiled her inner turmoil.

"It makes you sad, non? When ma papa et mama disappeared, I was sad. But now I am 'appy again to have such good friends like you. Jacqueline, my friend back dere, said that I was lucky to 'ave you. I told her what you ad bought for me. Then she was sad, so I stopped telling. Den I remember bout Jesus. I tell her dat. She smile a lot after dat."

"Oh, Camilla. You have such a sensitive spirit." Andrea gathered the little girl into her arms for a big hug. The few children Andrea knew never thought about another child's feelings.

Instead they called them names or bullied them.

"Where we go now?" asked Camilla.

"How would you like to go for a swim again this afternoon?" Brian decided this conversation needed some lightening up. "I spotted a beach not too far from the hotel. We could relax on the sand and enjoy swimming in the salty ocean before dinner."

"That sounds like a plan to me. Andrea picked up on Brian's good intentions. "Besides, I want to work on my tan some more. I kind of like the color I am turning."

"Pretty soon, we won't be able to tell you from the natives." Brian winked at her.

Andrea gave him a playful push. "You should talk. I don't think I've ever seen you with so much color before."

"Well we can't go back to the States looking as if we stayed indoors the whole time, can we?"

The trio walked along merrily trading teasing comment for teasing comment until they reached the edge of town. The closer they got to their hotel, the busier the streets became with bikes, mopeds, motorcycles, cars, and trucks, some pulling wagons. People seemed to be everywhere, which was not unusual for this time of day. Siesta was over. The stores were getting ready to reopen for the late afternoon commerce.

"We will have at least an hour or two to enjoy the water before we have to get ready for dinner." Andrea dodged a moped as she walked across the street heading toward the hotel. She turned her head to speak to her travel companions. "We'll need to shower before we dress to get rid of the salt from our bodies."

Camilla tugged on her arm. "Another bath! You Americans sure take many baths, n'est pas?"

Their laughter was interrupted as soon as they came in sight of the dive shop. They had to pass it to get to the hotel. A couple of men in suits as well as at least three uniformed policemen were looking at the body of a man who was lying on the dock. The trio moved closer. Andrea recognized their dive instructor. She gasped.

Brian directed them quickly away from the grizzly scene. The adults exchanged worried glances over the head of their charge and then looked toward the hotel. Any discussion would have to wait until Camilla was taken care of.

Andrea Wilton was beginning to think they had bit off more than they could chew. *What are we doing here?* She questioned herself, not for the first time. *We are dealing with killers, and we have no way to defend ourselves.*

****

Brian's thoughts almost mirrored hers. *Wait a minute. I know self defense. I could teach Andrea.* He also had something else up his sleeve.

"Andrea, you and Camilla go ahead to the hotel. I'll be along shortly." He ignored their puzzled looks as he strode purposefully toward the market place.

****

"Well, I guess we are on our own for a short while." She watched Brian walk away. Andrea grabbed the child's hand and headed in the direction of the hotel. They mounted the steps leading to the front door. Once inside, Andrea remembered Brian had suggested that their rooms be moved beside each other for easier access. She approached the concierge.

"Monsieur." Andrea turned hopeful eyes toward the concierge. "Monsieur Brian and I would like to have our rooms adjoining. Is that possible?"

"Oh, oui Mam'selle. We just 'ad a man leave the room next to Monsieur this morning. I would be 'appy to move your things to that room, non?"

"No, that's okay. I can do it myself. Can I have the key, please?'

"Oui, 'ere is the key. Will monsieur et mam'selle be coming to dinner this evening? Will you also bring the child?" He motioned toward the waif with his chin.

"Yes, we will, but first we want to go to the beach for a swim."

"Ah oui. It is 'ot today and a swim would be refreshing. I 'ope you like your new room, mam'selle."

Andrea took the key from the hotel owner. Camilla silently followed. When Andrea looked to see what was wrong, she noticed a troubled expression on the little girl's face. "What's wrong, Camilla?"

Camilla remained silent. She stepped into the elevator ahead of Andrea but remained quiet all the way to their floor and the door to their room. "Camilla something is bothering you. Tell me what it is."

Camilla started to cry. Andrea couldn't make sense of her muffled sobs. They sat on the side of the bed. Andrea held her until the sobs subsided. "What's the matter?"

"I will have to leave my new clothes with the room, non?"

"No, of course not. Those clothes are yours to keep until

you are too big to wear them anymore. We're simply moving our rooms together, so we can be a family, like a mother and father and our little girl, you."

Andrea knew that her explanation was pretty simple, but the child certainly didn't need to know the extent of the precautions these two felt were necessary in light of recent events. Just then a light knock sounded just before Brian entered. "You didn't lock the door. I…"

"I know. Camilla was so upset, I forgot. You weren't gone long."

"No, I knew exactly what I was looking for. I'll tell you all about it when Camilla is having her bath, later this afternoon."

"Oh, the reason Camilla's upset. I followed your suggestion and asked to have my room moved beside yours. I hope that's okay with you. The concierge said a man had moved out of there this morning, so the room was free. Here's the key. Camilla thought she would have to leave her new clothes with the room."

"Oh, sweetie, no. In fact I'll help you ladies move all your things to the new room right beside mine."

"Oui. Mam'selle Andrea explain we will be like family now, non? You papa and she mama to me, yes?"

Andrea felt her face flush even hotter than it had through the dance session. Oh boy. I'll have to watch what I say to Camilla from now on. "Er...Brian, I didn't mean…"

"Andrea, I know it's hard to explain things so the child understands but if you decide…"

"I won't." Andrea stared convincingly into his eyes.

"Oh." Was that sadness on his face? She couldn't tell. "Let's get busy then. We still want to go to the beach, don't we?"

Less than a half hour later, wearing bathing suits under shorts and t-shirts, they almost ran the short distance towards the water's edge. They tossed their towels down and plunged headlong into the cool surf. Camilla wore a life vest over her bathing suit this time, one borrowed from the hotel.

They splashed, threw water at each other, and danced in the surf as the waves pounded the shoreline. Camilla, held by her hands between the two adults, was lifted high over each wave that came ashore. Her enjoyment over simple pleasures had returned. *We are really going to miss this child when we drop her off at the orphanage tomorrow.*

The time raced by, as it seemed to do when they were having fun. Before they knew it, a cool breeze was coming ashore with the surf. It was time to return to the hotel, take showers, and dress for dinner. Some beaches had showers to wash off the salt, but this one, being so close to the hotel, did not. They quickly dried off as much water as they could, dressed in their shorts and t-shirts, and headed home.

Camilla didn't protest this time when Andrea suggested a bath. This room had a larger tub and a bed just for Camilla. It also had a small kitchenette, a convenience Andrea planned to use for breakfast, which would give the trio time for devotions before the day began. She hoped Brian would lead them.

Andrea showered quickly, dried off with the hotel's large fluffy towel and then stepped into a sleeveless dress purchased before the trip began. She was blowing her hair dry with Camilla safety ensconced amidst the bubbles when Brian knocked on the door between their rooms. With the blower running at full speed, she didn't hear anything until he was beside her. She jumped. Her heart just about leapt through her throat.

"Don't sneak up on me like that! I could have hit you with this hair dryer." She positioned the blower in a manner to strike him over the head.

Brian quirked his eyebrow at her with a grin designed to melt the hearts of all females. "You're quite the tigress when you get scared. Now I know why they haven't done any permanent damage." He enjoyed keeping her off guard, it seemed.

"I was not scared. I've just had it with people sneaking up on me."

"Well, I've got something a little more persuasive than a hair dryer. Here, I saw this the other day in the market place. I decided after what happened today to get one for each of us. Now, don't say no until you've heard me out. This is an electrical shock device called a stun gun. When you turn it on, it will immobilize a person long enough for you to get the upper hand but will do no permanent damage. In other words, it does not violate our desire to do things as Jesus would since it only inflicts momentary pain."

"Let me see that."

Andrea held the black object in her hand and felt the weight of it. It fit as if it were intended for her palm.

Brian directed her to turn it on and explained how effective it would be if someone came after her again. "We decided that the Lord would not use a gun to defend himself, but if He were to be in the situation we are in, He might use something to protect Himself that would not hurt His assailant a great deal but still get the job done. I know I'm rationalizing this, but we've got to do something. These men are not averse to killing someone. We've seen that today, if that was them involved. We know what happened to Max."

"I know! I know! I've been questioning our efforts here,

wondering if we should be armed. I know the Lord will protect us but…maybe this is His way of providing that protection. Andrea hefted the stun gun in her hand. She waved it around to see if she could handle it. .

"I agree so let's make sure we have these near us at all times. Oh and I also came across another dive shop we need to check out. It seems to be bigger with more equipment for rent or sale. I've given some thought to how we are going to follow a boat, under water, at night without being detected. I intend to check the Internet the first chance I get to see what would be most helpful. It will probably be expensive though."

"So what? The money Max left is for just this purpose. Since we no longer have a dive instructor for tomorrow morning, why don't we check out this shop before dinner?"

"Good idea. Oh, Hi Camilla. Did you have a good bath? Are your ears clean and your fingernails?" Brian teased the little girl as he looked behind the ears of the giggling waif. She had wrapped herself in one of the towels, which on her was large enough to act as a blanket. "I'll leave you ladies to finish getting dressed. The dive shop is just near the market, not far. Then we should make it an early night. We have church at 8 a.m., remember?"

"Church, what is church?" Camilla was all ears. She excitedly anticipated another new adventure. Brian quietly left the room and the explanations to Andrea.

"Church is a time when we let Jesus know how much we love Him. We read from the Bible and study what He would want to teach us. At home we go to a big building but here we will just be by ourselves." Andrea moved towards the closet, something else this room had that the other had not.

"Oh, I do love Jesus. I will show him tomorrow as well." Camilla stepped into clean underwear and then a little sundress that showed her coloring off to perfection. "I like this yellow one, n'est pas?" The child did a spin in front of the mirror.

Andrea finished styling her hair and with a glance in the mirror, decided make-up was not needed. Her complexion had turned a reddish brown making her brown eyes appear larger than before. She exuberated health, she thought, so settled for a little lipstick to compliment the color of her dress.

Camilla stared at her when Andrea stepped out of the bathroom. "You look very pretty mam'selle." Andrea detected a tinge of awe in her voice. "I think I would like to be so pretty when I am as old as you, non?"

"Camilla, you are already the prettiest little girl I know. When you grow as old as I, you will be far prettier, you'll see. Now, let's do something with your hair."

Chapter Twenty Four

The next morning began bright and early. Andrea and Camilla were awakened by the phone ringing and a voice announcing it was 7 a.m. Since Andrea had placed a request for the early morning wake-up call, she couldn't grumble, at least not too much anyway. Camilla wiped sleep from her eyes. Within seconds, she was bounding out of bed, ready to take on the world. *Children*. Andrea's eyes refused to focus yet.

"Let's get some breakfast before we get dressed for 'church', okay?" Andrea had stocked the kitchenette with cereal, milk, juice, and some cookies the night before.

"Okay. I'm 'ongry. Will monsieur Brian eat wit us?" Camilla stopped jumping on the bed. *Hmmm.* Andrea opened the tiny refrigerator to grab the bottle of orange juice. In this country, orange juice was the freshly squeezed kind and tasted as if the fruit had just been picked off the trees. "Yes he will, I guess. I'd better get dressed." She poured each of them a glass taking hers to the bathroom.

A knock sounded on the door that connected their room to Brian's. Camilla excitedly jumped off her chair, knocking over the glass of juice in her haste to be the first one at the door. Brian sent a questioning look toward Andrea who was mopping up the spilled juice. "Spill your juice. I guess you're not a morning person." He poured himself a glass of juice from the same container on the table.

"Camilla spilled this. I think she's actually excited about the visit to the orphanage." Andrea spoke for their ears alone. "Last night, while we were getting ready for bed that was all she could talk about … her new home as she calls it. I'm glad that she's so happy about this idea, but what if it doesn't work out?"

"We'll just have to find another solution, that's all. Let's eat." Brian grabbed a bowl and made himself right at home. Camilla finished her breakfast in record speed. With the last mouthful, she drank the rest of her juice. She started to climb down from the table. "Wait a minute, little lady. We need to talk."

"Oh, oui monsieur Brian," She planted her feet firmly on the floor ready to listen to anything he had to say. "We talk, non?"

"Yes well …. You know that today we visit the orphanage. Father Bertrand has not met you. We do not know if he will accept you yet, so you must not get your hopes up. We will only leave you there if we…" He pointed to Andrea and himself. "…think it's the best place for you. Do you understand?"

"Oh oui monsieur. I 'ave 'eard many good things about dat place. I think maybe my friends are dere. They disappeared a long time ago but maybe …." She shrugged her shoulders. "You never know."

The look on her face was comical to say the least as she

tried to behave in what she thought was a very grown-up manner. The adults couldn't fault her logic, nor could they stem her excitement as the morning progressed.

Brian led a time of worship and praise as he and Andrea taught Camilla some of the simpler choruses they knew. When they took out their Bibles to read the words of Jesus, Camilla finally sat as still as a church mouse. She raptly listened to every word, drinking in the newness of her faith and getting to know in a small way who Jesus was. Brian read the accounts of Jesus healing people and feeding the five thousand, all stories that brought a look of pure wonder on the face of the child.

"My Jesus does all dat!" She sat in rapt attention as Brian read the account of Jesus driving out the demons into the herd of swine. "People 'ere 'ave demons, I think." Her face reflected a memory best forgotten, Andrea surmised.

Worship time over, Brian left to do something else. Andrea began to pack Camilla's clothes into a small bag purchased for just that purpose. Both girls put on swim suits, with shorts as a cover-up. Andrea pulled a jacket from the closest and lay it on the bed beside Camilla's clothes. Everything was ready when they got back from the dive shop.

****

Brian quickly went downstairs to find a computer. He sat down, punched in the hook-up to the internet and began his search. He wanted to find out what some dive experts would recommend for their surveillance tomorrow night. Once they were in the water, following that boat of thugs, they did not want to get lost or lose track of the boat. There had to be a simple solution.

Within seconds he had an answer. Without explaining exactly why they needed this information, Brian received an answer from a dive shop in California. They provided him with enough information about the equipment they needed to keep their whereabouts underwater covert and give them help for a longer than usual swim. He printed off the information just as Andrea and Camilla stepped off the elevator.

The dive shop had a complete line of diving gear for sale, some which looked pretty expensive. There were other gadgets as well. It was to these items that Brian was drawn.

"Can I help you?" The man had a definite British accent.

"Yes, I am looking for a couple of rebreathers, two scooters, and a sonar navigation system. Do you have any of these in stock?" Brian read the list from the computer printout.

The dive shop owner looked at him, surprise written all over his face. His mind seemed to be calculating the cost of all these items. "As it turns out, I have everything you're looking for. Are you planning a long trip underwater or something?" The store owner's curiosity was aroused. Brian had his answer already prepared.

"We're planning some dives off the coast of the Dominican Republic. We just want to go prepared."

"Well you will certainly have the best equipment there is with this list of supplies. Have you used any of it before?"

"No, we thought you would be able to suggest an instructor for us, someone who could help us familiarize ourselves with these pieces."

"Well yes, Bertie over there has training in rebreathers and has used the scooter a number of times for treasure dives. Bertie can also help you with the sonar but I can't imagine that you would need that just for a simple dive. But if that's what you want…let's get you outfitted for your adventure."

****

While Brian went into another room toward the back of the shop with the sales clerk, Andrea selected two wetsuits that the sales clerk said would fit them. She also purchased booties, swim fins, and gloves. Just as she was about to select a vest, Brian approached from behind.

He whispered, "We won't need these vests. I am purchasing rebreathers for both of us. They will allow us to follow the boat undetected since a rebreather does not emit any bubbles. It will also allow us to stay under for a much longer period of time. We'll need training though, a requirement of purchase, which will give us some more dive time. You'll need to act as if you have hundreds of hours though instead of only a couple. If they suspect that we're novices, they won't sell us this equipment. Do you think you can handle that?"

"I'll do my best, Brian, you know that. If this is what we need, then so be it. How much?"

"Well, these are top of the line. We are looking at $12,000 each but the cost will be well worth it. I also want to purchase each of us a scooter, and one sonar navigation system. They have these in stock as well. That will add another $4000 to the bill. They take credit cards, but I told them that we would pay by check. They said they would phone our bank for verification and because they can't do that until tomorrow, they want us to leave the equipment here until our check has been verified. That should be tomorrow. Since the ceremony isn't until tomorrow night that will give us time for another workout with the equipment tomorrow afternoon."

Andrea felt giddy. Knowing they could purchase this stuff without worrying about how they were going to pay for it was a heady experience. "I'm curious, Brian. What did you tell the man about why we wanted this stuff? I assume he was somewhat curious."

"Well, yes he was. I told him we were going on a long dive in the Dominican Republic."

"Oh, I hate all these lies, don't you?"

"Yes I do, but we don't want to raise any suspicion. Since we're going to that country today anyway, I thought it would be a good cover. We can say we're going to explore some good dive sights and hire a guide."

"I think you definitely have some hidden talents for intrigue and mystery in that body of yours. Now let's get these purchases made so we still have time for a dive lesson … oops! … I mean training on the rebreathers," she whispered.

It took only a short time to write the check for everything. *And a hefty check it is.* Andrea decided to take Camilla back to stay with Mrs. Gevin again. This time the child didn't object to spending one last morning with her other friend. With promises to be back by lunchtime, Brian and Andrea set off in swim gear for the boat that was already loaded with their gear.

The trip to the dive sight didn't take nearly as long since looking at the beauty around them was not the objective of this particular dive. Andrea began practicing her deep and slow breathing the minute she hit the water to ward off the panic she had experienced the day before.

The rebreathers did not leave a trace of a bubble, as Brian had said, and they were no heavier in the water than regular tanks. They allowed each breath to recirculate within the system, be cleaned of carbon dioxide and made usable again. How that worked, Andrea could not comprehend, but she trusted the equipment to do its job.

****

Once his new pupils adapted to the rebreathers, Bertie

showed them how to use the scooters. Before long they were motoring all over the area but close enough together that Bertie could keep a close eye on them. He sensed they were not as practiced at scuba as they had implied, but he couldn't see any reason for worry. *Besides where they are going*, he thought, *they will have a good guide*.

With underwater signals, universal to dive instructors it appeared, Bertie demonstrated how to attach the sonar device to an object and then track it using another piece of equipment attached to his wrist. This item was battery operated with a ten hour run time. The instrument's display was highly visible underwater during the daytime so it was sure to be even more noticeable when all was dark and murky.

****

Their morning flew by. With the rebreathers, the duo did not have to surface within the hour, as was the case with the usual tanks, but Bertie was not using a rebreather. That hour gave them enough time, however, to learn what they needed. Surfacing as they had been taught, stopping every so often to allow their body to adjust to the change in depth, Brian and Andrea boarded the boat for the return trip to Port Au Prince. As Bertie doused their equipment in a barrel of fresh water, they sat at the back pretending to enjoy the scenery.

"Those rebreathers are just what we need. Our bubbles won't be seen and the scooter will help us keep up with the boat as long as it doesn't travel too fast. Somehow, I don't think that little motor we saw on the boat that night can go very fast. And that sonar device…it will shine clearly, I think." Brian checked his watch. 11:30 already. "We'll just have time for a quick lunch before meeting the boy from the orphanage."

Andrea's face held the seriousness of what they planned to do. "Brian if all this is a wild goose chase, I don't know what

I'll do. I just keep thinking of Trent and Diane with these guys. What could they want with them anyway?"

"All I know is that Trent was upset over something to do with Max the last time I spoke to him for any length of time about work. And that wasn't often." Brian sat back and sighed. He too hoped their mission was a success.

At the dock, they waved good-bye to Bertie. The man seemed much more personable than their last instructor. They arranged for another lesson the next day and then walked quickly to the hotel. Camilla was sitting on the veranda as before, with her friend. "Come, come, we must eat, so we not be late."

"This child has an over abundance of excitement running through her veins today." Mrs. Gevins shook her head and smiled a grandmotherly sort of smile. She accepted their thanks and walked ahead of them into the hotel.

Brian and Andrea laughed. They were so grateful that someone at the hotel cared as much for the little girl as they did. Back in their room, Andrea quickly dressed in shorts again while Camilla fidgeted on the bed. She had her bag of clothing in hand and was waiting not so patiently by the door long before Andrea was ready.

A hasty lunch in the hotel's dining room took the next half hour, and then they were off to wait at the designated spot for Troy. They spotted his jeep before he saw them approach, and it was then they tried once again to caution Camilla. "We don't know if this will work out, sweetie," spoke Brian. "Let's just have a wait and see attitude, shall we?"

"What is wait and see?"

"That means, we won't make a yes or no decision until we check everything out, okay?"

"Oh, oui monsieur, but I am so excited to be going where maybe my friends are."

"Oh boy, I give up." He grinned. Andrea led the way toward Troy. The teenager smiled in recognition when he spied Andrea but then looked curiously at Camilla. Andrea made the introductions making sure that Camilla was not made to feel awkward in any way with this young boy who seemed so intent in his scrutiny of her.

"So ma petite…" Troy bent to look her straight in the eye."…we go home to Father Bertrand, okay. He will give you good meals, warm clothing when it gets chilly, and cool clothing when it is so hot that it is hard to breath. Then he will make sure you learn to read, and how to use money, and a lot of other things to make a living when you are old like these two, non?'

Camilla smiled her delight at her new friend. It was amazing to watch such a young boy care so deeply for one as young as Camilla. "Troy, you have a great way with children." Andrea spoke out loud.

"Oui, mam'selle, I know how they feel. I've been there. We must go if we are to reach the border before six o'clock. New rules make it necessary to cross the border by then if we are to even go into the Dominican Republic these days." He threw up his hands in frustration and rolled his eyes. "Government rules, humpff!"

"Do you want us to follow in our car? We have a rented vehicle." Brian spoke for the first time.

"No, it is better that I drive. I know the rules and besides rented vehicles are not allowed into the country. You need some American cash with you however, to pay the fines and your American passports. Many times the police stop cars, which have Americans in them because the car is dirty or because we don't step on the brake fast enough. It is just their way to get extra for their job. The rules of the road are not so strictly enforced though."

They all piled into the cramped space in Troy's smallish car. Once everyone was settled Andrea decided to get to know this young man a little better. "How long have you lived in the Dominican Republic? Were you born in Haiti?"

"Oui mam'selle, I was born here. I was restavic, so I know how those with no parents feel. But Father Bertrand found me when I was four years old and helped me to be a better person than restavic. Now I don't steal anything except little children, non?" He chuckled at this last remark. Then he went on to tell his passengers about the trip ahead. "Santo Domingo is about 235 American miles from here, so we will be traveling a while. I will stop a couple of times to let Camilla stretch her legs since the small children get restless. At the border, you let me do the talking. They know me."

Over the next hour or so Andrea and Brian found out a lot from the young boy about the country they were going to be entering soon. The road they were on, the one that connected Port Au Prince to Santo Domingo, began at Jumani, just south of Port Au Prince. Quisqueya - the original name for the entire island, which the Dominican people still use today - was discovered December 5th. 1492, by Christopher Columbus. He called the island Hispaniola for Spain, a land mass of 29,457 square miles which later, under the Treaty of Ryswick in 1697, was occupied by two different nations, the Dominican Republic for Spain and Haiti for France. The western one-third of the island belonged to Haiti and consisted of about 10,641 square miles. As Andrea and Brian had already discovered, Haiti was very mountainous. The eastern two-thirds of the island belonged to the Dominican Republic and consisted of 18,816 square miles separated from Haiti with a north to south boundary 195 miles long. The Dominican Republic also included several offshore islands.

A long chronicle about the island's history filled the hours, as Troy's captivated audience made their way to the orphanage. He regaled them with stories of dictatorships and ruthless men who ruled with an iron fist. Their eyes took in all the sights they passed, but their minds were filled with facts about the country they were traveling towards.

Andrea and Brian looked over at Camilla who had fallen asleep, the history lesson not in the least interesting to her tiny mind. Brian's eyes winked at Andrea as Troy continued. "Rafael Leonidas Trujillo Molina became President in 1930… another dictatorship."

Troy's melodious voice filled the long trip. Andrea leaned her head on the back of the seat. Their morning's activities had taken its toll. She, too, was soon sound asleep.

****

Brian loved history…of any kind. "How can you keep so many facts straight? I love history but I always have trouble remembering dates and the proper sequence of events."

"Father Bertrand says that we learn from history how not to repeat mistakes made by our former leaders. He teaches us all about the history of our country so we can be better informed when we become adults. Maybe some of us will end up in a position to make a difference, non?"

"Father Bertrand sounds like a smart man."

"Would you like me to continue? Is good practice for me, non."

"Sure go ahead." Brian leaned back in preparation for the rest of the story. Troy knew the events of this country's colorful past to perfection, it seemed, as He regaled Brian with tales of this dictator and that. The American silently watched the passing scenery. The road they traveled led them through some territory that the couple had not yet explored. Camilla's sleeping form became restless as the lurching vehicle gave the ride the feel of a rocking chair. With the mountainous terrain, the drive was slower than was possible in the city so the time crawled by but the scenery was worth the trip. Flowers were in abundance and the animals seemed not to fear the vehicles along this route, coming often to the roadside to take a look see.

Before long, Andrea joined Brian in his perusal of the landscape. They had reached the border crossing. Restricting vehicles to one lane, the guards inspected the inhabitants of Troy DePuiz's car, noting the young Americans and the younger still Haitian native child. They did as they had always done when Troy brought a child across the border. They looked the other way. These adults did not like the Haitian system of restavic children so did whatever was necessary to help Father Bertrand give them a secure home.

"Senior y Senorita," spoke one of the guards. "You must remember, this border closes at 6 p.m. Dominican time and does not reopen until 8 a.m. the next morning. So if you arrive too late, you will be unable to cross the border until the next morning."

"We will remember." They spoke in unison. The car proceeded to enter the Dominican Republic for the first time. Where houses all along the route on the Haitian side of the border had been in deplorable condition, the homes here were well constructed. The yards were clean. Not all homes were large and expensive looking by any means, but they were well looked after. Andrea's hopes rose a notch or two, as did Brian's. This already looked like a good place for Camilla.

Chapter Twenty Five

The travelers continued to journey through lush tropical jungle, landscape dotted here and there with a clearing. Some homes were surrounded by fields of crops common to Haiti as well as the Dominican Republic. Here the plantations seemed to be better looked after as was the highway, which bypassed the fields. While Andrea had awakened when the car had come to a halt at the border, Camilla slept through most of the journey.

"How much longer before we arrive in Santo Domingo?" Brian was beginning to feel cramped. Since Camilla slept the whole time, they'd decided not to stop.

"Oh, maybe ten minutes or so, monsieur." Troy stretched his arms over the steering wheel. "Won't be long now."

"Good. As much as I am enjoying the scenery, I would like

to get back to Port Au Prince before 11 p.m. I didn't realize when we left that this trip was going to take so long."

"Really Brian." Andrea squiggled her body to a more comfortable position. "We can't just drop Camilla off and then rush back. She's just a little girl. I don't want to dump her somewhere just because it's convenient for us." Andrea folded her arms across her chest, clearly miffed at the idea of a speedy return.

"Ouch …. Where did that come from?" Brian turned to face his companion. "You don't think I care about her too? Don't you remember the real reason we came to this country?" The strain of the past few days was beginning to show on Brian's face, something Andrea had not noticed before. There were lines around his mouth and his eyes, lines that had not been present just a few short days ago.

"I'm sorry. Of course you care, and yes, I do remember. I just don't want to have to worry about our decision after the fact. If we could just take our time, at least for today, then we would know we left her in the right hands…" Andrea's eyes filled with tears. "…and could get on with our purpose for being here. After all, there's nothing we can do until tomorrow night anyway."

Brian grimaced. The last thing he wanted was to cause Andrea more anguish. "I guess I've just become impatient to get this thing over with. I'm not sure I feel comfortable with the course of action we have decided upon, and yet, I can't think of an alternative. I feel so responsible for you and Camilla. That must be a guy thing."

"Guy thing or not, I think that's sweet. But I made the decision to come here and I am part of the decision to do as we planned. If things don't progress quite as smoothly as we would wish them to, I certainly don't hold you responsible. We've taken every precaution, haven't we?"

Brian glanced over toward Troy to see if he was catching the drift of their conversation. He seemed oblivious to their comments as he drove with eyes looking straight ahead but given his quick intelligence, Brian nodded his concern to Andrea and they let their conversation lapse into silence. Both concentrated on the road and the landscape they were seeing, noticing some colorful birds for the first time.

Dozens or perhaps hundreds of trees along this stretch of the highway were in full bloom with blossoms ranging in size from petite red buds to large pink and orange flowers almost nine inches across. Tropical birds called to one another, their sounds unlike anything heard in the USA except for the zoos. "Is this place a park or something?" Andrea spoke for the first time since waking to their self appointed tour guide.

"Non, Mam'selle. This is just a cloud forest. We name it that because of the clouds of flowers everywhere. Some of the forests in Dominican Republic have been torn down, used for building homes or for firewood and farmland but here the forest remains large and healthy with over 200 species of birds."

"You certainly know a lot about your country." Brian marveled at the young man's memory.

"Father Bertrand tells us that we should know all there is to know about our country before we begin to learn about another. He also says that we can act as tourist guide sometimes when we are a little older. I am already a little older and have guided many visitors around our home."

Andrea smiled as she pictured the young boy guiding people through his country. "I think you'd probably make an excellent guide"

"Yes, and I bring the money home to Father Bertrand." This boy-man had grown up quickly for someone of his few years, yet he seemed to have purpose and strength about him.

The more the adults watched and listened, the more they felt this move to find a home for Camilla was the right one.

"We will be in Santo Domingo in just a few minutes," their guide explained, "but we will have to circle the city if we want to get to the orphanage before supper is served. *Merengue* is a festival that happens here every year at this time. It brings lots of people from all over the Caribbean and elsewhere to listen to famous people like Enrique Iglesias and many others."

He'd no sooner said that when Brian and Andrea began to see the outlines of large buildings and heavier automobile traffic. "What is all that noise?" asked a sleepy eyed Camilla.

"Wow, you're awake!" Andrea looked at the child. "You sure slept a long time, and you missed all the beautiful flowers and birds we passed."

"Can we eat soon?" Camilla ignored her guardian's comments caring little for scenery. She rubbed sleep from her eyes and peered wide eyed through the window at the tall buildings they were moving quickly past. Cars were everywhere, evidenced by a cacophony of honking horns. A man stuck his head out of his open car window, screaming at the top of his lungs when someone cut him off. Troy maneuvered the jeep onto a side street and continued away from the large city center. He displayed an adeptness that told of many previous trips.

Before long they pulled into a courtyard filled with children running, playing and chasing each other in one game or another. A large stone wall circumvented at least a couple of acres and protected the courtyard. Once Troy stopped the vehicle, children clamored to see who their visitors were and the new friend Troy brought to play with them. Camilla, in sharp contrast to her earlier sense of anticipation, moved closer to Andrea as she peered shyly back at all these strange faces.

"Shall we get out and meet some new friends?" Andrea

gently pulled the little girl with her as she slid across the seat and out the right hand door. Brian had already stepped out of the car. Andrea smiled toward Camilla, encouraging her to look at all the fun the children were having. They were surrounded by clean, well cared for buildings. Gardens, with every variety of flower, was also in evidence as well as a large vegetable garden.

Andrea was amazed at Camilla's timidity since she had been so open when they first met. "What's wrong, honey? Why are you afraid?"

"Maybe they don't like childs like me." Andrea remembered that in Haiti, Camilla had never felt comfortable with other children except those next door to her parent's home. She also remembered that other children harassed street children and treated them as if they were diseased.

"It'll be alright, Camilla. Most of these children were also street children and restavic before coming here. They know what it's like to have no home and no one to care for them." Just as she said that, a tall slim man wearing white pants and a white shirt approached from the direction of the largest of the three buildings in the compound. His face beamed a smile of welcome as he stepped closer, but it was for the child and not the adults. He knelt in front of her and smiled gently into her fearful eyes. His hands were roughened by hard labor, but they were gentle as they stroked Camilla's face.

"You are Camilla, and the perfect addition to this home. I have a bed all ready for you and a place for you to store your clothes. I will be your papa, and you will have many friends here. You will go to school with the other children and learn to be a great lady, I think." With that said, the man stood and extended his hand to Brian and Andrea. "My name is Father Bertrand. We are a family here, and I will love this one as much as I love all the rest. You must be Monsieur Strait and

Mam'selle Wilton. Welcome to our home. Would you like to see where your little one will live?"

"Oh yes." Andrea had tears in her eyes again as she watched the gentle priest. "We have not really told Camilla too much about your home, but we think this would be the best place for her since they will not let us take her with us when we go home. We have a lot of questions, though, before we make a final decision."

"But of course. I would be disappointed if you just dropped the child and left. Troy, lead the way. Camilla would you like to take my hand?" He extended his toward the child.

Camilla hung back for a second longer, a look of contemplation on her face. Then hesitantly, she reached for the strong hand held out to her. Her little hand became lost in the confines of the older man's. Apparently used to walking with little children, Father Bertrand kept his pace slow so the child could keep up. They walked toward the second largest building. The outside was covered in stucco that had been painted a pastel pink. The building contained two stories and had cheerful curtained windows every ten feet or so. The roof was lined in red Spanish tiles, a roof construction common to this area.

Once they entered, the cooler atmosphere was appreciated as everyone stepped out of the hot sun. Although not air-conditioned, the thick walls kept the building from over heating during the day and kept the inside warm during the night. "We pair our little ones with older girls who have been here for awhile, so they can care for them and see that they receive all we have to offer. Since some of these little ones have only known a life of little and have had to fight for every scrap of food they have eaten, sometimes they take from each other when there's no longer any need…at least for a while. Then they learn to trust us and what we can provide for them. The older ones protect the younger always." Father Bertrand was clearly pleased with his program.

He turned to the child. "Camilla, we have a place for you right beside Brendene. She came to us ten years ago and has made some remarkable progress. Brendene this is your little sister, Camilla." With that introduction, a large boned black girl stepped forward and bent down to place her face on the same level as the little girl's. She looked deeply into the child's eyes seeming to convey a secret message, one that Camilla responded to immediately.

"Come, mon Cherie." Brendene spoke with a strong Haitian accent. "Let's look where you will stay by me until you are older, n'est pas?" Camilla followed her to the side of a bed that had been draped with a large floral pink comforter. She touched the fabric and looked expectantly into the eyes of the older girl. "Yes, that is yours to take with you wherever you go, even outside if you want." Brendene continued to explain. "See each of the beds here have one that is similar but different than yours so that we all know who sleeps where. No one will take it from you or take anything else that we will place inside this little closet. This is your place, and these are your pieces of furniture. You now own them. That is, if your guardians decide that you may stay with us."

Although Andrea had brought along Camilla's suitcase stuffed with her new clothes, she had left it in the car until the final decision had been made. Camilla was visibly relaxed in the care of Brendene; she appeared to have lost her initial fear of new things and unfamiliar surroundings. She looked at Andrea now with a question on her face.

Andrea moved closer to the side of the bed and opened the locker-like cupboard. Inside were three shelves, low enough for the child to reach. Hooks along the back and the sides were also within easy reach of a child about Camilla's size. Located next to the bed, attached to the locker, was a table that served as a nightstand. On it was room for anything that the child held dear like photos of her family, a commodity not available to any of these children. Andrea purposed to see that she had a photo of her and Brian before they left that area of the world.

"Come on, cherie," Brendene held out her hand. "I will show you the restroom and where you will place your things in there." She led the way to a large room, which encompassed the entire end of the dorm like area. Inside were a number of cubicles for showering, located all along one wall, and a series of toilet stalls flanked by counter space with cabinets underneath. Brendene took Camilla to one cabinet and explained that she would be able to store all her towels, facecloths, brush and comb, as well as toothbrush there. She repeated, "This is your space. You own whatever you put in here, and for as long as you stay with us, you own the cabinet as well."

Andrea looked into the eyes of Father Bertrand for the first time since the tour began. He motioned for her to step outside which she did, followed closely by Brian who obviously had the same question on his mind that she did. "You noticed that we repeat ownership." Father Bertrand answered their unspoken concern. "These children have lost everything, what little they have owned. When they find something on the street that they try to lay claim to, someone steals it from them. The best way we can help them feel at home is to repeat over and over that these are their belongings, and they are. No one here will take these things from them, and they are free to do with them as they please."

Andrea and Brian looked at each other, tears of gratitude in their eyes. This was the sign they needed. Father Bertrand was truly a Godly man in every sense of the word. He was certainly interested in the welfare of his charges and had put into place ways to make them whole again. They returned to the dormitory building to discover that Camilla was in earnest conversation with another little girl who looked to be about the same age she was. Two older girls were looking on in interest and watching for any sign that one would hurt the other.

"Where do you get the supplies such as clothing and food or even school supplies for all these kids?" Brian waved his hand around the room.

"We receive donations from a series of churches in the United States and from Canada. Women's groups pack supplies and send them to us. We also receive some money from churches or from individuals such as you. The children also work for other people when they are old enough to raise money. We also sell a portion of the produce from our garden in the fall. God provides, as we need, it seems, and so we don't really want for much. The children's needs are few. As long as they are loved, they are happy, so that is why we partner the little ones with someone older who can make sure their life is stress-free."

Andrea was all ears. In a quick motion, she took Brian aside and between the two of them they committed to giving Father Bertrand money every month. They also decided to bring the matter of his orphanage to the attention of their church back home. In the meantime, Andrea wrote out a check as a way to begin their support.

Father Bertrand was overcome when he saw the amount on the check. He asked, "I take it that you both have decided to leave Camilla with us. We would be happy to keep her even if you could not give us this money but we are so grateful that the Lord has placed you in our lives, not just for the money you provide but also for your prayers. We try hard to do everything we can for these children who have been abandoned."

"Father, we are on a quest to find out why so many adults are disappearing in Haiti around Port au Prince. If we do find some of them alive, and they cannot find their children when they return, we will come for a visit with them. Maybe some of these children still have parents who are alive and can be reunited with them."

Just then, Camilla approached. She held out her hand for their farewell. Andrea's eyes began to tear and Brian's throat had a lump the size of an orange. Both had become very attached in the short time they had been part of her life. Now, however, they needed to let her stay where she would be with children her own age, where she would receive ongoing care from Father Bertrand and the other boys and girls at the orphanage.

Andrea picked Camilla up and began to give her a hug that she hoped the little girl would remember for the rest of her life. Tears were flowing freely now, although the child was not sure why the adults were so emotional. Even Brian could not contain his feelings, when he hugged the child. Letting her go was not going to be easy for either of them.

"Camilla, I have given Father Bertrand our address in the United States. If you need anything, you can write or phone us there, and we will see that you get it. Remember, we l-love y-you," Andrea forced herself to keep some control over her emotions even though she felt like sobbing her heart out. Camilla was so tiny to be left all alone here.

Brian gave Camilla one last squeeze then motioned for Troy to take them out of the compound so they could rent a car for the return voyage to Port au Prince. He put his arms around the shoulders of his companion. Andrea was sobbing but working hard to tell herself that Camilla was going to be all right. "Oh Brian, I am going to miss that little girl. I've never felt this way about a small child before, could never understand why some people seem to think they are the best thing since sliced bread."

Troy was very indignant. "You eat children like bread." Both Brian and Andrea burst into an emotional storm of another nature. They laughed so hard, in fact, that no one could have distinguished the real tears from their tears of laughter. Eventually they were able to slow their belly laughs to a normal pitch and explain what the phrase 'since sliced bread' meant to the teenager. They had a hard time trying to explain to a tired car rental agent, though, why they wanted to rent a vehicle, and where they were planning to take it.

Reaching the border crossing on time took a little ingenuity and a lot of prayer that police officers would not be in evidence, but the couple eventually made it with a half hour to spare. They crossed without incident and then continued on down the only highway that connected Santo Domingo with Port au Prince. Each silently worked hard at convincing themselves that Camilla was in a better place.

Chapter Twenty Six

The 235 miles between Santo Domingo and Port au Prince took Brian and Andrea over four and a half hours to complete. Although they arrived in the city as anticipated, neither felt in a very festive mood and not in the least bit tired.

"It's after eleven but let's do some sleuthing." Brian looked toward the hotel where Jason stood under the street light. "Jason hasn't seen us yet. The last couple of days we've accomplished some things, but with Camilla in tow, we've been restricted. Now…"

"I agree. We should be able to travel freely…for a while at least." Andrea liked the idea of following someone instead of someone following them. Since Jason seemed to always be on their horizon, he was the perfect choice. After a quick bite, they returned to their car and sat off to one side of the harbor road waiting to see if their 'friend' would leave for another location.

"While we're waiting, why don't we pray for Camilla. I miss her so much already." Praying with their eyes open was not new to either of them. Andrea started. "Lord, we know that Camilla is more precious to you than she has become to us. We also know that you guided our steps to Troy and down the path to the orphanage. Please protect her and give her the knowledge she needs to fend for herself. In Jesus name, I pray, Amen.

"Lord, I too pray your special blessing on Camilla, but also on Andrea and myself as we follow your leading to find Diane and Trent. Keep them safe wherever they are and protect us as well. Help us to find the way to them and keep us from harm while we dive tomorrow night. Amen." Just as he finished, Brian watched their quarry as he lit a cigarette. The lights were on in the rooms that Jason thought they occupied. Thanks to the concierge, their rooms appeared as if they were planning on staying in all night.

Brian and Andrea watched Jason walk over to a young boy. He handed him some cash. Jason pointed to the rooms on the second floor of the Al-B Oloffson Hotel, then got back into his car and turned on the ignition. Stepping on the gas pedal, he maneuvered into traffic and headed away from the harbor but into the business section of the city. Brian and Andrea followed a discrete distance behind in their rented vehicle until they saw Jason stop in front of the police station.

"Let's follow him and see who he talks to." Andrea already had a hand on the door handle of the car in a hurry to follow Jason inside the building. She slid out of the passenger side of the car just as Brian did the same on his side, and both quickly walked across the street. As they reached the entrance to the police station, they peered around the corner only to see Jason's pant leg disappear down a hallway to the right. They entered the building and walked up the short flight of stairs before peeking down the hall in the direction of their quarry.

They saw Jason enter a doorway and followed, making sure not to look too conspicuous. When they arrived outside the selected door, they saw the name of the police captain on the door. Brian raised his finger to cross his lips in a signal for silence. Andrea motioned that she knew that. They could hear voices inside.

Pretending to read a newspaper that he had brought with him, Brian lounged against the wall. Andrea bent over to straighten her pant leg.

"You had better be clear about what you can and cannot do in my city." The other voice spoke first. His gruff manner clearly stated who was in control, but Jason was not to be deterred.

"I think you will be a little more cordial when you see what I have brought you." Jason's familiar voice carried well through the closed door.

"Oh oui and what could that possibly be?"

"Here, see for yourself. I represent some people who would not take kindly if anything were to happen to someone connected with them and their plans."

"And just what might these plans be?" Each voice was so distinct that Brian and Andrea had no problem distinguishing who was speaking.

"You don't need to know the details. Just turn your head whenever one of the boys or I am in your city, that's all. And forget about pursuing any rumors you might hear about the ceremonies held in the clearing to the north of the city."

"Oh, ho, so you are the ones responsible for the disappearances. Well… we have too many of those cardboard box people anyway. Ha ha, cardboard box people! Makes them seem less valuable, non?"

"Just remember who's paying you to look the other way and we'll all be laughing someday."

"Oh, oui, we have a deal then. I will receive more of the same soon, non?"

"You will get the same amount every week, at this same time. In the meantime, can you keep an eye on two people for us? They are staying at the Al-B Oloffson Hotel and could be trouble for us. So far they seem to be having the time of their life as tourists, but I know they are up to something. The woman, Andrea Wilton, told me as much in the United States. The man, Brian Strait, is her accomplice. They are looking for some friends who happen to be helping us at the moment. We don't want them found."

Andrea gasped and then put her hand over her mouth. Jason did know where Trent and Diane were! She looked toward Brian who was also listening very intently to the conversation on the other side of the door.

"That will cost you extra, non?" The Haitian officer obviously wanted his fair share.

Jason sneered. "How much extra?"

"The same amount, I think…paid tomorrow before I begin that job."

"You'll have your money as soon as I get it. Don't get upset. I should have it by tomorrow night anyway."

"Then I start looking after the two Americans." Andrea and Brian heard a chair scraping. They moved swiftly towards the entrance of the building, out of sight. Jason emerged from the police captain's office just as they reached the stairwell. Andrea opened the outside door and they ran towards their vehicle parked one block away.

Brian and Andrea watched as Jason lifted his eyes to the bright moonlight as he stepped onto the sidewalk. He looked both ways, maybe sensing someone watching. They hoped not. Jason walked around to the driver's side of his black mustang, a car clearly not the same as the one seen in the U.S., but similar.

"He must really like Mustang convertibles." Andrea settled back in her seat for another clandestine trip following Jason. "Max was right. The police aren't to be trusted."

"Can you believe that police captain? He almost said that the people living in cardboard boxes needed to be exterminated. What kind of policeman would agree to something like that, and for a few bucks at best?" Brian clearly wanted to strangle someone.

"I don't think Jason just gave him a few dollars. Oops, speaking of Jason, there he goes. Let's follow to see where he leads us." They followed Jason back to the front of the hotel. He made sure the boy he'd paid was doing his job and then left without getting out of his car. He drove to the west side of the city in a manner that suggested that he knew exactly where he was going.

"I think Jason is planning to get the extra money for the police captain from those men who took the people during the last ceremony. Otherwise he would have been able to give it to him sooner. I'm sure he will be only too happy to give the job of following us to someone else." Brian seemed to be puzzled over this added information. Andrea concurred, however, since this seemed to be the most plausible explanation.

"That will give us time to execute the plan to follow their boat before we have someone else tailing us, someone we don't recognize." Andrea tried to put a positive light on this new development. "Tomorrow we have that lesson with all the new equipment. I wonder if they will question our use of it again. I can't imagine they care as long as they get paid."

"I gathered that as well. They seemed conscientious enough though to make sure we knew how to operate it."

"Yes, but they also make money on the lessons. Let's take our time tomorrow so we're really comfortable with all of it."

"Andrea, do you have any more concerns about what we're planning to do tomorrow night? We could maybe follow another way. I don't know how, but maybe we could think of something."

"No, this is the best way. If they catch us, we won't stand a chance of finding out where Trent and Diane are. Jason said they were working for his friends. Somehow I can't imagine that they are doing anything for those people willingly. Oh look, Jason's stopped in front of that house. I wonder who he knows there." As if on cue, a young woman emerged from the dark interior of the house. "Why, she can't be any more that about sixteen or seventeen."

Brian looked towards the house just as the young woman threw herself into Jason's arms. He walked into the house with her arms wrapped around his waist. Jason kissed her just before entering the building. The lights went out and all was quiet.

"How long are we going to stay here?" Andrea was disgusted. "It's obvious that he plans to spend the night."

"We might as well go to our hotel. We have a long day tomorrow." With that Brian pulled the car out of the shadows. They headed back to the Al-B Oloffson Hotel, parked behind the building at the staff entrance and entered through the back door. They bid the concierge goodnight and took the elevator to their floor.

Brian stopped with Andrea in front of her door. They looked at each other with the same feelings clearly visible in their eyes. Camilla was not with them anymore. He held the woman who had become a friend in such a short time. They both sighed deeply, missing their little friend immensely.

Brian was the first to speak. "I feel as if we left a part of ourselves back there. You must feel it even deeper since you shared your room with her."

Andrea leaned back to peer into his face. "It's hard to imagine how we'd feel if we'd kept her with us longer. It's only been a couple of days since we found her. I dread even going into my room without that bubbly spirit in there when I open my eyes tomorrow morning. However, it will make our job a lot easier if we don't have to worry about her."

Andrea didn't want to think about the little girl becoming a pawn in their game of cops and robbers, but she could very well be in danger just because of their quest to find the Michners. Brian shook his head as if reading her thoughts.

"She was such a sweet little girl for someone who had such a hard life." He shook his head. "See you tomorrow, bright and early, okay?"

"I'll be ready. Have a good night's sleep." Andrea walked into her silent room and locked the door behind her. She began to get undressed for bed, but then decided to check out the window to see if their watcher was still in the shadows. She opened the blinds and peered into the darkness. If he was there, she could see no sign of him. Staring into the blackness, she noticed something else though. Another little girl was combing through some garbage cans… another little girl who needed a home like Camilla had found.

"Dear Lord, how many of these children have to live on garbage and without proper care in this country. Please look after this one for the night and place someone in her life who will rescue her from the life she now leads. Also Father, keep Brian and I safe tomorrow and lead us to the place where Trent and Diane are. They have been missing for a long time. Father, keep them protected wherever they are until someone can rescue them. Amen."

****

While Andrea was praying about the Michners and the little waif at the garbage cans, Brian was going over their plan to follow the boat tomorrow night…if those men came back again. He knew they could not count on police support in this country, but did Max also mean that the police back home were not to be trusted as well? Maybe they needed to involve the FBI, he thought. No, he decided to himself. They didn't have enough evidence of foul play in the case of the Michners yet, but then he wondered if Lieutenant Kurshner had uncovered anything in the death of Max.

Taking the time difference into consideration, Brian decided to make a long distance call. When the police station answered on the fourth ring, he asked to speak to Lieutenant Kurshner and was put straight through. "Mr. Strait, I've been trying to reach you. Have you discovered anything else about your friends? Are they back from their vacation?"

"Vacation!! We told you they are not on vacation. They would have said something to us. Have you found out anything, or are you even looking?"

"We're looking, we're looking. Keep your shirt on. I was just testing you. We haven't uncovered anything in their disappearance, but we have some interesting news about Miss Wilton's friend, Max. Max visited the Caribbean at least four times every year, and he had a substantial bank account to which Miss Wilton has had access. Did you know that?"

"No…no.. I didn't. Why is that important?"

"We're not sure yet, but we think Miss Wilton knows more about this case than she lets on … and we think you're not telling us everything either. Why don't you come down to the station tomorrow morning and bring Miss Wilton with you?"

"Uh-h-h, we can't lieutenant. We're out of town. But we'll see you as soon as we get back." Brian hung up quickly deciding that now was not the time to confide in the lieutenant. They would have to wait until they discovered where the boat would lead them before calling in the authorities. Then it had better be the FBI since the Michners had been taken across state lines. Although he didn't know for sure that the police in the US were involved, he couldn't take the chance that they were.

Knocking gently on the door connecting his room to Andrea's, Brian whispered, "Andrea, are you asleep yet?"

"No, I'm just lying here thinking about tomorrow. Come on in." She sat up slightly just as Brian entered. "What is it?"

"I just talked to Lieutenant Kurshner. He thinks we both know more than we're telling them, and he knows about Max's bank account as well as your access to it. He wanted us to come down to the station tomorrow, but I told him we were out of town. I've been thinking about what we should do as far as involving the authorities. We know we can't trust the police here, and we aren't sure about the police back home. I think the

FBI would be our best bet if we find out something tangible tomorrow. What do you think?"

"First of all, have they found out anything about the Michners?"

"No, that's still a blank wall as far as the police go."

"Well, I agree that we don't know who we can trust. As far as I know, the FBI is the agency if someone has been taken against their will into another country. But you're also right that so far we have nothing to give them. Let's hope tomorrow is more fruitful than the last couple of days have been."

"I just wanted to fill you in. Go to sleep now and forget about tomorrow. Remember what the Bible says about worry. Take care of today and let tomorrow take care of itself, remember? Do you want to pray together about this stuff?"

"Oh, Brian that would be great." Andrea's bowed her head. Brian began, "Lord, we love You and we thank You for allowing us to see where Camilla will live and for allowing us to have a small amount of time with her. We ask You to love her through Father Bertrand. I ask now that You would protect Andrea and help her get a good night's rest. In Jesus name, Amen."

"Lord I too come to You tonight and thank You for allowing us to know Camilla. Help us to remember to seek help for the orphanage when we get back home and to send special gifts to Camilla from time to time to let her know we haven't forgotten her. Now Lord, I ask You to grant Brian additional wisdom as You have already done. Protect him tomorrow and give him Your rest tonight. Amen."

"Thanks Andrea. I've never prayed with a woman before except in groups at church. This is different, don't you think? I'm not sure where the Lord is leading us, but I am sure

He is leading us together. I mean, He is leading us somewhere … oh … I'm not sure what I mean. Good night again, and I'll see you tomorrow."

Andrea giggled when she saw the red coloring appear around Brian's collar. "Good night, Brian. Don't let the bed-bugs bite." When the door had closed behind him, she lay down with new thoughts filling her head. Did Brian think that they could be more than friends?

"I guess that wouldn't be such a bad idea." She spoke out loud and then giggled again before she turned off the light one final time. Her sleep was filled with dreams again, some not so awful this time.

Chapter Twenty Seven

Andrea opened her eyes. Her skin tingled with anticipation. Birds, many tropical, sang their melodious tunes just outside her hotel room window. She watched the sun's rays as they streaked through the louvered balcony doors across the bedroom floor. She could hear fruit vendors describing their juicy wares in the nearby market place. *Today could be the day when we'll discover where the Michners are*. She lay still a while longer wondering what the day had in store for them.

All the clues they'd uncovered seemed to lead to the voodoo ceremonies. Tonight, they planned to attend another one, prepared this time to follow that boat wherever it went. She rolled over on the bed, relishing a few last moments under the cool sheets before the day began in earnest. *The color on Brian's face last night. Could he be interested in me? I wonder where that will lead*. Her body quivered at the prospect.

****

Next door, Brian was also beginning his day. He stepped into the shower, enjoying the warm spray of water on his body. His roiling thoughts interrupted his shower concerto. Thoughts of what could go wrong tripped across his brain. "Lord, please remove any obstacles. Keep us safe. Amen" The mission they planned was dangerous. They were working against men not averse to using force, or more, to obtain what they wanted. The burden of responsibility weighed heavily on his shoulders, but he knew that if the Michners were here, they had no choice but to carry out their plans. *I hope we aren't in over our heads.* This thought was not a new one.

The warm water began to spray a little cooler as was the custom at this tiny hotel in Haiti. He knew it was time to shut it off or be exhilarated with a cold shower. Brian stepped gingerly out onto the tile floor and began drying off with one of the towels provided by the hotel. He knew this would be the coolest he would feel all day so he took his time dressing.

****

Andrea knocked on the door adjoining their rooms. When Brian answered she smiled. "Brian, good morning. Are you ready for breakfast?"

"I am. Are you ready for the busy day ahead of us?" Brian closed the door and then entered the hallway through her door.

"It's given me a lot to think about this morning. But I lay in bed for an extra few minutes just enjoying the sounds from outside…so tropical."

Before long they sat at their usual table in the dining room. Their waiter poured them fresh hot coffee, followed by fresh rolls and fruit for their breakfast. Their conversation was as light-hearted as if they were indeed just tourists. Appetites satisfied, the conversation turned to the day's tasks ahead.

"The first thing we need to do is complete another scuba lesson using the rebreathers and the scooters." Brian sipped his second cup of coffee. "We want to be really comfortable with this stuff before tonight, so we may need to spend a lot of time in the water today."

"You mean you want me to be more comfortable. I'm sorry I'm such a wimp. Do you think we could go down more than once today?" Andrea knew that diving in quick succession was definitely something to be concerned about.

"We can. Remember . . . if we spend a certain amount of time on the surface, we can calculate how long we can dive again. Each time will be shorter, but we will be able to go down more than once if we take the precautions they taught us." Brian signed for their breakfast. He held Andrea's chair for her while she rose.

"I remember. I wish that closed in feeling was not something I had to fight every time I went under the water. The thought of diving in pitch black water scares me to death." Andrea shivered.

"Do you want to stay on shore? Maybe it would be better if I went alone."

"No! I'm going. I'll just work really hard on conquering my fears, that's all." Andrea's stubborn streak had taken her beyond her comfort zone quite often. They exited the elevator and walked toward their rooms.

Inside, Andrea threw her bathing suit and a towel into a small, plastic lined, canvas bag along with a comb and her wallet, eliminating the need for a purse. She closed her door firmly; making sure the lock was engaged. Brian carried a similar bag when he emerged from his room. If anyone was watching, they were two happy tourists. Outside, the sunshine forgotten, a knot as big as the outdoors filled Andrea's stomach. Her fears were surfacing again.

"The scuba shop should have the okay on our check by now. We'll practice first...with the rebreathers, scooters, and the sonar. Afterwards we'll stash our equipment near the ceremony site, in the brush near the beach where the boat landed the first time." Brian looked at Andrea's ashen face.

"I'm so scared, Brian. Determined but scared. I hope I don't mess this up for us." Andrea's head dropped to her chest. She kicked at a stone on the sidewalk.

"Andrea, I'm scared too. Anyone going into battle is scared. They're fools if they aren't. It'll just keep our senses sharp, that's all. Now let's concentrate. As soon as those men leave the beach with their next victims, we can slip into the water and follow. I just hope they don't go faster than our equipment allows us to follow. At night, with no lights, I am counting on them going slower than if they were traveling during the day." Brian took her elbow to steer her across the street. The dive shop appeared on their right.

The more Brian outlined their plans, the more apprehensive Andrea became. "Until we confirmed that the police were not reliable, I still hoped we might enlist their help. Now..."

"We have no one to count on but ourselves...at least until we can give the FBI something solid to go on. I know this will not be the most pleasant experience. It's one thing to dive during the day when the water is lit up by the sunlight, but tonight... Are you sure you can handle this?" Brian watched her face closely for any sign that she needed to forego her involvement.

Strength and resolution were back in place. "I want to be there when we find the Michners. I will stay focused, and the practice this morning will certainly help." Andrea walked purposefully down the sidewalk again.

Boats were leaving the marina when they arrived, many on their way to their fishing grounds where they would spend the day. Others were charters taking tourists for some deep-sea fishing or scuba diving. Some were clearly rented pleasure crafts that tourists, who came to Haiti to either scuba dive on their own or just swim in the ocean, occupied. The parking lot near the marina was full. Brian and Andrea were glad they had left their car at the hotel.

They crossed the parking lot and walked down the dock toward the scuba office located to the right side of the marina. When they entered the door, their instructor greeted them with a big smile, happy to tell them they had indeed heard from the bank. Their check was cleared. "Today you will become proficient in the use of the rebreathers, non?"

"We can hardly wait." Andrea smiled at the man's enthusiasm. She and Brian withdrew to the dressing room area to put on their swimsuits. Andrea returned in a few minutes, resolve fully in place, if not anticipation.

****

Brian stepped to her side with his usual smile. He turned his head to look outside. Their young appendage, from the night before, was relaxing on a pile of canvas near the edge of the dock. *The boy obviously thinks that he knows we could be occupied for most of the day. He thinks he can relax a little.* To keep the boy guessing, as they loaded their gear onto the boat, he spoke loud enough for the kid to hear. "We may want to use regular tanks today as well." Andrea gave him a puzzled look. He tilted his head in the boy's direction. She smiled.

Walking past the boy to the water's edge, Brian helped Andrea into the boat. He sat across from her for the short ride to the reef for their dive. The water was as smooth as glass in the marina but it became a little choppy once they left the protected area. They were joined at the reef by other divers, doing the same thing…exploring the white sandy bottom and the colorful fish located in the hollows of the coral landscape.

Brian and Andrea's equipment would allow them to stay down much longer. They tossed their t-shits and shorts on a bench, strapped their rebreathers on and slipped their feet into fins. Masks and snorkels came next, just before their guide gave the signal for them to fall backward into the water from the side of the boat.

Fish of all colors streaked by. Sunbeams made ribbons through the clear water. Coral dotted the white sandy ocean floor. Brian watched the stream of bubbles from the other divers nearby. Nothing came from his or Andrea's tank. *We'll be invisible tonight.*

He watched Andrea extend her hand toward a nurse shark and then a sting ray. *Remember the warnings Andrea.* A lobster skittered away to hide in the coral. Andrea seemed engrossed in her surroundings. When a school of tiny silver fish swarmed around her head, she just knelt there on top of the white sand. *She's some kind of woman.*

****

The realization that she was not afraid any longer came as a surprise to Andrea. The light from the surface enabled her to view things quite a distance away, which left her feeling quite comfortable. She watched Brian a short distance away. He was doing the same things she was. Their guide's eyes were peeled for treasure, a common practice of island dwellers she was told.

She and Brian turned their focus to familiarizing themselves with their equipment. With the guide's help, Brian practiced lodging the sonar on the bottom of their boat. The instructor surfaced, gave the captain some instructions and then returned to Brian's side. The boat took off slowly. Andrea watched Brian use a scooter to follow. She decided to give that piece of equipment a try. She enjoyed the relaxing way it pulled her through the water while at the same time covering a great distance. *This will certainly make the dive tonight a little easier.*

Continuing to use the rebreather and the scooter, Andrea focused on her surroundings once again. The water was as clear at forty feet as it was at ten. Purplish sea fans waved in the currents and a larger fish swam by, totally oblivious to the human elements within their depths. Although the fans moved in a rhythmic dance to the ocean movements, those same currents were hardly felt by the divers.

Since he didn't have a rebreather, their instructor was on his second tank. Andrea signaled to him how confident she was. She felt way more comfortable than she did the last time. She watched him move farther away and continued to scrutinize the smooth strokes of his legs as they propelled him through the water. He had a certain rhythm; one that she knew would take her a long time to accomplish. The man was a good instructor. Brian was also to be trusted and a reliable dive partner. She knew she could count on him to keep her safe.

The instructor spotted an old Coca Cola bottle and then a crusty old coin, treasures he would clean up and store or sell, he'd told his students. His movements indicated he was not in any hurry to go topside, but Andrea knew the air on his second tank would soon run out.

Once aboard the boat, Brian listened to Andrea's breathless diatribe about the dive. "I think we've learned enough to accomplish our task. Let's go ashore, move the gear and then relax for the rest of the day."

Their instructor gave them a good progress report. When they arrived at the marina, their shadow was just waking from a nap. Brian watched him through hooded eyes. The boy seemed confident they knew nothing of him. Brian told the shop owner they would be back for the more advanced equipment.

"How are we going to lose that young man?" Andrea walked quickly beside Brian toward their hotel. "We don't want him to see us with all that equipment, do we? What if he tells Jason and they figure out that we're planning to follow tonight?"

"We sure don't want that to happen." Brian thought for a minute or two. "I know. Since the car is at the back of the hotel, why don't we make it look like we're bushed from our dive, that we plan to rest until lunch time. Once inside, we can go out the back way." With that said, Brian yawned, stretching his arms wide. Andrea followed suit. They both sighed.

Andrea spoke loudly enough for anyone nearby to hear. "I'm ready for a nap, too." They slowed their steps to reflect tired bodies as they reached the hotel, slowly lifting one foot and then another to trudge up the front steps. One look over their shoulders told them their act had paid off. Their young shadow took his stance on a bench across the street. He closed his eyes for another long rest.

Inside, Brian led the way past the concierge's desk, through the back door to their car. He got in the driver's side while Andrea piled into the passenger's seat for the short ride to the marina. It took them no time at all to complete the task of loading their equipment. They drove off looking toward the small bundle still seated on the bench in repose when they drove past the hotel. He never noticed a thing.

The trek to the clearing by car took longer. They followed an alternate route that circumvented the clearing to the beach side. They drove as far as they could, watching as branches from overhanging trees whipped past their windshield as if trying to snag them in the face. They heard animals scurry for cover, birds cackled and squeaked their annoyance at the intrusion. They parked the car, unloaded their gear, and followed the path they'd discovered a couple of days ago. Some brush alongside the path seemed the perfect place to hide everything. They moved the branches back in place and then returned to the car.

Returning to the hotel, they parked the car in the customary spot behind the hotel. Once inside, they decided on a quick lunch before really retiring. Andrea sat down at the table, took a long drink of water, and leaned back. "Brian, did you ever imagine that you would someday be doing all the things we're doing here in Haiti?"

"No, never in my wildest dreams. Now that we're here though, I kind of like this cops and robbers stuff. Imagine, we're being used by God to free our friends, and maybe stop people from disappearing here as well. We know Trent and Diane are still alive. Jason told the police captain as much last night. We might be seeing them tonight. I can't help but feel that God has led us this far. He'll lead us the rest of the way and protect us too, I believe."

"It's not only finding Trent and Diane, though. If we had not come here, we would not have been in a place where we could help Camilla. What about all those other children who browse through garbage cans for their next meal? I've been thinking. Maybe we should set up a foundation or something to provide a place for them off the streets. After all, we have all that money that Max left me. We've hardly put a dent in it yet."

"First of all, you have all that money. Max left it to you, not me. Besides, you don't have a home to return to thanks to all this. Or at least, I'm sure it's all tied together. You may need to use some of that money to rebuild or buy a new one.

We may not even have jobs when we go back, but it's your money. If you want to do something like that, then I think that's great."

****

Brian couldn't help but admire the heart of the woman across from him. He'd never discussed things like this with any of his other women friends but he was sure, they wouldn't think of anyone but themselves. *Why am I comparing Andrea to women I've dated? We're not dating.* He looked towards his companion and continued the conversation where it had left off.

"I don't know how you'd go about doing something like that. Why not wait until we're stateside, before making any decisions." Brian leaned his arms on the table.

"You're right, Brian. I really haven't given this much thought. I just feel so badly when I look out my window and see a tiny body scrounging in the garbage. But, yes, I'll wait until we are back home before making any decisions. I want to pray long and hard so I do what the Lord wants me to do."

"Mam'selle, Monsieur, you are coming back to the dining room this evening, yes? We 'ave another great band and lots of musique." The waiter returned with the salads. He placed them on the table and waited patiently for their answer.

"We'll see," Andrea took a forkful of the wonderfully fresh salad. The waiter left. Brian and Andrea had lots to think about. *Talk about going home seems so far into the future. We're in another world here.* So much had happened in the short week since they embarked on this journey.

Silent thoughts continued to plague them, as the couple made their way toward the elevator and their siesta. Before they had a chance to step into the elevator, however, a large black man wearing the uniform of the local police walked into the lobby. He moved towards the desk of the concierge at first, but then, when he spied the two Americans, he walked towards them with a purposeful stride.

"Monsieur Strait, Mam'selle Wilton, can I see your papers please?" He was very large and his presence commanded a lot of attention from other hotel guests.

"Sure, they're up in our rooms. Why do you want to see our passports? Have we done something wrong?" Brian was polite, but firm in his response to the man.

"Let's go on up then." The cop ignored his questions. He proceeded to enter the elevator with the young couple. His scrutiny made them feel very uncomfortable as they silently stepped out on their floor. There steps echoed down the hall.

Once inside Brian's room, without comment, the policeman took a cursory glance at his passport. Andrea went next door to get hers. The man glanced at her passport and then handed it back. "What is your purpose for being in Port Au Prince?"

"Just a vacation." Brian stood as tall as he could but his height didn't come near the man's ears.

Andrea spoke as calmly as she could. "Yes, you have beautiful waters for scuba diving, and we love the beach and the boats." Inside she was trembling but her answers were clear and concise, not showing in the slightest that she was intimidated by the man's questions.

"When do you plan to go home?" The policeman continued his interrogation.

"Oh, in a week or so. We're in no hurry." Andrea sat on a chair near Brian's bed.

"Well, we just want you to know that we are watching all Americans. We want you to have a good time, but when it is time, you need to leave for home. In fact, it would not be a bad idea if you left tomorrow instead of in a week or so." The large man almost filled the doorway as he made his move to leave.

"Oh and why is that?" Brian's voice spoke of his indignation at the policeman's unfriendly attitude. "We're not breaking any laws here. Why are you suggesting we leave tomorrow?"

"Just a suggestion, nothing more. Good day to you." With his cap in hand, he saluted and left the way he'd come. Instead of protecting its citizens, the police captain was loyal to a group of people sinister to the core.

"What was that all about, I wonder?" Andrea collapsed on Brian's bed with a sigh of relief.

"They just want us to know they know about us and are watching, I think. At least we know what he looks like. We should be able to sneak by him as easily as we did the kid today. Well…maybe not so easily, but we'll have to do the best we can tonight. We don't need them on our tails while we try to get to the bottom of all this. Let's rest, and we'll meet for dinner, okay? Andrea, are you okay? You look as if you've seen a ghost."

"I guess that visit scared me more than I thought. I feel all shaky inside. I'll be all right. Just give me a minute." She rose to her feet on legs that could have been a little steadier, but was soon at the door. "I need a good rest, I think."

Chapter Twenty Eight

As soon as Andrea had slipped into something more comfortable, she lay down on her bed with a small blanket covering her legs. Even with the heat of the day smothering any breeze that might have come through her window, Andrea liked to be covered.

She closed her eyes, but sleep didn't come quickly. Their plans for that night trampled all over her thoughts, leaving her nervous and excited all at the same time. Tonight they would know if the trail they were following would lead to the Michners. She missed Diane so much, the talks, the teasing. Diane would be all over her if she knew where her thoughts were leading with regards to Brian.

She needed to rest. Tonight required she have the strength to complete her mission. Andrea closed her eyes, prayed a short prayer for rest and focused again on her favorite praise chorus. Within minutes she was fast asleep.

Someone was knocking on her window. How could that be? She was on the tenth floor of her apartment building. She pulled the blanket over her ahead and kept her eyes closed. Whoever was out there was persistent. Knock. Knock. She heard the banging over and over again. She opened her eyes.

Someone was pounding on her door, not her window. That part had been a dream. Andrea rose quickly, walked to the door and listened. "Who's there?"

"It's Brian. We'd better get something to eat. It's almost time for us to leave."

Andrea looked at her watch. "Oh my. I did sleep. I'll be right with you." The realization that she had slept the afternoon away came as a surprise, but she was also thankful, feeling ready for her evening's test of courage.

She combed her hair, straightened her clothing, and grabbed a jacket before opening the door to her room. Brian was leaning against the wall waiting patiently. He smiled, tousled her hair – the effects of her recent combing completely undone – and motioned for her to follow him. They went down the stairs to the main lobby and into the dining room where, after a short wait, a hot, delicately spiced meal was placed before them.

Brian began the conversation, keeping it light. "I guess you were able to get some sleep after all. I rested but that was all."

"One minute I was working hard to relax so I could fall asleep and the next I was awakened by a loud person pounding on my door." She winked at Brian, clearly not as offended as her words indicated. "I can't remember when I've slept that soundly in the middle of the afternoon."

"Well, you obviously needed it. What shall we do tonight?" He asked in case someone was listening.

Following his lead, Andrea supplied all sorts of ideas and then, "Why don't we go for a moonlight picnic over by that waterfall and the swimming pond."

"That sounds like a great idea. I'll ask the concierge to pack us a light lunch while we go upstairs to get our bathing suits."

Andrea finished her meal first. Brian was content to follow her lead. They left the dining room and approached the man behind the desk in the lobby. Arrangements were made for a light snack; one they knew would probably never get eaten. They changed into swim suits under long pants and a shirt before leaving their rooms.

Once in the lobby again, the concierge was waiting with a box containing several items of food and a large bottle of raspberry flavored sparkling water. He whispered for their ears only, "You might want to go around the clearing on the north side of the pond. The ceremonies, they are scheduled for tonight."

"We know. We'll be careful." Brian and Andrea walked briskly out the back door, aware that someone was lurking in the shadows just beyond the front of the hotel. *These police are not so smart. They don't have the back door covered.*

Brian set their box of food into the back of their vehicle. He opened the door for Andrea. "In case I don't get another chance to tell you, Andrea, I've enjoyed being here with you. I admire your courage."

"I feel the same way." Andrea dropped her head and then looked at him again."You sound as if you expect something to go wrong."

"Not really or at least, I sure hope not. But in the past, I've often regretted not telling someone how I feel, only to discover it's too late. I didn't want anything to be left unsaid between us, just in case. . .well, you know what I mean."

"Yes, I do but we'll be alright. I have to hang onto that, or you'll never be able to get me into that dark water tonight."

Brian nodded his assurance that things would work out. He backed the vehicle out onto the street and then drove for a short way without turning on the headlights. At the edge of town, the black night forced them to illuminate their path. They hoped they were out of sight of any policemen. To keep their would-be pursuers at the hotel, both had left a light on in their rooms.

The moon was just beginning to peek from behind some large black clouds when Brian and Andrea pulled their vehicle to the side of the road near the clearing where the night's festivities would occur. They drove it into the bushes making sure it could not be seen by anyone approaching the grass covered field.

From out of the back seat, they gathered their basket of food just in case someone spotted them. They began the short hike to the water's edge where the boat would land when the ceremonies were in full swing. Using the trees and the night's darkness as cover, they prepared to put on their wet suits.

"I'm really glad we purchased wet suits." Andrea shivered. "It's chilly out here tonight." She pulled the tight rubber suit up her torso. It was a snug fit, but she knew that was so she could skim through the water unhindered by any loose fabric. Her body soon began to feel the warmth the suit gave her.

When Brian was comfortably suited up, he uncovered their hidden scuba equipment. Andrea watched as he prepared their equipment, keeping it hidden from the shoreline so when the thugs showed up they would not be able to see anything out of place.

"We can take this stuff out after the men leave for the clearing. By the time they return with their next victims, we'll be in the water waiting."

Andrea shuddered at the thought and then offered up a prayer for protection. She hunkered down behind a tree in preparation for their lengthy wait. Brian finished his preparations and joined her. They made themselves comfortable, not wanting a shift in their position to give them away at the wrong moment. Silence filled the bushes but a few minutes later, music could be heard from somewhere behind them. The ceremony had begun.

Hypnotic sounds beat on metal drums filled the air. A rhythmic tune was sung by participants, a tune that gathered momentum as the evening wore on. Andrea could imagine swaying bodies surrounding smoky bonfires, a sight she remembered from their first encounter with a voodoo ceremony. These people were blinded by a leader who did not care about them at all. In fact, he sold them for only a few cents to some very dangerous people. She would be very happy when his plot was exposed, and he was behind bars.

"Brian." Andrea whispered, letting her voice come out in little more than a breath. "How are we going to notify the authorities about what's going on. I've not really thought about how this will all work tonight, have you?"

"Yes, I have. I called the FBI this afternoon...while you were sleeping. I told them all about the note that led us here. They were a little curious about why we hadn't told the police about it back home but said that it was probable cause for them to land on the island. They told me to do nothing, not even to free Trent and Diane, until they are able to get there. Since we don't know where there is yet, we'll come back, and, using the compass directions, we'll be able to tell them where to go and what we've seen."

"Not free Trent and Diane! But…"

"We have no way to get them off the island. We'll have scuba gear but they won't so…"

"Oh Brian. I hadn't obviously thought all the details through. I just thought we would be leaving wherever we are going tonight with them. What happens if the FBI shows up and there's shooting and the Michners get killed?"

"We'll leave them with directions to a safer place on the island, or whatever this place is, before we leave. They may have to sneak away when they hear the commotion begin. I am certain the FBI will have enough men to make sure the bad guys are caught quickly. I also told the agent I talked to this afternoon that their son was with them, so they'll know who the Michners are when they see Jeffrey."

"Did the FBI say how quickly they could get there?"

"They are already on their way. They plan to anchor close by so that when I call, the message will be relayed directly to them and then…"

"I'm sure glad you're thinking. It just never occurred to me before now that we hadn't discussed …"

"Shh-h-h, I hear something." Just as Brian spoke, Andrea could hear the sound of a motor off in the distance. It was beginning.

The two amateur detectives moved closer to the ground and lay very still. Before long voices could be heard, some with a German accent, but others sounded more Haitian. *How could these people do this to their own?* Andrea remembered the poverty that was a way of life for many on this island. *I guess if I was hungry, I might be tempted to do something illegal too.* She hoped not.

The men beached their craft on shore, quieter now than they had been when they approached. They moved stealthily toward the music and through the trees without saying another word.

Once the sounds of footsteps ceased to be heard from their place of concealment, Brian motioned for Andrea to follow. They carefully moved their equipment from its hideaway. Andrea struggled with the weight of the scooter, half dragging, half lifting its bulk into the water. She and Brian assembled the rebreathers and strapped them on their backs as their instructor had taught them. With masks and snorkels in place over their foreheads, they stepped into the water.

"Wow, this feels really cold." Andrea shivered again as the cool seeped through her body.

"It's amazing how the water temperature changes when the sun isn't shining on it." Brian whispered as he attached the sonar device to the bottom of the boat. "I'm sure we'll become accustomed to the temperature soon." They immersed themselves almost completely to eliminate any shadow their bodies might create in the water with the moon so bright above them. Another wait!

This time their wait was short lived. They'd no sooner slunk down into the dark water than they could detect voices. Sound traveled well at night. The culprits weren't worried, their victims were in trances.

"Quickly, bring that woman here." A man with a gruff voice seemed to be in charge. Several figures appeared at the edge of the water. Two of them lowered an unconscious body into the boat. "Only one, harrumph." He cursed. "Heinz is not going to be happy, yah?"

"It couldn't be helped. That witch doctor sounded scared tonight. Did he tell you why?"

"Yah, he did." The leader spoke again. "It's those Americans. I told Jason to get rid of them. When Heinz finds out they are messing things up, he will deal with them himself."

"Let's get going." Another, higher pitched voice spoke in the darkness. "There's nothing we can do about this now." All three stepped into the boat. The motor started. The boat slowly moved from the shore. Brian checked to see that his sonar was working. Indeed it was, and even though they couldn't see anything, they could follow easily.

Andrea swallowed several times and then began breathing very slowly in an attempt to get her claustrophobic feelings under control. The water was so dark she could not see her hand in front of her face. She could feel her scooter though. Her rebreather was working beautifully. She sensed Brian's body right next to hers, almost touching, and was comforted by the thought that he was nearby.

Chapter Twenty Nine

The scooters pulled Brian and Andrea through the murky depths. Water flowed past, with an occasional fish that seemed like a flash of light and nothing more. Brian kept tabs on the direction the boat was headed with the sonar device so he could tell the FBI agents…if they were needed.

He glanced to his right. Andrea was keeping pace with him, a foot or two behind. *I wish there'd been some way to do this without involving her. I just hope I can keep her safe.* He really was beginning to care about her and that scared him almost more than the course they had embarked on to find the Michners.

Returning to focus on the task at hand, Brian watched first the compass and then the sonar detector. They were moving at a comfortable speed. *There's only so much fuel in that little motor so we can't be going very far.* The scooters had three hours of battery time. He glanced behind again. *Andrea's doing really well, considering.* They moved through some areas of coral. Thankful for the protection their wet suits offered them, the gloom of their underwater world made it nearly impossible for them to avoid hitting the sharp protruding spikes. Finally, they were in deeper water that left the way clear and free of any debris. Without a light source, other than the glow from the sonar detector on his wrist, there was little to see.

Brian noticed that their course had not altered a whole lot from the starting point, a straight line almost. *That piece of information will make it much easier when I call the FBI.* The scooters maximum speed was two and a half miles per hour. Apparently that speed was sufficient for the boat too.

****

By the time they'd been underwater for about a half hour, Andrea was feeling more comfortable. Being pulled by the scooter was almost relaxing, as long as she could see Brian beside her. She'd do this all over again if it meant finding the Michners. Just as she was about to pray for success, Brian stopped her forward motion with his hand on her scooter. The boat had stopped, he signaled.

Anticipation rose like a banner in her body. They turned off the scooters and kneeled in the water just behind the boat, waiting for the men to go up the shore or on the dock. They couldn't see, yet, whether they had beached the boat or tethered it to a dock. Andrea breathed a sigh of relief. They'd have to return the way they came, but it would be daylight or close to it by then…not so dark.

Andrea watched Brian slowly lift his head out of the water. He ducked under and motioned for her to follow. She raised her head. In the dim shadows, illuminated by the moon overhead, Andrea saw the piece of land that was their destination. The boat was tied to a dock. The three criminals dragged a body down the wooden planks covering it. Lights were located at regular intervals. Farther up the shoreline were several buildings, some larger than others, but plenty of places where a young family, like the Michners, could be held against their will.

Brian slowly swam toward the right side of the dock. Since it extended out into the water, there were several places underneath where they could secure their equipment from sight.

"What's next?" Andrea spoke in little more than a whisper.

"We'll wait until they're far enough ahead. Then we can safely begin our search of every building until we find the Michners, if they're even here. Remember, we don't know anything for certain." Brian began unfastening the harness of his rebreather as his scooter floated nearby.

The men moved toward a building to the left of the dock. Andrea and Brian rose from their crouched positions. They tethered their equipment, removed fins and masks and walked slowly ashore. Andrea pointed to the small round pebbles covering the beach. "Just like the one you found at the Michners." *That seems so long ago.*

"Let's get going." Brian was clearly anxious. "I want to know if we made the right decision. We have a lot of ground to cover before dawn." He crouched, ran up the shore and approached the first building.

"I can't see anything through the window, Brian." Andrea peered inside. "We'll have to see if the door is unlocked."

"Let's go this way. The longer we stay in the shadows, the better." Brian led the way around the side of the building. When they got to the other side, they noticed a large set of bars covering the windows, but no bars had covered the windows on the side closest to the beach. Strange!

They tried the door. In spite of the building's secure appearance, the handle gave way easily allowing the pair access to its interior. They stepped carefully inside. Rustling. Something or someone was in here. Both crouched low. Where could they hide? A dim light came on in the far corner of the large room.

"Who's there." A voice seemed to float through the air from somewhere in the direction of the light.

Andrea remained very still. She tried hard not to breathe more than necessary. Her heart raced almost choking off her air supply.

"Who's there." The voice again. This time he seemed a little closer. The light flooded the middle of the room, Andrea saw cages with people inside them. *What kind of place is this? There are people being held here like animals.*

Brian moved farther into the depths of the shadows grabbing Andrea's arm in the process to pull her with him. The voice materialized into a medium sized black man. Something was not right about the way he walked or about the way he looked.

Then they saw him more clearly. His dark skin was splotched with small patches of white, not so he looked two-toned, but enough that the white portions stood out in sharp contrast to the rest of his coloring. He also walked using a crude wooden crutch in one hand. He held a candle in the other.

Without giving away their hiding spot, Andrea peeked around the far edge of the box she hid behind. Faces were pressed against bars. *There has to be five or six people locked up here.* They wore tattered clothes. The fingers grasping the bars of their cages were spindly, as if food was scarce for them. Then she noticed the smell. *How can another human being make people live like this?*

****

Brian held his hand over his mouth and nose, trying not to gag. *The conditions here are deplorable.* He looked toward Andrea and shook his head. How were their friends handling this misery? Were their living arrangements as bad as this? *Please God, no.* Brian motioned for Andrea to slink further behind the boxes. They couldn't afford to be discovered yet. They needed to find the Michners. They waited.

A minute or two, with no further sounds, the man with the candle moved back into the shadows. "Go back to sleep." He spoke with a commanding voice but it looked as if he'd been treated just as badly as the people in cages. "It is nothing." He rattled the cages on his way past, and then all was quiet.

Minutes ticked by slowly. Andrea and Brian soon heard snoring. They stealthily crept outside, waited in the shadows to make sure they had not aroused anyone again, and then moved onto the next building.

"What is this place?" Andrea swiped at tears.

"I haven't got a clue. I'll bet, though, that some of those people are listed among the missing in Port Au Prince. I wish I knew what was going on here." Brian scurried to the door of the building they'd selected for their next search.

"I do too. I think we have stumbled across something very sinister. We need to get off this island before dawn, or we could be in big trouble." Andrea crouched beside the door waiting for Brian to try the lock. It didn't have any.

They opened the door as little as they could. Brian led the way inside. There were cages here too, filled with people. The moon was in just the right position to shine through the window. Their view of the deplorable conditions in which these people were kept was very clear.

Once they were outside again, Brian stopped near a large live oak tree dripping with moss. "Andrea, let's pray. God will lead us to the right building." He watched Andrea glance furtively right and left and then tuck her body further behind the tree. She looked expectantly toward him. Brian bowed his head. "Father, You know where the Michners are. You've brought us this far, please move us toward the right building. Please Lord, give us Your plan tonight, a plan that will help us get the Michners out of here and soon. Amen. Okay Andrea, let's hope…er…did you happen to see which building those men went into? I was so busy stowing our equipment, I missed where they went."

"Yes, I did. It's that large one over there." She moved behind Brian toward the next largest building on the compound. It was located between other smaller buildings. As they approached, the door creaked open.

"Take the body to the deep water and dump it." a voice said. "Make sure it does not end up on this shore as the last one did."

Brian and Andrea watched as two large men dragged a small body towards the water's edge along the dock. They threw it unceremoniously aboard the boat that had just led them to this island and then started the motor. They could hear it move off into the distance.

"I'll bet they'll be back soon." Brian's voice was growing hoarse from all the whispering. "Let's leave this building until last. We have time to wait until they've gone back to sleep. We still have lots of night left." Their black wetsuits kept them hidden in the shadows as they moved around to the back. There was the building Andrea had seen the three boatmen enter when they'd first arrived. But there was also a smaller building to the right and just slightly back from the larger one. Brian pointed to this one.

The door was locked. They moved to one side and noticed a small window had been left open. Brian crept forward and peered inside. A small light sat on a wooden crate beside a large bed. Three people seemed sound asleep. Their rough torn covers covered most of their bodies, but not enough to hide the fact that one of them was a small child.

"Look, Andrea." Brian motioned for her to look inside. "Do you think. . .?" He left the rest of the question unspoken. Andrea peeked through the same window. She turned excited eyes toward him. "Maybe…" She placed her hand over her beating heart. "Maybe…"

"Can you squeeze through this window?" Brian began pulling nearby boxes toward the spot where they stood. "You could climb on these."

****

Andrea looked at the window. "I think so but…" She began climbing. Brian assisted her as best he could.

"Try not to make any noise…in case…"

Just as Andrea stuck her head through the opening, a woman screamed. Andrea jumped and hit her head on the window sill. "Sh-h-h. We're here to help." Andrea jumped to the floor. She walked quickly toward the door. "Can you open this from inside?"

"Andrea! Is that you?" Andrea recognized that voice. Diane. "How did you find us?"

"Leave us alone." A man's voice sounded from the bed

Diane whispered, "It's Andrea."

"And Brian." Andrea supplied. Trent moved quickly from the bed to the window. Brian was lodged halfway through. He pulled his friend in the rest of the way.

Trent hugged both of them. "What are you doing here?"

Diane was sobbing uncontrollably on the bed beside little Jeffrey. "I-I-I thought we were all dead. Those men…"

"I know." Andrea hugged her. "We've come to get you out of here."

Brian sat on one of the two chairs in the room. "You scared us half to death. What's going on?"

Andrea and Diane continued to rock in each other's arms. Jeffrey still slept. Brian squeezed Trent's hand in a grateful gesture to have finally found them.

"Begin," Brian commanded. He motioned for Trent to sit.

"Well, we were just getting supper on the table…" Trent began as quietly as he could.

"We know. We found your house with food still in the pots and…" Brian placed his hands on the table trying to let Trent continue.

"Several men burst through the front door. They forced us to pack and then shoved me into their car and forced Diane to take ours. It all happened so quickly. They'd parked in our driveway so the neighbors…" Trent rested his head on his chest, his emotions clearly getting the better of him.

"That's why the neighbors saw nothing suspicious." Brian patted his hand. "Go on, buddy."

Diane was the next to speak. "We traveled all that day and into the next before reaching a little air field. There we were loaded into a small plane. We made one stop on some other island and then…"

"… we were brought here." Trent swiped his hand over his face.

"But why?" Andrea removed her arm from Diane's shoulders.

Diane looked toward the men sitting at the table. "Trent and Max Shuster developed a new drug the company was going to market as a pesticide. However, Max discovered that, if you changed the formula slightly, it could also be used as a biological weapon. He bragged about it to the wrong people. They offered him a gargantuan amount of money to complete the formula."

"I still don't understand." Brian looked into Trent's face.

"I guess Max told them about me. Anyway, they decided I was the one to finish the project. I thought we'd find Max here but…" Trent shoulders sagged visibly, defeat written all over his face.

"Max is dead." Andrea shuddered remembering all that blood.

Brian picked at a bread crumb on the table. "He delivered a note to Andrea just before someone shot him. That's how we got here. If he was working for them…"

"That's just it…he wasn't. He told me, that last day at work, that he'd decided not to work for these guys. They wanted to use the gas on poor black people all over the world. Max planned on returning their money but…"

"I guess that explains why they killed him." Brian sat back. "At least your living conditions are better than the poor people we saw in those cages."

"What people? We've not seen anyone since we got here except for the men who took us. They threatened to harm Diane and Jeffrey if I didn't do as I was told. I just couldn't be responsible for the deaths of millions of people. We were trying to formulate a plan to escape. Did you say there are other people on this island?" Trent got up and walked toward the window. "I've seen those other cabins when they come to get me in the morning but I thought they were empty."

"People who attend the voodoo ceremonies in Port Au Prince are being kidnapped. We followed them here tonight from one of the ceremonies. We saw them take a body out in the boat a little while ago and people are washing up on the beaches all the time…for the last six months anyway. Could they be using your drug on them, using them as guinea pigs?"

"Not that I know of. Like I said, I thought we were the only ones here…besides those bas…" Trent turned back toward the room. He hand balled into a fist. "I tried to make the formula harmless but…it's a pesticide…in large quantities…"

"Oh Trent." Diane scrambled into her husband's arms. "I didn't know…"

"I didn't want you to know. You had enough to handle." Trent held her close, finding comfort in the woman who'd been his soul-mate for so long. "You didn't need to know how bad it really was or…"

"I could have handled it." Diane walked over to the bed and looked at her sleeping son. "How long do you think we have before they'll catch on that you're stalling?"

"That doesn't matter now. We'll leave with…".

"We discovered a little about these people ourselves. They are very dangerous. They'll stop at nothing, it seems." Brian told the Michners about Andrea's house. "They tried really hard to discourage her and me from coming here. They've threatened her life many times but...she's one determined lady." Brian couldn't help but look at Andrea with a smile.

"O-o-oh." Diane smiled for the first time since they arrived. "I se-e-e-e."

"Never mind. We have things to do." Trent knew of his wife's attempts to pair these two up before. "What's your plan? What about all those other people? We can't leave them here."

Andrea ignored the question to ask one of her own. "Trent, besides being paid a lot of money by these thugs, did Max have access to other funds?"

"Max was a good investor. He knew the stock market backwards and forwards." Trent looked toward her with curiosity. "Why?"

"He left me about that much in a safety deposit box."

"American or Haitian?"

"American."

"Well, Max was paid by these guys in Haitian funds and he never converted it. The money he left you must be from his investments. Why would he leave you money?" Trent was really curious now.

"He wanted me to find his killers...and you guys too. That money was for that purpose but there's a lot there." Andrea rubbed her hand over her wet suit. "I'm getting hot."

"Andrea, I'm sorry our mess has become yours." Diane hugged her again. "You liked that little house."

"Girls, we need to formulate a plan here." Brian was reticent to interrupt, but knew they had to think of something before the sun came up.

"You don't have a plan?" Trent voice almost squeaked.

"Yes, we have. Sort of. We've been in touch with the FBI." Brian began to explain what they thought they'd do. "They want us to return to Port Au Prince alone, so they can handle the police work here. Is there a place you can hide on this island in case the shooting gets dangerous?"

"Yes, Diane discovered a grove of trees right outside the makeshift lab they built here. Jeffrey escaped from them one day. When she was looking for him, he was hiding in this bunch of trees. What they don't know is that there's a cave in those trees. It's a good thing Jeffrey hadn't found that but… well…we never would have found him if he had. Anyway, if we can get to that cave, we'll be safe. We've been working on a loose board back here." Trent showed them the board behind the bed, well hidden from prying eyes.

Andrea looked closely at her two friends. *What an ordeal. We'll need to get this done quickly.* Trent looked worn out. Diane seemed to have lost a lot of weight in the short time since all this began. Her eyes were sunken. She looked as if she hadn't had a shower in a long time. The conditions in that cabin were certainly primitive.

"We'll be back with the FBI agents as soon as they can get here. They are already on alert for our phone call." Brian placed his hand on Trent's shoulder. "Andrea and I need to return to the beach now. We have scuba equipment, so we can get back to Port Au Prince."

"Scuba equipment. You guys know how to dive."
Diane placed her hands on either side of her face.

"We can now." Andrea grinned. "We'll be back in a
flash."

The friends hugged each other again. Brian scurried out
the window and then reached up to help Andrea. They walked
cautiously to the beach and the hidden scuba gear.

Chapter Thirty

     Brian scurried from the trees toward the beach and the dock. Andrea followed carefully, moving in the near dawn hours toward the cold water. *Had those thugs returned after dumping the body?* They walked into the still black liquid, grabbed their equipment from its hiding place and began gearing up. First the rebreathers, mask, and snorkels and then the scooters. Just as they felt they were ready to sink into the murky depths again, they heard a motor approaching rather fast.

     Brian grabbed Andrea's hand and drew into the shadows under the dock. They sank as low as the water would allow and then waited. They watched the bow of the small craft appear at the end of the dock and then move slowly to the exact spot where they were hidden.

"Take the rope and tie us to the dock." The man who spoke yawned. The other grabbed the rope tied to the bow and jumped up onto the dock. The boat rocked.

"I'll be glad when we have the stuff and can get outta here. The boss seems to think we don't need to sleep but those black animals get ta sleep all night." He jumped to the dock. Footsteps moved across the boards over Brian and Andrea's head toward shore.

Andrea removed her regulator. "Phew, that was close."

"The sooner we get back, the sooner we can get the FBI over here and stop this craziness. Those guys have no love for black people that's for sure. I wonder if they're white supremacists." He shoved the regulator back in his mouth, moved out from under the dock in his crouched position.

"Whatever they are, they're sick. Their thinking is warped and evil." Andrea followed Brian as he walked slowly into deeper water. She replaced her regulator, and sank into the water, her scooter turned on and ready to go.

The return trip to the larger island of Haiti seemed much quicker since they knew exactly where they were headed and didn't have to follow anyone. By the time they arrived at the beach near the clearing and their car, the sun rays were peeking just over the horizon to the east. The sky was bright enough that anyone walking along that beach would have seen them emerge. But no one walked there at this time of day.

Brian pulled his scooter on shore. Andrea tried to lift hers but her arms felt as if they'd already done a ton of work. She had little strength to walk up the beach with the rebreather still on her back. Brian grabbed her scooter.

"Feeling a little tied, I guess?" He looked toward her.

"I feel as if a whole day to sleep would not be enough. All of a sudden, my energy is sapped." She removed her re-breather and set it on the ground, careful not to scratch this expensive piece of equipment.

"Me too. It's as if God gave us the energy for the task but now the task is over. Only it's not. We still have to get Trent and Diane off that island and before those thugs come to get Trent for the day." Brian entered the tree line on the path toward their vehicle.

****

Trent watched Brian and Andrea retreat to the beach and the water beyond. His heart went with them. How long before they'd be back with the authorities, he wondered? Would they get here before the men came to get him? He looked toward Diane and then moved closer, hoping the information he'd given Brian and Andrea wasn't causing her any more stress. He'd hoped to keep the worst from her but...

"Trent, I had no idea what you faced. I'm sorry. I wanted to blame someone and you were it, I guess. I can't believe we're in this situation. I can't believe that God would allow us to go through this." Diane melted into her husband's arms, the first time she'd done that since all this began. "I thought this was because of something you and Max had cooked up and now we're paying for it. I should've known better."

"Oh, Diane, how could you think I'd be part of this awful stuff? Max and I did talk about all the money we could make but not for a moment was I ever tempted to go along with his plans. I couldn't tell you then because of the secrecy at the lab and I couldn't tell you here because I didn't want you to worry any more than you already did every time they came to get me." He held her close, relishing the warmth of her body and her comforting arms. "Now, we have to get out of here…now. Those guys can't find us here when they come for me."

"But…"

"Get Jeffrey dressed. I'll move the bed and we'll get those boards in the wall loose if I have to tear them out with my bare hands." He pulled the bed away from the wall. The movement wakened the little tyke who'd slept through all the commotion in the early dawn hours.

"Mommy, Daddy. I awake." Jeffrey stretched. "It morning now?"

Diane laid his clothes on the bed beside her and began removing the t-shirt she'd allowed Jeffrey to sleep in the night before. "We have to get dressed, quietly. We're leaving this place and going someplace to hide. We'll see if the men will find us."

"Oh, you mean like hide and seek." Jeffrey giggled and then placed his hand over his mouth. S-h-h-h." He scooted across the bed to stand on the floor in front of his mother. "Me do." He held his hands out for the rest of his clothes.

"Okay, you get dressed while I pack a few things." Diane tried to smile but it froze on her face. Were they putting their son in more danger by leaving now?

"Trent, maybe…"

"Diane, if they come to get me, I won't be able to help you get out and the guys will be able to use me and you as a shield when the FBI comes for us. See?" He pushed the knife he held between the boards they'd been working on for the last two nights. He pried. "I need something stronger."

Diane pointed to the bed post."Could you use this as a battering ram? I know you'd have to be very quiet doing it but…"

"That might work." Trent quickly removed the end from the bed, tilted it and then rammed it against the board. The sound seemed so loud to them both. They stopped, listened for footsteps and then breathed a sigh of relief. Trent looked toward his handiwork. The first board was hanging slightly askew. He wiggled it some more and, sure enough, it gave way. Now for the other one.

It took them a few more minutes but then they had everything ready for their departure from the prison that had held them for over a week. Diane had a satchel packed with a few items of clothing and some food. "In case." She held it up for Trent's inspection.

"Let's go. Jeffrey, remember not a sound or they'll find us." Trent helped Diane through the opening first and then Jeffrey. He looked around at their makeshift home. *I won't be sad to leave this place.* He wiggled his body through the tiny space, barely large enough for Diane, never mind his larger frame. The rough hewn boards scratched his arms and shoulders, tore the only pair of pants he'd have until the rescue came, and then he was free. "Okay, let's find that cave."

****

"I'm just so anxious to get the Michners safely home." Andrea followed behind, lugging her rebreather. "I hated to see them in those conditions. Did you notice that sick look on Diane's face when we said they would have to stay behind? That's the hardest thing I have ever had to do."

Brian stopped and turned toward her, walking more slowly backwards. "That was hard but we had little choice. If that boat had been tied to the dock…maybe…but since it wasn't, we had no way to get them off that island."

"Well, well, look who's coming back from an early morning swim. Or should I say dive." Brian jumped and turned toward the sinister voice behind him. Andrea looked over his shoulder. Jason stood right beside their car, leaning on the driver's door.

"Jason…er…where did you come from?" Andrea squeezed past Brian on the narrow path.

"Yeah right. Like I'd let you get away with this stuff. You're not going to ruin my one chance to make it…to get richer than I ever dreamed. No way. Get over here. Drop your stuff and …"

Brian moved toward the passenger side of the car. "I'll get your clothes, Andrea."

"Where do you think you're going?" Jason pointed the gun he held toward Brian's face.

"I'm just getting Andrea's clothes. She's cold."

"Aw-w-w. Now ain't that just too bad." He looked toward Andrea again. "You guys have been nothing but trouble for me since the beginning." His temper began to rise. "I tried to be friends but you had to go and…"

Brian reached in through the open window. Andrea's purse was sitting on the front seat. He grabbed it and took the weapon out. He hid it in the palm of his hand before Jason could look toward him again.

Andrea's attention was focused on the gun. "Jason, you can't…I mean…You aren't going to shoot us, are you?"

"I should have done this right in the beginning. Then I wouldn't have to deal with this now. Where'd you guys go anyway?"

Brian moved around the hood of the car. "We just went for a night dive…practice, you know."

"Yeah, I'll bet. Now what're you up to?" His voice was trembling, his anger palpable. He raised the gun even higher, now pointed in Andrea's direction. "You tell me or I'll shoot her right here and now."

Brian reached out with the stun gun in his hand. He pressed the trigger and two wires streaked toward Jason's back. The wires stuck and Jason began to convulse. He dropped the gun and was lying on the ground before Andrea could blink.

"Grab the gun, Andrea. Keep it on him till I can find something to tie him up with. The FBI will want to question him and more, I'll bet." Brian raced to the car and popped the lid. "Here, you tie. I'll cover him so he won't hurt you. Tie his hands quickly before he comes to."

"That stun gun really works." Andrea wrapped the rope tightly around Jason's wrists and then pulled it toward his feet and did the same. In no time she had him trussed like a turkey ready for the oven.

"Great. Now let's hurry. It's already taken us longer than I wanted. Those thugs will be getting ready to go get Trent soon. Are you alright?"

"Yeah. I guess I'm getting used to this. Is that a good thing?" She laughed nervously and then smiled. Jason scowled, just beginning to focus. "I'll get dressed quickly." She walked to the passenger side of the car, grabbed her clothes and them went into the bushes, looking for some secluded spot to dress.

As soon as she returned to the car, Brian took his clothes and did the same. Jason was struggling with his ropes, trying to get loose it appeared. "I tied those pretty tight. You won't get loose. We plan to hand you over to the FBI. They're waiting for our phone call as we speak." Andrea kicked some dried leaves toward his face. "I can't believe that someone who works for General Warehouse could be so immoral. What you and your friends planned to do is incomprehensible."

"Oh get off your high horse. You think you're better than me. Well you're not. Little miss virgin…eh? Sleeping with some guy you've just met, yet. You're no saint."

"It's none of your business but Brian and I…"

"She's right. It's none of your business. Andrea you owe him no explanation. Let's get him loaded and then we can make that phone call." Brian dumped his wetsuit and the rest of the gear in the trunk. He then lifted Jason into the backseat with Andrea's help.

Brian picked up his cell phone. "Agent Menen, please." Andrea listened as Brian related the night's events to the FBI agent when he answered the phone. "Trent and Diane are on the island alright. They're being held in a building at the far left of the compound but they may not be there by the time we get back. Trent was going to try to get them to a safer place, a cave, so they wouldn't be in the line of fire."

Andrea looked into the backseat. Jason scowled again, his hatred tangible. She poked Brian, reminding him of Jason.

"Oh, we have one of the gang in custody already. He tried to kill us when we got back to the beach here." Brian listened for a couple of minutes. "Yeah, well we couldn't let him get away so we tied him up and he's in the backseat." He listened some more. "Yeah, the ropes will hold. We'll be right there." Brian took the receiver from his ear and gave it a look of astonishment before placing the instrument next to his ear again. "Why not? They're our friends. We're the ones who found them." Andrea surmised Agent Menen didn't want them involved any longer. "We're involved, whether you guys like it or not."

Brian continued to stare into space with an impatient look. Andrea figured they were being shoved aside in the investigation. Brian was not going to give in that easily it seemed. "No, we'll go with you. We'll stay out of the way. We know where Trent and Diane plan to hide. They'll go there for safety with their son Jeffrey." Then, "Good, we'll see you then." He hung up with a sense of accomplishment that even Andrea could see all over his face.

"They thought they could get us to stay behind."

"I figured that was what…" Andrea eyes jumped from Brian's face to the man in the back seat when he interrupted.

"You guys think you're so smart. Well the boss'll show them turkeys alright." Jason snorted his discuss.

"I don't think so, Jason. We outsmarted you, didn't we?" Andrea smacked her palms together in a 'that's that' gesture.

Brian ignored Jason and started the engine. "We'll meet them at the dock. That'll still give us time to get to the island before those men bring Trent and Diane their breakfast."

"Good," said Andrea. "There's no way I want to remain here while they raid that island."

"Apparently the warrants are made out for kidnapping only at this point since the Michners were reported missing over a week ago and the police are already involved at home. Once they have those men in custody, they will add murder and kidnapping here to the charges. Kidnapping is a federal offense which makes the FBI's involvement legitimate."

"Well, that makes sense. I don't care how they do it; I just want Trent and Diane off that island, safely at home with their son. Brian, we did it. I can't remember when I've been so tired and yet exhilarated at the same time."

Brian smiled toward the woman seated beside him. "Me, too."

"Oh get a grip." Jason snorted toward the couple in front of him.

Brian slammed on his brakes when they arrived at the dock. He hauled Jason out of the back seat just as another man, with a badge on a chain around his neck, parked himself to the right of the vehicle. Brian dragged Jason unceremoniously over to him. "I take it you're Agent Menen?"

"That's right. I'll take him now. You two get aboard. If we're going to make it to the island in a timely manner, we need to get underway." The man was all business. Brian and Andrea watched the stocky man remove the ropes tying Jason's feet and hands. He cuffed him instead. "Johnson, take this guy to the local jail until we get back. The police chief is also a suspect. Jail him too. Roberts, go with him."

Once everyone else was on board the motor launch, Andrea and Brian were introduced to the group of men and one woman who had been aboard when they approached the dock in Port Au Prince.

"How did you guys get here so fast?" asked Brian.

"We set up a communication center in the Dominican Republic, just off the shore where the two countries meet." Agent Menen waved his hand toward the ocean. "We headed out as soon as the sun rose. We knew you'd be calling soon."

"Well I'm glad you weren't too far away." Andrea shivered. She drew her arms over her chilled body. "Our friends are in danger. These men are ruthless and fanatical. They're trying to coerce Trent into making a chemical weapon against black people. Trent's been stalling but sooner or later they would have figured out that he had no intention of complying, even when his family was threatened. He just couldn't."

"That's right." Brian wrapped his arms across his chest, his back to the cabin door leading to the captain's wheelhouse. "They've threatened to kill Jeffrey and Diane in front of him."

"Well, we'll be there shortly. What time did you say they bring breakfast to the Michners?"

"They didn't say but I assume it's early. They may have already been there." Brian leaned against the worn wood.

Agent Menen spoke in a soft, yet authoritative voice. "We'll be there as quickly as we can. You guys just relax. When we get there you wait until we have the island secure before going off to get the Michner's, understand?"

****

Brian had supplied the exact coordinates to the island for the FBI agents to follow. He sat down on a bench towards the stern of the boat. There he'd be able to see everything going on. He'd be able to see the island as soon as it came into view. *I hope Trent and Diane are already out of that cabin.*

He rested his hand on the side of the vessel as it streaked through the water. Seagulls had already begun their search for food and were following, hoping he would throw some tidbit to them. The spray from the wake made by the boat was cool and refreshing in the early morning sunlight. *If it weren't for the mission we're on, I could enjoy this.* Andrea sat beside him.

They watched the federal officers prepare for their invasion of the island. They took off the baseball hats they'd been wearing and replaced them with helmets. Next they slipped bullet proof vests over starched white shirts. The vest had the letters FBI written clearly on both sides. Then they made sure their weapons were loaded.

The agent gave Andrea and he a vest to wear as well. "Just in case." The air was cool on top of the water unlike the feeling when they'd been wearing wetsuits and were under it.

"Andrea, are you going to be glad when this is all over?"

"Yeah, I will...only..." She smirked but then her face got a serious look. "I've enjoyed getting to know you. Now when we visit at the Michners, it'll feel more like a family."

Brian looked toward the water zipping past them. "I've enjoyed this adventure with you too. Maybe..." He fell silent. *We've been through a lot. I'm probably feeling the strain.* "Why don't we pray about what we'll encounter at the island... and for the Michners safety, of course?"

****

As soon as Andrea bowed her head Brian began. "Father God, please protect Trent and Diane. Help us find the Michners once the criminals are in custody. Lord, please keep the officers safe as well and Lord, help Andrea and I transition back to normal life when this is over. Amen."

Andrea shivered again but this time not from the cold. *I'm really not a brave woman. Not when it comes to confronting those guys and real bullets.* She was happy to let the agents do their job but…she'd help find the Michners. *Lord.* She prayed silently. *Protect us. Please keep each one safe and especially Trent, Diane and little Jeffrey. Help him to remain as quiet as his parents need him to be so they can get to safety.*

The bullet proof vest was longer than her torso. It did not bend easily so sitting was a problem. She lay back, trying to straighten her body but in a sitting fashion. She was so tired. The sun had warmed things considerably since they left the dock. *I wonder how Brian feels about all this coming to an end. Maybe we should spend a day or two just enjoying the tropics without having to wonder if we need to follow any clues.* She began to think about what she had facing her when she arrived back home. She'd not heard a thing from the real estate agent she'd contacted. She expected she'd be going home to a hotel room anyway since she had no furniture yet. Her mind drifted to her animals. *I wonder how they're doing. I've had no chance to call.*

"There's the island." An agent shouted over the sound of the engines. The boat slowed to a crawl through the water making almost no noise at all. The agent ducked behind the wooden sides, and it was then that Andrea noticed one of the men aboard was dressed as a fisherman. He was also black, the color of most of the islanders who fished these waters.

The boat moved closer. It appeared as if nothing inhabited the island. No one was about. Just before they reached a spot to the left of the dock, the man pretending to be a fisherman cut the engines. The boat pulled up close to the shore in water deep enough for it to float but shallow enough for the agents to scoot over the sides and walk ashore.

They moved as trained assault soldiers would, Andrea suspected. She and Brian followed close behind. They'd promised to stay clear of the buildings while the agents rounded up the culprits. They sat on a rock on the beach, waiting for their turn to move further up the shoreline.

Shots were fired. Shouts sounded everywhere. An explosion. It seemed to the two novices that a war was in progress. Andrea ducked her head. *Those guys are not giving up without a fight.* She peeked through half closed eyes. There were men racing in several different directions. *This is taking forever.*

But then all was quiet. Vested men escorted about four thugs toward the dock. *Now it's our turn.* Brian led the way. Andrea followed him around the nearest buildings toward the stand of trees that Trent had pointed out that morning. He held the branches for her and then scurried in a crouched position towards the dense underbrush that hid the cave. He pulled more branches aside. Andrea saw exactly what they were looking for. Removing their vests, to allow better access to the small opening, Brian continued to lead. The two crept through the entrance. Although pitch black, they could hear breathing.

"Trent, Diane, are you here?" Andrea couldn't keep quiet any longer. If someone else was in here, they'd have to deal with that later.

"Oh, Andrea, it's you." Diane's reply was little more than a whisper. "I was afraid they'd found us."

"Brian, am I glad to see you. What's happening outside?" Trent scooted over toward their rescuers.

Brian sat on his haunches. "We came with seven FBI agents, all well armed. They're rounding up those slime balls now, but they aren't going quietly, it seems."

"Unca Brian, Unca Brian." It seemed that Jeffrey finally recognized the voices of his friends in the darkness. He launched himself at his father's friend.

"Yes, big fella. I'm right here." Brian pushed Jeffrey back to his parents. "You stay with mommy and daddy until we get you out of this cave, okay?"

"We're hiding, Unca Brian." Jeffrey sat on his mother's lap.

"We know little one, we know." His mother gave him a big hug. "You've been so good. And so quiet. We need to be quiet a little longer, though."

Preparations were made to exit the confined space. Silently, Brian grabbed Diane's hand and led. The little group followed him out the entrance, Andrea close behind. Outside, Andrea stood and hugged Diane. She couldn't help but notice how thin her friend felt inside the tattered dress she wore. Diane legs buckled, her eyes flowing with tears held in check for so long. Trent moved quickly to her side. His concern was written all over his face. He, too, looked as if he hadn't eaten much since they were taken.

He and Brian shook hands. Then Brian lifted Jeffrey into his arms and gave him a big hug. Jeffrey giggled, but the adults cautioned him to stay very quiet. Everyone was to remain where they were until an agent came for them. They had no problem obeying that order.

There were several large rocks scattered all around the entrance to the cave. Everyone sat down to wait and listened. Shouts could be heard from English speaking men. No more shots were heard. The situation seemed to be under control. Everyone breathed a sigh of relief.

Footsteps. Snapping twigs. Everyone skittered for cover again. However, they soon found themselves looking into friendly eyes. The agent walked toward Trent and shook his hand. "I understand you have been in a bit of a situation here. We'll need you to give us a statement as soon as we get back to Port Au Prince. We've set up a command post there. Now let's get you folks out of here and some place where you can rest."

The FBI agent led the way. Trent and Diane watched as handcuffed men were loaded aboard a second boat that had materialized since the agents had come ashore. A third vessel, larger than the other two, was just offshore. Several small motor launches were transporting people from the cages to the ship that would return them to their homes. Once aboard the ship, they would receive medical attention, Andrea was told.

Brian and Andrea looked at the Michners as they walked gingerly over the rocks towards the boat waiting to transport them to freedom. Then they looked at each other. Andrea was feeling an overwhelming sense of accomplishment. She was sure that Brian was feeling the same thing. *We did it. We actually did it!*

Chapter Thirty One

Andrea knocked on the familiar storm door. It seemed like ages since she visited that Thursday night, just a couple of weeks ago. The morning was bright and sunny with chirping birds singing in the trees. The setting seemed to match the feeling she carried with her these days. Her friends were safe. The bad guys were locked away.

The two weeks since their return from Haiti had been very uneventful when compared to what they'd been through. She was still living in a hotel, one that allowed her to keep her dogs with her. She was more relaxed than she'd felt since the disappearance of the Michners.

Diane answered the door. "Andrea, come in. We were just sitting down for a cup of coffee. Join us."

The four friends had arranged this time to recap all the events that had occurred over the past month. There was plenty of evidence for the conviction of the group they now knew were neo-Nazis listed already on the FBI wanted posters, However, the evidence proving who had killed Max Shuster was sketchy at best.

Andrea followed Diane down the hall leading to the kitchen. Her friend seemed tense. Diane looked towards every doorway they passed. She jumped easily these days at any sudden noise. She pushed the door open, and the two women joined Brian and Trent for their conference.

"Hi Brian. Hi Trent." She looked toward Diane with concern. "We need to get more answers." She took the chair offered her. "Max wanted me to prove who killed him. So far we haven't got the proof that will convict anyone. Do you have any ideas?"

Trent was the first to speak. "Max was the one who contacted those men in the first place. I don't know where or how he found them, but before I knew it, they began coming into the lab on a regular basis. At least until Walter found out about it." Trent went on to explain that Walter, as the lab manager, controlled who entered and who left the section of the laboratory where secret research was done, the section of the lab where Trent and Max worked every day.

"Walter put a stop to their visits in a hurry, but Max took our research and sold it to them for all that money. The authorities found it in the Cayman's, another bank account Max had. About two months ago, Max started making regular trips to Haiti."

"Why didn't you tell someone?" Brian's curiosity was aroused.

"I couldn't. Max said these guys were ruthless. If I said anything to anyone, Diane and Jeffrey would suffer. I assumed he meant they would kill them so I kept quiet. I hoped they would fail in their attempts to use our research. In the beginning, I didn't even know what they hoped to gain by it. Max just kept saying it was worth more than we were getting paid at the lab."

"I can't believe the sweet guy who lived across the street was so greedy. I thought I was a good judge of character. I guess I was wrong." Andrea shook her head totally disgusted with the tears she had shed over this man. The whole thing had been his fault.

Trent leaned over to pat her hand trying hard to reassure her that she had no way of knowing the real Max. "Max was two people. He acted one way when other people were around. In fact, in the beginning, I thought he was a great guy too."

Brian had been quietly listening to his friend's story but now interjected with an observation of his own. "Most people who fall into sin, hide it very well in the beginning. It's when we become transparent to someone else that our true nature is revealed. That's why the Bible talks about the need for us to fellowship with other believers, so we can be accountable to someone else."

"That's so true. When Max began to travel down this road, I didn't suspect a thing. In fact, he kept me in the dark until he had already made the deal to sell our research." Trent frowned in remembrance of that time.

Diane placed her arms around her husband's shoulders. "Trent still blames himself for placing Jeffrey and I in danger."

"If I'd told someone as soon as Max approached me, when those men began showing up… none of this would've happened. All those people…" He hung his head and a tear slipped from beneath his closed eyelids. He sniffed his grief back into hiding.

"The man who was helping feed the people in the cages told the police that it wasn't you who killed those people. All you did was make them sick. Those creeps shot them when they got sick so they wouldn't have to take care of them." Andrea placed her hand on Trent's shoulder. "You did all you could to stop them without getting Diane and Jeffrey killed."

Brian looked toward his best friend. "Besides Trent, you just finished telling me there was no way of knowing how bad things were in the beginning nor how dangerous Jason and his buddies were."

Diane choked on her own tears, for her husband and for the nightmares they still had every night, especially Jeffrey. "Trent, you never suspected, not at first anyway, how bad this was going to get. How could you?"

"Enough, already." Brian's voice raised a notch. "It serves no purpose for us to continue blaming ourselves for what happened. Andrea, Max played you and he played Trent. Trent, you aren't responsible for his actions or your blindness to his alter ego. You are a victim here. Remember that."

Diane removed a pot of hot coffee from the coffee maker and refilled everyone's cup. Jeffrey was staying with a trusted friend, so the four of them could hash this all out before adding their input to the evidence that the police already had.

"The police were pretty angry with us for following the leads we had without telling them where we were going." Andrea admitted her own sense of guilt. "I thought Lieutenant Kurshner would throw his coffee mug at me when we arrived at the police station to give our statements."

"Max had made it clear we couldn't trust the police. I told Kurshner that." Brian recounted his own conversation with the angry officer. "I told him we weren't sure that meant the police in Haiti, or the U.S., or both. And I told him about seeing Jason bribe that police chief in Port Au Prince."

Andrea relaxed a little. "It felt really good when the lieutenant lay the suspicions we had about our police department to rest. I kind of wished we would have trusted them in the beginning. Ironically enough, Jason was the one who suggested just that. I just didn't know who we could count on."

"Max had thought of everything. He was the one who didn't trust the police, and of course, they would have thrown him in jail had they known what he was up to. He had his plan in place a long time before he was killed." Trent's face displayed the anger he felt for his former colleague.

"I know that now." Andrea leaned her elbows on the table and looked earnestly into the faces of her friends. "I still find it strange that he was able to get my signature on all those bonds. I wonder if, in the end, he had a touch of conscience or something?"

Trent smirked. "I doubt it. He was just making sure that no one got away with anything. I guess they had threatened to kill him too somewhere along the way. Anyhow, that money will be put to good use, won't it?"

"Can the police prove that Max's murder is tied into all this, aside from that thug's statement of course?" Diane sat on the remaining chair, her interest evident in the tilt of her head.

****

Trent glanced with great respect toward his wife. "They will follow the trail until they do. I'm sure." His admiring glance was not lost on his friends. "After all, this town has had

344

very few unsolved crimes. But then, they've had very few murders as well." His thoughts continued in the direction of their recent ordeal. Diane had surprised him with a strength he never knew she had. *She's my best friend, someone I know I can count on when the going gets tough. What a woman!*

****

"I have a feeling that someone in Port Au Prince saw Max with Jason or one of his buddies." Brian added his own opinion. "And it's also possible that someone saw that black Mustang he drove here all the time. I noticed it following us, so I'm sure someone else did too. The police just need to find that person."

"Max lived a lie and died because of it." Trent had the habit of turning philosophical once in a while. "When those guys insisted that I was needed for their plot to succeed, that ended Max's anonymity. I was one more person who knew how corrupt he was. Diane was kept away from their experiments, so she never met Max. I knew enough to put him behind bars for a long time. Once Max figured that out, he tried to kill me."

"He did?" Diane was as surprised by this revelation as everyone else. "You never told me that."

"It happened while we were still working together here. He wanted me to join him. He promised me a lot of money, but there was no way I wanted any part of his plan, especially since he was working with people so filled with hate for the black race. He threw a fit when I said no way and came at me with a knife."

"What did you do?" asked Diane.

"Walter came in, and Max pretended that he had dropped the knife. The next day we were taken to Haiti, and I was forced to participate. I slowed them down as much as I

345

could. I didn't know then that those people were being used as guinea pigs. They were dying." Trent bowed his head in sorrow for the part he had been forced to play in so many people losing their lives.

Silence filled the space of the next few minutes, and each one thought about the conditions in Haiti leading up to the atmosphere where people could disappear. No one did anything about it. Their ceremonies, hidden in the trees and under the mask of night, were the catalyst needed for evil to succeed.

"This afternoon, the district attorney will take our statements again. He's working very closely with the federal authorities, hoping for his chance to prosecute Jason for the murder of a citizen of this town. Jason and his men will also be charged with arson since they probably set fire to my house." Andrea recapped for the group the entire conversation she'd had with the D.A. yesterday.

"I'll be glad when all this is completely behind us, so we can get on with our lives." Brian pursed his lips in a thoughtful manner. "It's hard to concentrate with so much happening around us."

"I agree. I can't wait to put Max's money to good use." Andrea smiled for the first time since arriving at the Michners.

"When will they begin work on your house?" Diane had been instrumental in the decision to build Andrea's home on a piece of land nearby. "I'll bet you're anxious to get out of that hotel and into your own home again."

"You've got that right. The dogs and I are alright, but they have no place to wander free right now. The new place will have a large fenced back yard for them. And I would like to make the announcement. Brian and I are going into business together. We decided to open our own detective agency."

Diane and Trent squealed in delight, not so much for the business relationship as for the personal relationship they hoped would develop between their best friends. They hugged Brian and then Andrea while congratulating them on their decision. Questions rolled off their tongues, but Diane's matchmaking genes were about to explode. Her husband knew that look all too well so just rolled his eyes, happy that something pleasant was occupying his wife's mind again.

Epilogue

Andrea stumbled over the uneven gravel. The landscape was still not finished around her new home. It had been six months but the wait was worth it. She knew that when she moved in next week, it would have everything in place including all of the new furniture she had purchased since returning from Haiti.

Benitos Construction had done a wonderful job. They built her the perfect home. Andrea couldn't wait to move in. As she looked around, she spotted the construction foreman coming toward her. "Hi, Mark. I love the progress that I see on the house."

"Hi, Andrea. We'll begin landscaping later today. Is there anything in particular that you want done?"

"I've asked the landscape architect to keep the front yard pretty simple. I visualize flower gardens and a patio in the back yard. If the finished result is anything like his renderings, I will be satisfied. They encompassed everything I wanted and more. I also want the back yard fenced so Pokey and Patches can be free to roam within those boundaries. No more being tied up for them. Do you think you could have the fence done before we move in next week?"

"As long as the landscape company gets their work done, we can install the fence as well. We are almost done on the inside of the house and it won't take too long, maybe a couple of days, to do the fence. We could have sections completed, ready to install, by the time the grounds are done."

"That's great. I'm excited. Living in a temporary place can lose its luster after a while. Especially since I decided to put the dogs back in the kennels. I can't wait to have them home with me." The sun was just beginning to set as she watched the men leave the building for another day.

"I'll see you tomorrow then." She waved good-bye to the man who had become a friend during the past months.

****

"How's it going?" Brian startled her.

"Brian, don't sneak up on me like that! How are you? You walked so quietly I didn't hear you come up. The construction is just about finished, and I will be able to move in next week. I'm so excited!"

"You've waited a long time for a permanent place to call home. Have you got enough help moving in?"

"Yah, I'll be okay, but I can always use another pair of hands. Are you offering?" Andrea cocked her head to one side giving Brian that familiar glance he had come to expect from her. Since their return from Haiti, she'd worked hard to give him the impression that friendship was all she wanted, but … he was very hopeful.

Somehow his interest in anyone else paled when he compared them to this feisty young woman who would go to any lengths for a friend. That he'd found out when they were trying to find Trent and Diane. She was spirited, but careful as well, and their agency would succeed because of her.

" Ahem-m…Speaking of helpful," Brian interrupted his thoughts…again. "Angelia is the best secretary I've ever worked with. You were right in hiring her."

"I just had a feeling about her, and since we've begun getting some clients, we'll need all the office help we can get… so we can do the sleuthing, etc. etc. etc." Andrea turned and began to walk towards her car. "I need to go and take Patches and Pokey for a walk. They've been cooped up in that kennel all day. I'll be so glad when I can just open the back door and let them roam free again."

As they walked, she added, "I hope Shuster Detective Agency will be able to do all that we envision. When the Lord laid that plan on our hearts, I was a little skeptical, but it seems that our names have gotten out since the Haiti thing. By the way, what's new with Trent and Diane? I haven't had a chance to talk to her in the last week."

"A whole week! Wow, that's a record for you two isn't it?"

"Ve-ry funny. With building this new house, talking to organizations about Father Bertrand's orphanage, and getting all the necessary paperwork done to make us a legal agency, I haven't had time to think. When is your last day at Hartford Industries?"

"Tomorrow. Then I will be free to detect … or whatever it is that we will be asked to do. I am actually looking forward to this. Can you imagine who the Lord might place in our paths and what kind of problems we will be asked to solve? I have a hard time thinking of us as serious detectives, but it seems we have a knack for it."

Andrea chuckled as she recalled the first time she'd approached Brian with the idea of using some of Max's money to open their own agency. He had almost laughed out loud, but then he'd confessed he'd thought the same thing.

"The Holy Spirit is clearly in this thing, don't you think?" Andrea's sense of peace was almost overwhelming at times. She shook her head when she contemplated the changes that had taken place in her life. Never in her life had she imagined going down this path. "Walking with God is an adventure, all right."

Brian spoke his thoughts out loud. "I imagine we'll have plenty of opportunity to share our faith. I'm thinking that there are a lot of Christians around who will feel more comfortable asking us to become involved in their lives when they know we are Christians as well."

****

"I hope so. I quit my job at General Warehouse to help people." Brian knew that the position of personal secretary to Mr. Forrester had been given to someone else while Andrea was in Haiti. She would have been just a member of the secretary pool anyway. "The details for this new business have taken a lot of time. I hope that Angelia will be able to handle those details from here on so we can do what God has called us to do."

As they walked towards their respective cars, Andrea remembered some of those details. When they got back from

Haiti, she'd booked another hotel. This one allowed dogs but the process of building took too long so back they went to the kennel. That meant extra trips, just to be with them for a few minutes each day. *Oh well, by next week we'll all be much happier in our own place.*

Just before she got into her car, she said, "Why don't we go over to Trent and Diane's? They probably have enough food for two extra mouths, and I would like to catch up on how she's feeling."

"Great idea! Trent and I can plan that fishing trip that we've been meaning to take before winter sets in. Want to come with me or take separate cars?"

"No, I'll take my own car. I don't want to leave mine out here all night. I'll need it first thing in the morning. Besides, you live on the other side of town. I want to stop by the kennels to let the dogs out before it gets too dark. My babies need me!"

"Okay, okay, I'll see you at the Michner's." Brian chuckled as she watched him get in the driver's side of his car. He sped off in the direction of the Michner residence. She turned on the ignition and put her car in gear to follow close behind. *What a difference a few months can make in a person's life. Just a little over six months ago, I hardly knew Brian Strait, and now here I am, going into business with him. He's become my second best friend. I guess situations like we faced together can bring people close together.*

It took only about twenty minutes for Brian and Andrea to arrive at the Michners new home. Trent and Diane had returned home from Haiti to a house that they were not able to feel safe in again. They sold it two months ago and moved into a larger home on the other side of town. This one had a security system.

Andrea stepped out of her car but not before three year old Jeffrey had seen his two adoptive relatives arrive.

"Unca Brian, Aunty Andy," he squealed as he rushed out the front door with Trent and Diane close on his heels. They hardly ever let him out of their sight anymore, but their counselors said that time would help them relax their hold on him again.

Diane was beginning to look pregnant, a condition that had happened shortly after their return to a normal life again. The baby was due just after Christmas and everyone, including Andrea and Brian, was excited over the prospect of a new member in the family.

Diane hugged Andrea as Brian swung Jeffrey in a large circle over his head. "You sure have a lead foot." He chuckled toward Andrea. "How did you get here the same time as me almost when I started out long before you?"

"I know a short cut." She tossed her head with a new self assurance as she and Diane walked towards the front door.

"We were just about to sit down to eat." Diane was ever the perfect hostess. "There's plenty."

"I figured as much. You always cook for an army."

"Well, I never know when we might get company." Diane gave Andrea a playful punch on the arm, and they both laughed together.

Trent and Brian were already busy in conversation by the time they joined the women at the table. Jeffrey was occupied with his food almost immediately so the adults sat down to visit and enjoy Diane's great cooking. Trent and Brian huddled together making plans for their fishing trip.

"Look at the two of them." Diane nodded toward her husband, his head bowed in conversation with his best bud. "You'd think that's all they ever talked about, fishing! How is the house coming, Andrea?"

The rest of the evening progressed with the casual camaraderie expected when these two couples shared a meal together. Amidst laughter and the occasional ribbing, the four adults included Jeffrey as often as they could, making him feel important too. Diane had just served everyone dessert and coffee when the topic of the detective agency came up.

"How soon will you be able to handle some clients? A friend of ours is coming over tonight to discuss...well, it's something that we were going to talk to you guys about. Since you're here anyway, you can talk to him yourselves." Trent took a bite of the cheesecake Diane had set before him. "M-m-m." He gave her an appreciative look.

"We've already had some inquiries for a few simple jobs. Does your friend have someone missing?" Andrea spoke up before Brian could ask the same thing.

"Before you get into the details of this, I'll put Jeffrey to bed." Diane had noticed her son nodding off from time to time. "Go ahead, Trent, explain why we're interested."

"DJ belongs to a Christian motorcycle group." Trent sipped his coffee. "He's been with them for some time. They've been developing relationships with outlaw biker groups hoping to build friendships. Their goal is to share the Lord's love with these people any way they can. Well, a friend of his was murdered two days ago. He was wondering if you guys could find out who and why."

"Oh...no. Trent." Andrea sank back into the sofa cushions. "We don't know anything about bikers."

Just then the doorbell rang. Diane hollered from the other room. "I'll get it." She soon returned with a tall, long haired man dressed from head to toe in black leather. His strut, the walk of a tough biker, brought him over to the table as Trent pulled up another chair. His hair was tied back in a Steven Segal styled pony tail showing off pierced ears and a tattoo on the left side of his neck. Removing his jacket to reveal a black denim shirt with the sleeves cut off, he straddled the chair backwards. He held out his hand for Brian to shake as Trent introduced him.

"Brian, Andrea, this is Donald Wiebe or DJ as we all call him."

****

Donald grinned showing a definite set of dimples, a sharp contrast to his somber, no nonsense look. The look on the faces of the couple sitting with Trent was not unusual, especially in Christian circles. He had heard so much about how Andrea and Brian had saved the Michners that he felt as if he knew them already. It was clear; they were not sure how to respond to his presence though.

Taking their silence as a cue for more information, he stood up and turned around for everyone to see the crest on his back. There was a bright blue, red, and orange patch on his back identifying him as a Christian biker with the words 'Riding with the Son' clearly visible for all the world to see.

Brian rose and shook his hand. Then Andrea did the same. DJ enjoyed the intimidating image of testosterone he portrayed especially when he encountered the 'one percenters' or outlaw bikers.

"It's good to meet you both," he said. "I've heard all about you." His grin widened. "It seems Trent and Diane are your biggest supporters. They think you're the right people for this job." His happy-go-lucky mannerisms immediately became somber as he began to tell the story of his friend's murder.

About the Author

Barbara Ann Derksen is a prolific author with a few thousand articles, and several books to her credit. Her first book, *Mind Trap*, is a mystery, her favor-

ite genre. *Dance With A Broom*, a household management guide was released just before *Second to None*, a collection of stories submitted by Korean War vets, went to the publisher.

Straight Pipes, the first in a series of biker devotionals, was released in January 2007. Since then, she's written *Two-Up, Riding with the Lord. Chrome, Shining Faith* will be released in 2009.

Besides *Shih-Tzu Puppy Adventures,* Barbara has created a

Christmas story *Scruffles Finds a Home*, the story of a little field mouse who comes in out of the cold only to encounter a large man in a red suit.

She has written a second children's series Trumpeter Swan Adventures which is recorded on three audio CD's with a full color book included with each CD. Shih-Tzu Puppy Adventures is also available on CD although the stories are a little different than the book. Each CD series contains six stories designed to enthrall children between the ages of two through third grade.

Barbara Ann is represented by Hartline Literary Agency from Pittsburgh, Pennsylvania. Her books can be ordered through her website www.barbaraannderksen.com. and at www.amazon.com. Mind Trap and Second to None can be ordered through Barnes and Noble or Borders